THE BALANCE OF HEAVEN AND EARTH

A MAGISTRATE ZHU MYSTERY

LAURENCE WESTWOOD

JOCELYN !
HOPE YOU ENJOY

14/10/19

SHIKRA PRESS

1st Edition, October 2018

Published by **Shikra Press**
An imprint of Shikra Press Limited
Stratford-upon-Avon
United Kingdom

www.shikrapress.com

E-Book ISBN: 978-1-9164569-0-7

Paperback ISBN: 978-1-9164569-1-4

Hardback ISBN: 978-1-9164569-2-1

Cover design and artwork by www.samwall.com

For more information about the author and forthcoming titles:

www.laurencewestwood.com

CAST OF CHARACTERS

IN TRANQUIL MOUNTAIN

- **Magistrate Zhu:** new in town, seeking atonement
- **Jade Moon:** seamstress, perhaps a heroine reborn
- **Horse:** senior constable, big and very reliable
- **Fast Deng:** constable, very tricky
- **Slow Deng:** constable, also very tricky
- **Little Ox:** constable, small but very strong
- **Leaf:** orphan boy, always up for a fight
- **Madame Wu:** Magistrate's housekeeper, good with a knife
- **Senior Scribe Xu:** senior clerk, August Hall of Historical Records
- **Junior Scribe Li:** junior clerk with ambitions
- **Junior Scribe Ying:** a particularly stupid clerk
- **Physician Ji:** wise and kindly physician
- **Apothecary Hong:** expert pharmacologist, much travelled
- **Wondrous Boy:** son of Apothecary Hong
- **Patriarch Yang:** local aristocrat, owns extensive tea gardens
- **Patriarch Sun:** local aristocrat, owns extensive tea gardens
- **Patriarch Zhou:** local aristocrat, owns extensive tea gardens
- **Sensible Zhou:** Elder son of Patriarch Zhou, very sensible
- **Second Son Zhou:** Younger son of Patriarch Zhou, not at all sensible
- **Tea Inspector Fang:** agent for the Tea and Horse Agency, much disliked
- **Madame Tang:** seamstress, tough negotiator, mother of Jade Moon
- **Golden Orchid:** orphan girl, friend of Jade Moon

- **Madame Kong:** proprietor, Inn of Perpetual Happiness
- **Peach:** maid, Inn of Perpetual Happiness
- **Pearl:** maid, Inn of Perpetual Happiness
- **Chef Mo:** Head Chef, Inn of Perpetual Happiness
- **Madame Deng:** long-suffering mother of Fast Deng and Slow Deng
- **Butcher Deng:** local butcher, husband of Madame Deng
- **Pork Chop:** eldest son of Madame Deng
- **Rose:** Senior Scribe Xu's maid, plenty to say for herself
- **Miss Dai:** runs the Always Smiling Orphanage
- **Ritual Master Zhan:** spirit-medium and exorcist
- **High Priest Lü:** senior priest at the Temple
- **Sergeant Kang:** Imperial Army, leads the local militia
- **Soldier Du:** militia soldier
- **Schoolmaster Chu:** local schoolteacher
- **Studious Chu:**son of Schoolmaster Chu
- **Master Carpenter An:** best carpenter in town
- **Blacksmith He:** Horse's father
- **Mister Long:** proprietor, Inn of Harmonious Friendship
- **Mister Rong:** proprietor, Golden Lotus Tavern
- **Mister Gong:** in the wrong place at the wrong time
- **Eldest Song Gong:** eldest son of Mister Gong
- **Second Son Gong:** second son of Mister Gong
- **Third Son Gong:** third son of Mister Gong
- **Mister Wei:** neighbour of Mister Gong
- **Mister Chen:** neighbour of Mister Gong
- **Handsome Chen:** son of Mister Chen
- **Mister Shi:** neighbour of Mister Gong
- **Mister Mu:** neighbour of Mister Gong

DECEASED OR APPEARING AS GHOSTS

- **Magistrate Qian:** Magistrate Zhu's kindly predecessor
- **Minister Zhu:** Magistrate Zhu's father
- **Prince:** Jade Moon's father, heritage unknown
- **Constable Wei:** constable, comforter of widows
- **Woodblock Wu:** Little Ox's father
- **Tea Merchant Wen:** old friend of Tea Inspector Fang
- **Scary Face Fu:** whom no one seems to have heard of

IN CHENGDU

- **Prefect Kang:** Magistrate Zhu's boss, morally suspect
- **Silk Merchant Qi:** Magistrate Zhu's travel companion

- **Lady Yu (Sparrow):** Magistrate Zhu's sister
- **Minister Yu:** father-in-law of Lady Yu, Magistrate Zhu's sponsor
- **Mister Qu:** gardener, Zhu family estate

PROLOGUE

10TH MOON, 1083

*I*t had been unusually cold that autumn. And, on that day, a bitter wind blew from the mountains in the north, down the valley, following the course of the river to the market-town of Tranquil Mountain, where it rattled loose-fitting shutters and drew curses from the people who had the misfortune to be outside in such weather.

Jade Moon hurried along the Street of Heavenly Peace, head bowed against the wind and the cold, wishing she had taken her mother's advice and for once wrapped a scarf around her head. She trotted past the small groups of people talking in the street, shyly returning some of their smiles. She was headed for the market-square. She was to buy oil for the lamps, charcoal for the stove and a decent sized fish to share with her mother for dinner.

The market-square was crowded. But the people were not moving around as they usually did, looking for the best bargains, or talking and haggling with the market-traders and merchants. Instead they were gathered close together, all staring towards the northern end of the market-square, towards the August Hall of Historical Records. Being unusually tall for a woman, Jade Moon was able to peer over the heads of many people. She could see men pushing and shoving each other. Shouts and curses were clearly audible, carried on the wind. Stalls had fallen over and produce was strewn all over the ground.

"What is happening?" she asked, anxiety strangling the words in her throat. "Who is fighting?"

A woman, not known to her, who was holding a small child by the hand, turned to her with fearful eyes, and answered: "Bandits have come down from the mountains." The woman then hurried away, dragging the child behind her.

1

Jade Moon looked over the heads of the people again, staring with disbelief at what she was seeing. The fighting was getting worse. A man was struck and fell to the ground. His face was obscured, covered with blood, but she thought she knew him. Most of the regular market-traders she knew by name, and certainly many knew her mother well. Fists were flying, and then to her horror she caught sight of a blade.

"Where is Constable Wei when he is needed?" someone asked, nearby.

Then, many of the people around her began to disperse, their initial curiosity satisfied, wanting to be away from the trouble and back in the safety of their homes. No one was rushing to help the poor market-traders. No one was running to find Constable Wei.

Jade Moon turned, her heart pounding in her chest, and ran out of the market-square, jostling or pushing people aside as she did so, back up the Street of Heavenly Peace. Anger flooded through her. Good people – honest and hard-working people – were being attacked and beaten in broad daylight. How could this be? How could the people stand by and do nothing?

Bursting through the door of her home, she ignored the indignation of her mother, ran through to the backroom, and quickly reached for the long bundle wrapped in rough hemp cloth standing in the corner next to her bed. With trembling fingers, and amid a storm of shrill questions leaping off her mother's notoriously sharp tongue, she let the cloth fall to the floor, revealing a bow in ornate style. Then, in her travelling chest, and underneath her spare clothes which she threw out without a care how they landed, she uncovered a quiver, packed tight with the finest arrows.

Hoping the feathers were undamaged and praying the tension in the bow string was as it should be, she dropped the quiver on her bed, and pulled out three of the arrows, thinking the whole quiver would impede her. Then she was out of the house as fast as she could run, breathing hard, eyes weeping and stinging with the cold.

By the time she covered the short distance back to the market-square, her breath was coming in gasps. The fight had worsened, and people were running around, desperate to be away from there, but desperate also to protect their produce and the takings for the day. A few men lay on the ground. She saw one of the larger trouble-makers had knocked over Mister Peng, the spice merchant, and was now holding a knife to the old man's chest and shouting into his face. Mister Peng's hands were flailing wildly as he tried to extricate himself from the bandit's grasp.

Jade Moon planted her feet as solidly as she could, turning side on to the fighting, oblivious to the people shouting, crying and running around her. Brushing her long black hair out of her eyes, she prayed to the spirit of her father for strength, dropped the two spare arrows on the ground, and nocked the remaining arrow to the bow. Mustering all her intention, she lifted the bow in front of her. She drew the string back as far as she could, taking the strain across the muscles of her back. Trembling with the exertion, she fixed her eyes on the one point, concentrating as her father had shown her.

Then, with the sound of the melee receding from her mind, her breathing deepened and time slowed. And, in the silence that enveloped her, the arrow left the bow by itself.

CHAPTER 1

"At least something will happen now," said Fast Deng, excited by the news.

"Yeah, something bad," added Slow Deng, his twin brother.

Horse was not listening. Instead he looked out of the door of the jail. Not only was there fog, covering the town of Tranquil Mountain as if with a thick quilt, but a persistent rain had started to fall. He could not even see across the market-square, to the lanterns that were almost certainly lighting the entrance to the Inn of Perpetual Happiness. He smelled the cold, damp air, frowning as he did so. Somewhere out there, beyond the town and the valley, on the dangerous forested trail that snaked its way up and down hills between the Fifth District and Chengdu, was the new magistrate. Horse had walked that trail, as had most others in town, carrying tea to the tea markets of the great city. He could easily imagine what the new magistrate was suffering.

"Close the door, Horse," said Fast Deng.

"Yeah, and sit down," said Slow Deng. "Looking at the weather isn't going to improve it any."

The Deng brothers sat at a small, round, rough-looking table that had been reconstructed many times. They kept their elbows off it lest it collapse from their weight. Not that the twins were heavy. They were both slim youths, remarkably identical in body, clothing and habits. Those who studied them could just tell them apart, through observing Fast Deng's tendency to speak first, and his uncanny ability to arrive, wherever they were going, just a brief moment before his brother – hence, their names. Fast Deng had, of course, entered the world slightly before his brother, and never let his brother forget it.

5

Horse retook his seat next to Little Ox, the fourth and youngest constable – a short but stocky youth with large, sad eyes. Horse, as senior, had called the meeting. Late that afternoon he had visited the August Hall of Historical Records. Senior Scribe Xu had gravely informed him that a new magistrate was on the way from Chengdu, and would be arriving imminently. The constables were to look to their duties in the meantime, and make sure nothing was amiss in the jail. Apart from the Magistrate's name being Zhu, there was nothing more Senior Scribe Xu would – or could – tell him.

The constable's duties were, in truth, few. So, when Senior Scribe Xu mentioned duties, Horse knew he in fact referred to them all staying out of trouble.

Horse had only asked one question. "Senior Scribe Xu, are we going to keep our jobs?" Senior Scribe Xu refused to answer, instead ordering Horse to return to the jail. Horse felt nervous about the future, and the others could sense it. Horse was not normally one to suffer from his nerves.

"Buddha's Bones!" exclaimed Fast Deng, angrily. "I don't know what Senior Scribe Xu's trying to do. He knows there's nothing wrong here. He's just trying to frighten us. Or maybe he's frightened himself."

Horse put his finger to his lips, irritated by Fast Deng's loose mouth and lack of sense. They were not alone in the jail. Magistrate Qian's old house-keeper and cook, Madame Wu, was in the next room, in Magistrate Qian's old office. Apparently, she had received the same message from Senior Scribe Xu. She was at that moment cleaning the Magistrate's office and apartment in preparation for his arrival.

Despite orders received from Senior Scribe Xu to the contrary, after Magistrate Qian's death the constables had gone over every room looking for secret compartments and anything of interest or value. Nothing had been found, and what Madame Wu found to clean was a mystery. There was but a desk in the office, and a small bed, a few chairs and some empty cupboards in the apartment. Moreover, the internal walls were thin, and she was notorious for appearing in the doorway like an unwanted spectre, just as they were discussing something which could cause them potential embarrassment. Horse did not want to take the chance she would overhear them discussing Senior Scribe Xu, or even the new magistrate, in disrespectful tones. That would not be a good start to the new magistracy. They might find themselves in the cells rather than guarding them.

The constables were sitting around their only table in the large but gloomy jail-room, which also served as their kitchen, store, and dormitory. A corner section of the jail-room had been converted into small cells, four on either side of a short gangway, accessed by a stout wooden door. The cells had been constructed by Master Carpenter An and his sons a few years earlier. They were so solid it was a constant joke among the constables that if the jail ever fell down, the cells would be left standing. The jail-room was where the constables spent the majority of their lives, and all the possessions they owned were stored under their cots lined up against the far wall.

There was no privacy for them, or even security. To access the Magistrate's office and apartment, Madame Wu had to walk through the main gate, across a small forecourt, through the jail entrance, though the jail-room to a short corridor leading to the rear garden. Off the corridor was a doorway to the Magistrate's office, which in turn led into his apartment. The garden at the rear of the jail had been Magistrate Qian's pride and joy. He had often sat on one of the low stone benches whiling away the day, meditating and reading. The high wall surrounding the garden had afforded him some seclusion from the people. The double-gates in the far wall of the garden, which lead out onto the street behind the jail, were rusted shut. None of the constables had ever seen them open.

The four constables sat at the table listening intently. They thought they could hear Madame Wu muttering to herself as she moved around sweeping with her broom.

"Madame Wu doesn't hear too well anyway," whispered Slow Deng. "And what would she say? And who would she say it to? She hasn't any friends."

"It doesn't matter," replied Horse. "We must be careful." He fixed every one of them with his eyes, making certain his point was well made. "We must make sure we are seen to be sensible and responsible. The new magistrate must believe us to be good constables, even though we have no experience."

"It's alright for you, Horse," said Fast Deng. "You were hired by Constable Wei, though he's now cold and in his grave. You're big and strong; and you don't speak very fast so people think you're honest. If we're not really clever, me and my idiot brother and Little Ox will be out on our ears."

Horse stood up. There was nothing else to discuss. "Let's begin cleaning and tidying up again. At least let us look as if we're doing something. Whatever people say about us, I don't want us to be known as idlers."

Little Ox stood and looked around him, not knowing what Horse had in mind. The jail-room looked tidy and clean already. But then they were all momentarily startled when Madame Wu came shuffling into the jail-room, carrying her broom before her, on her way out of the building. She kept her head bowed, not looking at them, muttering to herself, and was soon out of the door.

Fast Deng made a sign with his hand to ward off evil and began to laugh, soon to be joined by his brother. Even Horse was forced to smile, but hating himself for it. Little Ox could not though. He always collected their food from Madame Wu, and though the food was not good – not even a fool would describe her as a competent cook – he saw how she worked harder than most. She was old, infirm, had no living children, and had had a hard life. Little Ox was certain this was enough to make anyone talk to themselves.

CHAPTER 2

EVENING, 17TH DAY OF THE 1ST MOON

"You are not yourself this evening," said Chef Mo, softly. He feared if he spoke too loud he would disturb the peace of the house, or the ghost that was rumoured to share its rooms with Senior Scribe Xu. The distinguished clerk's wife, dead these last ten years, was not quite minded yet to leave the house, Tranquil Mountain or her husband – most likely in that order. The house was, after all, very fine.

Senior Scribe Xu sighed. "You are quite right, Chef Mo. A courier arrived from Chengdu today. The content of the correspondence has quite disturbed me."

The two men sat on low wooden chairs at a small, square table. The table and chairs had been placed just inside of a rear door to the house, specifically so one could sit and admire the garden. The garden was not large, and not famous around town – there were others much more highly regarded for their symmetry and ornamental perfection – but a profusion of mountain flowers grew in it, all lovingly tended by Rose, Senior Scribe Xu's long-time maid. And there was a high wall around the garden providing a large measure of privacy and seclusion that was rare in town. That Senior Scribe Xu loved the garden was obvious to all who visited. Chef Mo wished that one day he would come to live in such a house with such a garden. He often had to struggle to conceal his envy.

The day had been warmer than of late but with evening the air had become chill and a heavy fog had descended. Chef Mo had broken away from his kitchen at the Inn of Perpetual Happiness, with a small flask of plum-flower wine in his pocket. He had cooked the first of the evening meals, and there would be many more to cook later on. But those who had not eaten yet were quite prepared to

8

wait, knowing Chef Mo had just gone to visit his friend, Senior Scribe Xu, and would be back before long.

"You are a good man, Senior Scribe Xu. I am sure with the assistance of your junior clerks, and advice from your dear wife, you will overcome any difficulties."

Senior Scribe Xu nodded gravely, and smiled at the remembrance of his wife. It was common knowledge to all that, despite her dark moods and vicious tongue, he still grieved for her, and often sought her advice at the family shrine in the house.

"Chef Mo, thank you for those kind words, but Prefect Kang has informed me by letter that a new magistrate has been appointed for this district. I am to show him every consideration, and educate him in how this district is administered."

"Ah," replied Chef Mo. He watched Senior Scribe Xu closely. Subtle emotions crossed and re-crossed the senior clerk's face. Chef Mo felt compassion for him. "Surely, Senior Scribe Xu, this is a cause for celebration. The added responsibility has weighed you down dreadfully these last months."

Senior Scribe Xu looked over at his friend, and smiled. He knew Chef Mo was right. He had been feeling unusually tired all through the winter months. He had tried to convince himself it was only his advancing years and therefore to be expected, but the last year had been unkind and he had found the sudden loss of both Magistrate Qian and Constable Wei hard to bear.

"Chef Mo, I seem to fear the unknown more than I do the continuation of my present burden, curious as that may seem. There are great perturbations in my mind. I don't know why. I do not serve as the best example to the junior clerks. That is quite certain."

Chef Mo grunted, quite used to Senior Scribe Xu's habit of self-deprecation. Chef Mo did not know anyone in town who did not consider the senior clerk the very model of correct behaviour. No one was more respected, not even the Patriarchs. There were very few who did not stop to greet the senior clerk when he walked around town, slightly stooped to hide his great height, dressed in a fine silk robe – a marked contrast to the grey trousers and blouses of the common people manufactured from rough hemp cloth or ramie, much as Chef Mo was dressed that very evening. Unlike most, though, Chef Mo had a tendency to roll up the sleeves of his shirt. He had found at a very young age that he would over-heat in the kitchen if he did not do this.

"Have the rumours been confirmed then, Senior Scribe Xu? Is the new magistrate due to arrive soon?"

"Yes, Chef Mo, quite soon…in the next few days to be exact…perhaps even tomorrow. The courier told me the Magistrate had joined up with the next caravan due in from Chengdu. Sergeant Kang is leading the caravan, so I don't believe the Magistrate will become lost, though he may lose his temper with Sergeant Kang. I am sure the Magistrate will not appreciate Sergeant Kang's rudeness. The Magistrate's name is Zhu."

"Ah," replied Chef Mo.

Now this was news. Rumours had been arising out of Chengdu for the last month that a new magistrate had been selected for the Fifth District, but until now no one had known his name. As Senior Scribe Xu had not bound him to secrecy,

Chef Mo felt himself free to speak of what he knew, and would do so later that evening – to much acclaim.

"However, Chef Mo, I am quite upset that Prefect Kang has not found time to afford me any useful description of Magistrate Zhu or even recommend him to me in any way," said Senior Scribe Xu, sadly. "I accept that a Prefect need not do this – of course, I trust Prefect Kang's judgement in all matters – but I do not know if Magistrate Zhu is young or old, or if he is talented or mediocre. What posts has he held before? Is he born, raised and educated in Chengdu prefecture or perhaps somewhere else? I am afraid I may have difficulty getting used to a new magistrate's working habits. You see, Chef Mo, Magistrate Qian was most unusual in not being a scholar, and was promoted from the common people for meritorious acts. And his tenure was so unusually long."

Senior Scribe Xu sighed, sipping at his wine.

"But Magistrate Qian was a good man, and a wise man," said Chef Mo. "You must not forget his particular talents, Senior Scribe Xu."

Senior Scribe Xu smiled. "Thank you for reminding me, Chef Mo. This district was very fortunate for his long tenure. You may not know, Chef Mo, but when I was young I worked as a junior clerk in Chengdu, and came into contact with a great many officials. Some few were compassionate men who carried out their duty with diligence and thoughtfulness. Most, however, lacked even a modicum of sensitivity and humaneness. They often turned out to be ambitious and uncouth. It is a terrible thing to say, I know, but it is true."

Chef Mo then understood Senior Scribe Xu's fear. He was thankful he was master of his own kitchen, and was not required to be tactful or speak respectfully all day, or have to work in the presence of such officials. He answered only to Madame Kong. This was no trouble at all as she was the best of women, and the best of proprietors.

"Senior Scribe Xu, perhaps this new magistrate will be as Magistrate Qian was. I am sure Prefect Kang….who, as Prefect, must be a wise man…would not send to us an official who would cause great unhappiness and disharmony."

Senior Scribe Xu sipped again from his wine cup, grateful for Chef Mo's consideration that evening. "I am sure you are right, Chef Mo. I apologise for burdening you with my troubles and fears. You and your wine have brought me much comfort this evening."

Chef Mo drained his cup, surprised that the flask of wine had lasted so short a time. He knew he should be getting back to the inn, but another thought occurred to him which had not seemed to occur to anyone else that day.

"Senior Scribe Xu, you are worried for Jade Moon!" he blurted out.

Senior Scribe Xu shifted in his seat uncomfortably, pointedly looking out into the garden.

"Forgive my rudeness, Senior Scribe Xu, sometimes I am rather slow and my thoughts take me and my mouth by surprise."

"No, don't apologise, Chef Mo. I am not offended by your observation. You have spoken the truth, and the truth – regardless of how painful it may be – is always acceptable between friends."

CHAPTER 3

*M*ister Gong wrapped his best heavy quilted coat around him as he hurried home. The hard, cold rain that pummelled his head and face smelt of mountains and snow. He bowed his head against the weather, cursing the inconvenience of it all, feeling the chill reach into him despite the two large flasks of rice-wine he had consumed that night.

His three sons had warned him about the weather. They had told him not to visit the Golden Lotus Tavern that night.

"Father, the fog is thick and it has already begun to rain," they had said, "and Mister Chen, who knows about these things, said it is only going to get worse. It's not a night for socialising."

But he had waved their warnings off, told them to shut their mouths and to look after their wives and children. A little bit of bad weather was not going to ruin the only enjoyment an old widower had.

And he had enjoyed himself. Most of the regulars at the Golden Lotus Tavern did not have as far to walk, so when he had arrived the tavern was already full to bursting, and he was fortunate to have had his favourite seat saved for him. He had talked and laughed and drank and gambled until very late, hoping the rain would let up, but finally, when it was almost midnight, and the weather was worse than ever, he knew he had to get home.

Mister Gong had stood up, satisfied he had had his say on all the important matters of the day, waved goodbye to his friends and the proprietor, Mister Rong, and, wrapping his coat around him, staggered out into the rain.

Any stranger to the town would have had difficulty that night finding their way, with the fog even obscuring the many street names written high on the street corners. Many of the lanterns hung out as a courtesy for people walking at night had also been doused by the rain. But finally, Mister Gong, soaked through and desperate for his bed, letting his old and tired feet guide him, turned the last corner into the Street of Thirty Tea Pickers, almost home. He stumbled as he did so, cursing the pains in his knees, trying to cover the last remaining paces to his front door quickly. He covered his eyes against a surprisingly strong squall of rain and then, without warning, collided with a man coming in the opposite direction.

"Forgive me, it is I, Mister Gong," he said, wondering who else would be stupid enough to be out on a night like this.

But the man did not answer. Mister Gong was taken roughly by the arms and thrown into the side of a house, twisting his back painfully, and collapsing to the street.

"Hey! It is I, Mister Gong!" he shouted, looking up through the rain, wanting to know who could be so rude, thinking it perhaps was a guard from the Sun residence who had become lost on his patrol around the residence walls.

He brushed the rainwater away from his eyes and peered up at his attacker. Horror took hold of his throat as he recognised the face of the man who stared down at him. A fist came towards him, which he could only partially deflect with hands thrown up in panic. The blow caught him on the side of the head, hard, again knocking him down, making him see stars. He spilt all the wine he had drunk that night out onto the street. He tried to crawl away, to get to his nearby door. But he was struck again and again, and then knew no more.

CHAPTER 4

MORNING, 18TH DAY OF THE 1ST MOON

"Sir, you must take hold of yourself!" insisted Sheriff Min. *"The girl is all that is important."*

"Sheriff Min, these were my friends. I trusted them. I thought them both correct and righteous men."

"Sir, you will have time to reflect later. We must act! We must do all we can to recover the girl!"

But he did not listen. He turned away from Sheriff Min. He turned away from all else he had known. He retreated into the darkness. There, few could find him. There, few could touch him.

He awoke.

An elderly man with fine, deep blue robes, a black silk hat and a long white beard was holding onto his wrists, taking his pulses. He tried to pull away but could not. The physician was stronger than he looked.

"I am not ill."

"That may be, Magistrate, but I understand you have travelled a long way, from Kaifeng – a journey to exhaust the strongest of men. I am Physician Ji, and it is only right that you let me examine you and make sure that all is as it should be."

"I had just closed my eyes to think," said Magistrate Zhu.

This was true. He had taken his seat at his desk in the office at the jail – a building that could only be described as rudimentary at best – with a view to considering his new surroundings and to wonder belatedly whether he had made the right decision. He was both figuratively, and in reality, at the furthest reaches of the Empire – far from his books and his study in the great house on the fine Zhu estate on the outskirts of Kaifeng. Was it too late to turn around and go home? Was it too late to choose another path?

"Magistrate, I do not believe you will have much time to think," said Physician Ji, finally releasing the Magistrate's wrists, satisfied that there was nothing chronically wrong – nothing that a few deep sleeps and a few wholesome meals would not put right. "I have to inform you there has been a murder."

Magistrate Zhu met the physician's eyes and noted for the first time that they were soft and kindly and truthful. He then looked beyond the physician to the four young constables whom he had met earlier, who had presented themselves to him at the gate, and who had shown him through to his office and his private apartment in the jail. None of them seemed to have any decent clothes to wear. What kind of place was this where the constables were hardly more than boys, and who did not possess a uniform of any sort between them?

"A murder – I understood this place to be a paradise," said Magistrate Zhu, caustically. He was still quite shaken that he had fallen asleep at his desk, and that Physician Ji had begun his examination of him without him being aware; an intrusion of privacy that could only be forgiven in a physician – but only just.

Paradise had been the exact description used by Silk Merchant Qi in regard to the town of Tranquil Mountain and the surrounding wild country which comprised all that was the Fifth District. The merchant had befriended him when he had travelled with the caravan from the city of Chengdu.

"Magistrate," had said Silk Merchant Qi, earlier that morning as they were descending the path from the forest down into the valley, "below us is Tranquil Mountain – the only town in all of the Fifth District. And see that each side of the valley above the town is lush with tea trees. These trees produce the best tea in all of Chengdu Prefecture, perhaps in all of Sichuan Province. One day, when I have finished being a merchant I would like to retire here – far from the noise and bustle of Chengdu. It is truly paradise."

Paradise! So far Magistrate Zhu had uncovered no evidence to support the merchant's extravagant claim.

Physician Ji was not offended by the Magistrate's ill-humour. By the swift examination of his eyes and tongue, the tone and quality of his skin, the smell of his body, and the taking of the pulses, he had not only determined the Magistrate was basically healthy, he has also ascertained many other things: that the young official had been born into a wealthy and privileged home; that he was comfortable with the trappings of power; that he had a sharp temper, an extraordinarily quick wit, and an impatience with all that dissatisfied him....but *was* compassionate just the same; and most interesting of all, that he was a man of secrets.

Inwardly, Physician Ji was overjoyed. Unlike most in town, he thought Tranquil Mountain could do with a bit of a shaking up. Too much dust had gathered through the years of Magistrate Qian's tenure. A young and vigorous official was possibly just what the people needed; especially now that there had been a mysterious murder. There was also the delicate and difficult matter of Jade Moon....

"Magistrate, as I am sure you are very aware, there is no corner of China that is not without its troubles," said Physician Ji.

"Bandits?" asked Magistrate Zhu, readjusting the long sleeves of his black travelling robes to cover up his wrists once more, uncomfortable that these robes were stained from the journey and even torn in places.

"Yes, sometimes bandits come here, Magistrate – when they cannot find easy pickings on the forest trails and when they are tired of starving. But this murder is something different, I think."

"Has the Examiner of Bodies been summoned?"

"We have no one of that title in Tranquil Mountain, Magistrate," replied Physician Ji, still amused. "I will be conducting the examination – together with Apothecary Hong, who is my friend. He is a very learned and observant man in his own right."

Magistrate Zhu blinked, hardly comprehending what he had just been told. "But, Physician, you are an expert in the ways of the living – how can you be expert too in the ways of the dead?"

Physician Ji laughed, stepping away from the Magistrate's side and looking around at the constables, wanting to include them in the joke. The constables were all very frightened and overawed by the arrival of the Magistrate. They needed some cheering up.

"Magistrate," said Physician Ji, "there are times, even in China, where we just have to muddle through, making the best use of what we have. Now I would advise you to wash quickly and compose yourself. The body of Mister Gong is being brought to the jail by his sons and neighbours. And Senior Scribe Xu has been summoned from the August Hall of Historical Records so notes can be taken. With bodies there is often not much time to lose."

CHAPTER 5

MORNING, 18TH DAY OF THE 1ST MOON

*T*he door flew open and Golden Orchid tumbled in off the street, her face alight with excitement. Jade Moon almost pricked her finger with the shock, but Golden Orchid merely giggled and pushed the door shut behind her.

"Come in like that when my mother is here, and you'll earn yourself a slap," snapped Jade Moon, her nerves getting the better of her.

Golden Orchid laughed, sat down on a cushion next to Jade Moon, and stared up at her through a mop of coarse black hair which kept falling into her eyes. Jade Moon had tied Golden Orchid's hair up earlier that morning with two strips of cloth that would not be missed – not bright red or yellow silk, but strips of frayed grey hemp. Golden Orchid had been proud of them though. What the young girl could not understand was why her mass of scruffy black hair kept working loose from the ribbons. She tried to push her hair back into place while Jade Moon stood, poured her a small cup of tea and placed a golden-brown sweet cake on a tiny food tray for her, as promised.

Jade Moon returned to her seat. "Now eat it slowly or you'll choke. And don't come running into the house again. If mother catches you she won't allow you to visit me at all."

Golden Orchid was nodding, but not really listening. Her focus of attention was on the cake she had been anticipating since early that morning. She bit into it greedily, loving the sweet taste. "Don't worry, Jade Moon," she said, speaking with her mouth full. "I saw your mother, Madame Tang, in the market-square. She was talking to the merchants already."

Madame Tang had left some time before, as soon as the caravan had been spotted approaching the town. She liked to get to the merchants as soon as possible, while they were still tired and dull-witted from their journey, and vulnerable to her aggressive bargaining.

The caravan was especially welcome that day. Jade Moon and her mother desperately needed to commence work on a new silk gown for the family Sun. Madame Tang had ordered the silk many days ago, paying in advance, and though the silk merchant had never let them down before, Madame Tang always had trouble sleeping the night before the caravan was due to arrive. There was always plenty of repair work given to them to complete, but nothing paid so well as the creation of new clothes. One such order a month – and it was rarely ever that – was enough to keep a roof over their heads and food on the table, with cash left over to be put aside for the bad months and the bad years that were certain to come around from time to time.

The silks brought from Chengdu were expensive and of the finest quality, which Madame Tang preferred. So her efforts to reduce the price she paid were often met with amusement by the silk merchants, and not a little respect. Madame Tang was a good customer, who always paid her bills, and who had the skill – notably passed onto her daughter – to do justice to the fine material. The merchants liked selling their silk to Madame Tang, and even enjoyed her hard style of bargaining.

"I have seen him," said Golden Orchid, sipping her hot tea carefully, the cake now a pleasurable memory.

Jade Moon had also poured herself a cup, and placed it on a small table to her side. She sat back down on her chair and picked up her needlework. She did not want Golden Orchid to see her drink the tea from the small cup, in case she saw the faint tremble in her fingers. The trembling had commenced that very morning since the shouted announcement in the street outside their house that the caravan was on its way. So she kept her fingers busy instead with her needlework.

"He is nothing like Magistrate Qian," said Golden Orchid, dissatisfied with Jade Moon's less than enthusiastic response.

After all, it was Jade Moon who had come to find her that morning and promised her a cake if she went with the other children to meet the caravan. A full description had been requested, and Golden Orchid was going to deliver, despite Jade Moon's obvious change of heart and mood. Jade Moon had befriended her a few months earlier, dragging her into the house off the street when she had heard a commotion and found Golden Orchid fighting with some young boys. Jade Moon had lectured her not to fight, and when she had found Golden Orchid to be an orphan, and in the charge of Miss Dai at the Always Smiling Orphanage, Jade Moon had said she could come round to visit whenever she wished. Jade Moon would give her titbits of food, or invite her to sit by the stove on the coldest of days despite her mother's protests – her mother having no good words for scruffy orphans.

Golden Orchid could not believe her luck, for her new friend was famous. But Golden Orchid soon learned that some days were better than others to visit, and that mother and daughter did not always get on. One moment Jade Moon would be laughing, her beautiful dark eyes bright and alive, the next she would have her head bowed down over her work, sullen and withdrawn. When those times came

Golden Orchid would slip quietly out and back onto the streets, glad to be away from the heavy atmosphere in the house. Golden Orchid watched Jade Moon closely, hoping it would not turn out to be one of those days, wanting to tell her story.

The whole town had been excited for days, not just in expectation of the caravan but about who was supposed to accompany it. Rumours had been circulating that a new magistrate was on his way, travelling with the caravan.

"How did you know it was the new magistrate?" asked Jade Moon, not looking at Golden Orchid, but peering closely at the tear in the blouse she was doing her best to repair.

"He had a black hat just like Senior Scribe Xu, and everybody said it was the Magistrate," said Golden Orchid pouting, unhappy to be doubted.

"There is another cake under the cloth," said Jade Moon, indicating another tray on the table next to the stove.

Golden Orchid jumped up, giggling again. She lifted the cloth, and sure enough there was another cake, and still warm to touch. She picked it off the tray and returned to her seat, biting into it quickly. The morning had definitely been profitable, but Golden Orchid was still anxious to tell her story and get away. She didn't want to be in the house when Madame Tang returned. She knew well that Madame Tang didn't like children, and with the new magistrate in town, her mood could be worse than Jade Moon's.

"Don't eat so quickly, Golden Orchid, you will make yourself sick. Now tell me exactly what you saw," said Jade Moon, still refusing to look up from her needlework.

Golden Orchid swallowed the cake in her mouth, and resisted putting the rest in right away.

"He had a black beard. He looked tired and miserable and his black robe was covered in mud. I thought he was old, but Leaf said he just looked old and wasn't really."

She put the rest of the cake in her mouth then, and used her sticky fingers to brush away a wayward lock of hair again. Leaf was a young boy Golden Orchid sometimes mentioned, whom Jade Moon took to be another child from the orphanage. Jade Moon understood Leaf wanted to be a constable so he hung around the jail as often as he could with Horse and Little Ox and the Deng brothers.

"The Magistrate didn't look happy. I don't think he wants to be here," added Golden Orchid, absently.

"Why do you say that? Is that what the people are saying?" asked Jade Moon, suddenly.

Golden Orchid shrugged her shoulders. "It's what I think. He just looked miserable. Some of the women watching said they thought him to be handsome. But he had a beard, so I don't think so."

Jade Moon looked over at her young friend, and frowned, seeing Golden Orchid's hair had worked its way loose again. She put down her needlework, and ordered Golden Orchid to turn around, so the ribbons could be retied and her hair brought back under control. Golden Orchid fidgeted, but liked the attention.

18

"Now don't play with the ribbons," said Jade Moon. "If they come loose again, your hair will cover your face and all the young boys will not see how pretty you are."

Golden Orchid laughed out loud, not caring about boys. But she did want to grow her hair as long as Jade Moon's, and wear it loose all the way down her back, and then walk about town without a headscarf.

"Describe him to me again," said Jade Moon.

Golden Orchid thought harder, wondering what further details she could speak about. "He has a black beard and a black hat and black robes. He was tall, but not as tall as Senior Scribe Xu – about as tall as you."

"I am not tall," replied Jade Moon.

"You are taller than most," replied Golden Orchid, unafraid. "You are the tallest woman in town."

Jade Moon smiled. "I am sure I am not. It is my long hair which makes me look tall. And I am not as tall as a man. Now describe him to me, don't tell me how tall he is."

"He has a thin face and eyes that see everything," was all Golden Orchid could think to add. "I was watching from the crowd and then he looked at me – just at me," exclaimed Golden Orchid. "I got frightened and then ran away."

Jade Moon laughed. Golden Orchid loved this, and thought of how beautiful her friend was when she laughed, which these days happened only rarely. Golden Orchid giggled, hoping the happy moment would continue. Then, deciding Madame Tang would be home soon, she jumped up, threw her arms around Jade Moon and kissed her on her cheek, and was gone through the door and out onto the street before Jade Moon could blink.

Jade Moon smiled, but felt cheated; she wished she had learned more. She stood and latched the door properly, hoping her mother would have more information, and would be prepared to share it without tears or tantrums.

~

When Madame Tang did arrive home a short while later, it was obvious to Jade Moon that all was not well. Her mother's face was pale and anxious. Jade Moon, with dread curdling her stomach, brewed some fresh tea, and put away the food her mother had placed upon the table. Madame Tang set her vast bulk down in the only chair in the small house which would support her. Tears slowly began to form in the corner of her eyes, and then began to roll down her chubby cheeks.

"Here is your tea, Mother," said Jade Moon, breathing deeply, trying to calm her own fears, silently cursing her trembling hands as she held out the cup to her mother.

Madame Tang accepted the cup of tea with a faint smile, and brushed away her tears. She sipped at the tea, still not speaking.

"The Magistrate has arrived," said Jade Moon, sitting down on her cushion, picking up the blouse once more, and inspecting the stitching that had taken her all morning to do.

"So you know," said Madame Tang irritated she was not the first to break the news. "Has that child been here again this morning?"

Jade Moon nodded. "Golden Orchid said the Magistrate had a beard."

"Is that all?" replied Madame Tang with a sneer. "You don't know anything, Daughter. There's been trouble at the August Hall of Historical Records. The new Magistrate walked right past the door even though Senior Scribe Xu had prepared for him a special reception. Daughter, can you believe it? Have you ever heard of anything so rude? I can only imagine Senior Scribe Xu's embarrassment."

Madame Tang began to cry again, and dabbed pointlessly at her eyes with her handkerchief, missing the majority of the tears.

"And there's more, much more," Madame Tang said between sobs. "This new magistrate is only about thirty years old. Thirty! Can you imagine it, Daughter? He could almost be my son. And he's from Kaifeng, the capital of all of China. He has travelled here....all this way! Has anyone ever heard of such a thing? Only thirty years old, and rude with it. What have we done to deserve this? What have we done?"

Jade Moon's was unable to answer. Fear had gripped her heart, her future shrouded in darkness.

"Oh, and there is something else, Daughter," said Madame Tang. "There's been a murder."

Jade Moon felt a wave of sadness move through her, thinking of the family, remembering that there were indeed some under Heaven who had greater problems than she. "Who, Mother?"

"Some old man named Gong – from over the river, near to the Sun residence, or so I'm told. He was out in the bad weather last night and got himself beaten for his trouble."

"Bandits?" asked Jade Moon with a shudder – difficult, old memories, rising to the surface.

Madame Tang shrugged. "Who can tell? There are some rough people in that part of town. It comes to something these days when some of the people act more like bandits than the bandits do!"

Madame Tang looked up at her daughter, so unlike her, so much more like her husband, dead now seven long years and more: brave, so very brave....and proud.

"Daughter, this young magistrate could spell our doom."

"I will not run, Mother," said Jade Moon, her expression set, her eyes fierce. "I will have faith in the law – the contract you were forced to sign was wrong...unfair."

"In Chengdu, maybe, we could forge a new life. Madame Kong said she would help us, would lend us cash to—"

"Mother, I will not run."

"Patriarch Zhou is so powerful, and that demon second son of his—"

"Mother, this is our home. This new magistrate will have to drag me away from you!"

Madame Tang wiped the tears from her eyes. Her daughter was a mystery to her; always had been, always would be. But there was no doubting that she was a Tang, that her blood would always run hot...even in the coldest of winters.

Madame Tang put down her cup of tea and stood. She retied the scarf around her head. "I will go out, and see if I can discover more. I will remind the people just who you are, Daughter, and just what you have done for them."

When the door shut behind her mother, Jade Moon stood for some time, feeling the trembling of her limbs, and the sense of injustice that pulsed within her with every beat of her heart.

CHAPTER 6

*W*as it not enough that the day had already begun so badly?

On his arrival in town with the caravan from Chengdu, the new Magistrate had walked straight past the August Hall of Historical Records, ignoring all tradition and protocol that he should first present himself there with his credentials. More importantly, he had ignored the special reception of food and drink the clerks had laid on for him, and had gone directly to the jail. If the rumours were true, he had then fallen immediately asleep at his desk.

And now word had been sent that there had been a murder – supposedly of an old man, on his way home from a tavern, just minding his own business, and wanting to get home to his family.

Had any tenure of any magistrate started in such a rude and ill-omened manner?

Senior Scribe Xu didn't think so.

He hurried across the market-square towards the jail, accompanied by Junior Scribe Li – the best and the brightest of his young clerks – who was clutching hastily grabbed paper and writing materials to his chest.

"Do we know the name of the murdered man?" asked Junior Scribe Li, his eyes wide with fear, either in anticipation of a first encounter with the new magistrate or with a dead body.

Senior Scribe Xu shook his head, still bitterly regretting the great expense he had gone to in laying out a reception for the Magistrate and the great embarrassment he had felt when he had stood in the doorway with the other clerks as they watched the caravan enter the market-square and the Magistrate – easily recognisable in the throng – not even glance their way. The Magistrate had walked directly to the jail, met the young constables at the gate, and then had disappeared inside. Senior Scribe had thought it possible the Magistrate might re-emerge; but, after some long and difficult moments, Senior Scribe Xu had led all his clerks back within the August Hall of Historical Records while wishing his friend, Magistrate Qian, was still alive, and that these new, disturbing events had not come to pass.

"Perhaps our new magistrate is overtired and not thinking," had said Junior Scribe Li, trying to be helpful.

"Or perhaps he just doesn't care," Senior Scribe Xu had muttered; but quietly, to himself. He did not want to frighten his young clerks.

On entering the gloom of the jail, Senior Scribe Xu put all these thoughts out of his mind. He found the jail-room crowded with men. Not only were the four young constables present, but also (he discovered their identities later) the neighbours of the deceased – there to observe the examination, both with sadness and unflinching fascination.

Physician Ji and Apothecary Hong had already begun their work. The naked body of an old man had been laid out on a long table, which Senior Scribe Xu guessed had been borrowed at some haste from a market-trader. At the head of the table, staring at the late-comers, was a hawk-eyed and bearded young man who, despite looking pale and drawn, and whose black robes were dirty and worn, and whose black silk hat did not sit as straight as it should, had the presence of one born into power and high office.

"Magistrate, forgive our lateness. I am Senior Scribe Xu. I am accompanied by Junior Scribe Li who is qualified to take the appropriate notes." Senior Scribe Xu bowed low. He hoped Junior Scribe Li was doing the same.

"Murder is the most heinous of crimes, Senior Scribe Xu. Do you not agree?" asked Magistrate Zhu, his tone barbed and cold.

Without thinking, Senior Scribe Xu nodded.

"Then why is it, Senior Scribe Xu, that I find only four constables in this district when there should be at least ten for a town of this size – and these four constables without uniforms or batons or swords or bows of any kind? And why are there no investigating sheriffs in post, when there should be at least one, better yet two? And why is there no official Examiner of Bodies to prepare for me a report on the causes of death?"

Physician Ji and Apothecary Hong, who had up to then been happily examining finger-nails, and poking and prodding the dead body, stopped what they were doing. All eyes looked to Senior Scribe Xu. There was more than the chill of death in the room.

At least for these questions, quite expected, Senior Scribe Xu had prepared some appropriate answers.

"Magistrate, Physician Ji is fully qualified and—"

"Senior Scribe Xu, I have never heard of a man who devotes his life to healing who also devotes his life to the causes of death," interrupted Magistrate Zhu. "In the whole of Kaifeng, which has more murders than you can dream of, there is not such a physician who spends his days examining bodies. I expect the truth is that there isn't the cash to fulfil such a post as Examiner of Bodies in Tranquil Mountain. Physician Ji has already explained to me that being ten days travel from

Chengdu we are too far to send for such a man, even though in any instance of suspected murder there should always be a second inquest or re-examination of the body by an Examiner from a neighbouring district."

"Magistrate, the body would be so decomposed that—"

"Senior Scribe Xu, irregularities in process give rise to irregular decisions. Irregular decisions give rise to injustice. The people expect that officials perform their allotted functions regardless of how far apart districts are."

"Yes, Magistrate, but Prefect Kang in Chengdu has given us special dispensation to—"

"And you should know, as a senior clerk, that as magistrate I should not even be present at an inquest. It is an abuse of process. That is why we have sheriffs: to investigate crimes, to gather evidence and witnesses, and to finally present them all to me so I can consider my judgement."

Without another word, Magistrate Zhu turned and walked from the room, towards his office and private apartment.

After some difficult moments, Physician Ji tugged at his long white beard to straighten it, and smiled at Senior Scribe Xu, his kindly eyes sparkling. "Senior Scribe Xu, I understand that Magistrate Zhu is most exhausted from his long journey. He has come not just from Chengdu but from Kaifeng and has been on the road some months – the winter months at that. He has also just explained to me that his expertise is in crimes of corruption, not murder. This is the first crime of violence he has been required to investigate – and to observe."

"And murder is always the most affecting of crimes," added Apothecary Hong. He was much younger than Physician Ji, clean-shaven, with sensitive eyes and hands. However, it was wrong to think him effeminate in any way. He was famous for having travelled far and wide in his younger years, in search of rare medicines – even into the barbarian lands.

"Thank you, Physician Ji and Apothecary Hong," replied Senior Scribe Xu, understanding the true meaning of their words, even if no one else in the room did.

"May I also introduce the sons of Mister Gong, whose father is sadly laid out on this table," said Physician Ji, pointing out the three men standing next to Horse, whose heads were bowed in grief.

Senior Scribe Xu nodded in their direction, thinking he had seen them around town.

"Apothecary Hong and I are in agreement, Senior Scribe Xu," continued Physician Ji, "though it must be said the facts were already known to me. I was informed late last night by Eldest Son Gong that his father, Mister Gong, had been attacked outside their house in the Street of Thirty Tea Pickers near to Patriarch Sun's residence. I attended the house sometime after midnight and found Mister Gong already unconscious. He had been struck repeatedly about the head. In the time I was there he did not regain consciousness, and I had the sad task of explaining to Eldest Son Gong and his brothers that my skills do not extend to the miraculous. I understand that he finally succumbed just before dawn."

Senior Scribe Xu looked down at the naked body, and then at all of the sad faces gathered around the table. He could see that Mister Gong, whoever he had been in life, had been well-loved by his sons and his neighbours. "Did no one see anything?"

Physician Ji shrugged and looked to Eldest Son Gong, who knew it was time for him to speak up on behalf of his father. Eldest Son Gong faced Senior Scribe Xu and bowed, and then said: "There was no one in the street when we found my father just outside the door. The fog was thick and the rain heavy. We had become so worried we had decided to go out to search for him. He was an hour overdue. Our father said only one thing before he spoke no more – 'Scary Face Fu.'"

"Scary Face Fu?" Senior Scribe Xu looked to Physician Ji, who shrugged again, then to Apothecary Hong, who sadly shook his head, and finally to the young constables, Horse in particular.

"No one has ever heard of such a man, Senior Scribe Xu," said Horse, slowly and deliberately.

Junior Scribe Li quickly made a note of this – of the unusual name, and that such a person was not known to exist in town. He stifled a shudder, not wanting to seem weak in such illustrious company.

Physician Ji once more addressed Senior Scribe Xu. "I will prepare a full report and make a copy for you as well as the magistrate, so you can then prepare the official certificate of death. We have almost finished. The body can then be taken away by the sons of Mister Gong to await the proper arrangements for burial. I do not think you need stay."

Senior Scribe Xu nodded, relieved he could get away from the jail. And from the eyes of Magistrate Zhu which, though the Magistrate was no longer in the room, he still felt were boring into him.

"And I will speak again to Magistrate Zhu about the way it is here....that this is not Kaifeng," added Physician Ji. "A small town has many benefits, but adequate funding for public posts is not one of them."

Senior Scribe Xu smiled, grateful for anything that Physician Ji or even Apothecary Hong's could do. "Nothing must be allowed to interfere with the tea harvest," he said, softly.

"Of course," replied Physician Ji, to which there were murmurs of agreement from all around the room, even from the grieving sons of the murdered Mister Gong.

The first tea harvest was due soon – a fact that the Magistrate would soon have to be informed of. Murder was sad and tragic, and the Gong family would never be the same again, but, compared to tea, it was just the passing of a small dark cloud across the face of the sun.

CHAPTER 7

"*P*hysician Ji, I apologise for my bad temper. It is my one weakness," said Magistrate Zhu, sitting once more behind his desk.

"No apology is needed, Magistrate. However, I insist that you rest for a while before beginning your thinking on the death of Mister Gong. Any long journey is an ordeal. The spirit often takes some time to catch up with the body. When I first came to Tranquil Mountain, I slept for three days and dreamed of my former home in Hangzhou. This is all perfectly natural and not a cause for concern."

"Physician Ji, I do not have that luxury of time. You have seen there has been a murder. There are no sheriffs to investigate and I have only youths for constables. I must commence my work immediately."

Physician Ji smiled again and shook his head. "Whether you start work immediately or rest for a few hours, this will not bring Mister Gong back to life. Please do as I say, Magistrate. You should undertake no physical labour or arduous mental activity until this evening at the earliest. Contact should also be avoided with women for at least a month. I have found them to be especially tiring to a man's mind. And certainly you should keep control of your emotions during this period. Emotions could open one of the many gates of your body to disease. Set your constables to work. They have been sitting around idle for almost a year – and idleness, as you know, is not good for young men."

Magistrate Zhu saw no sense in this. What use were constables without uniforms or weapons, and who were just boys?

As if he could hear Magistrate Zhu's thoughts, Physician Ji said: "In the time of Magistrate Qian, there was but one constable – Constable Wei. His main contribution to the good of Tranquil Mountain was keeping certain widows happy, if you understand my meaning. But, just before he died – barely a month before Magistrate Qian's death – he recruited Horse to be his replacement. If anyone in Tranquil Mountain now speaks fondly of Constable Wei it is for this one last act. Though Horse is born of a blacksmith and is big and muscular in every respect, he was never intended to be a blacksmith, you see. And, though it is true that the Deng brothers have deserved reputations as rascals, I am quite sure some timely guidance from you can set them on the golden path to maturity. As for Little Ox, the youngest, well there is a story there. He was Horse's choice. Little Ox was with his father on business in Chengdu, when the father suddenly took ill and died. Little Ox walked back from Chengdu alone, and with little food and water. There are great reserves of courage in that young man."

Magistrate Zhu remembered his own journey from Chengdu, along the hazardous trail. He would not soon forget the ever-present dread precipitated by the dense, dark forest. The trees were often so tall they obscured the sky above. But he had been fortunate. His fear had been mitigated by the presence of the rough and ill-tempered Sergeant Kang, by the other militia guards, and by merchants and the ever-cheery porters that made up the rest of the caravan.

"He was alone?"

"Yes, he could not wait for the caravan, having no cash to live on in Chengdu. It is good to know such a story, I think – and that all youths soon grow to be men. Now, Magistrate, you must rest."

Physician Ji then lifted his satchel from the floor by its strap, placed it on his lap and opened it. He sifted through a number of small, white paper packets, and smiled when he found what he was looking for, replacing the remainder back in the satchel.

"You have some medicine for me?" asked Magistrate Zhu, hoping that whatever was in the packet would remove the tiredness he felt in every muscle and every bone.

"No, Magistrate, not exactly – but it will be beneficial for you," replied Physician Ji. "The contents of this packet are for Madame Wu. You must understand that Madame Wu has had a long and difficult life and you, to recover, must eat. Horse will give her this tonic as a gift from you. Preferably, I would prescribe a month of eating only food cooked by Chef Mo – he has such a wonderful touch – but if I did this, greater disharmonies would result in your life. Do you follow?"

Magistrate Zhu did not. "Who is Madame Wu?"

"She is your house-keeper and cook, of course. Now I am sure Horse will bring you some tea. You must rise, wash, shave, and change out of your travelling clothes. Madame Wu will clean them and return them to you. Then you must rest all the hours of the day."

"Physician Ji, I thank you for your advice, well-intended I am sure, but I must be about my work."

"Magistrate Zhu, please listen to me," replied Physician Ji, seriously. "This district has survived almost a whole year without a magistrate. If you do not abide by my instructions you may follow Magistrate Qian into the ground before your time. Please take my advice; I assure you it does not come cheap."

27

～

After Physician Ji had gone, and with Magistrate Zhu still sitting at his desk, unable yet to get up to wash and change, the largest of the constables appeared in the doorway, a cup of tea in his hands. Magistrate Zhu pointed to the corner of his desk where Horse could place the cup, which he did with the utmost care. The orange-green liquid steamed. Magistrate Zhu knew it would be hot and refreshing.

"Tranquil Mountain tea, the very best of teas," Silk Merchant Qi had often said on the trail. "Certainly not as fine as the great white teas reserved for the Imperial Family, but, for me, the finest I have ever tasted or could ever afford."

Magistrate Zhu stared at Horse, studying him. That the youth was nervous was evident; but not as nervous as Magistrate Zhu expected him to be. He sensed a natural calmness with the youth, and an unusual caution. This was a surprise. Magistrate Zhu was well aware that neither trait came easily to himself.

"You are senior?"

"Yes, Magistrate – my name is Horse."

"Your family name?"

"He, Magistrate – my father is Blacksmith He."

"Tell me, Senior Constable He, are murders commonplace in this town?"

Horse knew that murders happened from time to time, but could not rightly say whether these murders happened more frequently in Tranquil Mountain than any other place in China. "I cannot say, Magistrate."

"You cannot say, Senior Constable?"

Horse nodded. He felt intense dissatisfaction radiate from Magistrate Zhu, whose mood seemed not to have improved from the time of the examination of Mister Gong's body.

"Then let me ask you this, Senior Constable He," continued Magistrate Zhu, with some force. "There are two schools of thought in respect of the application of the law. The first school states that the common people are fundamentally good-natured, that the law only exists to guide people back to the correct path when they err and that punishments should be light and merciful. The second school states that the common people are out for whatever they can get, capable of committing any crime; and that these evil impulses of the common people can only be kept in check by the issuing of the harshest penalties. To which of these schools of thought do you subscribe?"

Horse knew he was been tested, but – though he had tried to follow every word – did not fully understand the test.

"Well, Senior Constable?"

Horse knew he could hesitate no longer, that his job may vanish if he offered no answer. "Magistrate, I cannot rightly say. Both...."

"....schools of thought...."

"Yes, Magistrate – both schools of thought seem not quite right to me."

"Explain!"

"Magistrate, in Tranquil Mountain, the people just do their best to get along. That is all I know. That is all I think there is to know. Sometimes people do bad things, sometimes people do good things – and sometimes people do both good and bad things on the same day. Other than that, Magistrate, there is nothing more I can say."

For reasons he could not quite understand, Magistrate Zhu became calm for the first time in many months. He looked deep into Horse's eyes, and began to reassess the legacy – the constables – that had been left to him. Horse did not blink, or waver, or speak more words than he had to. Horse was a revelation to Magistrate Zhu after months spent on the road with chattering merchants and gibbering porters. He felt a glimmer of hope arise in his chest, and no little curiosity towards the people of this far-flung market-town at the very edge of the world. As a northerner, Magistrate Zhu had always believed all southerners to be overly emotional and incapable of sensible thought – and that surely border towns such as Tranquil Mountain would be infected with all manner of barbaric practices. Now he was no longer sure.

"That will be all, Senior Constable He."

"Yes, Magistrate."

Magistrate Zhu watched the large youth make an awkward bow, and then turn and walk out of the office. After a few moments spent deep in thought, Magistrate Zhu reached for his tea.

CHAPTER 8

EVENING, 18TH DAY OF THE 1ST MOON

Senior Scribe Xu arrived at the Yang residence early that evening, as prearranged with the Patriarchs – the heads of the three noble families, the Yang, the Zhou and the Sun, who truly owned much of the town and most of the tea gardens and provided much of its governance. Unlike many other parts of China, it was the Patriarchs who collected the taxes on behalf of the Prefecture here – not the Magistrate. An archaic system to be sure, but the Magistrate had other responsibilities: not only had he to administer to the legal needs of the people, he was required to make sure, when it had been harvested, that all of the tea was transported to Chengdu – and nothing was more important than that.

This evening the Patriarchs wished to speak with Senior Scribe Xu about the Magistrate's appointment and learn as much as they could from his first impressions.

The Patriarchs were already seated in Patriarch Yang's favourite banquet room, which was exquisitely and richly decorated with embroidered screens depicting various scenes from the life of the Lord Buddha. The room always made Senior Scribe Xu uncomfortable. It belonged more in a temple or monastery rather than the house of a landowner. But historically, the Yang family had been energetic patrons of Serene Tiger Monastery from its very inception. He knew Patriarch Yang to be very proud of those links and liked to show them off at every available occasion.

With difficulty, Senior Scribe Xu seated his tall frame down on one of the cushions. Patriarch Yang preferred the use of large cushions to chairs, and to eat dinner off a low, long table. This was a matter of constant complaint and friction between Patriarch Yang and the other Patriarchs, and Senior Scribe Xu could do nothing to intervene. If the subject was ever raised, Patriarch Yang would casually comment that what was good enough for his father and grandfather was good enough for him. The conversation would then be ended. But, in the privacy of their own homes, the other Patriarchs would carp on about Patriarch Yang's eccentricity and rudeness. They assumed Patriarch Yang enjoyed watching them struggle up from the cushions after a meal, instead of allowing them a graceful rising from a chair.

Patriarch Yang was the most senior of the Patriarchs in age, rank and property holdings. He exuded the strength and vitality of a man twenty years his junior. Only the white hair under his silk hat, and the many lines radiating out from the corners of his eyes, revealed the truth of his great age.

Senior Scribe Xu had the greatest respect for Patriarch Yang. He would happily spend time in his presence, regardless of the old man's affectation for keeping an unsheathed sword at his side at all times. This affectation, as far as anyone knew, was not a carry-over from more violent times: Patriarch Yang's father had done the same, as had his father before him. Tradition was very important for Patriarch Yang.

Patriarchs Zhou and Patriarch Sun were at least ten years younger than Patriarch Yang. Patriarch Zhou was a bad-tempered heavy-set man, with a well-earned reputation for stubbornness and inflexibility. Patriarch Sun was quieter, slim and immaculately groomed, preferring robes of the brightest yellow or green silks, rather than the white, black or brown robes worn by the others. Patriarch Sun was perhaps the philosopher of the Patriarchs, preferring to think rather than talk. Senior Scribe Xu considered him a rather cold fish, but believed this could be more to do with his sensitivity to the fact that – comparatively speaking – the Sun family was the most recent arrival to the district, having bought up land and property only seventy years ago. The other Patriarchs would often raise this point if Patriarch Sun was apt to disagree on any matter, using the fact as a weapon of leverage or embarrassment to get their own way.

Senior Scribe Xu could not say which man frightened him more. Each of the Patriarchs wielded tremendous power and influence and, it was said, Patriarch Yang and Patriarch Zhou maintained extensive business interests in Chengdu and beyond. They were not men to be treated with disrespect – a fact Magistrate Qian never, ever, forgot.

"Well, Senior Scribe Xu? What do you make of him?" asked Patriarch Yang. "Zhu is not a family name I know."

Senior Scribe Xu was busy arranging his robes for comfort and decorum, conscious that the eyes of the Patriarchs were upon him. Struggling for words, and not wanting to be the bearer of bad news, he decided to be as opaque as possible. "He is not like Magistrate Qian at all," he said simply.

Patriarch Zhou grunted. "We've learned that much ourselves. We hear your little reception in the August Hall of Historical Records didn't go according to plan."

Senior Scribe Xu picked up the cup in front of him, and sipped at the rice-wine, wishing to alleviate the dryness of his throat. "You are quite correct, Patriarch Zhou," he said. "I admit to being not quite recovered."

Patriarch Zhou turned to Patriarch Yang. "See, did I not tell you? Prefect Kang is up to something. What's he doing sending us this insolent puppy? This magistrate won't have the good sense to keep his nose out of what does not concern him."

Patriarch Zhou's temper was already up and his face set tight like a mask. Senior Scribe Xu was already beginning to fear that the dinner would not be a comfortable affair.

"I'm not in complete agreement with Patriarch Zhou, though I am concerned," said Patriarch Sun. "It may be, that in providing us a young magistrate, Prefect Kang is sending us a message that he is happy for him to be moulded to our particular traditions and methods. His rudeness to Senior Scribe Xu and the clerks may just be an aberration – a product of his journey and physical exhaustion – and perhaps the fear of taking up an important position. The energies of young men – even officials – are volatile, and easily misplaced."

Patriarch Yang nodded his agreement. "I'm of this opinion also. And I must disagree with Patriarch Zhou over Prefect Kang's talent for manipulation. I don't believe he has any such talent – bribes, lavish parties, and dancing girls are more his style than in selecting officials to undermine us."

Shocked by Patriarch Yang's indecorous words, Senior Scribe Xu sipped more wine from his cup to cover his embarrassment.

Unconvinced, Patriarch Zhou turned to Senior Scribe Xu and said: "I'm certain you know more than you are telling us."

Senior Scribe Xu did not doubt for a moment the Patriarchs already knew about the letter received from a distant cousin of his, who worked in the Ministry of Justice in Chengdu. The letter had arrived by the very same caravan that had brought the Magistrate. So he chose to be as open as possible to save future confusion. But first he had to defend Prefect Kang, who was in theory anyway, his direct superior.

"Patriarchs, I am sure Prefect Kang put much thought to the selection of an appropriate magistrate for this district. He would not send us a man who was incapable or not up to the task, nor would he send us someone insensitive to our local concerns. But I have also to tell you that I have received a letter written in regard of Magistrate Zhu which may contain useful information. I would urge caution in referring to this letter in the future. The letter is a breach of trust and confidence, and though we can be grateful for what it tells us, I cannot condone its writing or its transmission."

"Yes, yes, Senior Scribe Xu," said Patriarch Zhou, impatiently. "What did the letter say?"

Quite used to the Patriarchs general disregard for his feelings, he tried hard not to be offended by Patriarch Zhou's harsh words. But he hoped all of the Patriarchs would be more careful when they met the Magistrate for the first time.

"Patriarchs, this magistrate is not from Chengdu – he is from Kaifeng," he continued. "Prefect Kang awarded him a magistracy based on a recommendation from a certain Minister Yu. There is some reason to believe Prefect Kang is wary of Magistrate Zhu and has sent him here to keep him away from Chengdu."

"Why would Prefect Kang be wary of him? Is this young puppy of the Imperial Family....related to the Son of Heaven himself?" asked Patriarch Zhou, the words rushing out of him.

"He is the son of Minister Zhu – an important minister at one time," replied Senior Scribe Xu.

"I have never heard of him," said Patriarch Yang.

"Nor I," said Patriarch Sun.

This did not come as much of a surprise to Senior Scribe Xu. The Patriarchs' knowledge of political events in Kaifeng was vague at best. They were understandably only concerned with those issues which directly affected their personal business affairs.

"If he's from an important family, what's he doing here?" asked Patriarch Zhou, scratching his head. "And why should Prefect Kang be frightened of him? Isn't Prefect Kang also from Kaifeng? Surely he has his own contacts."

Senior Scribe Xu pressed on, desperate to make his point. "Patriarchs, the letter also makes reference to Magistrate Zhu previously holding posts in the Ministry of Justice and the Censorate, so—"

"So, accepting the magistracy of a rural frontier district is a step backwards," interrupted Patriarch Sun.

Patriarch Yang turned to Senior Scribe Xu. "The Censorate investigate corrupt officials, don't they?"

"Among other things," replied Senior Scribe Xu, offering no further comment. He felt he had said quite enough.

"Do you think Magistrate Zhu is here for a purpose, Senior Scribe Xu?" asked Patriarch Yang.

But Patriarch Zhou did not give him time to answer. "We are speaking about a young puppy!" he exclaimed.

In the silence that followed Patriarch Zhou's outburst, Senior Scribe Xu became aware of Patriarch Yang's granddaughter, Jasmine, entering the room. She filled his wine cup for him, and gracefully moved around the table doing the same for each of the Patriarchs.

Jasmine was Patriarch Yang's favourite. She was famous for her beauty, and was rarely seen out of the Yang residence. It was common knowledge Patriarch Yang continued to find impediments to a good marriage for her, even though she was now seventeen. Many said the old Patriarch did not want to be parted from her.

Senior Scribe Xu always found the young girl quite charming, but was well aware of gossip that portrayed her as dim-witted – not necessarily the best of catches for a husband in need of useful advice. Some said Patriarch Yang ought to act soon before Jasmine's beauty faded, and potential suitors vanished into the mists.

It was Patriarch Sun who broke the silence. "If what Senior Scribe Xu says is true, and if this young magistrate has previously held positions in the Ministry of Justice and the Censorate, and is but thirty years old, and has passed the civil service exam at an early age, then he must be considered a precocious talent. But the question we need to ask ourselves is: why is he here? I cannot accept it is merely to gain experience of life in a frontier district, or that he has a particular interest in tea. We should suspect an ulterior motive. Prefect Kang may be aware of this young man's mission or he may not. He might have been ordered to facilitate Magistrate Zhu's position here, and then step out of the way. Alternatively, we could think more kindly of this Magistrate Zhu, and consider he has fallen on hard times and has been required to accept any position offered to him. But surely there are a thousand vacant positions between here and Kaifeng. I suspect he has been sent to either to look at how we do things here and report back to Kaifeng, to prepare the ground to take some sort of action against us, or to take a surreptitious look at our seriously flawed Prefect."

Patriarch Sun fell quiet. Senior Scribe Xu shivered, feeling cold and tired.

Patriarch Yang turned once more to Senior Scribe Xu. "Well, is Patriarch Sun's assessment correct?"

Senior Scribe Xu sighed, feeling distinctly unhappy. "I don't know, Patriarch Yang. But to me it seems unlikely. However, I have also received a memorandum today from the Tea and Horse Agency. Tea Inspector Fang is on his way. He may even arrive tomorrow or the next day. He is moving across the countryside with some speed, and did not wait for the next caravan. The clerk from the Agency made it very clear that Tea Inspector Fang was very much looking forward to meeting Magistrate Zhu."

"But he was not due here for some days, not until the first harvest," said Patriarch Zhou, horrified. "Is this new magistrate here to promote Agency business then? What more can they do to us?"

"I've heard rumours, from other prefectures, that landowners have been forced to sell their tea gardens to the Agency," said Patriarch Sun.

Senior Scribe Xu was aghast. He had not heard this, but there was no doubting the sincerity in Patriarch Sun's voice...or the slight trace of fear.

"Well, we won't know what this new magistrate of ours has in mind until he deigns to speak to us," said Patriarch Yang. "Do you know when that will be, Senior Scribe Xu?"

Senior Scribe Xu fidgeted on his cushion, unable to answer the question. Then he said: "I will arrange a meeting at everybody's earliest convenience."

They all sat in silence for a while, reflecting on Patriarch Sun's considered observations. Senior Scribe Xu found himself to be sceptical. Surely he would have heard rumours or whispers of such a move by the Tea and Horse Agency. Forced takeovers of tea gardens would be unprecedented and wholly unnecessary. But then, what did he know for sure?

The meeting concluded after drinks and food, with not one mention by the Patriarchs of the murder of Mister Gong. Such mundane matters were beneath them. Senior Scribe Xu wandered home to his fine house on the Street of Thieves, content at least that this miserable day was almost behind him even if disturbing thoughts continued to cross his mind.

A new magistrate who was rude and thoughtless and who possessed a bad temper, who hailed from a noble and probably wealthy family in Kaifeng, who once had held an important position as a Censor investigating corruption, but who now had taken up the simple and unexacting post of a rural magistrate in the remote south-west of China – what did it all mean? And was it purely coincidence that his arrival was preceded by an unusual murder?

On passing through the gate to his house, Senior Scribe Xu made sure it was properly locked behind him.

CHAPTER 9

To the astonishment of the constables, after drinking his tea the Magistrate had spent some time in his private rooms at the jail unpacking his belongings – most of which appeared to be fine robes and books – and had then promptly fallen asleep in a chair. That had been in the early afternoon. He was still asleep now, and had left no instructions for what they all should do that evening.

So Horse had left the Deng brothers to guard the jail and to attend to any of the Magistrate's needs if he did wake up, and Horse had walked with Little Ox to the house of Mister Gong. Horse wanted to ease his conscience for allowing a murder to happen, by spending time at the Gong household, sitting outside on a stool, guarding the house from whatever demons, ghosts, or men that might be tormenting the Gong family, possibly intent on further murder.

Little Ox sat with him, looking nervously up and down the street. The visibility was excellent though it was now fully dark. Only a light mist had come down that evening and many people on the Street of Thirty Tea Pickers had purchased new lanterns or put more than one lantern up above their doors, hoping to ward off whatever evil was around.

"I think we are looking for a man," Horse said, bluntly.

"In the forest I saw things," said Little Ox, shaking his head.

"You should listen to Little Ox, Horse," said Eldest Son Gong, who had just brought a seat from inside the house to join them. His two brothers, Second Son Gong and Third Son Gong, had done likewise.

"Yes, Horse. We're grateful to you and Little Ox for spending time at our house," said Second Son Gong. "This ghost or demon could be very strong. We might need all the help we can get to defeat it."

Third Son Gong nodded in agreement. Though each of the brothers was almost ten years older than Horse and Little Ox, and each had a wife and children, and none of them was weak or feeble, Horse's great size and calm manner, and Little Ox's known courage in facing the demons of the forest alone, were welcome additions to their street for the evening.

The consensus was that, as no one had ever heard of anyone called Scary Face Fu, it must be some demon or ghost sent to plague the Gong family for reasons yet unknown. Not that Horse agreed with the consensus. Yes, he was certain demons and ghosts existed, and could easily accept that the ghost of Magistrate Qian still inhabited the jail – a fact sworn to by the Deng brothers – but from Physician Ji's whispered comments to Apothecary Hong during the course of their examination of Mister Gong's body, the bruising to Mister Gong's head and face were most likely to be caused by the impact of a fist and a boot. Horse was convinced that Scary Face Fu, if that was the killer's name, was indeed a man. Not that the Deng brothers could be convinced of this, or even Little Ox.

"No man would have been out on a night like that," had said Fast Deng.

"Absolutely," had agreed Slow Deng.

That Mister Gong had been out that night seemed to be beside the point. But, when Little Ox had described his time spent in the forest walking back from Chengdu, and spoken of seeing and hearing all manner of strange spectres and creatures, who could argue? And who could say such terrible things would not come to town?

Earlier, when Horse and Little Ox had first arrived at the house, they had accepted cups of tea, and listened as Eldest Son Gong and his brothers explained how a monk from Serene Tiger Monastery, which was situated far up the valley, and a priest from the Temple in town, had been paid to come and offer their blessings. Charms had been painted on the walls of the house to ward off evil, and incense and artemesia purchased to burn within, with a view to purifying the air. Horse did not understand about these things, but Little Ox had nodded, having some knowledge.

Horse said the family must do what they could to protect themselves, but added that it was his view that it was a man they were looking for as the murderer. The Gong brothers accepted this without comment, but Horse knew he was wasting his breath. The brothers looked exhausted with grief and worry over what their family could have done to attract such evil, working all day in the tea gardens on the Sun estate and now preparing to stay up all night, homemade clubs in their hands, to do what they could to protect their wives and children. But the brothers seemed to be much heartened by the constables' presence, though both he and Little Ox had come without weapons and, although Horse did not mention this, without the Magistrate's order or blessing.

Soon, neighbours also came out of their houses, bringing their kitchen knives and home-made clubs with them, placing their stools next to the Gong brothers. They were mainly older men, and Eldest Son Gong introduced them all to Horse and Little Ox.

"This is Mister Wei, and Mister Chen and his son, Handsome Chen, and Mister Shi, who is the oldest man on our street, and that is Mister Mu."

"Horse, it's good you're here," said Mister Wei. "I used to be a soldier before taking a job as a guard for Patriarch Sun. But now I'm retired from that as well. People have to understand that sometimes fighting is the only way. And demons have to know that decent people won't stand for being murdered in the street. It's not right. But if this demon is really strong, Mister Chen can read to it and bore it to death. How about that, Mister Chen?"

Mister Chen laughed. He was a genial man, who had taken his seat next to his young son, Handsome Chen, and gripped a book in his lap. "It is poetry, Mister Wei. I am not sure if demons are frightened of poetry."

Mister Wei smiled. "Who cares? We will kill the demon anyway for what it did to Mister Gong. And if it's a man, then the Magistrate will find him, won't he, Horse?"

Horse nodded. "I believe the Magistrate is very clever." How he knew this he could not say, but even the Deng brothers had agreed with this assessment without reservation.

"See, what did I tell you boys?" Mister Wei directed his words at the Gong brothers. "This murdering bastard is as good as caught. You know this Magistrate's far smarter than Magistrate Qian. And he won't stand for any nonsense. Look at how he put Senior Scribe Xu in his place quoting the law. I don't remember Magistrate Qian ever quoting the law. And Magistrate Zhu is young and vigorous too, and I've heard he is the son of a very rich family in Kaifeng. The women will be queuing up outside the door of the jail by tomorrow. Horse, you and Little Ox and those hoodlums the Deng brothers will have to spend all your time fighting these women off instead of fighting demons and criminals."

"Mister Wei, you should not speak like that in front of my son," said Mister Chen. "He is only thirteen years old and does not need to be confused by thoughts of women."

"Mister Chen, I am fifty-two years old," replied Mister Wei, "and I am still confused by thoughts of women. Why should your son be spared this mental anguish?"

"Mister Wei, you must listen to Mister Chen. He is quite right," said Mister Shi. "Such lascivious talk might attract the demon."

Mister Wei snorted. "What do you know about demons, old man? I've fought the cannibals in the forests to the south. I've sat listening with my knees knocking together as the savages swarmed around us, talking in their language of the birds. And those savages could conjure demons out of thin air. I tell you laughter is the only cure for demons. This is why Physician Ji and Apothecary Hong are always so healthy. It's not their medicines and potions, but their happy discussions at lunch every day. Did you see how they examined Mister Gong's body? I am sorry to bring this up boys...and there's hardly a moment goes by without me thinking about it with tears in my eyes...but Physician Ji and Apothecary Hong really knew what they were doing."

"The Magistrate was angry about Mister Gong's death," said Mister Shi. "I saw it in his face. I believe he has a righteous temper. I think he will not rest until this demon or man is caught and executed."

"The Magistrate did seem very angry," said Mister Chen. "I have read about clever and brave and angry magistrates in my books. There are many stories about their great deeds. I believe we are lucky to have such a magistrate."

"That's right," agreed Mister Wei. "And we're lucky to have four fine constables...or two at least. Like most I can't quite fathom what Magistrate Qian was doing recruiting those Deng brothers. No offence meant, Horse, but they can be tricky."

"They are not so bad," said Little Ox, seeing the need to defend the twins as Horse was still finding speech hard to come by.

"Horse, you should give Jade Moon her bow and arrows back, and let her sit with us. She'd put an arrow in the demon's eye," continued Mister Wei.

"I agree," said Mister Mu, simply, the first he had spoken all evening.

CHAPTER 10

The banging of the drum at the Temple signifying dawn and the start of a new day had been sounded before Rose had left her own house, provoking her to curse at how slow she had been that morning. She had worked for many years for the Yang estate and had always been up in the tea gardens well before the dawn. But somehow, either the problems of age or the time spent speaking with her husband about the goings-on in town, seemed to slow her down more and more each morning. By the time she unlatched the gate to Senior Scribe Xu's house, the sun was already climbing in the sky.

Not that Senior Scribe Xu knew whether she started on time or not. Being the senior clerk, he always chose to set a good example. He was always at his desk in the August Hall of Historical Records – except in the times of the greatest festivals – well before dawn each day.

Rose sang to herself as she worked her way slowly from one room to the other, dusting and sweeping as she went, ignoring the pain in the joints of her fingers – a legacy of picking the leaves of the tea trees for so many years. She was proud to be Senior Scribe Xu's house-keeper, and very grateful to the gods for giving her a new life after leaving the tea gardens behind.

It was some time before she went into his study, thinking she was alone in the house. To her shock and amazement, she found Senior Scribe Xu sitting in his chair, looking like he had not even gone to bed.

"My goodness, Senior Scribe Xu, you are home! Are you unwell? Should I summon Physician Ji?"

Senior Scribe Xu, who had not noticed Rose come into his study, turned to her, quite surprised that someone was speaking to him. "No, no, I am quite well, thank you, Rose."

Which was a lie, Rose could see, even with her poor eyesight. For even if his body was healthy, his mind certainly was not – which according to Physician Ji was one and the same.

Of course Rose knew what the problem was: the new, young Magistrate – who by all accounts had severely embarrassed Senior Scribe Xu by not attending the reception prepared for him in the August Hall of Historical Records. The Magistrate had also embarrassed Senior Scribe Xu in the jail, in front of Physician Ji and Apothecary Hong and the sons and neighbours of the dead Mister Gong....oh, and, of course, in front of those four boys playing at being constables....by being rude and by quoting law – something that the great Magistrate Qian had never deigned to do...to anybody.

Not that a new magistrate was unwelcome. Like Physician Ji, Rose was of the opinion that Tranquil Mountain needed a bit of a shake, to remove the accumulated dust of the years. Magistrate Qian, though he had been a wonderful man, had been a touch too soft and too respectful to the Patriarchs for her liking. A young magistrate with a temper, and of a wealthy family, and from Kaifeng – which as everybody knew was situated directly under Heaven – and who could effortlessly quote law, was maybe just what they all needed.

"Shall I fix you some breakfast then, Senior Scribe Xu?"

"No, no, please don't bother yourself, Rose. I intend to go to work."

"Today?"

He stared at her, and blinked, as if he had not quite understood what she had said or the sarcastic tone in which she had said it.

She sighed, and leaned her broom up against his desk. "Senior Scribe Xu, you must forget yesterday, and be especially forgiving. This new magistrate is youthful and full of energy. Although from what I hear he has been asleep much of the time since he arrived. But you should know that he is not Magistrate Qian. Now, I know you and Magistrate Qian were the best of friends, but you have mourned his passing long enough. You must make friends with Magistrate Zhu. If you and Magistrate Zhu cannot work in harmony, then how is there to be harmony in Tranquil Mountain?"

"Rose, it is not so simple," replied Senior Scribe Xu, with a sigh. "He is but thirty years, and by all accounts noble-born. And I am fifty-six, the son of a clerk, who was the son of a clerk before him. How could we ever be friends?"

Rose snorted with contempt. "I am sixty-three years, and a former tea-picker, and yet we talk."

"This new magistrate is arrogant and has a temper."

"Most men have tempers, Senior Scribe Xu. You are quite unusual in that you don't. Why only yesterday, Mister Gu...you may not know him, but he and his wife live but a few doors down the street from me...well, he took his shoes off in a rage and threw them in White Dragon River – just because his wife refused to cook him fish that night for dinner!"

"He threw his shoes in the river? But that is stupid. He will need them."

"And you will need this Magistrate too, Senior Scribe Xu. So go and see him, make friends with him....invite him to dinner. Take him to the Inn of Perpetual Happiness. Let Chef Mo cook for him. The expense will be worth it, I am sure. He would thank you for such an invite. Everyone knows that Madame Wu, his house-keeper, killed her first husband with her cooking."

"That is just an evil rumour, Rose."

"It's the truth, Senior Scribe Xu!"

Senior Scribe Xu pondered Rose's advice. It was sound. It had been a long night, full of his wife's vitriol and desire for vengeance for what the Magistrate had done to him...to them. Still, he knew this new magistrate was not going to be easy to befriend. His own relationship with Magistrate Qian, who had been the kindest of men, had been built up over twenty years. It was commonly understood that officials and clerks never saw eye to eye...on anything. Officials were in post to give orders and make policy; clerks were in post to make sure those orders and those policies were carried out regardless of their stupidity or impossibility – or at least carried out with the least amount of harm to the people. So officials grew to believe clerks were obstructive, and clerks grew to believe that officials were mostly tyrannical and impractical. That anything was ever achieved in China at all was a miracle.

"I will invite him to dinner, as you say, Rose."

Rose nodded, satisfied, and took up her broom again. "Good."

"And I will go to work and calm the minds of the junior scribes."

"And you will speak up for Jade Moon to the Magistrate?"

Senior Scribe Xu sighed again. "Yes, I will do that. I promised as much to Magistrate Qian before he died."

"Good, and you can tell this young Magistrate Zhu that before long we will also find a wife for him. Many have already noted with some disquiet that he is unmarried. It is foolish for a man to marry before twenty years of age, but disas-trous if he is not married before thirty."

Senior Scribe Xu shook his head, and spoke then with all seriousness. "Rose, a magistrate is not allowed to take a wife, or a concubine, or even a new maid from any family in the district over which he is presiding. This is to guard against corruption, and to prevent families showering a magistrate with their daughters as gifts to gain influence."

Rose waved a hand at Senior Scribe Xu and laughed. "Are you quoting law to me now, Senior Scribe Xu? I have never heard such nonsense! Every man needs a wife. How else is he to make good decisions? Now sit right there and I will fix you some breakfast. A man cannot go out to work without some good food inside of him. How the Magistrate is going to make one good decision with Madame Wu cooking for him I do not know. I've heard that those four boys playing at consta-bles have had stomach upsets all year – not that I've much sympathy. Though I have to say that Horse has grown into a big, handsome man. Many of the women about town are saying so. And that small one....Little Ox, I think he is called....well, many are saying good things about him too, that he has more metal in him than most in this flea-bitten town."

Rose left Senior Scribe Xu sitting in his study and walked out into the hall, heading for the kitchen. As she did so she felt a rush of cold air brush past her face. Without thinking she raised a hand and made a sign to ward off evil. "Bitch! If I had the cash I'd get Ritual Master Zhan in this house when Senior Scribe Xu is at work. I'd have you exorcised for all eternity!"

Rose had never liked Madame Xu, even when she had been alive.

CHAPTER 11

*P*hysician Ji was glad to see Magistrate Zhu sitting on a small stone bench in the garden at the rear of the jail, being warmed by the early morning sunshine. He had arrived later than he had wished, wanting to be at the jail at dawn but delayed by a full night's work treating the sick of the town. Many of the people were complaining of nervous stomachs due to the arrival of the new magistrate and the unfortunate – and blown up out of all proportion – perceived disharmony between the Magistrate and Senior Scribe Xu.

"Physician Ji, it is not an auspicious start, is it?" This had been spoken by a certain Mister Wang, of the Street of White Lanterns, who had been vomiting up his dinner all night.

Physician Ji's reply to Mister Wang was the same he said to all he had treated that night: "There is nothing to fear. It is Heaven's will that Magistrate Zhu has been sent to us. Let us just wait and see. Even the best of births is accompanied with some pain and blood."

"Magistrate Zhu, you are looking much better!" exclaimed Physician Ji. "Have you eaten breakfast this morning?"

Horse quickly placed a stool for Physician Ji to sit upon to conduct his examination of the Magistrate, then stood well back to afford the two men privacy, but still to be in earshot if the Magistrate were to issue an immediate instruction.

"Physician Ji, I have eaten breakfast this morning, but I find it sits painfully in my stomach. The meat was difficult to identify."

"Ah," said Physician Ji. "Pork or chicken or rabbit would be most usual."

"Really? I could not be sure."

"And was it delicately spiced? I did ask Horse to instruct Madame Wu to forgo

44

most spices. Just as southerners cannot stomach the stodgy food of the north – the dumplings and the blood and offal soup – so northerners, such as you, Magistrate, would have difficulty with our many spices."

"Physician Ji, I cannot say I remember that much about it."

In good humour, surprised and delighted by the Magistrate's wit, Physician Ji took Magistrate Zhu's offered wrists again to take the pulses. He then examined the tone of the skin, the brightness of the eyes and the colour of the tongue, and pronounced himself very satisfied – except for the underlying lingering issue he had noticed the day before, something from the past, something unsettling, something lying deep in the emotional recesses of the mind.

"Good, Magistrate, very good…but only light work for the next few days."

"Physician Ji, there has been a murder."

"And you will solve it I am sure, Magistrate – in good time. But for now I wish to tell you a story."

"A story? Now?"

"Magistrate, please humour me – stories are the stuff of life, are they not?"

Magistrate Zhu nodded, assenting – intrigued.

"I was born in Hangzhou, and at the age of fifteen – for by that time I already knew what I wished to be – I was apprenticed to Master Physician Shi. He taught me well and praised me often. He died when I was twenty-five years of age. By then I was able to take over his practice and found myself in much demand. Before the first year was out I had made a lot of cash, and my fame was spreading throughout Hangzhou.

"Then a young girl was brought to me. She was suffering with severe pains in her head, and the local ritual master, a Daoist priest of some renown, had advised the girl's father there was nothing that could be done. The demons were too strong, he had said. In my pride I disagreed. Though I cannot speak about the demons that may or may not have been present, I found the girl's pulses to be weak and minute – an almost total absence of blood and *qi*. To this day I do not know why, but I told the father I could cure the girl. But the medicines I sold him did nothing, and she was dead within a few days."

"But how does this story – sad as it is – relate to me?" asked Magistrate Zhu. "I am not young…nor am I a girl…nor am I ill."

"Magistrate, the point of my story is not the fate of the girl. Because of my failure, I grew embittered and resentful and angry towards the family of the girl. I thought perhaps they had brought her to me, to ruin my business. I myself developed unusual symptoms. I would grow dizzy in sunlight, and suffered many bad headaches. I was often sick to my stomach."

"Did the family blame you? Did they petition the courts?"

"Not that I knew of, Magistrate. I never saw the family again. But the point of my story is that emotions can unbalance the flow of the *qi* and of the blood throughout the body, just as extremes of cold, heat or damp can do. You would not stand for long in a biting wind, so why would you subject yourself to constant and debilitating emotion? Now there are physicians who will dismiss the emotions, saying that emotions are trapped in the body and are released by the very illness itself. But I would say to these men: 'Think about the illnesses of women, and how difficult they are to cure. Is this not because women are more prone to emotion?' Magistrate, these men would then have no answer for me."

"Physician Ji, what did you do? How did you cure yourself?" asked Magistrate Zhu, fascinated.

"I left Hangzhou. I gave up my wealth and possessions, and travelled far and wide, until I came here. I left my resentments and strong emotion behind me and found, as the months went by, my health to be recovered. I have lost patients to death since, but now I do not pride myself on being able to alleviate all suffering. And I no longer promise miraculous cures. I am also careful not to involve myself in situations which could induce powerful emotions. I have not had a serious illness since. Apothecary Hong says it also helps that I never married or had children. I trust his wisdom in this. Alas he has done both, and on many occasions I have seen him quite agitated, and quite physically weak."

"I understand the meaning of your story, Physician Ji, and why you have told it. You think somehow it pertains to me. But I don't believe I suffer from such excessive emotion, and I certainly do not possess the mind of a woman."

"Magistrate, sometimes a journey or a great distance gives us the opportunity to reconsider our lives, to make peace with the past – and to begin anew. That is all I wished to say."

"Then thank you, Physician Ji, for your time. Please send to me your account when it is prepared. I will send one of the constables to your house with the cash."

"Yes, of course, Magistrate – and you will have my report on your desk before midday on the unnatural death of Mister Gong."

"I am grateful – though you should know I will be writing to Chengdu as soon as I am able to request that a proper Examiner of Bodies is sent here."

Physician Ji nodded, smiling, serene in the knowledge that even if the letter was sent, no Examiner of Bodies would be forthcoming, nor probably an official reply.

"Oh, Magistrate, one final thing. The health of your constables is also a concern of mine. A few proper clothes would not go amiss on them."

CHAPTER 12

MORNING, 19TH DAY OF THE 1ST MOON

"*P*ig on a stick!" exclaimed Fast Deng.

"Two pigs on a stick!" exclaimed Slow Deng, laughing.

The constables were all walking down the Street of Heavenly Peace. Horse was in the lead, knowing he had to be brave. Madame Tang was not easily confronted, not even in the bright light of day.

"Yeah, that sly old fox, Physician Ji, really tricked the Magistrate," said Fast Deng.

"Didn't even see it coming," said Slow Deng, shaking his head. "We really owe him – we really do!"

Finally at the house, Horse knocked softly on the door, hoping the encounter would go well. After a brief pause, the door opened slowly. Jade Moon stood there looking at them, her eyes blinking, adjusting to the bright light of the day. She was as tall and as beautiful as Horse remembered, though he hadn't seen her for some time. A shadow crossed her face as she recognised them all, fearing what they had come to do.

"The Magistrate has sent us to buy clothes," Horse said quickly, regretting that he had caused any fear in her.

Jade Moon nodded, relieved, not ever wanting to vent the vitriol that so easily rose up in her throat upon Horse. She did not know a more decent youth. She smiled and beckoned them all inside.

Madame Tang's house was as dark and gloomy as the jail-room. Sunlight barely forced its way through a small window by the door, heavily filtered by the oiled paper. Madame Tang and Jade Moon worked by the flickering light of oil lamps. That they turned out such work of wonderful intricacy and colour was a marvel to everyone in town.

"I am sorry for scaring you," said Horse.

"I will get tea," replied Jade Moon, not wanting to look at him.

"Who's there?" asked her mother from the back room, which served as bedroom, kitchen and living apartment. Jade Moon and her mother used the front room of the house as their workshop.

When Madame Tang appeared in the doorway, Horse struggled to find the words to explain their visit. Madame Tang's hand went to her mouth, her eyes darting between each of them, fearful and angry.

"Mother, don't worry," said Jade Moon, pushing past her to brew the tea. "The constables are just here to buy some clothes from us."

Madame Tang recovered quickly. Walking up to Horse, and though barely up to his wide shoulders, she shook her fist in his face.

"You should know better, young man! Coming here, frightening me and my daughter like this without sending word first you wanted to buy clothes. Now sit yourselves down on the floor where I can see you. And don't think I don't recognise you two, Fast Deng and Slow Deng. You may think you're constables, and Heaven's gift to China, but your mother is a great friend of mine. You have ruined her life. Boys should be a blessing and not turn out to be a curse. Twins are always suspect, but twin boys – what a curse for your poor mother! Now keep your hands where I can see them. I don't want you stealing everything I own!"

"Mother, don't be so rude!" said Jade Moon, sharply, returning with a tray of four cups. She bent down to each of the constables in turn, who had sat down on the floor immediately after Madame Tang had told them to. Jade Moon let them each take a cup of tea off the tray.

"And who is that?" Madame Tang asked, pointing at Little Ox, who wanted to shrivel up and not be observed in the dark corner he had found.

"Mother," said Jade Moon, sitting down in her seat, "you know very well who that is. It is Little Ox, son of Woodblock Wu."

"What? Woodblock Wu, the idiot who died penniless in Chengdu?" she asked, peering at Little Ox carefully.

"Yes, Mother. Little Ox is very brave," said Jade Moon. "He walked all the way back from Chengdu on his own. Now sit in your chair and let us hear what Horse has to say."

Madame Tang let her weight sink slowly in her chair, looking at the constables suspiciously. Horse felt confused and breathless, not liking Madame Tang's eyes upon him. Madame Tang had always had that effect on him. She had come many times to his father's smithy to buy needles of all shapes and sizes, often dragging Jade Moon along with her. Even his father, who was the strongest man he knew, was frightened of Madame Tang and her tongue. He would sell the needles to Madame Tang for next to nothing and not complain. Jade Moon, who was a year older than Horse, had always been pleasant, and always smiled at him. When he was young he had thought her a princess because she was so tall and looked different to the other girls and let her hair fall freely. But that was before the trouble, and before his own father had thrown him out. Now Horse was a constable, and Jade Moon was rarely seen around town.

"Well?" asked Madame Tang. "What reason do you have coming here, all four of you? I am sure the people are saying that you've come to arrest us, to drag us before the new magistrate—"

"Mother!" snapped Jade Moon. "Let Horse speak!"

Horse looked from one to the other. Mother and daughter were so different: the mother short, ill-tempered, over-weight, and happy always to comment on other people's business; and Jade Moon tall, elegant, mysterious and aloof. Some even said Jade Moon couldn't be Madame Tang's daughter, that Madame Tang had kidnapped her as a young girl or had found her wandering abandoned by the road-side. But there *was* a similarity about mother and daughter...perhaps a shared toughness and fire behind the eyes. And Horse suspected that, if necessary, Jade Moon's tongue could be just as sharp as her mother's. He was not minded to pick a fight with either of them.

"Madame Tang," said Horse, "we didn't mean to worry you. We need uniforms – that is all. The Magistrate said our clothes are a disgrace."

Madame Tang looked them all up and down. Even the Deng brothers who would happily brag about all their brave adventures around town would not look up and meet her eyes.

"Of course you need clothes. All boys need clothes, because you don't look after what you've got. Boys are a constant drain on their parents' funds. But what are you doing here? My daughter and I do fine work....exquisite work. We embroider for the Patriarchs, and we create the finest silk robes outside of Chengdu. We don't have time to make repairs to the worn clothes of stupid boys."

"Mother, be nice!" exclaimed Jade Moon, her patience with her mother's rudeness wearing thin.

Horse understood that Madame Tang was not being entirely truthful. Astute as she was, Madame Tang would take on work from everyone. And though not cheap, she and her daughter were the only seamstresses of real quality in town. Most often people repaired their own clothes, and even the wives, daughters and granddaughters of the Patriarchs practised needlework and embroidery. But none could match Madame Tang and Jade Moon for skill and speed. There were many for whom Madame Tang's high prices were well worth paying.

"I have a letter of promise of payment from the Magistrate," said Horse. He held it up for Madame Tang to see, but she snatched it from him quickly, and began to read it.

"The Magistrate is paying?" she asked.

"Yes, Madame Tang," replied Horse, simply, not betraying the excitement he felt within or his astonishment, or that of the others, when the Magistrate had called them into his office and had ordered them to have proper uniforms made and *at his personal expense*.

"We cannot do the work quickly," Madame Tang said, to delay her decision. "We have far too much to do."

"Madame Tang, the Magistrate said we should have uniforms as soon as possible, and boots because we will have to do lots of walking around town," said Horse, hopefully.

"Then this Magistrate makes no sense," replied Madame Tang, harshly. "Does he think we sit around waiting for him to send us work? And last I heard the Magistrate spends all his time sleeping."

"Mother, show some respect!" said Jade Moon, fuming, frustrated with her mother's continuing rudeness.

Horse didn't want to witness an argument between mother and daughter, especially between Madame Tang and Jade Moon, but he was grateful for Jade Moon's intervention. Madame Tang was wrong to talk about the Magistrate that way. As senior constable, he knew he should have corrected her himself.

Madame Tang turned her attention to Jade Moon.

"Daughter, how are we going to do this work? I cannot work all hours of the day. My eyes won't let me. They weep enough as it is. And you certainly cannot do the work. You have that robe to complete for the family Sun. And these boys want boots as well. We don't make boots."

"But we can help them, Mother. You can go to a cobbler and get boots made for a good price. We can make the uniforms. And they should have leather jerkins as well, like soldiers, to give them some protection against arrows."

"Arrows! When are these four idiots ever going to fight bandits? They'll run away at the first sign of trouble like most of the men in this town."

"Mother, you know that's not true," replied Jade Moon, with a dismissive wave of her hand.

Madame Tang turned her attention back to Horse. "Listen, young man, we'll do the work, but it will not be cheap. We'll only do it because it's for the Magistrate, who does not know any better but to waste cash on you four scoundrels. And uniforms won't change a thing. A fool is still a fool even if he is dressed in good clothes."

"Mother!"

"Now stand up all of you," continued Madame Tang, "and let Jade Moon measure you."

Madame Tang returned to the back room, taking the Magistrate's letter with her, thinking of what she should charge him for the work. The work would be good. Of course it would. Everyone should know she and Jade Moon had made their uniforms. But how much profit to make – especially with what was soon to come to pass, the judgement she had so long expected and feared? Too much profit and the judgement would certainly go against them; too little and it could be thought they were trying to buy favour. Oh, why was life so difficult?

CHAPTER 13

*T*hough she was *now* of another family, the Lady Yu was not to be denied. She waved away the servants and the gardeners and the maids as they each tried to bow to her and obstruct her path. Finally, only Mister Qu, the senior estate manager, stood between her and her goal.

"My Lady, please do not do this," he pleaded, bowing very low.

"Would you stand between me and my brother?" she asked, coldly.

Mister Qu faded away into the shadows, and Lady Yu walked on, happy to be back in the great house, but sad also that she could not stay and enjoy once more its gardens and views. She walked into her brother's study, intention set, words pre-arranged in her mind.

"Brother, you dishonour me and my new family when you do not reply to the great Minister Yu's communiqués. Have you lost your sense of courtesy as well as your mind and your honour?"

He lifted his eyes from the paper on his desk. Just that month he had begun to catalogue all the books in the great house, writing a short summary of the content of each book and adding a personal comment as to its value to the committed scholar and also to that of the general reader. He was also in the process of working his way down a list of books supplied to him by a merchant who had come to call not three days earlier. The merchant had the best of connections, he had been assured. "Whatever you desire, I can obtain it for you," the merchant had said. And looking at the list, there were many books that were indeed desirable.

"Sparrow!" he exclaimed, surprised.

"I am now the Lady Yu, or is your mind so gone you do not remember?"

He put down his ink-brush, liking her spirit, glad she had come.

"The boys?"

"Both well, thank you," she replied, "which is more than I can say for you. Your eyes are dark, your face is as white as mare's milk, and you seem to have forgotten how to shave properly. And look at your robes...have you no seamstresses among the maids? What would our father say?"

"Our father is dead."

"He should live on in you. You carry his name, Brother!"

"I am not worthy of that name."

"That may be, but honour can be regained. The Minister Yu has written to you saying so."

"I do not recall any such letters," he replied flatly.

"Then should I return to my home and tell my boys that their uncle has become an idiot who cannot remember the simplest of things?"

"The Minister Yu does not understand. He does not know what I have done. He should not extend his help to me. He will be tainted by my crimes."

"Brother, haven't you heard? The Emperor Shenzong is dead. His sixth son, still a young boy, has taken the throne and the name Zhezong. A fresh wind is blowing across China, bringing many new beginnings. Go see the Minister Yu. He has found a position for you in the South. You must not waste your life. You must not waste your education. The people need good men. China needs good men. And I need you to be a good man. I wish to be able to tell my boys of what they should aspire to. Go see the Minister Yu. He has told me you should travel to Chengdu."

"Chengdu?"

"Yes, you must leave Kaifeng for a year or two. Regain your honour and then come back and resume your career. You must do this for me. You must find atonement, brother. I cannot rest if our father's spirit is not at peace. If you have to shave your head and be a monk and do good works, then you must do it."

"I am not a monk or a priest. I know only the law."

"Then practise the law—"

"Sparrow, I am not worthy—"

"Then make yourself worthy. And write to me as often as you can so I will know where you are under Heaven. And write of the people you are presiding over, and of the people who come to you for assistance. I need to see with your eyes, Brother....how else can I know the world?"

"Sparrow, I—"

But she was already gone. He stood up at his desk and looked at the sprawl of papers and books around him. There are much better men than me, he thought.

Much better men.

Men such as Sheriff Min.

～

Magistrate Zhu woke from the dream. He opened his eyes, realising he had once more fallen asleep at his desk. An old woman, with a face like a shrivelled prune, studded with hard, gleaming eyes, and with grey hair pulled back tight into a bun at the back of her head, was staring down at him. In her hands she held a broom as if it was a weapon. Magistrate Zhu felt fear, regretting sending all the constables away at once to purchase uniforms.

The old woman spoke, or maybe issued a curse, but in a language or dialect he couldn't understand. And then she was gone, as if she had never been there at all. He rubbed his tired eyes, his fear slowly dissipating.

"What sort of place have you forced me to come to, Sparrow?" he asked of his sister, now so very far away.

Then he started to consider the paperwork laid out before him.

CHAPTER 14

Senior Scribe Xu had decided to act on the instant, on Rose's recommendation, and face his fears. The people would expect that he at least try to work in harmony with the new magistrate. He had attired himself in his favourite robes of turquoise silk and called in first at the August Hall of Historical Records to assure the clerks he was not taken ill – and also to retrieve Magistrate Qian's letter from the archives.

Naturally, Junior Scribe Li had volunteered to accompany him. And, naturally, Junior Scribe Li had both bowed and accepted – with some noticeable relief – that this was something he had to do alone. Officials did not respond well to delegations of clerks. All officials, good and bad, young or old, were prone to bad tempers and the giving of bizarre orders when confronted in such a manner.

As he had walked across the market-square, many of the market-traders and people out to shop for their day's food, or even just to chat and gossip, called out to him 'Good Morning, Senior Scribe Xu!' and 'What a pleasant day it is, Senior Scribe Xu!' all the while marking his progress to the jail. He had smiled and nodded to them all, trying to keep calm. He wondered why it was that in China, the only civilised nation under Heaven, clerks and officials found so much to disagree upon.

Much to his surprise, Senior Scribe Xu found the jail-room empty, the constables nowhere to be seen. He stepped into the gloom, waiting for his eyes to adjust, feeling nervous, anxious about the rumour that had just reached the August Hall of Historical Records, that Madame Wu had been seen arriving at the jail – her first visit to clean since the arrival of the Magistrate. He hoped that Magistrate Zhu had not tried to speak to her, or think of her as typical of all who lived in Tranquil Mountain.

Senior Scribe Xu stepped cautiously though the jail-room, listening as he went, wondering if the Magistrate was still in bed, but when he came to the doorway of the Magistrate's office, he found the Magistrate at his desk, reading papers by the narrow shaft of sunlight that entered the room through the small window up above and behind him.

"Magistrate, I must apologise for the short-comings of this district," said Senior Scribe Xu, bowing low. He then waited some time for Magistrate Zhu's response.

The Magistrate looked better than he had at their previous meeting. He had washed and shaved, though dark circles still garnished the undersides of his eyes, and the skin of his thin, angular face had almost a translucent quality about it. Magistrate Zhu was dressed only in plain black robes and Senior Scribe Xu suddenly regretted his own choice of fine turquoise silk. What had he been thinking?

"Senior Scribe Xu, please do not apologise for things that are outside of your control," said Magistrate Zhu, finally looking up from his papers. "Please sit down."

Senior Scribe Xu was grateful for that little consideration. His long back had been hurting him that morning after a night spent sitting in his chair in his study. He took the small seat that was available in front of the Magistrate's desk. He thought back to the last time he had done that in this room, when Magistrate Qian had been still alive. An intense grief struck him when he realised that his friend – his great friend – had now been lying cold in the ground for almost a year.

"Senior Scribe Xu, are you taken ill?"

Senior Scribe Xu shook his head, not relishing that Magistrate Zhu's eyes were again boring in to him. "Forgive me, Magistrate – no, I am not ill. I am aging, that is all. I am sometimes taken over by memories of the past. It is sentiment only – nothing to be concerned about. But let me compliment you on your recovery. You are looking much improved."

"Thank you."

They both became silent for a while and Senior Scribe Xu, reflecting on the small size of the office and the Magistrate's poor apartment adjoining it of only one living space and one small bedroom, felt forced to apologise again.

"Magistrate, please forgive us the rough lodgings. I am sure you would have expected better."

Magistrate Zhu smiled, momentarily mitigating the fierceness of his stare. "Was Magistrate Qian comfortable here?"

"Oh yes, Magistrate Zhu. He loved this jail and the small garden. But he was born of a rural district himself and used to such—"

"And I am not?"

Horrified, Senior Scribe Xu could only open his mouth and wonder how he could be so stupid so soon. But then he was surprised to see Magistrate Zhu laugh, and wave away any intended criticism with a subtle flick of his right hand.

"Senior Scribe Xu, don't be concerned. I have accepted my fate and situation.

However, just because I have reasoned that every man has to be somewhere under Heaven, does not mean that I shall be just as accepting of bad administrative practices or abuses of proper judicial procedure."

"Of course, Magistrate," agreed Senior Scribe Xu, fear assaulting his belly again.

"Though I assure you that I will endeavour to recognise that under Heaven nothing is perfect, and that sometimes we all have to make the best of what we have."

Magistrate Zhu smiled again, warmly, and Senior Scribe Xu could only nod, as if sagely, hoping that would suffice. He was having trouble keeping up with the Magistrate's quick changes of mood and tone. He wondered if he was being teased....or even tormented.

"Tell me about Magistrate Qian. I understand from the constables that he had an unusually long tenure here....twenty years or thereabouts. Of course, I am here for one year only, when I hope to return to Kaifeng."

"Ah, yes, he was a great man. But not a scholar such as you, Magistrate – not even a graduate of the civil service exam."

"Then he was given the post on merit?"

"Exactly, Magistrate. He was sheriff of a district in the south....in the Luzhou Prefecture, I believe. That is a wild and lawless place. It is full of bandits and wild barbarians. One day many bandits came into the town and the constables ran. And the magistrate and the clerks too, I am sad to say. But Sheriff Qian, as he was then, did not run. He took up his sword and defended the people and took many heads that day. He was made a magistrate by the Prefect of Luzhou. I think he wished to stay there but...."

"You do not need to tell the rest of the story, Senior Scribe Xu," interrupted Magistrate Zhu. "Though he had done his duty he had embarrassed too many who did not. Magistrate Qian was sent here to Chengdu Prefecture for his pains in the hope that his great feat would soon be forgotten." Magistrate Zhu's tone had become dry and caustic.

"We did not forget, Magistrate. We were glad to have him here for he was wise as well as brave."

"I am sure," said Magistrate Zhu, looking back down at his papers, his mood suddenly become gloomy and downcast.

Senior Scribe Xu bit his lip, growing increasingly concerned at his inability to keep up with Magistrate Zhu's mercurial emotions. Had he upset him again?

"Magistrate, I do not mean to say that we are not glad that you are here now to guide us in—"

"Senior Scribe Xu, you should understand that I am not of such a meritorious character as Magistrate Qian. In the past I have made mistakes."

Senior Scribe Xu looked down at the floor, not wanting to be seen to pass judgement on the Magistrate's words, though fascinated by what they might mean. In the silence that again followed, he suddenly remembered the letter and reached into the sleeve of his robe, withdrew it, and presented it to Magistrate Zhu.

"This is not your resignation, I hope, Senior Scribe Xu," Magistrate Zhu said, softly.

"Oh no, Magistrate, it is for you…written by Magistrate Qian just before he died…words of encouragement, I think, for his successor."

"Or advice?"

Senior Scribe Xu felt Magistrate Zhu's sharp eyes on him once more, and felt forced to tell the truth. "I think so, Magistrate."

Magistrate Zhu placed the letter flat on his desk, his obvious intention to read it later; a fact that disappointed Senior Scribe Xu. He had been holding onto the letter for a whole year and never known its contents. He hoped Magistrate Qian had made a recommendation as to his own good character.

Magistrate Zhu coughed gently, then began to speak again. "Senior Scribe Xu, I ought to apologise for my own ill temper at the time of our first meeting – at the examination of Mister Gong. I was tired, yes, but it is no excuse. It is a defect of character I freely admit to. I should have realised that all was not well here in this district, that few of the necessary posts would be filled. My meeting with Prefect Kang was concluded perhaps far too quickly. He said only that I should come here with some haste, to join up with the caravan about to leave the next morning from Chengdu's Western gate. I think perhaps he wanted rid of me. I do not think that even if Prefect Kang and I both lived for a thousand years we would ever become friends. His manner was most abrasive."

"Ah," said Senior Scribe Xu.

"Have you met him?"

"Prefect Kang?"

"Yes."

Senior Scribe Xu considered his answer carefully, not wanting to make a mistake that could never be corrected. He had met Prefect Kang twice, but many years in the past. Prefect Kang was even then a nasty, little rat-faced man, whose black silk hats fitted him badly, falling down over his eyes, whose advancement was due only to a remarkable administrative ability and friends in Kaifeng as well as in Chengdu. Senior Scribe Xu hoped these friends were satisfied now, for the Prefect's corruptions and predilection for parties and dancing girls were, after a few short months in office, already infamous.

"Your silence is enough, Senior Scribe Xu." Magistrate Zhu sighed. "What I have been told is this: that, unlike almost every other magistrate in China, I am not in charge of collecting tax. I believe there is an archaic system in place, where the local nobility, the…."

"Patriarchs, Magistrate."

"Yes, the Patriarchs, collect the tax twice yearly. I have also been told that I must be sensitive to the numbers of barbarians moving back and forth across the borders for purposes of trade and not upset them unduly; that I must generally take care what I do and say as the people of this province – returned only to the empire barely a hundred years ago, and then by force – do not consider themselves wholly under the protection of the Emperor."

Perturbed, Senior Scribe Xu said: "I am sure that is not true, Magistrate."

"Is there not a local saying, Senior Scribe Xu: *In Sichuan the mountains are high, and the Emperor is far away?*"

"Yes, Magistrate, but—"

Magistrate Zhu put his hand up to stop Senior Scribe Xu's words. "I also understand I am here to support the work of the...." Magistrate Zhu looked down at some of the papers on his desk, lifting one after the other until he found the right note. "....ah, yes, the Tea and Horse Agency." He looked to Senior Scribe Xu for confirmation he had the correct name.

Senior Scribe Xu nodded, very aware that Tea Inspector Fang was on his way, and was due to arrive like a plague at any moment.

"I am sure you will advise me of my duties to this agency when the time comes."

"The porterage list, Magistrate."

"Pardon?"

"You have to compile the porterage list, Magistrate – the roster of people fit and able to carry the tea to market in Chengdu. There are not enough mules, you understand. And there are some people who would hide in their homes and not do their duty to the district. This list is most important."

"And a murder is not? Surely, I have first to find the killer of Mister Gong."

Senior Scribe Xu bowed his head, knowing full well that the death of an old man, regrettable though that might be, was nothing as to the movement of the tea. It could be the only thing that Tea Inspector Fang and the Patriarchs would find agreement on.

"Senior Scribe Xu, ask your clerks to search the archives for any mention of a Scary Face Fu. The name seems to be unknown to my constables and to the people they have spoken to. I take it your census records are up to date."

"Magistrate, there is no such person listed in the current census. We have checked already."

"Ah, but have you checked all of the archives? Who is to say that this name is not an alias – or perhaps someone who has recently returned to town and is being sheltered by a friend? I understand that all people....even criminals....tend to frequent those places known to them. Though I am experienced only in the investigation of corruption you should know that the techniques of investigation are the same. I have yet to find the legal case histories I brought with me. They are still somewhere in my luggage. I also brought with me the notes I made while under the tutelage of Judge Pei, my great mentor at the Ministry of Justice in Kaifeng, who...."

Senior Scribe Xu stopped listening for a time. He was thinking of the work involved in sifting through the archives for just one name. How far back did Magistrate Zhu want them to go: a year, five years, ten, fifty? And should they just examine the census records, or also the records of taxation, the records of contracts, the records of birth and death, the records of legal dispute and punishment as well as the records – patchy at best – of those barbarians that bothered to ask permission to come into China, mostly from Tibet, to trade?

"Senior Scribe Xu, am I boring you?"

"Forgive me, Magistrate, no....there is much on my mind."

"Then you should get back to work."

"Yes, Magistrate, thank you, I shall."

"Oh, and before you go, I should inform you that I have just learned from the constables that you personally have been paying for their food prepared by Madame Wu, in view of the fact they have had no salaries. I assume from this that not only are you a man of some decency, but also the Patriarchs do not wish to do their duty and pay for the upkeep of four constables, let alone the ten or twenty that a district of this size really needs?"

"It is a long story, Magistrate, but historically there was only one constable, which was Constable Wei. But then he died. And then Magistrate Qian may have grown confused in his final days and—"

"Yes, yes, Senior Scribe Xu, just be informed that I will reimburse you, and begin paying the constables from my own personal funds until I speak to these Patriarchs, when I will raise the subject of the constables...probably most forcefully."

Senior Scribe Xu stood and bowed, though he felt suddenly faint. Magistrate Zhu had returned to looking once more through his papers, and Senior Scribe Xu had to steel himself then to do what he had come to do.

"Magistrate, I would like to invite you to dinner."

Magistrate Zhu glanced up at Senior Scribe Xu, a look of astonishment on his face.

"Magistrate, I know you have been ordered to rest by Physician Ji, but you do not even have to leave this jail. I have already spoken to Chef Mo, who cooks for Madame Kong, who owns the Inn of Perpetual Happiness. He can have a fine meal delivered here this evening. And I thought that we could speak more. There is a legal matter...a dispute really...that requires your immediate attention and, I think, a most delicate touch."

Senior Scribe Xu thought Magistrate Zhu hesitated longer than was usually polite. He decided to persuade him. "Chef Mo is as dissimilar a cook to Madame Wu as one could get, Magistrate Zhu."

"Then I accept, Senior Scribe Xu."

"I am glad, Magistrate." Senior Scribe Xu bowed deeply, and turned to leave the office. When he was already past the doorway and almost back in the jail-room, Magistrate Zhu called after him: "Do not forget to search the archives for the name, Scary Face Fu!"

Senior Scribe Xu smiled as broadly as he could as he walked back across the market-square. He wanted the people to know that his first proper meeting with the new magistrate had gone as well as humanly possible.

CHAPTER 15

*T*he Deng brothers thought the day was going rather well: they had all survived an encounter with Madame Tang and was each to get a uniform and new boots paid for by the Magistrate. But then Horse, who had finished his tea rather quickly, something obviously preying on his mind, stood up and said: "I have to ask Magistrate Zhu a question."

Before Fast Deng or Slow Deng could recover from their shock and react, Horse was already in the Magistrate's office. And it only seemed like three shakes of the dice when Horse returned, saying that the Magistrate wanted to speak to them all.

"I have only a vague recollection of my arrival," he said. "So I think now that introductions should be made again. My name is Magistrate Zhu, and I am from Kaifeng. Though we speak the same language my words do not always sound the same as yours. In the north we say the same words but speak them often in a different way. So you must speak slowly and clearly so that I always understand you. Moreover, I have read that southerners are prone to emotional instability and irrationality. So I insist that around me you cultivate a serene and yet purposeful outlook every day. You may be amused to learn that one of my travelling companions from Chengdu, Silk Merchant Qi, explained to me that southerners consider all northerners dour and miserable." Magistrate Zhu smiled, giving the impression that he believed this to be true. "So for my own part I will cultivate as happy and as outward a disposition as I can. Are we in agreement?"

The four constables, frightened to be in such proximity to the Magistrate, hardly able to raise their heads, stayed silent.

"Good, good," said Magistrate Zhu. "Now, I have been asked an important question by the Senior Constable here...." He pointed at Horse. "But before I answer it, please tell me your names so I can write them down and commit them to memory and something of your upbringing. Let us start with you, Senior Constable, as your name is already known to me."

""Magistrate ...I am the third son of Blacksmith He. I was clumsy around the smithy. My hands are large and strong but not clever. Constable Wei came to the house when my father said I had to leave. Constable Wei brought me here to the jail. And Magistrate Qian said it was fine that I sleep here, and—"

"Your father had decided to throw you out?"

"Yes, Magistrate. He said I would never be a blacksmith. He said I had to find other work. I was going to join the Imperial Army or the militia. Sergeant Kang and Constable Wei had a big argument about this after I arrived at the jail, and—"

"Is the Sergeant Kang you speak of the same man who led my caravan?" asked Magistrate Zhu. He remembered the sour-faced soldier, who had sat on an old and tired looking pony at the head of the caravan all the way from Chengdu, who had done his utmost not to help anyone at any stage of the difficult journey – confirming for Magistrate Zhu everything bad he had ever thought about soldiers.

"Yes, Magistrate, that is Sergeant Kang. He was very angry and said that Constable Wei had stolen me away."

"But you are happy to be a constable?"

Horse nodded. The last year of inactivity – especially the criticism of the people that all they did was sit at the jail and do nothing – had been a great trial. But now everything was different. They now had a magistrate to give them guidance. "I am *very* happy to be a constable."

"Good, good, Senior Constable He. I am glad to hear it."

Magistrate Zhu then looked at the twins, finding it hard to discover any dissimilarity whatsoever. This was going to be a problem, he thought. "And you two? How were you recruited?"

"Magistrate, we are the Deng brothers – we volunteered!" exclaimed Fast Deng, happily.

"Absolutely, Magistrate," confirmed Slow Deng. "We volunteered because we want to serve the people."

"Serve the people...yes, exactly that, Magistrate."

"Exactly that!"

Horse couldn't quite believe what he was hearing. He turned his head to look at the Deng brothers, to see the expression on their faces as they had told the Magistrate something far less than the truth. They had got into so much trouble around town that their mother had gone to Senior Scribe Xu and legally disowned them and then thrown them out of the house. Somehow, with great trickery with words, they had convinced Magistrate Qian to recruit them.

"And what does your father do?" asked Magistrate Zhu, simply, as if he suspected nothing untoward.

"He is a butcher," said Fast Deng.

"He has a shop across the market-square, near to the Temple," said Slow Deng.

"Our elder brother, Pork Chop, is going to inherit the business."

"He is not as bright as us."

"He likes the blood and—"

"—the squealing of the pigs and—"

"Good, good," interrupted Magistrate Zhu firmly. "But before I let you continue as constables you must explain to me why I have a memorial on my desk describing your many crimes. I will not say who has written this memorial, except that it was at the top of the pile of correspondence I am required to read, quite detailed, more than explicit, and disturbing to me in every way!"

The Deng brothers would have turned and run, the Magistrate's mood having changed so quickly from one of cordial interest to savage inquisition, had they not been prepared for this very moment. They knew who had written the memorial, of course: Senior Scribe Xu, with one-sided anecdotes given to him from the many, many unforgiving people around town.

"Magistrate, we are not criminals," said Fast Deng.

"We are the opposite of criminals," added Slow Deng.

Magistrate Zhu picked up a piece of paper from his desk and began to read out the list slowly.

"Illegal gambling in the street with fighting crickets. Running amok in the Temple and being disrespectful to the priests. Breaking Mister Jin's door on the Street of Golden Butterflies. Stealing food from Chef Mo's kitchen. Fighting with other youths in the market-square. Throwing a rock through the window of the August Hall of Historical Records. Creating a disturbance in the middle of the night in the Street of Happy Circumstance. Making fun of a young monk. Shouting profanities at your mother. Stealing a barrel of wine from the Inn of Harmonious Friendship. The list is quite lengthy. Need I go on?"

Fast Deng laughed. "Ah, Magistrate, that was before."

"Yes, before," intoned Slow Deng.

"Before what?" asked Magistrate Zhu, relaxing back in his chair, finding himself amused, his forced judicial anger dissipating as he was enveloped by the Deng brothers' cheeriness.

"Before we were reborn, Magistrate!" stated Fast Deng.

"Yes, reborn!" agreed Slow Deng.

"We became so disenchanted with our behaviour."

"Terrible behaviour!"

"That one night we prayed all the hours of night."

"In the dark, Magistrate!"

"And by the morning we were reborn."

"Absolutely, reborn!"

"And we went to Magistrate Qian."

"And convinced Magistrate Qian of our rebirth....which was easy because it was true."

Magistrate Zhu put down the piece of paper, keeping the smile off his face. "Did this night of sober reflection on your short life of crime coincide with your mother throwing you out of the family home?"

This insightful question was unexpected. Fast Deng and Slow Deng glanced at each other. They would have to remember in future that Magistrate Zhu was not like the old and kindly Magistrate Qian – not in any way. They silently agreed on the truth – or a version thereof....

"Magistrate, sometimes a terrible shock brings enlightenment."

"Yes, Magistrate – the monks who come to town often say so."

"Our mother threw us out of the house and broke our hearts."

"And in our sadness we were reborn."

Magistrate Zhu pondered this, letting the twins suffer for a while, though his decision had been made already. Then he said: "All people make mistakes, myself included. Magistrate Qian saw fit to trust you. And I have not yet had occasion to doubt his wisdom. So I will let you continue as constables, answering not only to me but to Senior Constable He in all things. See that you behave, and know that for six months at least you shall be on probation, and I shall be watching you."

"Yes, Magistrate!" the twins exclaimed together, more than pleased.

"And in future," continued Magistrate Zhu, "in the telling of stories, make sure you use the proper words. In that way will you be more convincing. Rebirth is something monks speak of. In the administration of justice we speak of 'renewal'."

"Yes, Magistrate – renewal," said Fast Deng, grinning.

"We are the most renewed of young men," said Slow Deng, overjoyed.

Magistrate Zhu nodded, made a note with his ink-brush on the paper before him and said: "Hereafter, you shall call each other Constable Deng and Constable Deng – but never forget that this may only be a temporary state of affairs."

Horse was pleased for the brothers, but wise enough to know that if the Deng brothers got into trouble in the future, he, as senior, would get into trouble as well. He would have to watch them like a hawk.

Magistrate Zhu then turned to Little Ox. "Ah, I think I know something of you already, that your father is dead and that you walked all the way back from Chengdu...through the great forest...on your own."

Magistrate Zhu paused then, considering Little Ox carefully. Horse, fearing that Little Ox – not the easiest of speakers – would have very little to say, decided to speak for him.

"Magistrate, this is Little Ox whose family name is Wu. He is not related to Madame Wu, your house-keeper and cook. His father was Woodblock Wu, who cut woodblocks and took them to Chengdu so books could be printed from them. He—"

"Senior Constable, let him speak for himself," said Magistrate Zhu, not taking his eyes from Little Ox. "Constable Wu, is your mother dead as well?"

"Yes, Magistrate," replied Little Ox, speaking carefully. "When I got back from Chengdu she had died from fever. I have no brothers or sisters and did not know how to carry on the business. There are many people who cut woodblocks and take them to Chengdu. I sat on the step of my house and did not know how to pay the rent. Horse...please excuse me, Magistrate...Senior Constable He came to me. He took me to Magistrate Qian, who said I could become a constable and live here."

Magistrate Zhu stopped taking notes, and placed his ink-brush by the side of his papers. "And is being a constable really what you wish to do?"

"Yes, Magistrate," replied Little Ox. But then he surprised them all and continued to speak. "But none of us know what we should do....to be good constables. The people make fun of us and say we are lazy when we are not, and that we do not know how to catch murderers or fight bandits or demons. Magistrate Qian said we must all be brave and keep the peace. But none of us know how this peace can be kept."

Again amused, Magistrate Zhu could not help but smile. But he was moved also, seeing the sincerity in the young man's expression. "This is the same question that has just been put to me by Senior Constable He, though put in a different way. He asked me what it is to be a constable? A profound question, I think, and one I have never considered before, but one I am pleased to attempt to answer now."

Magistrate Zhu placed his hand on a large book that rested on his desk beside his papers. "This, Constables, is the most important book in my possession. It is the laws of China, known as the Song Penal Code. I consult this book to consider which offences a criminal may have committed and to determine the appropriate punishment to fit the crime. Many of our laws were written by the sages, perhaps as far back as the Golden Age. But they were finally collected together by a host of great scholars in one book, at the time of the Tang Dynasty.

"Now this book does not tell you what it is to be a good constable, or even how I should be a good magistrate. In fact it says little about the true meaning of our work at all. There have been many words written on the subject of justice, and many competing theories developed by great men. But let me tell you what I believe to be true, what has been proven to me by my own work and experience...and by my own failures.

"There is a balance to be maintained at all times – the balance of Heaven and Earth. If this balance is not maintained then the people will suffer famine, flood, earthquake, plague or any other such horror you can name. Dynasties and empires can fail if this balance is undone. And this is not just the responsibility of the Emperor – the Son of Heaven – or even of the great men who walk the halls of the finest palaces in Kaifeng. Even the simplest or poorest man in China has a part to play in preserving this balance.

"You should know that I have come to believe that injustice is the primary cause of any imbalance between Heaven and Earth. It takes just one innocent man to be punished for a crime he did not commit, or for one guilty man to go undiscovered and to walk abroad in this land unpunished, for suffering to be brought down upon all of us. This is the moral responsibility that has been laid upon our heads, we who have chosen to enforce the law.

"Naturally, mine is the greater responsibility. I am the magistrate. But you, as constables, are responsible too. This is why we must find the killer of Mister Gong with all haste – not just for the sake of his family or the peace of Mister Gong's spirit in the afterlife. It is because the balance of Heaven and Earth demands this of us. Do you all understand?"

Horse felt his hands and knees trembling, having understood much more of the Magistrate's words than he had expected to. "Yes, Magistrate," he replied, firmly, for all of them.

"And as I sit in my office and consider every legal petition placed before me," continued Magistrate Zhu, "you are to go out into the town, on patrol, being my eyes and ears among the people, and – this is most important! – you are to be my voice on occasion as well. A sharp word from one of you may stop a miscreant in his tracks, before any crime is committed or any damage is done. As enforcers of the law, we do not just punish – we guide also! So, Constables, be about your business and leave me in peace a while to reflect more on the wrongful death of poor Mister Gong."

CHAPTER 16

MIDDAY, 19TH DAY OF THE 1ST MOON

"*B*uddha's bones!" exclaimed Fast Deng.

"Magistrate Qian's bones!" exclaimed Slow Deng.

It was not long after their meeting with the Magistrate. They were all sitting at the table, their tea long gone cold, their minds all profoundly disturbed.

"Why didn't you tell us, Horse?" asked Fast Deng, angrily. "Why did we have to wait until now – until the Magistrate arrived – to find out Heaven was watching our every move?"

"Yeah, Horse, you could've got us killed," said Slow Deng.

"Or other people," added Little Ox, unhelpfully.

"And we're on probation," said Fast Deng.

"Yes, killed while on probation! Not a happy thought!" added Slow Deng.

Horse was also angry, and bemused, and at a loss to respond to them.

"Didn't Constable Wei mention anything of this?" asked Fast Deng. "Magistrate Qian was dying when we met with him. It was no wonder something this important slipped his mind. He told us to behave ourselves and—"

"—do right by the people, whatever that means," interrupted Slow Deng.

"Yeah, he never said if we made a mistake, or gave the wrong person a smack, there'd be famines and floods and plagues and that the town would fall into the pig-sticking river," said Fast Deng.

"The Magistrate never said that," replied Horse, sharply, irritated by the Deng brothers' whining. Couldn't they see *he* was more responsible than they, because as senior constable he was responsible for *their* behaviour?

Little Ox looked on in worried silence, not quite knowing what to think. He would defend Horse to anybody. Horse was the best friend anyone could have, but still the Deng brothers had a point.

Horse tried to remember the little Constable Wei had explained to him, in the short time they had had together before he died. "Constable Wei just told me that constables break up fights and catch bad people."

"So is that all Constable Wei said, that 'we catch bad people'?" Fast Deng deliberately mocked Horse's slow and deep voice.

Slow Deng punched his brother's arm, worried Fast Deng had gone too far. None of them knew the limits of Horse's temper and Slow Deng didn't want to find out now. He was sure Horse could pick them both up with ease, one under each arm, and knock their heads together.

But Horse didn't rise to the bait. "Constable Wei didn't tell me much about anything," he said, softly. "All we did was walk around town and the valley. He stopped and talked to people. He went into people's houses and ate their food. Then he would call on Widow Han or Widow Jiang, and I would wait outside until he came out. Then we would walk some more."

"We should call on Widow Han and Widow Jiang ourselves. They might be able to teach us how to be good constables," said Fast Deng.

"And other stuff," said Slow Deng.

This was too funny for the constables to stay angry or keep hurling recriminations at each other. Even Horse had to smile. The Deng brothers nearly fell off their chairs laughing. Little Ox covered his mouth with his hands.

It was only as the laughter died down that they realised the Magistrate was in the jail-room with them, hovering in the doorway. The table was nearly knocked over in their haste to stand up straight and then to bow and then to stand up straight once more.

"Forgive me for disturbing your tea, constables. I forgot to inform you that you are now to be paid salaries. You, as senior," he said, pointing towards Horse, "will be paid one and a half strings of cash every month. The other constables: one string of cash every month. I will arrange the first payment to be made in the next few days, the cash to be collected from the clerks at the August Hall of Historical Records. You must spend the cash wisely, or better still save it. It is not to be wasted on wine or on unsavoury women."

Magistrate Zhu opened his mouth, as if he was going to expand on the subject, but then, thinking better of it, he turned and vanished back into his office.

For a while all Fast Deng could hear was the thumping of his heart, wondering how much the Magistrate had overheard, but then he clapped his hands together with glee. "Why didn't he say this at the very start, before all that other complicated nonsense?"

Slow Deng was already thinking ahead, convinced that their prospects had improved almost beyond measure. "Now that we have salaries the girls will come running, won't they?"

Horse sat back down, feeling weary to his very soul, a pain forming in his head, just behind his eyes. He suspected his troubles had only just begun.

"I'll make some more tea," said Little Ox.

Tea was appropriate for any occasion – even one as great as this.

CHAPTER 17

AFTERNOON, 19TH DAY OF THE 1ST MOON

Magistrate

As you read this, no doubt I am already in the afterlife. I send you my sincerest best regards from wherever my spirit resides. I had wished to greet you in person and welcome you to the Fifth District, and share a pot of tea, but my health is failing day by day, and I expect no new appointment to be made until after I am cold and in the ground. They say there is a shortage of men of quality, but I say there is not. Instead there is a lack of determination to govern this prefecture and this province properly. Fortunes are being made by greedy men. Officials spend too much time socialising with dancing girls. The needs of the people go unfulfilled. It was ever thus.

I trust you have arrived safely, and there has not been too much of a hiatus between my death and your arrival. No district should be without a magistrate for long, even a small district such as this. I beg you to have patience with these people, and with the Patriarchs. The people here value their separateness even from Chengdu. I urge you to be steadfast, but gentle; receptive to their concerns, but then confident and unshakeable in your judgements. I am certain the people will respect such an approach.

As I lie on my death-bed, I find I have become especially sensitive to the subtle energies balancing Heaven and Earth. Change is coming and great difficulties will have to be overcome. Is this a true premonition of evil? I do not know, but I do believe I am not up to the task. I think I am being removed by Heaven to make way

68

for a magistrate with more wisdom and courage than I. Wherever you have come from, I am certain you are not here by chance. It saddens me that I will never speak with you in this life.

If it is allowed, I will give you what aid I can from the afterlife. That I solemnly swear.

Now, there are some matters of a practical nature I must discuss with you.

The first concerns the tradition of very public Courts and hearings in the Fifth District. I am certain you will <u>not</u> have been made aware of this by the authorities in Chengdu. They prefer to turn a blind eye to the administration of justice in the more remote districts, and I am sure such a practice would have come as quite a shock to you on arrival. Before you act in any way to curb this tradition please consider first what I have to say.

Up to about one hundred years ago, there were no officials or clerks in this district. The local Patriarchs administered to the people and presided over criminal courts and adjudicated in civil disputes. Banditry was suppressed by the Patriarchs' personal guards and local volunteers.

When Sichuan Province was brought back within the empire, this was a situation which could not, of course, continue. But change is painful, even if that change is for the benefit of the people. When the first magistrate arrived – his name was Magistrate Gao, and I believe his life and thoughts are worthy of study – he took it upon himself to implement correct judicial procedures. But he did not interfere with the local right of the people to attend Court in the Temple. I will let you be the judge of whether his decision was wise. At first I did not think so and I resisted this experience in my mind. But through the years I have come to appreciate the nature of these public Courts and found value in being able to give moral guidance <u>directly</u> into the minds of the people.

I urge you to continue with this tradition, though it will trouble you at first. Do not be concerned with judicial review by the circuit judicial intendant, whoever he now might be. I have always been able to demonstrate that my decisions have not been unduly affected by the people. However, please note that I have still conducted the examination of witnesses and defendants in private. It is the semblance of the public Court I urge you to continue. I am certain you will have the moral strength not to be swayed by public opinion when you attempt to read out your judgements. You may also be concerned about public disturbances. Do not be. The people treat this tradition with great reverence. The loss of this tradition, though perhaps inevitable in the long term, will be of great sadness to them.

I have been so impressed with the effect of these public Courts that through the years I have considered writing a memorial to the Ministry of Justice, recommending their institution in all other districts in the Chengdu Prefecture, and then, if successful, all across China. That I have not done so should be seen as my natural reluctance to display my lack of education and poor talents as a writer and maker of arguments. Perhaps you would consider such a memorial when your tenure comes to an end?

I wish now to comment on the clerks.

It is unfortunate there is not a full complement of clerks in the district, and none who specialise in legal matters or who are trained in legal research. However, through my difficult beginnings in the district I was forced to rely on the assistance of Senior Scribe Xu. I have found him to be a staunch ally and have come to value his advice. He has indeed become a loyal and beloved friend. I advise you not to overlook his talents or underestimate his worth.

I must also speak about the constables.

There are four young men I have come to employ in the last few months, who, with good fortune, will be at the jail on your arrival awaiting your command. These youths were not employed on a whim. And though there may be many in the district who will inform you that their employment was a symptom of my senility or illness, I assure you it was not. I see in each of them great potential to be of service to the people of this district. I recommend each of them to you.

Finally, I have to mention a dispute that has dogged my final months and contributed much to my failing health. This is the dispute between the Family Zhou, one of the three noble families in the district, and a certain Madame Tang. The dispute concerns the failure to perform a contract.

I have been unable to write a judgement that does not seem to offend my conscience, or indeed Heaven, in some manner. Because I do not wish to influence your thinking unduly, I have destroyed all my personal papers and notes in regard to this dispute, preferring you to start afresh. Forgive me for this. All I ask is that you consider and examine Jade Moon <u>most carefully</u> before coming to a decision. I find her fascinating and unsettling in equal measure, and fear the consequences of a wrongful judgement. I will say no more.

My sincerest best wishes to you and your family,

Magistrate Qian
Fifth District, Chengdu Prefecture
1ˢᵗ day of the 2ⁿᵈ Moon, 1085

Magistrate Zhu laid the letter down on the desk, having been given much food for thought. Public courts? Who had heard of such a thing? But what was it that Prefect Kang had told him? *"Try not to interfere with local traditions, Magistrate Zhu!"* He frowned, thinking he would cross that bridge when he came to it.

The calligraphy of the letter had been poor, forgivable only in that Magistrate Qian had written it when only a few days from his death. But the mind behind the characters had been sound.

"Yes, I would have liked to have shared a pot of tea with you, Magistrate Qian," he spoke out loud.

CHAPTER 18

EVENING, 19TH DAY OF THE 1ST MOON

"Senior Scribe Xu, I have some anxiety over the kinds of food served in the south. I have a constant fear that I may be poisoned by strong spices and pungent herbs."

"Oh no, Magistrate, do not fear. Chef Mo is the most subtle and delicate of cooks. I eat at the Inn of Perpetual Happiness at least seven times a month, and have done so since the death of my wife. Never, in that time, have I had to consult a healer or physician. I am certain Chef Mo is responsible for this great wonder of my good health. I am convinced – though I have great respect for Physician Ji – that Chef Mo's is the greater art."

"Do you really think so?"

"Magistrate, I have no doubt."

They were sitting in Magistrate Zhu's apartment at the jail, with Horse standing by to take Senior Scribe Xu's order for food over to Chef Mo at the Inn of Perpetual Happiness. Horse had never known this to happen before, that Chef Mo would send servants out to deliver food. But then there was a new magistrate in town, and as everybody was saying, it was important that Magistrate Zhu and Senior Scribe Xu become, if not friends, then at least tolerant of one another. A good meal shared was sure to help.

"Would you allow me to order for us both, Magistrate?"

Magistrate Zhu hesitated, lacking confidence, having eaten so very badly at wayside taverns and lodging-houses all the way from Kaifeng. And he was now at the mercy of Madame Wu, who seemed able to effortlessly remove any goodness or flavour from the food she prepared.

"Yes, Senior Scribe Xu, you will know what is best. I will trust your judgement."

Senior Scribe Xu wrote the order quickly, and passed the note to Horse, pleased with himself. However, it was a ruse. He had already discussed at length with Chef Mo what should be prepared. He had told Chef Mo just to wait for a few moments before having the servants run the food over from the inn, so as not to make the Magistrate overly suspicious. Already, servants had delivered a table and a decoration of mountain flowers for the meal – much to Magistrate Zhu's great delight.

After Horse had vanished with the note, Senior Scribe Xu commented on the fine weather of the day and how the Magistrate's vitality seemed to be improving by the hour. Not that the Magistrate was interested in speaking more on his health. Instead, after a time, when Senior Scribe Xu was worried that he had run out of subjects for easy discussion, Magistrate Zhu quite surprised him by mentioning a name that Senior Scribe Xu had wished he hadn't yet heard.

"Jade Moon – please tell me about her," said Magistrate Zhu.

"Who?"

"Jade Moon. In his letter Magistrate Qian made reference to a sensitive legal dispute concerning this young woman."

Senior Scribe Xu licked his lips nervously, wondering how much Magistrate Qian had written. "Ah, she is quite a puzzle, Magistrate."

"You think her more than a common girl?"

"She and her mother are seamstresses in the possession of great skill, Magistrate. There are none better in town. In fact, I understand you have employed them to create the constables' uniforms."

Magistrate Zhu was taken aback, appalled that his senior constable had contracted on his behalf with seamstresses, who were caught up in a legal dispute he was required to now adjudge. He tried to calm himself, remembering the constables' lack of legal understanding.

"Magistrate, are you unwell?"

"Senior Scribe Xu, if I had known this fact, I would have gone elsewhere for the constables' uniforms."

Senior Scribe Xu shook his head, as plates of food were placed before them, filling the room with a wonderful aroma of venison in a sweet, dark sauce. The Magistrate, taken up with the subject of Jade Moon, had not noticed the remarkable speed of preparation of the food.

"Magistrate, you could not have gone elsewhere. Naturally, all the women in town do needlework for their families...the Patriarchs' wives and daughters are especially talented...but for the constables' uniforms there was really nowhere else to turn. However, I would not be surprised if Madame Tang had tried to make a good impression with you. I suspect Horse got a more than fair price."

"Senior Constable He," corrected Magistrate Zhu.

"Yes, of course Magistrate, my apologies."

Magistrate Zhu spooned some of the food into his mouth. He felt the venison melt on his tongue and the sauce invade all his senses with pleasure. Involuntarily he closed his eyes and found himself far away. It was truly a wonderful moment.

They sat in silence for a while eating slowly. Senior Scribe Xu felt quite emotional that Magistrate Zhu obviously appreciated what was being placed before him. Though the food was of the usual extraordinary standard, he felt himself to be drawn more to the expressions of joy and wonder on the Magistrate's face than to concentrating on what was happening on his own tongue.

"Let us speak of the dispute between Madame Tang and Patriarch Zhou," said Magistrate Zhu finally. "I would ask you to deliver the file – what exists of it, anyway – to me tomorrow morning. I understand that Magistrate Qian destroyed much of his own papers, but the original petitions should still exist."

"Oh, yes, Magistrate – in fact there are two petitions and a counter-petition in the file. Magistrate Qian did do a great deal of work. He interviewed witnesses, and spoke at length to all the people concerned. I believe there were even harsh words exchanged between Magistrate Qian and Patriarch Zhou. It is a pity Magistrate Qian destroyed all his fine work."

"Yes, and no, Senior Scribe Xu. It does give me a fresh start. I am torn between thinking the destruction of the papers was a demonstration of Magistrate Qian's trust and faith in me, or a manifestation of his frustration in not being able to solve this dispute."

Senior Scribe Xu believed it to be the latter. In his final days, lying on his death-bed, Magistrate Qian had begun to express great emotion about the dispute.

"Magistrate, though I cannot be sure, I believe he was sympathetic to Madame Tang."

"Did he discuss the case with you often?"

"No, Magistrate, but he was a compassionate man. And he certainly demonstrated compassion for Jade Moon."

"How so?"

Senior Scribe Xu thought carefully, wishing he could take back those last few words. "Magistrate, perhaps I misspoke. But to me he always spoke of Jade Moon in the kindest of fashions. I believe Magistrate Qian did not have as much sympathy in regard to the mother, Madame Tang, and thought her to be much the author of her own misfortune. However, there are others who believe the Family Zhou are going to bring destruction upon us all by their...and these are not my words, Magistrate...pig-headedness and pride. These people – and they are many and quite vocal – say Madame Tang should be released from the contract, and that this should be done regardless of any loss incurred by the Family Zhou. It is a most depressing situation."

"What are your thoughts, Senior Scribe Xu?"

"Magistrate, I believe Jade Moon to be a remarkable young woman, and worthy of careful consideration."

More trays of food were put in front of them, and Magistrate Zhu commenced eating again, feeling life and strength return to his body.

"Senior Scribe Xu, could you please tell the story in your own words? Do not be concerned about falling into subjectivity or sentimentalism. Let us call it a personal introduction to the case."

"Yes, Magistrate, I would be glad to speak of it. Some years ago, seven or eight I think – I cannot be sure without consulting the census records – Madame

Tang and her daughter arrived in Tranquil Mountain. They decided to stay. Oh, and Madame Tang is a widow, that is most important. She does not speak of her dead husband, though it is widely known that he was a barbarian – not a Tibetan, I believe, but one of the barbarians to the north."

"Barbarian? So the daughter, this Jade Moon, is half-barbarian?"

"Oh yes, Magistrate. She is now nineteen years of age."

"Then, Senior Scribe Xu, we should refer to her properly as Miss Tang and not by her given name."

"Yes, of course, Magistrate. But she is certainly not fully Chinese. She is tall for a woman – not as tall as me, of course, but very striking. She wears her hair long and loose and down her back, which the other women about town do not always appreciate. Not that Miss Tang is seen about town very often these days. Perhaps the way she wears her hair is a barbarian custom. Her mother is always well dressed and wears her hair up quite properly in a chignon."

"Then I would say the mother is to blame for not teaching her daughter proper codes of dress."

"Yes, I expect so, Magistrate. Now, when Madame Tang and her daughter arrived in town they had no cash, just enough to find lodging. It seems Madame Tang wanted to set up in business, rather than enter a life of service as a maid. She approached the Patriarchs for credit. But because she was not known, or because she could not easily demonstrate her skill without materials, no credit was offered."

"That is understandable."

"Yes, Magistrate, but, when Madame Tang visited the Zhou residence with Jade Moon – who, you must remember, was only about twelve years old at the time – Second Son Zhou, the youngest son of Patriarch Zhou, took an instant liking to the girl. He prevailed upon his father, and an incredible contract was struck. Madame Tang sold her daughter, Jade Moon, to be a concubine for Second Son Zhou, for an advance of cash to buy raw materials and tools. She also got a reduced lease on a house, large enough to serve as a workshop as well as a place to live. Patriarch Zhou accepted an argument from Madame Tang that her daughter would be taught further skills as a seamstress by her, and would be better able to serve the Family Zhou as a concubine at the age of seventeen. Jade Moon...please excuse me, I mean Miss Tang...was, according to the contract, to join the Family Zhou as concubine on her seventeenth birthday."

"Was stamp tax paid on the contract?"

"Yes, of course Magistrate, everything about the contract was done correctly. But Madame Tang had no cash, so Patriarch Zhou paid the whole four percent tax."

"Is there a copy of the contract in the file?"

"No, Magistrate. The copy kept by us at the August Hall of Historical Records was borrowed by Magistrate Qian and then, I believe, destroyed in the burning of his papers. Madame Tang or Patriarch Zhou should still have their copies."

Magistrate Zhu frowned, unhappy. "Please go on, Senior Scribe Xu."

"I had personal concerns with the legality of the contract. I do not approve of the selling of children. I believed, at the time, that it was unlawful for a free woman to be sold into service or slavery. But Magistrate Qian said in this instance that law had not been breached."

Magistrate Zhu nodded. "He is quite correct. The Song Penal Code indeed makes it an offence for a free man or woman to be sold into slavery to pay off a debt. But a concubine is not a slave. I admit that a concubine is not as honoured as a wife, but Miss Tang should surely have no complaints. To be a concubine to a noble family is to be in a place of honour."

"Yes, Magistrate, and the contract was extremely beneficial to Madame Tang. She and Jade Moon were able to eat and live while setting up a business, buying hemp and silk, and creating clothes and embroideries to sell. They were very successful. You must understand, Magistrate, Madame Tang proved to be no novice. Soon the business was thriving and she became notorious among the merchants for her negotiating skills. She was able to sell clothing to all the best families, including to the Patriarchs and their wives. Both mother and daughter are as skilled as any seamstress I have ever seen in Chengdu, if not more so, and yet their prices are much more attractive."

"And their success is due to this contract?"

"Indeed, Magistrate, without the contract they would have starved or been forced into a life of service. Some years later, I cannot remember when, I heard Madame Tang had gone to Patriarch Zhou and asked to be released from the contract. She had saved enough to pay cash to—"

"To buy herself and her daughter out of the contract?"

"Yes, Magistrate, that is exactly it. I do not know what Patriarch Zhou's feelings on this were at the time. But Miss Tang was older by then and Second Son Zhou had grown even more enamoured of her. He persuaded his father not to alter the contract."

"Even though Miss Tang is of barbarian appearance?"

"Quite so, Magistrate. And he is not alone. There are many who think she is quite beautiful, if not a little exotic."

"This is extraordinary."

"Yes, Magistrate, but there is more. There is a counter-petition in the file from Madame Tang that states that her daughter is not her daughter."

"Not her daughter?"

"There is talk of the supernatural."

"Ah."

"Magistrate, please wait until I finish my story. There is much more I have to explain. About two years ago bandits came down from the mountains. These bandits were army deserters – half-starved and very desperate men. They came into town carrying knives and started an altercation in the market-square. They fought with the market-traders and tried to steal food. Traders were hurt. Sergeant Kang and his militia soldiers were in their barracks sleeping or away guarding the caravans, and Constable Wei was nowhere to be seen. Many questions were asked afterward I can tell you, Magistrate."

"Was anybody killed?" asked Magistrate Zhu.

"Oh no, Magistrate, that is the miracle. The head bandit, who went by the name of Bad Teeth Tong, was about to plunge a knife into Mister Peng, a trader in spices, when he was taken by an arrow straight in the heart. He was dead before he hit the ground. Physician Ji wrote this in his report."

"Was it a hunter who killed this bandit?"

"No, Magistrate, it was the girl, Jade Moon...Madame Tang's daughter! And she was then just a short time from her seventeenth birthday."

Magistrate Zhu dropped his spoon on the table, a look of horror on his face. "Miss Tang...who is a young woman and a seamstress and the daughter of Madame Tang...shot a bandit dead with an arrow?"

Senior Scribe Xu nodded, feeling an intense satisfaction from the telling of this story.

"Where did she get the bow and arrows? Surely the common people are not allowed to be armed here?"

"Oh no, Magistrate, it is not allowed except for the hunters. Magistrate Qian confiscated the bow and arrows. They are in the store in the jail, I believe."

"Good, very good," replied Magistrate Zhu, still shaken by the story. "Then where did she get the weapons?"

"No one truly knows. Magistrate Qian interviewed Miss Tang at length afterwards, but I was not present and I did not get to read any notes taken. As you can imagine I was quite distressed by the events. Did I tell you the other bandits were chased through the town by the people? Not one of the bandits survived. They were all thrown in the river. It was a calamitous day."

"Are bandits common in this district?"

"They can be, Magistrate, though most are cowardly and attack people only on the trails outside of town. Which was why it was all so shocking. I saw the body of the bandit-leader with my own eyes. Bad Teeth Tong was lying dead, in a pool of his blood, his eyes staring open at the sky. The arrow stuck out of the centre of his chest. I shall never forget it, Magistrate. My dreams were quite disturbed for some time after. Magistrate Qian had arrived belatedly, waving his sword in the air, trying to calm the people, and prevent further mayhem. He was angry, Magistrate. Did I say that Constable Wei was nowhere to be seen?"

"But what about the girl, Miss Tang? Did you see her in the market-square?"

"Ah, Magistrate, again it was a sight I will never forget until I die. She was standing there alone, looking upon what she had done. I cannot describe the expression on her face – I have not the skill with words – but many say a goddess had descended into her."

"A goddess?"

"Yes, Magistrate, this is most important. As I said, she was almost seventeen, Magistrate, and many people believed they had seen a miracle...an act of Heaven. Mister Peng, who has since sadly passed away from natural causes, said at the time he saw the light of a goddess behind Jade Moon's eyes. And the people – some of them, at least – believed him."

Magistrate Zhu nodded. "And Madame Tang sought to take advantage of this event?"

Senior Scribe Xu laughed and smiled. "Yes, Magistrate, perhaps that is what she did. On Jade Moon's seventeenth birthday, Madame Tang refused to send her daughter to the Zhou residence. Patriarch Zhou sent men to Madame Tang's house to collect her, but they were turned away by a great crowd protesting this. Patriarch Zhou was not willing to shed blood and become infamous in the eyes of the people. He ordered his men back. So he then put a petition to Magistrate Qian to have the contract completed. Magistrate Qian then had two petitions: one from Madame Tang claiming her daughter was no longer her daughter so she could not in good conscience send her to the Family Zhou, and one from Patriarch Zhou asking for Miss Tang to be delivered up to him."

"Fascinating."

"Exactly, Magistrate. But there is also a third petition in the file."

"A third petition?"

"Yes, Magistrate – a terrible accusation. It has further inflamed emotions across town. Some months after, Second Son Zhou went to Madame Tang's house when she was not there, ostensibly to collect the rent. What happened then nobody knows, but Second Son Zhou came running out of the house with a cut to his face. Second Son Zhou accuses Miss Tang of putting a knife to his face and threatening him with murder."

"Did he not choose to reject Miss Tang then?" asked Magistrate Zhu, astonished.

"No, Magistrate – some say Second Son Zhou is quite peculiar."

"And where is Magistrate Qian's judgement on this criminal petition? I take it he would have dealt with this accusation with the appropriate alacrity."

Senior Scribe Xu sighed. He looked down at his plate, realising that somewhere in the middle of his story, the food he thought he had been eating had been replaced by the servants with something entirely different. He looked back up at Magistrate Zhu feeling suddenly sad.

"Magistrate, this criminal petition has not even been considered yet. Magistrate Qian decided to consider all the petitions together, much to the fury of Patriarch Zhou. A year later nothing had been resolved and then Magistrate Qian took ill and died. I offered Patriarch Zhou the choice of taking his complaints to the Prefect in Chengdu but he declined. I cannot blame him. Chengdu is so far away, and how long would he have to wait for the Prefect to consider a simple contractual dispute? Patriarch Zhou resolved to be patient until a new magistrate came to town. But he didn't think we would have to wait so long."

"All disputes, no matter how complicated, can be resolved quickly and easily if the magistrate or judge considers every aspect carefully and rationally," said Magistrate Zhu. "I am at a loss to understand why Magistrate Qian could not do this."

"Many people say this dispute contributed to his ill-health and premature death," said Senior Scribe Xu, sadly.

"Premature? I thought you said Magistrate Qian was quite advanced in years."

"Quite so, Magistrate, but he was well loved, and many hoped his tenure would go on for many more years."

Magistrate Zhu nodded sympathetically, privately pleased he would have to rule on such a locally important dispute. He could make his mark immediately. He could demonstrate the correct approach to such problems, whether they were considered intractable by others or not.

"Senior Scribe Xu, this food is quite excellent. I have not eaten better."

"I am glad, Magistrate."

"In fact I am feeling so recovered, I wish you to approach the Patriarchs and set a date for a meeting. I wish to discuss some important matters with them."

"Of course, Magistrate," replied Senior Scribe Xu, smiling, his happiness in the evening complete.

"Then, as I am continuing my investigation into the death of Mister Gong, I will deal swiftly with the dispute between this Madame Tang and the Family Zhou."

Senior Scribe Xu smiled and nodded, wondering if the Magistrate's confidence was properly justified.

I t was the best time of their lives.

They had all heard of Chef Mo's incredible talent but none of the constables had ever partaken of it. Like many of the common people in town, they had never had the cash. Or the benefit of an invite from Madame Kong, who, though a slight and pretty woman, ran the Inn of Perpetual Happiness with an iron hand and a mind to cater to those travellers and local patrons who were the most affluent and important.

And it was not just leftovers that they were eating. The constables had been sitting at their table, drinking tea, having pushed aside Madame Wu's latest offering for dinner, when the servants from the inn had placed food trays in front of them on which were placed all sorts of delicacies, and bowls into which was poured the greatest broth that had ever been prepared under Heaven: Chef Mo's 'Broth of a Hundred Flavours'.

"There must be some mistake," had said Horse, disbelieving.

But the servants had smiled, shaken their heads, and assured them that the food had been provided free by Madame Kong, who had wished the atmosphere of the *whole* jail to be as harmonious as possible, so that the Magistrate and Senior Scribe Xu could speak freely.

The Deng brothers needed no further encouragement, and tucked in. And soon Little Ox and Horse were also filling their mouths, and finding their senses overcome with the most wonderful scents and spices.

When Leaf put his head around the door, even the Deng brothers didn't complain when Horse took a bowl, filled it with some of the food and gave it to him – the child's eyes each as large as the full moon. Yes, it was true that Miss Dai of the Always Smiling Orphanage always put three meals on the table for the children, but it had to be said that the portions were never great and her cooking just barely acceptable.

So there they were, all happy and complete, when Chef Mo looked in the door, much to the sudden consternation of the Deng brothers. In the past they had been chased away from his kitchen at the point of a meat cleaver for attempting to take food that was not theirs. But such things were to be forgotten in the importance of the moment.

"How is the meeting going?" asked Chef Mo, his voice a whisper.

"I think they are becoming the best of friends," replied Horse, believing it to be true. When he had last looked in, they had both seemed to be talking animatedly about something or other, not a cross word or difficult silence between them.

Chef Mo laughed, and wiped a heavily-muscled forearm across his brow. Though the evening was not warm, and the mist was already beginning to descend, Chef Mo was sweating profusely, either from nervousness or his cooking exertions. "Then maybe there is hope for us all," he said, accepting a cup of tea from Little Ox, who had seen just what was needed.

CHAPTER 19

*H*orse bowed deeply, surprised to find the Magistrate still at his desk at this hour and after a long evening spent speaking with Senior Scribe Xu.

"Magistrate, do you need anything? Constable Wu could prepare you some tea."

Magistrate Zhu shook his head. "Are you going out on patrol, Senior Constable? I am aware that I have yet to speak to you about this...about how we are to cope with just four constables."

The subject of patrolling and keeping the peace was a difficult one for Horse. Constable Wei had made his rounds in the early evening, and then only by moving from tavern to tavern, or visiting with friends at their homes. And then he had died suddenly, and no patrolling had been done while Horse had taken care of the ailing Magistrate Qian. After the death of Magistrate Qian, when asked, Senior Scribe Xu had been circumspect. "Do what you think best, Horse, but if you arrest anyone there is no one here to pass judgement, and don't forget that the Deng brothers are not welcome in many parts of town or in any taverns if you should wish to break up fights."

There was also the problem that, though all four of them had grown up in Tranquil Mountain, many of the streets in the poorer parts of the town were densely packed – warrens almost – very easy to get lost within, especially at night when the mist came down. And if they were patrolling at night and patrolling in the day, when would they sleep? The last time the Deng brothers had kept to their cots in the day, Madame Wu had caught Slow Deng on the side of the head with her broom, fetching up a nasty lump – her signal disapproval, they assumed, of anyone who was weak or feeble enough to sleep during the daylight hours.

"Magistrate, we do need guidance. I do not know when we should arrest people. There is sometimes much drunkenness, especially at the time of the festivals and after the tea harvests. Youths often fight in the streets. Sometimes they fall into the river and are never seen again. Sergeant Kang's militia soldiers are rowdy and upset many people. And Magistrate, though I try to be respectful, I have found that people do not speak much to any of us. I think that constables are not well liked."

"Unhappily, this is a universal truth, Senior Constable. Though you may find it hard to believe, in some parts of the empire it is sometimes hard to tell the difference between the constables and the criminals, so alike are they in their behaviour. The people are often right to be suspicious. But I will speak to you at length about your duties, and endeavour to find you batons and swords with which to carry them out. Were you going out now?"

"I was going out with Little Ox...please excuse me, Constable Wu....to sit with the sons of Mister Gong. They fear their family is cursed – that a ghost or demon has killed their father."

Magistrate Zhu sighed, and placed his ink-brush down on the desk. Horse assumed he was writing a report or a letter of some kind.

"Senior Constable, it is a pity that my exhaustion has caused me to remain here and to neglect my duty. Otherwise I should come out with you and speak again to the sons of Mister Gong. Perhaps tomorrow. But let us be clear on one thing: a man murdered Mister Gong. It would be unusual for a woman to beat a man in such a way, and out on the street. A woman's preferred weapons are those of the weak and the underhand: poison or a knife.

"You may ask: why not a ghost or a demon? It is true that I have read of strange cases from all across China, of ghosts, and of demons who can take the shapes of animals or men – but in the case of Mister Gong I do not think so. Surely a ghost would appear in a house, and not the street, and surely a demon would not come into town...unless...." Magistrate Zhu paused to think deeply for a moment, his eyes caught up in watching the flickering of the flame on the oil-lamp perched on the edge of his desk. "....unless it had been invited to do so, I suppose, through necromancy." He looked towards Horse, inviting comment.

"Magistrate, I also believe the murderer of Mister Gong to be a man."

Magistrate Zhu raised his eyebrows. "You do?"

"Yes, Magistrate, and that the murderer – this Scary Face Fu – was known somehow to Mister Gong."

"And why do you believe this, Senior Constable?" asked Magistrate Zhu gently, smiling.

Horse searched deep within himself. Somehow, just from listening to the Magistrate these last few moments, certainty had come to him. But how to explain this?

"Magistrate, I trust the examination made by Physician Ji. And Apothecary Hong, who assisted him, has travelled in all the barbarian lands, even over the mountains to the west. He has seen many things and can tell many stories. Neither of them believes it to be a demon, because…I think…a demon would have taken Mister Gong's body away. And if it had been a ghost, then surely Mister Gong's heart would have simply stopped. There would have been no need to give him a beating. That is what I think, Magistrate."

Impressed, and with a strange excitement coursing through his veins, Magistrate Zhu almost stood up and offered to go out with Horse that night. But he had to remind himself that restraint now would lend him greater stamina for the days to come.

"Senior Constable, I am in agreement with all that you have said. So we are looking for a man, this Scary Face Fu – a man who supposedly does not exist, because no one has ever heard of him. I have already asked Senior Scribe Xu to have the clerks scour the archives, though personally I do not have much hope. The name is unusual, not one wished for, I think. Perhaps an alias. So I want you to consider this instead: that Mister Gong was killed because of who he was, or because of something that he had done for which the murderer wanted vengeance, or because of something he knew or had seen that night. You should know that it would not be unusual for a man who had committed the crime of corruption to also commit murder – though that is the more serious crime – if he is frightened of being found out. Judge Pei, my legal mentor in Kaifeng, used to say: a crime may appear senseless to the righteous man, but it will always make sense to a criminal. Do you understand?"

Horse was not sure, and his head was beginning to ache. He was beginning to suspect that Magistrate Zhu was the cleverest man he had ever met, cleverer even than Studious Chu, the son of Schoolmaster Chu, who read books and scrolls, and thought many great thoughts, from morning until night.

Magistrate Zhu stood up, warming to his subject. "We must also consider geography. Most often the murderer lives in the vicinity of the murdered – perhaps the next house, or the next street, or he attends the same tavern or prays at the same temple. So we must always remember to think of this when we are investigating. It is rare for a murderer to travel many miles just to kill, except for banditry. And, as we already know, Mister Gong still had coins in his pocket, so he was not attacked for purposes of robbery. And because of the theory of geography, we must even consider the family—"

"Magistrate," interrupted Horse, surprising himself, and finding it necessary to apologise immediately. "Please forgive me, but the sons of Mister Gong are good men."

"Yes, I agree, for I have met them too. But you should be aware that this crime does happen, though thankfully rarely. Plotting the murder of one's parents is one of the ten great abominations, even if the plot is unsuccessful. It is the fourth abomination, in fact, and is called contumacy, because the crime casts aside our deepest principles concerning family."

Horse spoke the word 'contumacy' in his mind, never having heard it before. He committed it to memory

"Now as to the matter of time," continued Magistrate Zhu, "we must think more creatively. A murderous grudge could be formed ten, twenty or even thirty years before the crime of murder is ever committed. The reason for the crime need not be found on the day of the murder. So did Mister Gong, though he had become a respected father and grandfather, do something to someone in the past – even unwittingly – to earn that person's enmity; an enmity that festered, corrupting a man so that he was willing then to commit murder?"

Horse nodded, understanding this as a true fact, remembering instances from his own childhood where he was chastised by his father for no good reason, instances that burned within him – continued to burn within him – for years.

"Good, so tonight, Senior Constable, when you are sitting with the sons of Mister Gong, do not think too much on ghosts or demons. But listen to anything that may be said. It may be only a simple thing and not recognised for what it is by the speaker, but it may be of the utmost importance."

Horse breathed deeply, feeling a terrible burden had been placed on him. He bowed deeply to Magistrate Zhu.

"Oh, and Senior Constable, before you go, I must censure you on something you have done. You have contracted on my behalf with a certain Madame Tang for the making of your uniforms. However, I am required to make judgement on a legal dispute involving her and her daughter."

Horse felt a chill reach into his heart.

"I will not punish you, Senior Constable, but you must recognise your mistake. Your action could be misinterpreted, that I might be persuaded to show undue favour. Do not cancel the contract now, but be wary in the future. To enforce the law we must stand slightly apart from the people. It is a small price to pay to gain the approval of Heaven."

Horse bowed again, and quickly left the office, resolving never to make that mistake again.

CHAPTER 20

*J*unior Scribe Li lay awake in bed, too anxious to sleep. Despite the ridiculous extravagance, he had decided to keep one oil-lamp burning by his bedside – though he gained little comfort from it. His eyes kept straying to the latch on the door of his small house. It would be a simple thing for a murderer to burst in and do for him as had been done for Mister Gong.

It would have been better, he thought, if he were married. He had heard that the voice of a wife often gave courage to a husband, whether that courage was wanted or not. But at twenty-three years old, he still lived alone. He was not as yet that advanced in his career as a clerk to be earning a salary attractive to the sort of women of whom his parents would approve.

Junior Scribe Li sat up in bed, studying the latch to his door carefully, certain for a few terrible moments that it had in fact moved. He climbed out of bed, walked the few steps to the door, and tested the latch, breathing only when he had satisfied himself it was as secure as it was ever going to be. Yes, it was true that they had a new magistrate in town, and certainly it was a good thing that he and Senior Scribe Xu had shared a fine meal that very evening, and were said now to be the firmest of friends, but it should not be forgotten that there was a murderer walking the streets.

There had been other murders in Tranquil Mountain in the last year, after the death of Magistrate Qian and before the arrival of Magistrate Zhu. But each had been solved quite easily. A certain Mister Han had murdered his wife, and had then calmly gone to the house of Senior Scribe Xu and confessed what he had done, saying that he had been thinking about it for twenty years. Senior Scribe Xu had sent him to Chengdu for trial the next morning, escorted by Sergeant Kang. Fortunately, Mister Han's children were grown, and though they would have to live with the family shame, they could at least take care of themselves.

The other murder was committed by Mister Wang on his great friend Mister Feng, when a night of drinking and gambling had gone terribly wrong. Mister Wang had thrown himself in White Dragon River afterward before anybody could stop him – not that many had tried to do so.

"Inseparable in life, as in death," Senior Scribe Xu had written at the end of his report, which Junior Scribe Li had read thoroughly as part of his education in style and content, before placing in the archives.

But now they had an *unsolved* murder. And Junior Scribe Li could not get the memory of Mister Gong's naked body laid out on the table out of his mind. It could so easily have been him, or anybody. Everyone now knew that Mister Gong had been a good man who had raised a fine, respectable family, and had no enemies under Heaven.

And all the Magistrate had done so far to find the murderer was to ask them, the clerks, to trawl through the archives (which was so vast that nobody knew for certain how many records were contained within it) and look for the name Scary Face Fu.

"We may as well throw rocks at the clouds," had said Junior Scribe Ying, who was older even than Senior Scribe Xu. But he had remained a junior clerk all his life for possessing a bad mouth and for having...*bouts of utter incompetence and stupidity*...as Junior Scribe Li had read once when stumbling about in the personnel records by mistake.

Still, most privately agreed with Junior Scribe Ying on this matter, believing that, if the Magistrate was competent at all, then surely he would have caught the murderer by now and all by himself.

Junior Scribe Li lay back down in bed. He pulled the quilt up to his neck, feeling cold and without hope for the future. He thought on the archives, hoping that the image of record set upon record would lull him to sleep. Then he thought only of the legal records, from which Senior Scribe Xu would soon be extracting the file on Jade Moon, and sending it to Magistrate Zhu for consideration and wondering, just wondering....

The legal records!

Junior Scribe Li's mind began to race again. Surely, that was the smallest of the sections of the archives. And if Scary Face Fu existed, and is not a ghost or a demon, and is a bad man and has been to Tranquil Mountain before (how else would he know his way around the streets at night in the fog?) then there might be a judgement already against him – admittedly, possibly, in another name. Or perhaps there was correspondence sent to Magistrate Qian from Chengdu that a madman by the name of Scary Face Fu was about in the Prefecture, and should be approached only with caution by the common people, and arrested on sight or killed – whichever was easier – by the constables or the militia.

Junior Scribe Li jumped out of bed, thinking he would go that moment to the August Hall of Historical Records, to begin a thorough examination of the legal records. But then he remembered it was still night, that a heavy mist had settled again, and that Scary Face Fu, whoever he was, was still out there. For Junior Scribe Li, now very excited, the dawn could not come soon enough.

CHAPTER 21

MORNING, 20TH DAY OF THE 1ST MOON

Honoured Sister

I hope this letter finds you and your sons in good health. Please give my sincerest regards to your husband, and to your esteemed father-in-law, the Minister Yu.

I know I have not written since leaving Chengdu, but the journey to the Fifth District was arduous, and the difficult trail not conducive to writing.

I wish you were nearby, so I could come and visit and speak to you of what I have found here. I am on the very edge of the empire. Only snow-covered mountains separate me from the barbarian host in the land of Tibet. Can you believe that this is where Heaven has sent me to find atonement?

There has been no magistrate in this district for almost a year, and seemingly no sheriffs ever. I believe that the people have greatly suffered for it. What happens when officialdom is absent? I am sure you would say: "Surely life goes on" and would expect the common people to get by.

And I would agree that on my arrival I saw a bustling market-town, with the people going about their business as if they lived in the heart of Kaifeng itself. But it did not take long for me to encounter problems. There had been a murder, and this very evening I have been informed of a delicate legal dispute. Though we Chinese are a moral and civilised people, you would be quite wrong if you argue – as you tend to do from time to time – that the people do not need continual moral guidance. Please accept it when I say that they do.

To my dismay there is no house reserved for the magistrate, but just a small apartment at the rear of the jail. I am sure you would laugh when I tell you that if there were prisoners in the cells, and if they were prone to mad fits or screaming, I should be kept awake by them. I have been reminded, quite pointedly I think, that my predecessor survived a tenure of twenty years in this rural squalor – for that certainly is what it is – and so I have kept the majority of my thoughts to myself. I have chosen to see this arrangement as temporary, in the sense that my tenure will be over within the year.

As the Minister Yu said to me, "You have to begin again. You have to accept whatever is given you, and discover your humility. Once you have done this, and regained your honour, then you can be once more of great service to China."

I think of him as the wisest of men, but surely an optimist.

I have not spoken of this before, but prior to leaving our father's estate – forgive me, but I still cannot think of it as mine – I was sitting at my desk, dreaming of the great journey I was to undertake. Then, outside the window, I noticed a small owl, perched on the gatepost, looking at me. How long we stared at each other I do not know, but it was no brief length of time before he flew away and disappeared into the twilight sky. A premonition of death? I admit I did think so. And I was loath to speak of it before now. This accounts for my melancholy in my final visit with you, when you tried to cheer me with amusing stories of the antics of my nephews.

But I was discussing this strange event with a kindly merchant on the trail to the Fifth District, a certain Silk Merchant Qi. He explained that the owl might be a sign only of a change of life, or a journey from which one does not return. 'Magistrate,' he said, 'if I could spend my remaining days in Tranquil Mountain then I would consider myself a happy man.' But then Silk Merchant Qi has not seen the great Zhu estate, or the wondrous Imperial Way of Kaifeng that is more than three hundred paces wide, and the canals planted with lotus flowers bordered with trees of peach, pear and apricot.

I do not know why I have spoken of this now to you, and I do not wish to worry you, but I often entertain fears I will never return to Kaifeng. I am sure it is nothing, and that it will not be long before I see you and the boys again.

I know you like stories of the streets, and of the common people, so let me tell you first of my constables. To keep the peace in this whole district I have but four, and the eldest is but eighteen years of age! When I arrived these youths were dressed in rags. They have no weapons, and I suspect that they cannot read or write the simplest of characters. Normally, I would have sent them packing, back to their parents; but where should I get replacements? Do not laugh when I write that volunteers are not exactly queuing outside the jail to sign up. Is this not another challenge for me, sent by Heaven? However, I am glad I did not send them away. In truth, I have found these four young men to have some inner substance, and with my guidance will, I assure you, become decent men and fine constables.

The eldest, Senior Constable He, has a most unusual mind. He asks questions – insightful questions. And he has a presence to him, which is both reassuring and calming. The local people call him Horse. I am not sure why this is so. It is possible it is because he is physically very large and muscular, or that he appears slow and to have a plodding nature. I must admit I thought this at first, but then I saw his slowness was the product of a cautious nature and not of his intellect.

The other three constables are younger. Two are twins, going by the name of Deng, and I confess I cannot as yet tell them apart. They are slim, and quick. They have a reputation about town as rascals, and have been thrown out of their family home. My predecessor recruited them despite this knowledge. I am happy to defer to his judgement, for Magistrate Qian was, I believe, a good and wise man and knew these rural people well.

The youngest constable is but sixteen, and would probably be considered too short to be a constable in Kaifeng. He is an orphan, of the family name Wu. Supposedly he once walked all the way from Chengdu on his own through the great forests to the Fifth District, following the death of his father from an illness – a most courageous act. He has sad eyes, but makes the most wonderful tea.

Oh, did I not already tell you, sister? Tea is all anybody in this district wishes to talk about. Perhaps if I stay here long enough I may too become a grower of tea, and learn to speak in a southern dialect!

Sister, I will write again very soon when I am able.

Magistrate Zhu
*   Fifth District, Chengdu Prefecture*

M agistrate Zhu laid down his ink-brush and considered the letter, not sure if he was satisfied with it; wanting to communicate his fears but also not wishing to frighten his sister unduly.

Though it was commonly accepted that a daughter or a sister was never properly family – always destined to join with another family through marriage – he could not help but think of Sparrow as a Zhu rather than a Yu. Fiery and outspoken, and with a mind to act in the most adventurous of ways, she was nothing like the withdrawn and deeply conservative Minster Yu or even like his eldest son, to whom Sparrow was married. He was so bland that he appeared to Magistrate Zhu as if he were but a blank piece of paper.

The Yu family had been their father's choice for her. At the time, Magistrate Zhu had opposed the marriage. He would have chosen better, he thought.

How old was Sparrow now? Twenty-one? Twenty-two? It disturbed him that he could not remember. He folded the letter and applied his personal and official seals, content at least that the letter would wing its way to Kaifeng with the rapidity of all official correspondence – the only boon perhaps of his isolated and lowly posting.

CHAPTER 22

LATE MORNING, 20TH DAY OF THE 1ST MOON

"*M*agistrate, look at this fine plant. Is it not wonderful?"

Tea Inspector Fang reached out to the tea tree. He ran his fingers lightly over the leaves, affecting a reverential love for the tea tree in front of everybody. He invited Magistrate Zhu to step closer to do the same.

Magistrate Zhu hesitated, self-conscious, very aware of the common people gathered around them – the men and women who normally spent their whole day tending the tea gardens that extended up and down the valley. The people had come close when they had seen Tea Inspector Fang leading the Magistrate off the trail and into the tea gardens belonging to Patriarch Sun. Some of Patriarch Sun's guards were also present, but they did not interfere, wary of both the Magistrate and Tea Inspector Fang. They knew there was nowhere Tea Inspector Fang was not allowed to roam, even onto private property, and, as for the Magistrate, surely the same was true for him. But Patriarch Sun's guards did not have to like it. They hadn't been warned about such an inspection. And one guard was already sprinting back to the Sun residence to tell Patriarch Sun what was happening.

Magistrate Zhu leaned closer to the tea tree but did not touch it. He did not enjoy nature as some officials prided themselves on doing. He had seen more than enough of the flora and fauna of China on his great journey to the south, and he had better things to do with his time than stand in the midst of a tea garden, surrounded by the waist-high tea trees, with a warm sun beating down on him.

"Tea Inspector Fang, I do not understand what you expect me to learn from examining this plant. I am impatient to know why you have dragged me and my constables out here. And we are causing confusion to the workers. Has some crime occurred here that I should know about?"

Tea Inspector Fang placed his hands upon his hips and roared with laughter. "Magistrate, this tea tree is not a crime – it is a miracle of nature! It is the very life-blood of this district, and of all China. I have brought you here so you shall understand why."

"Ah," replied Magistrate Zhu, less than impressed, wanting desperately to be back at his desk.

~

Magistrate Zhu had woken at dawn determined to make a list of the things he needed to accomplish that day. Firstly, he wished to impress on Senior Scribe Xu the need to hurry up the search of the archives for the name Scary Face Fu. Secondly, he wanted to visit the home of Mister Gong, and impress upon the family that they need not fear ghosts or demons. He thought he may perhaps learn something useful himself by understanding the geography of their home and the history of their family. And thirdly, he would begin to read the file on the young woman, Jade Moon, so he could at least begin an initial consideration of that dispute.

But before he had had even a chance to prepare the ink and his writing materials with which to make the list, he caught a slight movement at the doorway to his office.

"Come here!" he ordered, furious to be so rudely disturbed.

A young boy put his head around the doorway, his face pale and frightened. Seeing Magistrate Zhu's anger, the boy threw himself down in front of the desk, and actually placed his forehead on the floor – as if Magistrate Zhu was the Emperor himself.

"Please....Magistrate, sir....please I want to be a constable and have a uniform and eat great meals all the time," said the boy. His words were high-pitched and came out in a rush, offending Magistrate Zhu's ears.

However, Magistrate Zhu's initial anger dissolved into amusement and then he began to consider how difficult it was to find volunteers to be constables. The work was dangerous, poorly paid, had terrible hours, and, as Horse had rightly pointed out, constables were never very popular with the people.

"How old are you, boy?"

"Eleven, Magistrate, sir! Maybe twelve....or if you wish me to be thirteen years, then I think I could be that age too, if that—"

"A man does not become a man until fifteen years of age," said Magistrate Zhu, bluntly. "What is your name and where do you live?"

"Leaf, Magistrate, sir...and I live sometimes at Miss Dai's Always Smiling Orphanage...though most of the time I am out on the streets, day and night, helping Horse and Little Ox and those Deng brothers keep the peace, and—"

"You are an orphan?"

"Yes, Magistrate, sir," lied Leaf, hoping the gods would not strike him down.

"And your family name?"

"I don't know, Magistrate, sir," Leaf lied, again.

Magistrate Zhu pondered what he should do. Though the boy was young, and an orphan, he did not want to reject such a natural and instinctive commitment to public service. He was also concerned about treating the constables he had as servants. He had never known a time when he had lacked for administrative and physical help – even with putting on his own robes. He was still thinking when Horse appeared in the doorway, amazed and not a little concerned by Leaf's presence in the Magistrate's office.

"Magistrate, forgive me, but—"

"Senior Constable, please take this boy into the garden and give him a good wash. By the time you return I will have a note written to Senior Scribe Xu, requesting the file on the young woman, Miss Tang. I wish this young boy to act as runner and messenger for this jail until he is fifteen and old enough to be a constable. He is not to go out on patrol and must be returned to the orphanage at dusk every evening. But he can be fed here by Madame Wu during the day."

Magistrate Zhu tried to read Horse's expression, to see whether the young constable agreed with his decision. But if Horse had a view, it was not to be revealed on his face. Instead he merely nodded, physically picked the boy Leaf up off the floor, and took him into the garden to wash his face.

The boy was soon returned, looking much cleaner, Horse holding onto his collar as if the boy was prone to wild and unpredictable movements.

"Do you know where the August Hall of Historical Records is?"

Leaf nodded. "Yes, Magistrate, sir."

Magistrate Zhu extended his hand, passing the note to Leaf, who clutched the folded paper within tight fists as if he could lose it right there, in the Magistrate's office.

"Now listen to me, boy. You are to deliver this note without taking detours, and to wait for the file to be placed in your hands. You are not to open the file, but to bring it immediately back to me. The clerks will keep you waiting I am sure. I have never known a clerk to respond quicker than a snail's pace for anything, no matter how important. But cultivate patience, which is a supreme virtue. And do not be concerned if the clerks are rude to you. This would not be unusual – they are rude even to officials."

With Leaf dismissed, and Magistrate Zhu feeling rather pleased with himself, he decided to begin again writing his list of things he wished to accomplish that day. As he was pondering his words, he heard a great noise, like an animal bellowing in the jail-room.

"Magistrate! Magistrate! Where are you? Come out from where you are hiding!"

So loud was the voice, Magistrate Zhu's heart began to thump. Was the jail under attack by bandits? He ran through to the jail-room hoping the constables had not abandoned him, prepared for the worst, and was most surprised to see a stocky brute of a man, middle-aged, badly shaven and sporting the most extraordinary grey close-cropped hair, beaming from ear to ear. More surprising still, was that his four constables had lined up and were bowing to this man, showing him the greatest respect.

"Ah, Magistrate Zhu, at last!" the man roared again, laughing. "I thought these young scamps had done away with you. I have at last arrived. We have so much to discuss."

Magistrate Zhu was astonished, and said the first thing that came to mind: "You have no hat."

The man laughed again, and ran a hand through his short hair.

"Ah, Magistrate you don't know how hard I have tried. My fingers are thick and stupid, for which I suppose I have my parents to blame. I don't have the finesse to tie the strings to a silk hat such as yours, and Madame Kong has confiscated my two best turbans this very morning. She says they are too soiled for me to wear in public. What can a man do? Now if you passed a law that forbade women from speaking at all, then we would all be better off, wouldn't we? But believe me you should try it. Take your hat off. You would find it very liberating."

Magistrate Zhu turned to Horse for an explanation.

"Magistrate, Tea Inspector Fang has just arrived in town this morning."

"This morning?"

"Yes, Magistrate," said Horse. "Tea Inspector Fang does not always travel with a caravan."

"Magistrate, don't just stand there, you must come with me," said Tea Inspector Fang. "There is something I must show you so that we may understand each other. And bring along your constables. Madame Kong has told me all about them and about the new uniforms they are to get. I am sure they will look quite splendid. Between you and me, I don't think Senior Scribe Xu had it in him to run a constabulary. He would not have thought of uniforms. He spends far too much time preening himself. But enough of this! Come, and bring your constables. They must see what it is they are employed to protect."

"But Tea Inspector Fang, I have a murder to concern myself with."

"Nonsense, Magistrate, what is a murder compared to the importance of tea!" exclaimed Tea Inspector Fang, not to be dissuaded.

~

For reasons he could not understand (he would later rationalise his compliance with Tea Inspector Fang's request by recalling Prefect Kang's instruction that he should offer the Tea and Horse Agency every assistance he could) he followed Tea Inspector Fang out of the jail without even changing his robe or taking cognisance of the weather. He soon found himself following the Tea Inspector across the market-square, over the Bridge of Eternal Union – which spanned the narrow but fast moving White Dragon River that split the valley and town in two – and down the main street towards the East Gate. Two miserable-faced men with swords accompanied Tea Inspector Fang, one on each side of him. Horse told Magistrate Zhu they were the brothers Bian – Tea Inspector Fang's long time bodyguards.

Tea Inspector Fang set such a great pace that Magistrate Zhu found his breath coming in gasps. He had never known anyone to walk so fast, and with such purpose, and be able to wave and greet people on the street as he did so.

95

"Senior Constable, does this man know all of these people intimately?" Magistrate Zhu asked.

"Magistrate, everybody knows Tea Inspector Fang. But the people wave back at him only because it is expected of them, I think." Horse then regretted these words and said: "Please excuse me, Magistrate."

But Magistrate Zhu shook off Horse's attempted apology, grateful that his senior constable was at least demonstrating some insight into the nature of people.

Soon they were through the East Gate and climbing the trail up the valley side. Fortunately, Tea Inspector Fang did not climb far. He peeled off into the tea gardens belonging to – Magistrate Zhu soon discovered – Patriarch Sun, and invited Magistrate Zhu to join him. The people tending the tea trees gathered about them, curious to know what was happening.

"Magistrate, touch the leaf, it won't bite you!" said Tea Inspector Fang. "Touch something which is far more valuable than jade or gold, or a fair princess' skin. Touch this leaf, and you touch the beating heart of China."

"Tea Inspector Fang, I do not see the point of this," said Magistrate Zhu breathlessly. "We are disturbing the work that is going on in this tea garden. And we have not sought the permission from the owner of this tea garden to wander around like this."

"Nonsense, Magistrate. Don't concern yourself with Patriarch Sun. I am Tea Inspector Fang, and you are Magistrate Zhu. If there ever were two gentlemen who could do what they liked in this district, then we are it. Now indulge me and touch this fine tea tree. Feel the life within it. Feel its beating heart. To understand me you must understand this tea tree. To understand this district, and the people who live here, you must understand this tea tree. To understand China, you must understand this tea tree. This little tree keeps the Emperor on his throne and the northern barbarians at bay. Without this little tree, your laws and edicts, your books and collections of poetry, and your observations on politics, economics and education, are all meaningless. This little tree *is* China."

Irritated, sceptical, and thinking Tea Inspector Fang to be quite deranged, Magistrate Zhu did as he was asked. He reached out and touched a single dark green leaf, finding it leathery and cool to the touch and with a slight serration at its edge. He half expected some great vision to take hold of his mind and to be possessed with some great insight into Tea Inspector Fang's strangeness, but no such great event happened. Instead, he was more convinced than ever that Tea Inspector Fang was wasting his time and making him look like a fool in front of the common people.

"What did I tell you? Is it not the most perfect experience?" asked Tea Inspector Fang.

"You cannot have brought me all this way just to touch a plant, Tea Inspector Fang. I am not one of those scholars fascinated by the natural world. What is it you require of me to know?"

"Ah, Magistrate, you are a very serious man – but serious about the wrong things, I suspect. Now, I heard about you in Chengdu, and I have come rushing all this way to meet you. Most years, I arrive just in time for the first harvest to be transported to Chengdu. But not this year! I wanted to arrive early to meet you, and to see if it's true what they say about you."

"Are people talking about me?" asked Magistrate Zhu, concerned.

"Of course, Magistrate. You should know there is always whispering in the corridors of power. They say you passed the civil service exam at a ridiculously early age. They say that you spent time in the Ministry of Justice, and at the Censorate, that you then vanished for a few years. Why this is I don't know. But now you are a rural magistrate in a frontier district for which you have that idiot Prefect Kang to blame. But look around you, Magistrate. Fortune has been kind to you. It has brought you to one of the most wondrous places in all of China!"

Magistrate Zhu felt the blood drain out of his face at the mention of his own past. Almost everyone – his constables, Tea Inspector Fang's guards and many of the people who worked in the tea garden – would have heard. And Tea Inspector Fang's liberal criticism of Prefect Kang – though probably well directed and honest – had to be answered.

"Tea Inspector, your lack of respect—"

"Magistrate," laughed Tea Inspector Fang, "I am known for my candour. Important men such as us have no time for protocol and false politeness. You have been sent here because Prefect Kang is frightened of you, and I am here because I am not frightened of anyone. So, Magistrate, I am certain you and I are going to be the best of friends. You may not appreciate this tea tree yet – there is plenty of time for me to convince you of its many virtues – but first I understand you are to meet with the Patriarchs tonight."

"I am?" Magistrate Zhu thought quickly, believing he had only asked Senior Scribe Xu to *arrange* a meeting.

"Yes, it is quite the talk of the town already. So, it is important I speak to you first. My arrival this morning is indeed fortuitous. So before you go to sit down with three cantankerous and short-sighted old men, let me tell you a story."

"Tea Inspector Fang, I do not have time for stories. Perhaps we can dine together one evening when—"

"Magistrate, it's not that kind of story. There will be poison spread about me this evening by the Patriarchs. There are some truths you must first be made aware of. Let me first ask you a question: do you own a horse?"

"Yes, of course. I could not have travelled so far without one. It is stabled at...." Magistrate Zhu paused, realising he could not remember what he had done with his horse. He was certain he had been riding it when he had first joined the caravan. But then the trail had become twisting and steep, good only for mules, and he had dismounted and....he made a mental note to make enquiries in a few days time.

"I am glad to hear it, Magistrate. But how many other horses do you see around here?"

Magistrate Zhu looked about him, seeing no horses at all – not that he expected to see any in a tea garden.

"Now, Magistrate, what does this scarcity of horses tell you?"

"Tea Inspector Fang, it doesn't tell me anything as I have little interest in the welfare of horses. Perhaps horses are too expensive for the people here to own."

"Expensive, yes, but that is just another word for scarcity, Magistrate."

"Then, I will point out that this scarcity is local. I have seen many horse-markets in Kaifeng. And horses are still expensive in Kaifeng."

"I am sure they are, but do you know it is the Tibetans who bring the horses to market in Kaifeng? Think about that Magistrate. I expect you have a fine horse, but I am certain it was not born and reared in China. We have neither the pasture land nor the skill to rear such fine beasts. And the horses we do manage to raise are sick, weak, and certainly not up to the struggles of life in the Imperial Army."

"I will take your word for it, Tea Inspector Fang. But why is this important to me?" asked Magistrate Zhu, impatiently.

"Magistrate, there is an important connection between tea and horses – far more important that most people realise," replied Tea Inspector Fang. "Think about China, Magistrate. We are indeed the Middle Kingdom. We are surrounded on all sides by barbarians who wish to take everything we have."

"Please get to the point, Tea Inspector Fang," said Magistrate Zhu, sharply.

"Magistrate, without horses, there would be no China!" said Tea Inspector Fang emphatically. "Without horses there is no cavalry, and without cavalry there is no defence against the northern barbarians, the Xi Xia and the Liao. We need horses to fight horses, Magistrate. The barbarians of the steppe spend all their lives in the saddle, from their birthing to the day they drop stone dead to the ground. If we don't have horses, the barbarians will ride over Kaifeng in a heart-beat. This is my point, Magistrate!"

"Tea Inspector Fang, this is all very interesting, but I am a magistrate, not a general. The defence of the empire does not concern me."

"Oh, but it does Magistrate….far more than you think. I ask you: where do we get the horses for our cavalry to defend Kaifeng and our northern borders?"

"You have already said the Tibetans bring the horses to market," replied Magistrate Zhu.

"So you have been listening, Magistrate. This is good," replied Tea Inspector Fang. He pointed to the mountains, his hand sweeping from the west to the north-west. "Over there are the great grasslands of Tibet. We have made a curious bargain with barbarians, so we might defend ourselves against other barbarians. Did you know the Tibetans and the Xi Xia and the Liao are all cousins?"

"I did not, Tea Inspector Fang."

"Magistrate, the Tibetans breed the horses and we must purchase them if we are to defend ourselves against the Xi Xia and the Liao. And we do not have the cash to pay for them. Did you know that two thirds of our taxes are spent keeping the Imperial Army in the field? What use is such a large army without horses? We must give the Tibetans what they want in exchange for the horses. And, Magis-trate, what the Tibetans want, more than anything else, is tea."

Tea Inspector Fang looked back at the tea tree, and Magistrate Zhu followed his gaze, suddenly seeing the tea tree with fresh eyes.

"But what is your role, Tea Inspector Fang? Why has this Tea and Horse Agency been created? Surely the Patriarchs would supply tea to the Tibetans."

"Magistrate, before the Tea and Horse Agency was created – by imperial edict, I might add – the Patriarchs used to sell their tea to the highest bidder. In those days the tea buyers would exchange the tea for any kind of goods, not necessarily horses to sell to the army. Now the Agency buys all of the tea, and the majority of that tea is exchanged for horses. The Agency *guarantees* the horses that are supplied to the Imperial Army and delivers much needed cash into the imperial coffers. So you see, I am as much a defender of China as any soldier cooped up in some frozen northern border fort."

Tea Inspector Fang laughed, shaking his fist to the north, at imaginary armies of barbarians. Then he continued.

"Magistrate, the Patriarchs don't see the real importance of tea. They wish only to make as much cash as they can. The Patriarchs are not concerned with China and the good of her people. They are concerned only with profit. They would just sell their tea to the highest bidder. But the tea is too important for such men to decide on how it should be sold. I buy it *all* for the Agency. We must keep the Tibetans hungry and the market buoyant. Do you see? I am here to make sure there is no flouting of Agency rules, to remind the Patriarchs of their duty to grow the best of teas and to send it *all* to Chengdu, and to remind you of *your* duty to the Agency."

"Duty? What duty?" Magistrate Zhu took a sharp intake of breath. "Tea Inspector Fang, my only duty at this moment is to solve the murder of Mister Gong."

"Magistrate, murders happen in China all the time. The completion of the porterage list is all that should concern you. The people must transport the tea to Chengdu when it is harvested. And the people will only do this if you take all the names of the fit and able, and order them to carry the tea. There are always some who will feign illness or run away and hide. Only you can prepare the list. You are the magistrate. The people will do as you order."

Magistrate Zhu had forgotten the porterage list, and all that Senior Scribe Xu had said of it.

"The harvest will be very soon, Magistrate, depending on the weather," continued Tea Inspector Fang. "So you have a few days to do the work. Once the list is done, then you can worry about your petty murders."

Tea Inspector Fang laughed, and walked off back the trail followed by his guards, with not even a parting bow. Magistrate Zhu fumed. He was embarrassed to be treated so impolitely in front of all the people, and especially in front of his constables.

"Magistrate?"

Magistrate Zhu turned, seeing it was Horse who had spoken. "Yes?"

"Magistrate, we should go also, and let the people get back to work. The guards do not like us here. Patriarch Sun might come and make a complaint."

Magistrate Zhu nodded, valuing the wisdom of his senior constable.

CHAPTER 23

"*M*agistrate, I have been looking forward to meeting with you and sitting down to tea – but at your invitation, of course. However, this afternoon I am leaving once more for Chengdu, with the caravan. I have a client. His eldest son has been taken ill. He explains in his letter to me that he believes it to be a case of the worst malpractice. I understand his son has been dabbling in things that should be left well enough alone."

Ritual Master Zhan was the epitome of grace. Almost as tall as Senior Scribe Xu, yet more willowy, it seemed he almost glided towards Magistrate Zhu, with hardly a rustle of his green silk robes decorated with iridescent embroidered king-fishers. There was a perfume about him, something that Magistrate Zhu did not like in a man, but there was no mistaking the intelligence that lay behind the dark eyes.

"Please sit, Ritual Master Zhan. Constable Wu will bring tea out to us. I regret I have no food to offer you. Lunch was served a while earlier."

Magistrate Zhu had been sitting in the garden, his head swimming with thoughts of Mister Gong, tea, horses, and the file on Jade Moon that sat next to him on the stone bench as yet unopened, when another unexpected guest had arrived. Horse had come into the garden with some haste, explaining that Ritual Master Zhan was waiting in the jail-room, hoping for an audience. Magistrate Zhu, not yet recovered from Tea Inspector Fang's lecture – could it be called anything else? – was on the verge of refusing, when Horse spoke up, saying: "Magistrate, even Physician Ji listens carefully when Ritual Master Zhan opens his mouth to speak."

So Magistrate Zhu had assented, and Ritual Master Zhan had appeared in the garden, closely trailed by three very young boys, younger even than his new messenger, Leaf.

"Ritual Master Zhan, who are these boys? Are they your sons?" To Magistrate Zhu the children looked healthy and well-fed, but each wore the gravest of expressions he had ever seen in a child.

Ritual Master Zhan smiled, looking at the boys with pride. "No, Magistrate, they are not my sons. I have never married or taken a concubine. I am dedicated to my work. It is my experience that women dilute a man's conviction. The constant prattling of women causes indecision and eventually wears down the mind. I find by the time they are very old, most married men have become insensible."

"Ah," replied Magistrate Zhu, pondering this reply.

"But these young boys perform a great service for me. They are my instruments."

"Ah," said Magistrate Zhu again, not understanding.

"Magistrate, I am not a priest who hides away in Temples, conducting marriage and funeral ceremonies, safe in the knowledge that the Temple or the cemetery has been built on consecrated ground. I go where I am needed. My work is much more important than accepting the sacrifices of the people, blessing them, and lighting incense."

"More important than the proper conduct of sacred rites?" asked Magistrate Zhu.

"Oh yes, Magistrate. Though the work of the Temple priests is to be applauded, I choose to take a more active role in the community. I am a healer and exorcist. I travel far and wide in the practice of my craft. If the people are afflicted then I must go to their aid."

"And the children help you in your work?"

"They are my spirit-mediums, Magistrate – my eyes into the darker realms. They sit with the afflicted. They interpret the signs for me. They see what I cannot see with my physical eyes, and tell me the name of the enemy....or at least describe his nature."

"The enemy?"

"Yes, Magistrate, the enemy: the demon who chooses to possess and torment poor souls, who creates depression or mental instability, or who lays these souls low with mysterious or chronic illnesses. I am surprised you are not more familiar with the nature of my work – district magistrates often make great use of me, and not necessarily just to work with their own families."

"Ah yes, Ritual Master, but to date my own work has been more concerned with more mundane breaches of the law."

"Of course, Magistrate, I didn't mean to imply you were ill-informed."

They were interrupted by Little Ox, who carried with him a tray of tea. He set it down on the small bench next to Ritual Master Zhan.

"Constable Wu, would you please take the children into the jail," requested Magistrate Zhu. "Give them something to drink if they wish it, and buy them some honey-cakes from the market if they are hungry. That is, if I have your permission, Ritual Master Zhan."

"Yes, of course, you are kind, Magistrate. They are due to eat later this evening, but you know young boys I expect. They eat anything that is put in front of them, and at any time."

Little Ox herded the children back into the jail, disconcerted by their presence. The three boys did not laugh or cry as other children would, or speak when they should not.

"Magistrate, I have come to give you my thoughts on a matter of some delicacy."

"Delicacy?"

Ritual Master Zhan nodded, and sipped his tea, feeling refreshed by the warm liquid. "Yes, you are to rule soon on a contractual dispute between a seamstress and a family of some importance."

"Ah, Ritual Master Zhan, you are speaking of the dispute between Patriarch Zhou and Madame Tang, and the contracted concubinage of her daughter. I have the file beside me, but I have yet to begin my considerations – or even meet with the concerned parties."

But Ritual Master Zhan commenced to speak as if he had not even heard Magistrate Zhu's words.

"It is a dispute everyone in town knows about, and many beyond. In fact, when I am in Chengdu I am sure there will be people who will ask me if Jade Moon has killed any more bandits with a single arrow shot from a hundred paces, or stuck a knife into the faces of any more men possessed by amorous thoughts. I assure you, her fame is far greater than mine."

"This young woman is famous?"

Ritual Master Zhan nodded, leaned closer and spoke softly and in serious tones. "Magistrate, you must understand that Patriarch Zhou and his sons have already consulted me at some length on the essential nature of Jade Moon."

"I think I prefer you to refer to her as Miss Tang," corrected Magistrate Zhu.

"Yes, of course, Magistrate. And I must tell you I am already bound by contract with the Family Zhou."

"By contract?"

"Yes, Magistrate, though of course I am not precluded from speaking to you of the details. When Miss Tang is taken into the Zhou household as concubine, I am to perform the exorcism....if required."

Magistrate Zhu was speechless for a short time. "You believe Miss Tang is possessed by a demon?" He glanced quickly at the file on the bench next to him, thinking it might leap up at him.

"Magistrate, Patriarch Zhou summoned me more than two years ago and asked for my services. You must understand this was just after Miss Tang had killed Bad Teeth Tong and was due to enter the Zhou household as concubine. The contractual dispute had not then begun. Patriarch Zhou had heard the rumours about Miss Tang, and feared for his family."

"But what were you contracted to do?"

"Magistrate, it is quite simple. I would ask for Miss Tang to be left in a room by herself. She could have food and water if she wished, but no wine. I would then send in my three boys to sit with her, study her and even converse with her. I leave this very much to them. Children are much more sensitive to the needs of the day,

I think. Then, when they are finished – after one, two or even three days in the most stubborn of cases – they would leave the room and tell me what they have discovered....if anything at all."

"You would not hurt her?"

"No, Magistrate, though it has been known for the afflicted to cause harm to themselves. Some also die in the middle of an exorcism ritual, their physical strength depleted. The battle between good and evil often weakens the heart."

"Ritual Master Zhan, I would like your opinion then regarding Miss Tang. You understand that I have yet to meet her myself. But Senior Scribe Xu has already mentioned to me that some of the common people believe she is possessed of a supernatural quality. Not that I think this is pertinent to the contractual dispute: her qualities, supernatural or otherwise, are irrelevant in law. Might you indulge me in your thoughts, Ritual Master Zhan?"

"I cannot speak about the law, Magistrate – I would never dream to do so – but you must not dismiss the beliefs of the people so quickly. Some things under Heaven are not governed by your law. I fight demons almost every day who laugh at our law, and at the laws enforced by the magistrates and judges in the afterlife."

"But Ritual Master Zhan, I have read somewhere that the work of exorcists and demon hunters often parallels my own work – that you can restrain demons with the application of supernatural laws?"

"Ah, yes, Magistrate...I see what you are saying. You are better informed than most." Ritual Master Zhan thought for a short time before speaking again. "Perhaps, I meant to say that there are some men and women for whom a higher law is applicable than one that is written in your law books."

"How could there be a higher law than the Song Penal Code?"

"I don't know, Magistrate, but I would think that the wise men who wrote the Song Penal Code would not have met a young woman quite like Jade Moon."

"Miss Tang," corrected Magistrate Zhu.

"Yes, of course, Magistrate."

"Then what are your thoughts on her?"

"Yes, Magistrate, well...without allowing my boys to study her or converse with her, I believe there are two matters we can consider right now: her temperament and her genealogy. First let us think on her genealogy. She is half-barbarian. If she is possessed by a demon, or some mischievous faery or spirit, then this spirit may be unknown to me, or the possession may be subtle, or temporary, or unusual."

"But since she is half-Chinese, could not a barbarian shaman have a similar problem in that the demon is known to us but not known to them?"

"Quite so, Magistrate, that is very perceptive of you. I say this only to demonstrate that jumping to conclusions one way or the other about Miss Tang could be dangerous. I may find her clean of demonic possession because my boys do not recognise the barbarian demon within her. Or my boys may say she is possessed because her barbarian temperament has fooled them into thinking she is possessed when she is not. Also, women – especially young women – are notoriously difficult to diagnose. They are prone to such fluctuating emotions that an inexperienced exorcist may think they are possessed when in fact it is just a normal day.

Alternatively, and because of their highly volatile nature, young women are especially vulnerable to demonic possession and hauntings of every kind. You will understand when I tell you, that as much caution is required in coming to my judgements as is to yours."

"I am speechless with admiration for your analysis, Ritual Master Zhan. I am glad you came to speak to me before you left for Chengdu," said Magistrate Zhu, with obvious sincerity.

Ritual Master Zhan laughed softly, enjoying the compliment. Then he said: "Even if my boys spent a month with her, they may not be able to describe properly what they find. But there is another way, Magistrate. There is another analysis we can do. Answer me this: when she killed Bad Teeth Tong with one arrow to his heart, shot from a hundred paces, did Miss Tang do good or evil?"

Surprised by the question, Magistrate Zhu replied without thinking. "Again, I must remind you that I have not read the file, but I have been led to understand by Senior Scribe Xu that she saved many lives that day."

"Undoubtedly, Magistrate, which is a good thing, is it not? It was certainly not the act of the demonically possessed. Demons rarely do acts of courage or kindness, except when practising to deceive. And there was no deception there. Bad Teeth Tong was very much dead."

Magistrate Zhu was cheered by this, and felt a great weight lifting from his heart. "So, Ritual Master Zhan, you would say and with confidence, that you believe Miss Tang has no supernatural quality?"

"No, Magistrate, I didn't say that – not at all. I am in fact of the opinion that she is possessed, but by a special kind of supernaturalness, and one that should be taken heed of."

"But—"

"Please, Magistrate, let me finish, because what I have to say is important. It is my contention that the fate of this town is in the balance and cannot be separated from the fate of Miss Tang. Once I had signed the contract with Patriarch Zhou I tried to explain this, but he wouldn't listen. And neither would that fool son of his, Second Son Zhou. If you think you have met some idiots before, wait until you meet him. It is as if between his ears there is but a void. The Family Zhou is not over-endowed with intelligence. Except, that is, for Sensible Zhou, the elder son. When he comes into his inheritance most people in this town will breathe a sigh of relief, and many pray at the Temple and make offerings for his continued good health. I will tell you now what I told Patriarch Zhou. And I am sure you will take more notice. Forget what the people say, and forget how unusual Miss Tang is – physically and temperamentally. Forget that her father was a barbarian, and forget that her mother is as shrewd and calculating a woman as you would ever be likely to meet. Magistrate, you only need to consider what people do. Miss Tang stood still and defended the people when all around was panic and confusion. Miss Tang defended her home and her person when Second Son Zhou came to call, when any other woman would have cowered in the corner or really stuck a knife in his ribs for his stupidity. She did neither. What is one little cut beneath the eye? And finally, one last piece of evidence for you. You should see her embroideries. One hangs in the Inn of Perpetual Happiness, Senior Scribe Xu has another, and there is at least one in each of the Patriarchs' residences, whether they admit to it or not. You will never have seen such sublime skill, Magistrate. To have perfected such an art and at such a young age, she must have lived before."

"Lived before?"

"Magistrate, there is no doubt in my mind she is a great heroine reborn!"

"A great heroine?"

"Yes, Magistrate, but for what purpose I do not know. I am certain Bad Teeth Tong is not the end of it. And I told Patriarch Zhou this, after I had taken the advance of his cash. I said to him he was a fool to take such a strange young woman into his house as a concubine. 'You cannot trap such a spirit,' I told him, with as much force as I could muster. 'It is an offence against nature and against Heaven.' But, Magistrate, he wouldn't listen, fool that he is. Mark my words, if you order Miss Tang to take up her concubinage in the Zhou residence, and to lie in Second Son Zhou's bed, then, by the time I return here from Chengdu, all the buildings in Tranquil Mountain will have been reduced to dust and the forest would have grown back all over the valley to cover up this great crime."

Magistrate Zhu shook his head in wonderment. "But the contract—"

"Magistrate, don't worry. I have great faith in you. I am sure you will catch Mister Gong's murderer, as I am sure you will come to the correct decision about Miss Tang."

～

Soon after Ritual Master Zhan said his farewells, Magistrate Zhu was left to look down at the file next to him with real suspicion, wondering just what Magistrate Qian had endowed to him.

He sat alone in the garden, thinking he should be up and about, but found he could not move. Leaf came running, almost falling over as he came to a halt, trying to bow before he had truly stopped moving. He then proudly handed a small note to him. It was from Senior Scribe Xu, a written invite to the Yang residence to attend a formal reception with the Patriarchs.

He had assumed, when Prefect Kang had made his order, and made him magistrate of a rural district, that his greatest enemy would be boredom. He was beginning to form a different opinion. There was much to do. Indeed, too much to do to waste time exchanging pleasantries with the local nobility. For now, the Patriarchs would have to contend with his absence and make their own entertainment that evening.

CHAPTER 24

EVENING, 20TH DAY OF THE 1ST MOON

*S*enior Scribe Xu gulped down his rice-wine, wishing he could drown himself in the cup. The meeting with the Patriarchs had begun. Well, not exactly. For the Magistrate had sent a letter of apology and regret, saying that pressing legal matters were preventing his attendance that evening, but that he hoped to meet with all the Patriarchs sometime in the next few days.

The letter had been sent to Senior Scribe Xu and, feeling faint and nauseous, he had had no choice – as he was due to attend the meeting anyway – but to pass the content of the message on to the Patriarchs in person.

Patriarch Yang sat on his cushions at the head of the table, his great sword laid at his side. Patriarch Zhou and Patriarch Sun sat down one long side, across the table from Senior Scribe Xu. There were no women in sight – a fact Senior Scribe Xu was very grateful for. Instead, just one man-servant poured the wine, and this servant seemed not to notice the vitriol pouring forth from Patriarch Zhou's and Patriarch Sun's mouths.

"They were on my land! Both of them!" spat Patriarch Sun. His eyes were cold, and his face flushed an unnatural dark hue. Senior Scribe Xu also noted Patriarch Sun's hands were trembling.

"We have all been fools," said Patriarch Zhou, bitterly. "This Magistrate never meant to meet with us before the arrival of Tea Inspector Fang. They're probably old friends. Think of how much cash the Tea and Horse Agency must send back to Kaifeng. The Ministers probably want more, and the Magistrate has been sent to get it."

"They were on my land, Patriarch Yang," repeated Patriarch Sun. "I have reports. They were looking all around, probably deciding how much land they were going to take away from me. It is as though we have been invaded again and we don't even know it."

Patriarch Sun was referring to a common topic of discussion: the bloody annexation of Sichuan by the Imperial Army over one hundred years before, when the province of Sichuan was returned to the empire – the legacy of which was much lasting bitterness and resentment.

"Yes, this is true," interjected Patriarch Zhou again. "They think of us as mere farmers."

"Patriarch Zhou is right, this cannot go on," said Patriarch Sun, impressed that, for once, he and Patriarch Zhou were of one mind. "They are planning to take my land, I know it. The Agency has wanted my land for a long time. They want all our land. They resent having to pay any cash at all for the tea. There are far too many coincidences here...far too many. This will be a year of treachery and violence, believe me."

Senior Scribe Xu gulped the rest of his wine down, hoping it would do something to ease the shaking of his own limbs and the dryness of his throat. He hoped the evening would pass by in a blur, that in the morning he would remember none of it.

He had been attending meetings with the Patriarchs for over twenty years, ever since he had been appointed as senior clerk to the Fifth District with the directive to clean up the district's then disastrous administration. Even then, in happier times, the Patriarchs had been isolated and fearful. After 1074, the year that heralded the creation of the Tea and Horse Agency, their worst fears had been realised, and Tea Inspector Fang had become a constant visitor to their nightmares.

For his part, Senior Scribe Xu had become more sympathetic to the Patriarchs as the years had rolled by. He saw for himself how one-sided their relationship was with the authorities in Chengdu. The only benefits they ever saw for the taxes taken from them were Sergeant Kang's few militia, and an ever decreasing public purse to spend on maintaining the administration of the district, with just enough cash left over for public works to stop the district and town from falling into complete disrepair. It was no wonder the Patriarchs wished they could roll back the years to when the province was autonomous, and they were allowed to grow their tea in peace, and sell to the highest bidder.

The whole day had been a challenge for Senior Scribe Xu, trying to keep all his worries and fears for Jade Moon at bay and, much to his surprise, having had to pass over her file into the hands of a boy who now purported to be the Magistrate's new messenger. This was much to the amusement of the junior clerks who had teased the boy mercilessly on his lack of height, lack of literacy, and lack of parentage. It was well known he was one of Miss Dai's from the Always Smiling Orphanage.

It was a credit to the boy that he did not cry or run, but merely stood his ground, hands on his narrow hips, scowling until Senior Scribe Xu had given him Jade Moon's file in person and sent him on his way.

On top of the worries about Jade Moon, he had been hoping for a good meeting that evening between the Magistrate and the Patriarchs. And a miracle to occur in that one of the clerks would stumble across the name of Scary Face Fu in the archives. No such discovery had been made, and now there was to be no meeting between the Patriarchs and the Magistrate.

Then there had been the arrival of Tea Inspector Fang.

"When Tea Inspector Fang arrives, the dogs slink away and the crows fly off towards the mountains," had said Junior Scribe Li, loudly, sparking much discussion and noise-making by all the clerks in the main hall. Senior Scribe Xu had been forced to leave his office and to caution the clerks on their raucousness and general idleness, and to remind them that in difficult times the common people looked to the clerks for guidance on how to behave.

∾

"Patriarch Sun, you must control yourself. You are thinking too much as always," growled Patriarch Yang, finally deciding he had heard enough. "Tea Inspector Fang is playing politics. He is trying to impress the Magistrate with his inflated self-importance...that is all!"

"Patriarch Yang, I must respectfully disagree," said Patriarch Sun.

His eyes flitted from Patriarch Yang to Patriarch Zhou and back again, desperate to make his point. Senior Scribe Xu had never seen Patriarch Sun so angry or nervous.

"Tea Inspector Fang may be a loud-mouth and a villain," continued Patriarch Sun, "but he is not stupid. We know the Agency answers to Kaifeng more than it does to Chengdu. This must be why this Magistrate is here, and has come all the way from Kaifeng. This is why Prefect Kang is frightened of him. We should be as frightened. We have become as ciphers in our own lands."

Patriarch Zhou grunted. "He is right, Patriarch Yang. It's obvious now what this Magistrate thinks of us. And we all know Tea Inspector Fang wants rid of us. We must do something, before it is too late."

Bothered by the words of his fellow patriarchs, Patriarch Yang looked to Senior Scribe Xu to make sense of it all for him. "What do you think, Senior Scribe Xu? What is your assessment of the situation?"

Patriarch Yang's question took Senior Scribe Xu by surprise. He had his wine cup to his lips again, and almost spilled the wine down his robe.

"P-Patriarchs," he stammered, "I don't rightly know. My thoughts are chaotic. My opinion of the Magistrate changes every moment of every day. He confuses me with his thinking and his actions."

"Is he receiving orders from Kaifeng? Do we know that much?" asked Patriarch Zhou harshly.

"I have not come across any unusual correspondence," replied Senior Scribe Xu. "The Magistrate has received no letters, and so far he has written only to his sister, I believe. That letter has gone with the caravan this afternoon."

"Could he be writing in code and this sister in reality be a minister instead?" asked Patriarch Sun.

"Yes, could that be true, Senior Scribe Xu?" asked Patriarch Zhou. "You have spoken to him...dined with him even. You must give us your assessment of his character."

Senior Scribe Xu swallowed more wine, disliking the taste. It was not Patriarch Yang's best. "Patriarchs, I am not a good judge of character."

"Senior Scribe Xu, you must do better than that," grunted Patriarch Yang.

"Then I think he doesn't care about any of our problems - just the law!" Senior Scribe Xu blurted out, before covering his face with his hands.

Astonished, the Patriarchs all looked at Senior Scribe Xu. They had always thought of him as a weak man, but never before overly emotional.

"See, I told you we can't trust this magistrate," said Patriarch Sun, believing – as did the others – that Senior Scribe Xu had just spoken a terrible truth.

CHAPTER 25

*H*orse stood on the street corner with Magistrate Zhu, feeling very badly dressed, never more aware of the rips and fraying edges of his clothes. Though Jade Moon and her mother could sew like the wind, it would be days before their uniforms would be ready. For the journey out that evening the Magistrate had not chosen his usual black, non-descript robes. Instead he had spent some time getting himself ready and then appeared in the jail-room clothed in the most marvellous vermillion robes. Even the Deng brothers had been impressed, volunteering quite vocally to accompany the Magistrate wherever he wanted to go.

"I wish to go to the house of Mister Gong," the Magistrate had said, simply.

Horse wanted to argue against this, believing it unseemly that a magistrate should be walking the streets at night.

"Magistrate, a heavy fog has come down this evening, and Mister Gong's house is some way. It is across the Bridge of Eternal Union again, not far from Patriarch Sun's residence."

"Good, then the weather conditions are not different from what they were on the night of the murder," Magistrate Zhu had replied, quite cheerfully.

Horse could do nothing but acquiesce. But he indicated to the others that they should all accompany the Magistrate – for his protection. There was still a murderer out there, somewhere. Though he did not know much about being a constable, he knew enough not to ever let the Magistrate come to harm.

The Magistrate had been, Horse thought, in a strange mood all afternoon. He wondered what Ritual Master Zhan had said, about Jade Moon in particular. Late in the afternoon, when he had gone into the Magistrate's office to enquire whether he wished Little Ox to prepare more tea, Horse had found him reading and re-reading the file sent over by Senior Scribe Xu.

Horse had stood there silent for a while, biting his lip, wishing he had a better facility with words, that he could say what was on his heart, that the Family Zhou was wrong to make Jade Moon be a concubine, that Jade Moon was not as some portrayed her – violent and out of control.

Instead, when the Magistrate looked up and acknowledged his presence, and shook his head at the suggestion of more tea, he began to quote the law again – specifically in regard to barbarians.

"Senior Constable, in terms of the law and the treatment of legal petitions we must always show the utmost care with barbarians. Yes, there are sensitivities that must be recognised, especially in the border districts, as we don't want the barbarians that are peaceable to become unsettled. They must not think that they have been specially selected for rough treatment or punishment for criminal or civil infractions.

"But, Senior Constable, there is a much deeper problem. Barbarians are not like us Chinese. They are not civilised. They do not possess our moral capacity. When a Chinese man has done wrong, all that has happened is that he has failed to live up to his natural, moral capacity. The law can then be usefully applied, wrongful behaviour corrected, the criminal renewed, and the balance between Heaven and Earth maintained. But with barbarians it is much more difficult. For even when the law is stated to them, they may not even understand what they have done wrong. To be blunt, in terms of their natural morality, they are closer to animals than to us civilised Chinese. Often it pays to be lenient. It is better to fine a barbarian and send him on his way, than to order a beating with a light or heavy rod as I would do to a Chinese who had committed a similar wrong. That is not to say a more serious offence should be ignored."

The Magistrate had then returned to reading Jade Moon's file, and Horse had retreated back to the jail-room to think on the meaning of these words.

It was only when they were standing near to Mister Gong's house, tendrils of mist floating in the air around them, that it suddenly dawned on Horse just who the Magistrate had been speaking about – Jade Moon! Horse had forgotten that Jade Moon's father, a man that no one had ever seen and certainly knew nothing about, had been a barbarian, which meant that Jade Moon was half-barbarian. Did that also mean that Jade Moon was only half-moral? Horse was not sure, but thinking back now on the Magistrate's words, he began to have some slight glimmer of hope that the Magistrate was minded, because of her ancestry, to treat her with kindness.

"Senior Constable, are you asleep?"

Horse turned towards the Magistrate, realising too late that the Magistrate had been speaking to him. "Forgive me, Magistrate, I was thinking."

"Ah, and what was it you were thinking about?"

Horse knew he could not lie to a magistrate, that any falsehood would be quickly set upon. "Magistrate, I was thinking about your words earlier, about how the barbarians lack moral capacity." The words were not easy, but he had done his best to commit them to memory.

Magistrate Zhu peered at him closely. Despite the fog, the many new lanterns above the doors now made the Street of Thirty Tea Pickers one of the brightest streets in town at night. "You were listening?"

"Yes, Magistrate. Was that wrong? Should I have closed my ears?"

"No, no – not at all. But I have spoken many times in the past to officials and to clerks and had the most difficulty in getting them to remember anything I have said. I am pleased, very pleased. But for the moment let us use our minds to consider geography...the geography of a murder. What do we see around us?"

Horse looked about him, and at Little Ox and the Deng brothers who were milling around the cross-roads, peering carefully at windows and doors, not having any idea of what they were doing but trying desperately to impress the Magistrate.

"Magistrate, this is the cross-roads of the Street of Thirty Tea Pickers to our right and the Street of Twenty Tea Pickers to our left; in front of us is the Street of the Glorious Family Sun, and behind us the Street of Happy Homes. At the start of the Street of Thirty Tea Pickers, on our right, is the house of Mister Gong. The high wall opposite, on the corner, and running far into the distance surrounds the Sun residence."

Through the fog, Horse could just about see the large, ornate, entrance gate to the Sun residence, well lit with lanterns, guards on duty outside, who were returning their interest and their stares.

"And what do you notice?" asked Magistrate Zhu

Horse shrugged. "It is not raining as it was on the night of the murder."

"Yes, that is true. But I was thinking on how quiet the streets are – no passers-by. Are the people so frightened they all stay in their homes?"

"Magistrate, there are no taverns in these streets. They are normally quiet after dark. And the guards for the Sun residence often patrol the high wall protecting the house. They are all mercenaries. Even Sergeant Kang's militia are frightened of them. They often push people out of the way and bully them."

Magistrate Zhu was appalled. "And this is stood for?"

Horse shrugged, knowing it just to be a fact of life. He decided then to speak on what was known, to get him away from the difficult subject of the Patriarchs.

"Magistrate, the sons of Mister Gong have spoken to all the neighbours, on every street nearby. No one saw anything."

"And at the tavern....the...."

"Golden Lotus Tavern."

"Ah, yes. Have you been there?"

"No, Magistrate, but some of the men from the tavern have been out to sit with the Gong brothers. Mister Rong the proprietor is very upset. He has known Mister Gong thirty years. He had taken himself to his bed in his grief. All of them say Mister Gong had no enemies."

When they had first arrived at the Street of Thirty Tea Pickers, Magistrate Zhu had gone into the house of Mister Gong, to the amazement of all, including many neighbours who immediately gathered into and around the house. Magistrate Zhu had, in no uncertain terms, spoken of his ardent belief that they were looking for a man, not a ghost, and that neither the family nor the street was subject to any kind of supernatural curse.

"The evidence for this is quite overwhelming," had said Magistrate Zhu. Some of the women then began to cry with relief.

Horse noted though, that the Magistrate made no mention of why Mister Gong had been singled out for such an attack, even by a real, physical man, and how the Magistrate looked most carefully into the faces of everyone who was present – even the women.

"I will not rest until I discover this murderer," Magistrate Zhu had then said, with such conviction that the sons of Mister Gong, bowed deeply, wept openly and thanked him from the bottom of their hearts. They offered him whatever sweets and pastries they had in the house – all politely refused – and then did as the Magistrate requested, locking themselves in their home for the night. The neighbours and friends had also returned to their own houses, and made sure their doors were latched. Regardless, Horse was certain that many eyes still looked at them, peering out from behind the paper of the windows, peeled back as surreptitiously as possible.

"These streets do not lead anywhere special, do they, Senior Constable? There is no place a stranger or traveller would obviously be visiting."

"No, Magistrate."

This was a fact that had also occurred to Horse, when he had first learned of the murder. And more so on the last two evenings when he had sat out in the street with Little Ox and the Gong brothers, on guard.

"Unless someone was travelling home, like Mister Gong," continued Magistrate Zhu, "or come to visit the Sun residence, perhaps. But why? And why at night? I had assumed that people came to town just with the caravans, for security. But since Tea Inspector Fang came to town only with those bodyguards, this has set me to thinking. Someone could have come to town…for reasons that we do not yet know or understand…possibly using the atrocious weather to mask what they were about. Is there anything around here of any value? I suspect that the Sun estate is wealthy, and the family would have many heirlooms."

Horse had no doubt of this, but that was not what came first to Horse's mind. "Magistrate, the tea harvest is soon. In the past bandits have tried to steal the tea. It is very valuable. When the tea is harvested it is stored on the Yang, Zhou and Sun estates before it is taken to Chengdu."

"So, Mister Gong could have been killed because he saw something he should not – bandits scouting the Sun residence, perhaps, with a view to committing criminality. But let us consider this carefully. Surely it would be easier to raid a caravan on the trail, take some of the tea and then disappear into the forest. The high wall around the Sun residence is tough to scale. And I can see that the gates are well guarded."

Horse was disappointed, hoping the murder of Mister Gong almost solved, and that the Magistrate would have a wonderful plan with which to trap tea-bandits.

But the Magistrate was not finished. "Senior Constable, we would also have to accept that the bandits beat Mister Gong to silence him, to keep his mouth shut about what he had seen. This begs further questions. How did he know one of their names to be Scary Face Fu? Did he overhear the name? Possible, but I think unlikely. Has Mister Gong associated with bandits in the past? I think not." Magistrate Zhu looked down the Street of the Glorious Family Sun and considered the gate and the guards. "Have you spoken to those men? Is it possible, even from there, that they might have heard or seen something? Sound travels far at night, even in fog and rain, I think."

Horse had attempted to speak to the guards the previous evening, but they had sent him on his way, none too gently. "They are rough men, Magistrate. They do not care about the death of Mister Gong."

Horse worried for a moment that Magistrate Zhu was going to speak to the guards himself, and cause a commotion outside the great house of Patriarch Sun. But the Magistrate just restricted himself to staring intently at the guards, and then at the doors of the houses around him.

"Magistrate?"

"Senior Constable, this is not a place for passers-by or for chance encounters. The answer is here. I know it. And I feel it in my bones that Mister Gong knew his murderer, or, more realistically, *knew of* his murderer."

Horse then felt moved to make a point. "Magistrate, even though the guards are rough they have never murdered anyone. Patriarch Sun would not allow it. He is an important man. He would not consort with criminals."

"Consort?"

Magistrate Zhu laughed out loud. Horse felt a great heat come to his face. He was very conscious of the Deng brothers nearby, who no doubt had heard and would tease him for trying to use such a clever word to the Magistrate.

"Senior Constable, you are young and inexperienced in the ways of the world. I agree that important men should be always law-abiding and have the wellbeing of the people uppermost in their minds. But I am afraid it is not true. The Golden Age is long gone. I fear that the sages, if they were alive now, would be taken ill with horror at what China has become. I will speak of this more in the months to come. You are still young but, as a constable, it is right that you know."

"Yes, Magistrate."

"However, for now, I have seen enough…or at least enough to consider and to formulate how we should continue with our investigations. Is Senior Scribe Xu's house far? I wish to speak to him again with some urgency."

"Senior Scribe Xu's house is back over the bridge, in the north of the town, not far from the residence of Patriarch Yang. It is some distance."

Senior Scribe Xu actually lived in a fine house on the unfortunately-named Street of Thieves. But Horse did not want to say this name out loud in case the Magistrate thought things he should not.

"Then let us get started, Senior Constable – unless there is some other problem?"

Which there was. Horse had a feeling that Senior Scribe Xu would not be up to receiving guests. The talk of the town – brought earlier that evening to the jail by Leaf – was that the Magistrate's refusal to attend the Yang residence and meet with the Patriarchs had caused the senior clerk not a little embarrassment.

"Magistrate, it is getting late," said Horse, trying to dissuade Magistrate Zhu from making the visit.

But Magistrate Zhu laughed again. The walk that evening and the consideration of the circumstances of Mister Gong's murder had evidently, and most oddly, put him in some good humour. "Senior Constable, let us go, for Senior Scribe Xu does not strike me as one who spends his evenings carousing with friends."

Which was true, Horse thought glumly. But he also remembered that Magistrate Qian never once called on Senior Scribe Xu at home in the evening, and they had been the best of friends. He exchanged concerned and meaningful glances with the other constables, and began to lead the way.

CHAPTER 26

*I*t was some relief to Horse when Rose opened the gate to Senior Scribe Xu's home. If alone, Senior Scribe Xu may not have heard or have bothered to come to the door himself, not unless he was expecting his friend, Chef Mo. Horse gently picked up Rose who, on first sight of the Magistrate, had thrown herself on the ground. He whispered to her to fetch Senior Scribe Xu. She whispered back, with real panic in her eyes, that although it was indeed true that Senior Scribe Xu had returned from the Yang residence, it was also true that he was not quite himself.

Nevertheless, she vanished into the house with some rapidity, leaving Horse to guide the Magistrate across the small courtyard and into the entrance hall. Little Ox and the Deng brothers had been left outside on the street, Horse knowing full well that Senior Scribe Xu would never have condoned the presence of the Deng brothers on his property. Little Ox had to suffer as a consequence, Horse not wanting the Deng brothers to feel singled out.

"This is a fine house," said Magistrate Zhu, thinking it one of the best he had seen in town.

Fearing what the Magistrate might suspect, experienced as he was in the investigation of corrupt officials and clerks, Horse felt it best to explain.

"Magistrate, Senior Scribe Xu came here many years ago – I think at the same time as Magistrate Qian. Senior Scribe Xu had had a serious illness in Chengdu. He came here for his health, to be close to the mountains and the good air."

"Ah."

"Madame Xu, his wife, had a great dowry – which paid for the house."

"She must have been disappointed then to only marry a clerk," said Magistrate Zhu absently, walking further down the hall than was usual when waiting for the host to appear.

"I do not know of such things, Magistrate," replied Horse, feeling uncomfortable, thinking…feeling…that Magistrate Zhu was in the mood for a confrontation. He wondered what Senior Scribe Xu could possibly have done wrong since he had last met the Magistrate.

Magistrate Zhu stopped in front of a small vase with a cobalt-blue glaze, placed carefully in a small alcove so it caught the light from the nearest oil-lamp.

"I think it was a gift from Tea Inspector Fang, Magistrate," said Horse.

"A gift for completing the porterage list for the tea last year, after Magistrate Qian had died?"

"I do not know, Magistrate," Horse replied, truthfully, feeling more uncomfortable, hoping that the Magistrate did not consider such a gift inappropriate – or worse, a bribe.

Intending to deflect the Magistrate's attention, and seeing also an opportunity to do some good that evening, Horse stepped forward and pointed to the opposite wall on the hall. There a small silk embroidered screen was mounted, also well situated to catch the light of the oil-lamp.

"Magistrate, please look at this."

Magistrate Zhu turned, then stepped forward, closer to the embroidery. He became fascinated by the subtle blend of colours, admiring the tremendous skill and hours of effort that had gone into such a creation.

"You have a good eye, Senior Constable – it is quite beautiful."

"It is of a magnolia plant."

"Yes, I see that. You have been here before then…to this house?"

"Yes, Magistrate, when Magistrate Qian was still alive. I have heard there is no better embroidery in the whole of Tranquil Mountain."

"Cash well spent, I think, Senior Constable. I have to admit that Senior Scribe Xu is a man of fine taste – in food as well in art."

"Jade Moon did it – when she was fifteen."

Magistrate Zhu was surprised. "The young barbarian woman? Miss Tang?"

"Yes, Magistrate, forgive me…Miss Tang."

The Magistrate opened his mouth to speak, perhaps to say something else about the embroidery or Jade Moon, but was interrupted.

"Magistrate! Magistrate! Forgive me keeping you so long! I was preparing myself for bed."

Horse was horrified. Rose had been speaking truthfully. Senior Scribe Xu was definitely not himself. His clothes were quite dishevelled, and his hat was missing, his greying hair quite unkempt. Moreover, he appeared to have difficulty standing, so much so that Rose was standing next to him, supporting him – something that Horse had never ever seen.

"My apologies, Senior Scribe Xu for the lateness of the hour. Something has been preying on my mind and could not wait. But…forgive me…have you been taken ill?"

"A little, Magistrate – just a strange turn. Nothing to worry about though. Come follow me to my study. Rose was just preparing some tea."

Senior Scribe Xu was helped through the doorway of one of the rooms off the hall.

Magistrate Zhu frowned, then turned to Horse, and asked in a whisper: "Senior Constable, could his illness be an excess of wine?"

Horse could not doubt what his own eyes had seen. But felt bound to defend Senior Scribe Xu – one of the few in town who had continued to be kind to him and to the other constables after the death of Magistrate Qian.

"Such a thing has never before been known, Magistrate," he said, deflecting the question.

～

I n Senior Scribe Xu's study, with all seated – Senior Scribe Xu finding much benefit from being in his chair – and with Rose having served tea and, Horse suspected, still hovering nearby outside the door, Magistrate Zhu began.

"Senior Scribe Xu, I confess my mind is troubled this evening."

"Ah."

"Tea Inspector Fang has spoken to me of the importance of the tea, and how it is necessary for this tea to be exchanged for Tibetan horses – horses that are needed by the Imperial Army to defend the northern borders against the barbarian hordes."

"Ah."

"So the tea is grown for a noble cause...a necessary cause."

"Yes, a necessary cause," repeated Senior Scribe Xu, nodding, his eyes glassy.

"And yet I sensed that Tea Inspector Fang is disliked...even feared. There is no doubt he is quite rude."

"Yes, quite rude, Magistrate."

"And his manners uncouth."

"Yes, quite uncouth, Magistrate."

"But I sense some deeper problem here...some reason that I have been sent to the Fifth District, when my skills could perhaps have been put to greater use in Chengdu, for example. Would you care to elucidate?"

"Magistrate, I am just a clerk."

"You are a senior clerk, and I think hardly a piece of official paper escapes your attention. Why have I been sent here? I suspect it is not just to bring law to the people?"

Senior Scribe Xu's mind felt stupid. Patriarch Yang's wine, and his great consumption of it that evening, had caused some serious damage. Not even Rose's ministrations, her towelling of his face and neck with icy water not long drawn from White Dragon River, had done much to regain his sensibilities. But for some reason he was very aware of a great emotion behind Magistrate Zhu's eyes and a feeling in his own heart, that all was not well with the young official.

And whether it was the wine still coursing through his veins, or just this sudden understanding or sympathy for Magistrate Zhu, Senior Scribe Xu

118

wondered whether his initial fear of the Magistrate had led them all to some awful misperception. Was it possible that this arrogant young official had *not* been sent by Kaifeng to complete some terrible mission, such as the seizing of the tea gardens into government control? Was it possible that Magistrate Zhu was innocent of all the things that had been suspected of him, not only by the Patriarchs, but also by him and his clerks?

Whether it was the wine in his body, or the internal distress he thought the Magistrate was in, Senior Scribe Xu suddenly felt moved to speak.

"Magistrate, I must tell you what happened in 1074."

"1074?"

"Yes, Magistrate, that was the year the Tea and Horse Agency was created – by imperial edict."

"I was still wrapped up in my studies at the time."

"Of course, Magistrate. Well, that year was a year of terrible trouble. Before, this place was happy and prosperous, as were many of the other tea-growing districts. With four good tea harvests a year, plenty of cash was made by the Patriarchs. They then paid good wages to the people, and actually spent cash on the upkeep of the town. You have already seen that many of the streets are paved with stone – a legacy of a better time."

"And some of your houses are very fine...such as your own."

"Thank you, Magistrate – though my home has not been the same since the death of my wonderful wife."

Horse was convinced he heard a cough of dissent from Rose, lurking outside in the hallway. But he chose to ignore it, trying to concentrate hard on the words that Senior Scribe Xu was speaking, memorizing history, so he might fully understand himself the place in which he lived.

"Magistrate," continued Senior Scribe Xu, "the Tea and Horse Agency said that, by law, only they would buy up all the tea. This put all the private tea buyers out of work. There was trouble in many places, even rioting in some districts. Not here, though, Magistrate – not in Tranquil Mountain. But there was great unhappiness and discontent. And to keep the tea valuable, the men from the Agency said there must only be two harvests a year. The Patriarchs protested. They argued that this policy would reduce the income for everybody and impoverish the whole district. But they were not listened to. All we could do was wring our hands in frustration and anguish, and mourn a comfortable life that was now over. Tea Inspector Fang, who had been a private tea buyer was seen by the Agency to have useful skills and recruited. He began to visit then, and to throw his weight around. Some said he enjoyed pushing our noses further into the dirt. But through the years I think he has become not so bad. And the people have come to tolerate him, if not exactly to enjoy him. He visits often, especially at the times of the harvests, just to make sure that the law is obeyed."

"And Magistrate Qian stood by and did nothing, when all this came to pass?"

"Magistrate, what could he do? It was his role to see that the new rules were enforced. And this is your role also, Magistrate. A magistrate always enforces the law, doesn't he?"

Magistrate Zhu shook his head. "If a law oppresses the people, how can it be called a law?"

Senior Scribe Xu was astonished, never hearing such words before. Had the Magistrate just expressed sedition? Had the Magistrate just questioned the wisdom of the wisest men in all China, the Emperor's best ministers, the men who made policy, and the law for all the land?

"Magistrate, surely you have no choice."

"Prefect Kang told me nothing of the policy of this Tea and Horse Agency. He just commanded me to support their work. Whether the people are accepting or not, does not make a policy right."

"But Magistrate, Prefect Kang would assume that you would understand, that this is all for the good of China...that sacrifices must be made by noble and common-born alike."

Magistrate Zhu felt weary. "Senior Scribe Xu, the law, though great, is not written by Heaven. The Patriarchs could draft a petition. They could contest the law that created the Agency."

"But would this not take many years to consider, Magistrate? And the people of this district may attract the worst kind of attention, and perhaps be labelled trouble-makers. And such a petition may need attendance by the Patriarchs in Kaifeng, before the highest courts in China. I am sure the Patriarchs would be grateful for your concern, and you should certainly speak of your concern to them. But a petition is not practical. Forgive me, I did not mean to quote law that I do not understand, but sometimes the people have to accept a lesser evil to prevent a greater. Magistrate, this is why the Patriarchs do not care about the murders of old men, or even about Jade Moon. The tea must be grown, and harvested and then sent to Chengdu. Nothing else matters. For to make a little cash is better than making none at all."

"I understand, Senior Scribe Xu."

"If perhaps all the barbarians that surround us would go away, and not prey on us so much, then awful choices would not have to be made, and laws not enacted to impoverish the people."

"Yes, that is true, Senior Scribe Xu. But Tea Inspector Fang does not look impoverished, and I am certain that men – corrupt men – in Chengdu and Kaifeng do very well out of this arrangement."

"That would be music to the Patriarchs' ears, Magistrate, but those are dangerous words."

"Are they? Magistrates and judges have criticised even the Emperor in the past for bad policies and bad laws."

"But did they keep their heads, Magistrate?"

Magistrate Zhu saw the anguish in the face of the senior clerk and decided to accept the point, with a gentle laugh. "Some did, some didn't." He eased himself out of the chair. "You have made things very clear, Senior Scribe Xu. I thank you for that. I will begin work on the porterage list soon, though I may have to come to you for advice."

"Yes, of course, Magistrate."

"However, I will continue my investigations into the death of Mister Gong.

And I will summon the Family Zhou, and Miss Tang and her mother, to give evidence to me in regard to their dispute tomorrow. The death of an old man may mean little to the Patriarchs or to Tea Inspector Fang or to the people in comparison to tea, but it means much to me. For lesser evils, if they are ignored, lead to greater evils. But I appreciate your candour this evening, Senior Scribe Xu. I will not forget."

CHAPTER 27

EVENING – NIGHT, 20TH/21ST DAY OF THE 1ST MOON

*J*unior Scribe Li had achieved nothing useful that day. Though, like the other clerks, he had his usual work to accomplish – the never-ending stream of paperwork that had to be created, read, annotated, moved from desk to desk, and eventually filed – he had done less than most in following the Magistrate's orders to search the archives for the name Scary Face Fu.

The problem had been that he had not wanted anybody to comprehend his insight of the previous night, that the answer lay somewhere within the legal records. So he had shown less method than he should. He had sifted chaotically through the census records of some years before, concentrating on an area of town near the southern gate, then moved onto the records of contract of the year 1082, and then onto the records of births and deaths in the year 1079. It was not long before this nonsense was spotted by Senior Scribe Xu – who missed very little – and he was reprimanded in front of the others.

"Junior Scribe Li, you must calm yourself!" snapped Senior Scribe Xu. "Have you forgotten all your training?"

Junior Scribe Li accepted this admonishment with good grace, as part and parcel of the deception he was making. Though he was rattled a short while later when he realised some of the other young clerks were smirking, those idiots hoping that his star was falling from the sky.

He would show them!

At last, when the sun sank below the horizon, the August Hall of Historical Records began to clear – the junior clerks wanting to get home to their homes, their families and most especially their evening meals. Soon, he alone was left at his desk, his single oil-lamp illuminating the great hall.

"Junior Scribe Li, only so much work can be done in a day," said Senior Scribe Xu, approaching his desk, his key to the main door in his hand.

"I wish to remain slightly later, Senior Scribe Xu – to make up for my foolishness earlier this day."

His mind on many things, Senior Scribe Xu did not argue. He nodded, smiled, and placed the key on the desk before Junior Scribe Li.

Once the senior clerk had vacated the building and slammed the door shut behind him, Junior Scribe Li had an intense moment of doubt. The hall was large, full of shadows. There were no stories of ghosts wandering the hall, but who was to say what might happen to a lonely clerk in the middle of the night?

Junior Scribe Li breathed deeply, knowing he was committed to this course of action – ambition always necessitated the taking of risks. He got up from his desk, locked the main door, and then took his oil-lamp with him as he went in search of the legal records.

Little did he know then, that the sun would be almost on the rise before he would stumble upon that for which he was looking.

CHAPTER 28

"*M*adame Tang! Madame Tang!"

Madame Tang dragged herself away from conversation with Madame Qu, who was having a great deal of difficulty with her mother-in-law – aged, bed-ridden, and nasty to boot – and looked to see who was trying to attract her attention. It was Madame Deng, her second best friend in Tranquil Mountain after Madame Kong, who was approaching her through the crowd, a most anxious look on her face.

"Madame Deng, what is it? Have those twin boys of yours been found out for what they are by the new magistrate?"

"Oh, Madame Tang, I thank the gods every day that I have a good husband in Butcher Deng, and a wonderful eldest son in Pork Chop – though he is a trifle slow. Even Physician Ji said a bad wind was blowing the day I gave birth to the twins. But that they are still employed by Magistrate Zhu…well, I can't explain it…and as you know, this Magistrate Zhu, though young, rude and heartless is apparently no fool."

"Then what have you heard that has so affected you?"

"Oh, Madame Tang, the twins came to the shop this morning, just to boast to Pork Chop about the uniforms that you are making them. But they also told him that the Magistrate is to summon you and Jade Moon to the jail…this very morning. You are to explain yourselves and that stinking contract you were forced to sign!"

Madame Deng, knowing full well what to expect, reached out with strong arms to support Madame Tang. She then called out to the market-traders for a chair on which to set down Madame Tang's vast bulk.

124

When this had been achieved, and a small crowd had gathered around, and water, tea and wine offered to restore Madame Tang to health, Madame Deng said: "Madame Tang, you must go see Madame Kong. You must ask her to accompany you. She knows how to handle important men. Look how she handles Tea Inspector Fang – and he is a brute."

Madame Tang looked at her friend, tears blurring her eyes, and replied: "Oh, Madame Deng, I have made so many mistakes in my life."

~

S he had first seen him in the market-square. The late snow had been melting, churned up into muddy slush as people hurried about their daily tasks. The day was like any other, but Madame Tang would remember that she had been thinking then a lot about her mother and father, both recently dead, and was, as a consequence, more emotional than she should have been.

There had been an entertainer in the market-square that day, an archer, who performed impressive tricks for the crowd. Vegetables were thrown into the air and, well before they landed, they would be pierced through with an arrow. Madame Tang had thought it a terrible waste of food, but had clapped with all the others. And the archer had smiled and laughed and bowed to the people.

"Never have I seen such skill," said a merchant next to her, throwing coins to the archer, who would pluck them from the air with the same dexterity with which he handled his bow.

Madame Tang had never seen such skill either, and had never set eyes on such an impressive man before. He was tall, dressed gaudily with bright red trousers and high leather boots. He wore his hair long, but tied behind him, out of the way of the bow. But it was his eyes that truly transfixed her. They seemed to see everything, to look through her and into her at the same time, as he asked in imperfect Chinese, and with a curious accent, what trick the people would like him to perform next.

"He is from the northern wastes," said a man next to her, speaking to his wife, who had asked the question.

"No, I think from Korea," said another. "His accent is odd."

"No, he's Liao – look at his clothes."

"He's Xi Xia – any fool can see that."

Madame Tang would never know. The archer would never speak of it, saying the past was dead, and that if one did not speak of it then the past could not follow you. She had believed him then because he spoke with conviction. Never was a man so wrong.

Eventually the day had grown old, and a cold wind had begun to whip across the market-square. The crowd dispersed. Madame Tang was left alone looking on, and the archer came over to her, smiling, sending a shiver down her spine. He asked her in that odd accent of his, if she had enjoyed what she had seen. But all she could reply was that, entertaining though the tricks were, it was not proper work for a man.

She asked if he had a place to stay that night. She told him that she and her

125

sister often rented out the back room of their house to travellers to raise extra cash. She said it would cost extra if he wanted to eat as well. He opened his palm, showing the coins he had earned that day, which were plenty, and so he followed her home, back to the house, which was also a shop, where she and her sister carried out their business as seamstresses.

~

A month later Madame Tang was married. And her sister, in tears, had left with all her possessions, to set up in business on the other side of town, taking with her most of their clients.

"I will not live in the same house as a barbarian, especially one who does not work," her sister had said.

Madame Tang had thought her jealous at the time – her sister was older by a year and had yet not found a husband – but in the years that followed Madame Tang realised her mistake.

Madame Tang, whose name then was Miss Tang, decided to perpetuate the name of her family, being unable to pronounce her new husband's barbarian name, or for that matter wanting to be known by it.

The archer, her husband, whom she called Prince because of the upright and haughty manner in which he carried himself, seemed to have no trade. After their marriage, she forbade him to show off his skills in the market-square. It was only men without ambition who acted in street plays or entertained the people, she told him. First she repaired his clothes which, though fine at a distance owing to their bright colours, were actually ragged and torn. Then she sent him out to seek proper work, ordering him to leave his bow and arrows behind at the house.

"A tall, strong and handsome man such as you will have no difficulty in finding a job," she had told him.

So he had gone out and did not return until dark. When he did return he would not speak, and when she had served dinner, he continued to sit in silence, refusing to look at her. He did not leave the house again for three days. After the sudden death of her father and mother, it was the second time in her life Madame Tang had truly known fear. She submerged herself in her work, knowing it must be of the finest quality or else her sister would steal all of the business to be had in town.

On the fourth day, Prince left the house before dawn, taking his bow and arrows with him. She stayed in the shop, fearing he was performing again in the market-square and bringing shame upon their new-formed family. But the one or two women that came by to pick up their repaired clothes, or order new dresses, did not mention that they had seen him. They asked only after her sister, knowing full well the sisters did not now speak. Madame Tang's sister was, in fact, to be married herself – to a very prosperous and *very* Chinese merchant!

"She was always prettier than me," Madame Tang had told her customers by way of explanation.

Prince returned early in the evening. By his gait and the smell upon his breath, she knew he had been drinking wine. But he was smiling, and he said – though with some difficulty as he found the Chinese words hard – that he was to join a caravan going west as a guard. He would return within the month with a caravan coming east. He then handed over some coins, which were his advance payment. In the morning he was gone. Trying not to think or worry, or wonder what else she could do, Madame Tang worked in the days that followed from dawn until dusk, and then well into the night, charging as little as she could to attract more custom. In this way the days went quickly, and to the customers who asked, she explained that her husband was fearlessly guarding some very important men.

Prince returned as promised at the end of the month, looking quite content. He placed his bow and quiver of arrows in the corner of the room, gave her a small purse full of coins, ate his dinner and then went out – she was certain to the tavern. It was early morning before he came home.

~

J ade Moon was born late that year, as happy, as boisterous and as healthy a child as one could wish for – except that she was a daughter. It had been a difficult time for Madame Tang: she had had to work right up to the birth, and her husband was away again, as was now usual. But the midwife had come – as promised, in return for a free dress – and the baby had finally been born, a full day and night after the pains had begun. Madame Tang had named her for the moon that had then been in the sky, but for days afterward feared the return of her husband.

"This is your daughter," she said, when he came through the door, watching his face for his reaction. Her husband had then taken the baby in his arms, held her up in front of his face, nodded, and smiled, and then laughed, placing the baby back in Madame Tang's arms. He then sat down to his dinner. Later, he gave her a purse containing coins, and went out into the night.

~

I t was only years later that Madame Tang understood the blessing she had been given. Yes, Jade Moon was a girl, but she was the happiest child anyone could wish for, laughing and singing songs her father had taught her, all day and often into the night. She was also intelligent, eyes sparking with life, and her fingers demonstrated a remarkable dexterity with the needle.

"I show her once, and she remembers," Madame Tang would say to her customers, who all doted on the pretty girl, giving her sweets when they came to the shop.

And never was Jade Moon happier than when her father came home after many days away. She would struggle to help him carry his bow and his quiver of arrows around the room, and he would clap and laugh, and marvel at his daughter, who despite her mother's constant disciplining would insist on wearing her hair long in the style of the barbarians and of her father.

"She will wear her hair up like a lady when she is older, "Madame Tang would tell her customers, embarrassed by the wilfulness of her child.

One day her husband gave Jade Moon a small bow, and he taught her how to stand, and how to draw back the string. Madame Tang had shouted at them, but they had gone off together out of the house, returning only much later, with Jade Moon looking flushed but happy. The bow stayed by her bed at all times then, even when her father left with the next caravan.

"Young women do not shoot arrows," Madame Tang had said. But Jade Moon had laughed, and continued to sing her songs as she practised with the needle. In the time before her husband returned next, Madame Tang began to teach Jade Moon her numbers and the characters with which she would need to do business.

As the years went by Madame Tang's business prospered, and Jade Moon, by the time she was eleven years, was as tall as many men. She was strong as well, and quite capable of doing all of the chores around the house when Prince was away.

"More young men will be using your shop soon, Madame Tang," some of the women would say, nodding towards Jade Moon, who would sit on a large cushion in full view of the people in the street, working away with needle and thread.

Madame Tang would then consider her daughter, see the fineness of her complexion, the brightness of her smile, the sharpness of the eye, but also the haughtiness and high cheekbones of the father. Madame Tang could not describe her daughter as pretty, not really seeing what the other women saw. But there was no doubt she had an indefinable quality – a certain exotic air about her. Was this was what her customers meant?

"She's too clever to get married," Madame Tang would reply. "Men don't like women who are clever, no matter how good natured and happy they are. I am sure she will take over my business in a few years when my fingers are old and stiff, and then she will take care of her mother."

Madame Tang was also sure there were not many men about town who would take a young woman as a wife who was the product of the union between a Chinese and barbarian – though she had heard that men on the northern frontier were not that fussy. But those men, whoever they were, would not be good enough for Jade Moon. Madame Tang was quite sure of that.

In that year, her husband came home with the caravan, brushing the first snow flakes of the winter off his shoulders. Jade Moon had gone to him, taking his bow and quiver from him as always, and they had sat down to dinner. He then handed over his bag of coins, got up and went out, saying to Jade Moon before he went, that they would practise again in the morning with *his* bow to strengthen her muscles. Madame Tang had frowned and tutted, thinking as Jade Moon was almost a women this should stop, regardless of what the barbarian women might do on the northern steppe.

Later, strange men came to the door, carrying her husband between them. "He fell in the street on leaving the tavern," they said, and could give no further explanation.

Jade Moon ran for Physician Mu who came quickly. He made his examination, shook his head, and said there was no hope. "Madame Tang, it is because he is barbarian and far from home. I have heard of this before. He is not in his own country, and has left his true heart behind. What he has in his chest is too weak to sustain him any longer. He will be in the afterlife before morning, I fear."

Physician Mu was proved right. In the middle of the night, with Madame Tang and Jade Moon looking on in silence, Prince breathed his last.

Madame Tang looked across the room at her husband's possessions in the corner. "We will sell his bow and the arrows to pay for the funeral. They have unusual decoration and will fetch a good price."

But Jade Moon had run and stood in front of them, barring her mother's way, tears rolling her face and shaking her head.

"You will not, Mother," was all she said in a voice unnaturally adult and harsh. Her face, which was normally happy and open, from that night became hard and closed. Then, in the days that followed, Jade Moon no longer sang, and talked less and less, until Madame Tang began to believe her daughter had become almost mute.

Finally, after months of this misery, and no word of condolence from her sister, Madame Tang had said: "Daughter, there is no happiness for us in this town. We will leave and go where the weather is warmer."

So they began the longest walk south, taking what possessions they could and all the cash they had saved. Jade Moon carried her father's bow and quiver wrapped in hemp cloth across her back, and spoke very few words the whole journey. For Madame Tang it was the hardest time. She prayed often to the spirit of her own father, whom she now called Grandfather Tang, for help. They walked with the caravans for protection, and they saw life as Prince had seen it, on the trails and in the forests. Fear of attack by bandits was a constant in their lives, but as the cash dwindled in her purse, this was superseded by the fear they would never reach Chengdu, where it was said the streets were paved with jade and gold, where there were wondrous parks and gardens, and the people were so rich they could afford to buy new robes of the finest silk every month.

Their days then were of struggle and hardship on the road, and Madame Tang feared her feet would collapse under her. She was grateful for her daughter's great strength, often carrying their bags for them both, never moaning or crying.

One day, a merchant, half in jest Madame Tang thought, offered fifty strings of cash for Jade Moon. Madame Tang told him, and without hesitation, that a good parent would never sell a child no matter how difficult life had become.

"One hundred strings of cash, then," said the merchant, but Madame Tang turned her back on him, and walked away, and would not speak to Jade Moon of what the merchant had offered.

∾

I n the early summer they reached Chengdu. Madame Tang had very little cash left. To her great distress, after asking around, Madame Tang found numerous seamstresses working in the city. Though the prices they charged were in many cases exorbitant and often scandalous, some of the women had skill almost as great as her own. In despair, Madame Tang rented a small room for the night in a dingy guest house. At dinner, a maid told her of a town, far out on the frontier, in a backwater district.

"If you are an exceptional seamstress, Madame Tang, you should go there. They have none that I know of. Everyone knows that the people with cash in Tranquil Mountain send to Chengdu for their best clothes. A good businesswoman could undercut them all if she lived in that town. The people are a bit insular and rural, and there are too many foreigners and barbarians for my liking, but it is a place to live, is it not?"

"Submit to your fate," Grandfather Tang had said once, when Madame Tang and her brother and her sister were sat down to dinner. Her brother had submitted to his, having gone north with the army, and never returned. Her sister had gone her own way now, married well and prospered. So be it. Tranquil Mountain would be their new home, just because a young and friendly maid had spoken of it – in the time of their greatest need.

So, and with just a few coins left in her purse, Madame Tang had taken Jade Moon and joined with the first caravan she found leaving Chengdu, cursing the thousand bad decisions of her life, but determined not to fail, not to let circumstance conquer them…ever.

~

I t was only very slowly that Madame Tang, centre of attention that she was in the market-square, recovered the uses of her senses.

"Madame Tang, you must go see Madame Kong, and then get home to Jade Moon," insisted Madame Deng. "You do not want the Magistrate to come looking for you. Imagine what would happen if he entered your house when you were not there. Jade Moon is such a lovely girl. I think of her as the daughter I never had. Madame Kong feels the same I am sure. But Jade Moon has a bad temper and would sooner stick a knife in the Magistrate or shoot him full of arrows than pay him the proper respect."

"This magistrate does not yet deserve our respect!" exclaimed Madame Tang, almost spitting the words out.

The small crowd around them backed away slightly, though they should not have been surprised at Madame Tang's vehemence. After all, she was well known for her strong opinions and emotions. And it also had to be said there was much agreement with her words. So far, the Magistrate had not been seen much around town, had not spoken to the people at the Temple, had not met with the Patriarchs, had not solved the murder of Mister Gong, and had only been seen chatting to Tea Inspector Fang – none of which had so far filled the people with any confidence.

And as many commented in the market-square later that morning: "Heaven doesn't stand for any nonsense from arrogant officials, and neither will Jade Moon."

But Madame Tang did not hear this. Madame Deng had already supported her across the square to the Inn of Perpetual Happiness to seek comfort in the wisdom and friendship of Madame Kong.

CHAPTER 29

"Father," she prayed, at the family shrine, "please give me the strength to face this new magistrate. I understand it was the will of Heaven that Magistrate Qian, who was a good man, was taken from us…but guide me now in what I should say and do. I am afraid. I—"

The door burst open, and Golden Orchid ran in, and threw herself down on the ground beside her. Angry to be disturbed in her quiet time, when her mother had gone out to the market-square, Jade Moon opened her mouth to admonish the child. But she could not. Golden Orchid's eyes were especially mischievous that morning.

"What is it? What have you heard?"

Golden Orchid shook her head giggling. Jade Moon hoped for a moment that Magistrate Zhu had already ruled in her favour, using some special law known only to officials from Kaifeng – a law that could release her from the terror of her future. But she knew it was a stupid hope, and pushed it out of her mind.

"Tell me, Golden Orchid, what have you heard? Tell me or I will send you back to Miss Dai's orphanage without one single honey-cake."

"It is not what I have heard, but what I have got." Golden Orchid giggled as she held up a folded note. "Leaf gave it to me. He was too frightened to come here because of your mother. It is from the Magistrate. Leaf says that the Magistrate has written to ask you to come before him later this morning."

Jade Moon took the note from Golden Orchid, deciding not to open it in front of the young girl. "Please fetch my mother to me," she said instead, her tone grave, commanding. "She is in the market-square."

Golden Orchid jumped up and ran to the door, but not before – and without permission – grabbing a cake from the tray. "Leaf also says that the Magistrate is the cleverest man in the whole of China. He says it's true because Horse says it's true," she laughed, before disappearing out onto the street.

"That may not be enough," mused Jade Moon, unwilling still to open the note, having heard already from her mother that Magistrate Zhu was very clever, but rude, arrogant, uncharitable, temperamental, a hater of women, and – even worse – unconcerned with the plight of the common people. All this her mother had picked up from the people in the market-place; true or false, she could not tell.

She knelt down at the shrine again. "Father, please give me your courage."

∽

A s a young girl, Jade Moon would hear her mother carping whenever her father came home from guarding the merchants and their caravans on the never-ending grasslands and deserts in the far north.

"Is this all you have earned?" she would ask, snatching the purse of coins from his outstretched hand. "Is this all that is due to me when I have slaved day and night running my sewing business and bringing up a child on my own?"

Her father would never reply. He would merely shrug, wink at Jade Moon behind her mother's back, eat his dinner, and then go out to the tavern.

"Men always hide some of what they earn so they always have enough to drink and gamble," her mother would say afterwards. "They would rather see their wives and children starve before they forgo their pleasures."

However, Jade Moon would not be too concerned, knowing that each of her parents loved her, even if they did not care much for each other. Jade Moon was glad to get up each day and sew and work with her mother and glad when her father returned from his great journeys, so she could spend some time with him, and could learn from him. When he was at home he would always take her to the outskirts of town, and teach her to shoot the bow. As she grew, he made her bigger and bigger bows, and by the time she was twelve years old, her bow was almost as large as his, and she almost as tall as he.

Curiously, her mother would not speak of this practice. Possibly she had spoken of it many years before when Jade Moon did not remember, and it had been the only time her husband had stood up to her, and it had frightened her. Regardless of the truth, her mother would look the other way. Even now it seemed as if it were just yesterday, when her father leaned close to her face, whispering to her, as she readied to shoot.

"Remember, if your heart is pure, your mind open, your gaze steady, and your concentration total – then you will not miss."

She would release the arrow, and it would appear in the centre of the target as if by magic. And she would be amazed, revelling in this skill, and in the love and confidence of her father, though he made her shoot and shoot and shoot until her arms shook and back ached.

At the end of the day, he would walk her home, and sometimes he would say: "I treasure only one thing in this world." Then he would grow silent and sad, and she would not know what he meant by those words. Other times he would laugh, and clap his hands together and say: "You felt it, didn't you? You felt the breath of Heaven upon you as you released the arrow."

She would nod, and laugh, not knowing what he meant, but wanting him to be happy, always.

Then, one day, some of the men of the town had brought him back from the tavern and laid him out on the bed, pale and almost lifeless. She had stood over him, not recognising him at first, wanting to know why these men had brought a sick stranger into the house. Her mother had wailed and cried and pulled hair from her head, and later, as morning came, gathered up his clothes and the few rings he wore on his fingers to sell to raise cash for the funeral. Jade Moon had taken his bow and arrows in her arms, screaming at her mother if she came too close, refusing those to be sold also. Her mother had cursed her as a stupid child, but had come no closer and instead had gone to the merchant who had employed her husband and made threats saying it was overwork that had killed her husband.

The merchant, who was a kindly man, did not argue. He came to the house later, and arranged for the body to be taken away and buried, saying fine words to Jade Moon about her father.

"Young girl, one day out in the desert, barbarians came – thirty of them on horses. Your father rode out to meet them while the other guards quailed like women behind the carts and the mules. Five barbarians fell from their saddles before the rest turned and fled. I couldn't believe my eyes. Five! And all in the blink of an eye. Your mother named him well. He was a prince among men. I will gladly pay for his funeral, and will honour his spirit until the day I die."

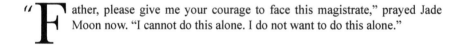

"Father, please give me your courage to face this magistrate," prayed Jade Moon now. "I cannot do this alone. I do not want to do this alone."

CHAPTER 30

"Father, this is wonderful news," said Sensible Zhou. "This speaks well of this Magistrate's character. Magistrate Qian never invited us to the jail to put our case. We must do this immediately."

Patriarch Zhou laughed, and pointed a finger at his elder son. "What do you know of Magistrates? He is from Kaifeng, which is a nest of vipers. He plays games with us, that is all. What if he denies our petition for that she-wolf, Jade Moon, and then judges we should be paid even less for our tea, or that we should be removed from our lands, making a fact out of Patriarch Sun's nightmares? Have you thought of that?"

"Father, you should not jump to such conclusions."

"You are a fool," replied Patriarch Zhou. "You should have been there last night. The Magistrate treated us like the common people by not attending our meeting."

"Father, I must respectfully disagree. I have heard in Kaifeng that officials are the most important men. Magistrate Zhu just doesn't yet understand who we are or comprehend the importance of our traditions. I hear he is a landowner too, just like us. I believe we can find common ground and mutual respect."

"Bah! Mutual respect, what nonsense is that? You speak like a woman, not like my son."

Sensible Zhou sighed, knowing his words were wasted.

"I don't trust the Magistrate," said Second Son Zhou, picking at his teeth.

"See, your younger brother understands more than you, Sensible Zhou," said Patriarch Zhou, proudly. "He is not fooled. The Magistrate has first to earn our respect before we can begin to trust him. These officials are all slippery as fish, and as dangerous and unpredictable as dragons. How is it you are called 'Sensible' and do not see this?"

Patriarch Zhou threw the note he had just received from Magistrate Zhu onto the floor. Sensible Zhou bent down and picked it up and read it quickly for himself. And he was glad he did.

"Father, we must hurry. The Magistrate is asking for Second Son Zhou to attend the jail immediately. He is to be examined in regard to the petition against Jade Moon – our petition."

Patriarch Zhou's response was, to Sensible Zhou, very predictable. "No son of mine should attend the jail like a common person or criminal!" he bellowed, face flushed with rage.

"Father, it is in response to our own petition," said Sensible Zhou, trying to calm him. "If we do not attend, then it may be the law that the Magistrate can discard our petition, regardless of our status as a family. I agree you should not go, but I can accompany Second Son Zhou, and make sure Second Son Zhou's words are not misinterpreted or twisted by the Magistrate."

Patriarch Zhou fumed, knowing that Magistrate Qian would not have summoned them in this way, but also knowing – at least in this one thing – that Sensible Zhou was right. He turned to Second Son Zhou and said: "Don't let the Magistrate trip you up with clever words. Let your brother speak in your defence. He is older, so if a mistake is made, it is him I will hold to account. And remember to tell the Magistrate that the she-wolf put a knife in your face and drew blood... our family's blood. There must be punishment for this."

⁓

"I went to Madame Tang's home, which is leased from my father, to collect the rent for the month. Unfortunately, Madame Tang was not there. But Jade Moon was there, and—"

"Second Son Zhou, please refer to Madame Tang's daughter as Miss Tang," interrupted Magistrate Zhu. "I have found that if the parties to a dispute refer to each other with civility, then the disputes are more easily resolved. Now let me just confirm the three petitions I have in the file. First, there is the petition made by your father, that Madame Tang should honour the contract for the concubinage of her daughter, Miss Tang. Second, there is the counter-petition made by Madame Tang, stating that her daughter is no longer her daughter, that she has now developed a supernatural quality and can no longer force her to do anything against her will. And thirdly there is a petition, once again made by your father, Patriarch Zhou – a criminal petition this time – alleging an assault made by Miss Tang against your person, Second Son Zhou, in Madame Tang's home. Is this all correct?"

"Yes, Magistrate," answered Sensible Zhou, handing over their copy of the contract for the Magistrate to hold onto and to study.

Magistrate Zhu was taking his own notes at his desk, having not yet come to a decision to send a request to Senior Scribe Xu for the use of one of the junior clerks. It made the process more long-winded, and did not improve his temper, but the frequent pauses he requested – so his calligraphy could catch up with the spoken word – gave him more time to think. "Second Son Zhou, please continue to describe the assault on your person. I must dispense with the criminal allegations before considering the contractual dispute."

"Yes, well, Miss Tang—"

"And refer to me as Magistrate when you speak to me," interrupted Magistrate Zhu, again. "You will find me more attentive if you do so."

If Magistrate Zhu would have glanced up when he said this, he would have seen the look of pure hatred on the face of Second Son Zhou, and the smile that fleetingly crossed Horse's face as he took up station behind the two Zhou brothers at the back of the office. Horse had done his best to be polite to both brothers when they arrived at the jail. Though he did not know or care about Sensible Zhou, except that he was well-regarded as the heir to the Zhou estate and due much respect, he loathed Second Son Zhou for what he had tried to do to Jade Moon.

"Yes, Magistrate," said Second Son Zhou. "Jade Moon...excuse me, Miss Tang...attacked me as I entered the house. She flew at me like a wild cat, though my father says she is a she-wolf. I did not know what to do. She held a knife to my face and she cursed like a soldier. I was lucky to escape with my life. I reported then to my father what had happened."

"The petition states that Miss Tang threatened you with murder, Second Son Zhou. Is this true? So far you have said Miss Tang flew into a rage and attacked you with a knife. But did she really threaten murder? That is a most serious allegation."

"She had a knife, Magistrate. She put it in my face and cut me."

Second Son Zhou, pointed to a small scar under his right eye. Magistrate Zhu stopped writing for a moment and peered carefully at Second Son Zhou's face.

The brothers, who were sitting close together in front of his desk, looked to Magistrate Zhu as if they could have been born of different mothers – which he supposed was entirely possible, as he knew nothing of the family history. Sensible Zhou's features were solid and his eyes slow and solemn. But Second Son Zhou was slim, and his eyes quick and sly. Sensible Zhou was wearing dark brown robes, whereas Second Son Zhou was dressed in robes of crimson, expensively decorated with dragons and with what Magistrate Zhu took for alchemical designs. Second Son Zhou could have been visiting an expensive courtesan rather than attending an official examination.

And Magistrate Zhu had noted with amusement and curiosity the emotions moving across the face of his normally placid senior constable when he had showed the two men into the room. Horse did not like Second Son Zhou, and made no secret of it. Magistrate Zhu already sensed Horse to be a very good judge of character – which was valuable – but he would have to caution him to hide his emotions more.

Magistrate Zhu tapped his fingertips on the desk. "Second Son Zhou, I understand Miss Tang threatened you with a knife but the petition states quite clearly that you were threatened with murder. Did Miss Tang speak or just curse when she brandished the knife in your face?"

"She spoke or screeched...I am quite sure of that, Magistrate," replied Second Son Zhou. "But I don't remember her exact words. I was in fear for my life. She said she would blind me, or rip my heart out...something like that, I am sure. What does it matter? She wanted to kill me that was certain. She should be punished...beaten, for what she did. She should be sent to us. I will teach her how to behave."

"Second Son Zhou, you must do your utmost to remember Miss Tang's exact actions and words. Threatening murder is potentially a capital offence. It is imperative I understand what she was saying to you."

"Magistrate," said Sensible Zhou. "We do not want this girl executed. We merely want—"

"Sensible Zhou," interrupted Magistrate Zhu, "your family has brought this petition, and I will offer up my judgement. The penalty I impose, if I find that Miss Tang has broken the law, will be determined by me, and me alone. You have no influence in that regard. Do you understand?"

Sensible Zhou blinked, and nodded. He knew his brother should not have been at Madame Tang's house. His brother's stupidity could have cost Jade Moon her life and, more importantly, whatever remained of the goodwill of the people towards the Family Zhou.

"Magistrate, it all happened so quickly," continued Second Son Zhou. "I walked through the door, and she was on me like a crazed tigress, pushing a knife into my face."

"You said wild cat."

"Excuse me, Magistrate?"

"Second Son Zhou, you referred to Miss Tang earlier as a wild cat, and now you say crazed tigress. Though it is a minor matter, and I usually ignore such emotive descriptions, you should take greater care with your words. Now, please tell me, is it usual for you to collect the rent?"

"Magistrate, I—"

"It is, Magistrate," interrupted Sensible Zhou, answering for his brother. Sensible Zhou did not like lying, and especially to the Magistrate, but he knew he had to take hold of this examination before his brother unravelled in front of him. "The rent is collected by me, by my brother, or by our more trusted guards and man-servants. We also make regular visits to all of our properties, often without warning. The tenants are prone to damaging the houses or making alterations without permission. Magistrate, you will find such terms in the tenancy contracts."

"Thank you, Sensible Zhou," said Magistrate Zhu, "but please let Second Son Zhou answer my questions. But I will turn to you if I find him completely incapable. Now, Second Son Zhou, what sort of knife did Miss Tang brandish?"

Second Son Zhou shrugged. "I don't know, Magistrate....a cooking knife, perhaps? It was long and sharp, and the bitch cut me." He pointed again to the short scar under his right eye.

"What day of the month is the rent usually collected?" asked Magistrate Zhu.

Before Second Son Zhou could answer, Sensible Zhou interrupted once more, realising the Magistrate was trying to trick his younger brother.

"Magistrate, it varies," he exclaimed.

Magistrate Zhu nodded, and made further notes. Sensible Zhou breathed deeply, thankful at least this was not a lie. Rent collections were made on any day during the month, and were a constant source of contention with the tenants. But other work had to be done, and often there was no choice.

"Did Miss Tang know who you were?" asked Magistrate Zhu, returning his gaze to Second Son Zhou.

"Of course, Magistrate," Second Son Zhou replied with some irritation. "I am the son of Patriarch Zhou. Everyone knows who I am."

"Are you certain, Second Son Zhou? I have found that among the common people, women tend to notice only what goes on in their own homes or in their own streets. They may avert their eyes when men of importance walk by. Could Miss Tang have confused you for a robber or worse, breaking into her home and—"

"Magistrate, my brother is very well known around town. In no way could he be mistaken for a robber," interjected Sensible Zhou. "See how he is dressed now – like a gentleman. Do robbers wear hats and robes of the finest silk? And everyone knows that robbers come by night. Miss Tang attacked him in the morning. This girl has no excuse, none at all."

Magistrate Zhu felt his face flush, but otherwise did his best to keep his temper. "Sensible Zhou, do not teach me my profession. It is true that most robbers attack under the cover and anonymity of night, but I have found daylight does not always preclude such activity, whatever you may think. Now, does your brother remember anything else of value to my investigation?"

"I don't want her marked in any way. No tattoos," said Second Son Zhou. "She must be as she is now when she comes to me as concubine."

Magistrate Zhu felt his temper almost break through to the surface.

"Second Son Zhou, you have sent in your petition and described the events as you experienced them. You must live with the consequences. If you have nothing further to add, my examination is concluded for today, though I may have more questions at a later date."

～

On the way back to the residence, Sensible Zhou felt frustrated and unhappy. Even with his help, the examination had not gone to plan, *and* he had been forced to be rude and objectionable to the Magistrate when his intention on entering the jail had been the opposite. There was no doubt in his mind the Magistrate knew exactly why Second Son Zhou had gone to Madame Tang's house, and what he had been intending – not that that was any excuse for Jade Moon's appalling and violent behaviour. How this would affect the judgement he did not know. But then a sudden thought cheered him slightly. What if the Magistrate did order Jade Moon to trial in Chengdu before the Prefect, and to face execution? If executed, wouldn't that be a good thing for all? Wouldn't that save his family from having the curse of that she-wolf under their roof as a concubine, and preserve the Family Zhou line from his father and brother's stupidity?

Sensible Zhou was so cheered by this he was moved to say: "Second Son, you have been a fool, and always will be a fool, and it's a pity that Jade Moon didn't cut your throat. Our family would be better off."

There was no reply. Second Son Zhou looked in front of him, pretending not to hear, still pouting from his uncomfortable encounter with the Magistrate.

CHAPTER 31

"*J*ade Moon, you must put your best silk dress on. And today you must wrap a scarf around your head and cover your hair," said Madame Tang. "The Magistrate mustn't think I've neglected to teach you how to dress."

Madame Tang bustled around the room trying to get herself ready, constantly adjusting her own pale yellow silk dress around her ample body, and tucking in the hair that kept working loose from under her headscarf.

The wearing of their best silk dresses had been Madame Kong's brilliant idea. Madame Tang had thought first to wear her poorest clothes, made from the roughest hemp and coloured in the drabbest of greys, to elicit as much sympathy from the Magistrate as possible. Wasn't sympathy the best a woman could hope for from such a man? But Madame Kong had been of a different opinion, and was adamant they should all look their very best.

"Let the Magistrate see that you are a woman of substance, Madame Tang – an artisan of uncommon skill. Women of substance do not have their daughters taken away from them and forced into concubinage."

Madame Tang could not but agree. And, after all, Madame Kong knew a thing or two about important men and catering to their needs, owning and managing as she did such a fine establishment as the Inn of Perpetual Happiness and maintaining a more than close relationship with Tea Inspector Fang – not the easiest of men to care for.

The difficulty though, that day, was in getting Jade Moon to dress properly. So far she had shown no sign of changing her clothes, and Madame Tang's nerves were beginning to get the better of her, so much so that tears were not far from her eyes. Jade Moon's mood had been infuriating all that morning. When Madame Tang had returned from Madame Kong's with the plan settled, Jade Moon had suddenly decided she did not want to cooperate.

"Jade Moon, both Madame Kong and I are decided upon this!" shouted Madame Tang. "The Magistrate has demanded to see you, as well as that stupid contract. When he sees how pretty you are, he is bound to be moved to be compassionate toward you."

But Jade Moon had turned her back on her mother. She sat in the corner on her seat with her needlework – work that Madame Tang had to admit needed to be done urgently – dressed only in a light blouse and her old working trousers. Madame Tang had laid out the peach-hued silk dress she had made for Jade Moon two years earlier, after that dreadful incident with the bandit-leader, Bad Teeth Tong. The dress had never ever been worn. Jade Moon had not once tried it on.

There was a short, sharp knock at the door. Madame Kong entered quickly, wearing her best pale green dress, looking radiant. Madame Tang would have known, even if they had not been dressing for the Magistrate, that Tea Inspector Fang had arrived the day before.

"Madame Tang, it is time," said Madame Kong, breathlessly. "I have heard that Magistrate Zhu has just met with Sensible Zhou and Second Son Zhou. We must now show willing as well."

Madame Kong then noticed Jade Moon's state of unreadiness, and sighed. "Oh, Jade Moon, why aren't you wearing the beautiful dress your mother made for you?"

"Madame Kong, you wouldn't believe the morning I have had with this girl," said Madame Tang. "I am of a mind to let her go to the Family Zhou after all. She is not much company for me as it is. Sometimes she doesn't speak to me for days."

"I will not dress as someone I am not!"

Both Madame Tang and Madame Kong were taken aback by Jade Moon's sudden outburst and sharpness of tone. And Jade Moon wasn't quite finished yet.

"The Magistrate will have to see me as I am – a seamstress – and not some… some…dancing girl!"

Madame Kong knew she could dress Jade Moon in next to nothing and still she wouldn't look like a dancing girl. Her height, her stark barbarian beauty, her long unbound hair and the manner in which her nostrils flared when she was angry – all these spoke more of a warrior-princess than a young woman educated solely for the entertainment of men. But perhaps in this matter Jade Moon was right, thought Madame Kong. Sometimes it was hard to figure men out. Yes, Magistrate Zhu could be impressed by fine clothes, but he could be just as easily impressed the attire of a young woman who worked all the hours under Heaven just to make a living.

"Madame Tang," said Madame Kong, "it is too late for Jade Moon to dress properly now. Perhaps it is just as important that Jade Moon feels comfortable in front of this magistrate. And there is still hope. The Magistrate may not be what you both expect. Tea Inspector Fang already thinks highly of him, and it is most rare for him to think highly of anyone."

"Madame Kong, what have you heard?" asked Madame Tang, her voice shrill.

"Madame Tang, there is no time and I have no specific detail. But Tea Inspector Fang says that Magistrate Zhu is a deep thinker. It has given me hope for Jade Moon. Come Jade Moon, put on your light jacket, we must go. No matter how we are all dressed, we cannot afford to be late."

Madame Tang shook her head, annoyed that Jade Moon was putting on her jacket, and just because Madame Kong had merely asked her to.

They filed out of the house. Jade Moon shut the door behind them, and hurried to catch up as Madame Kong and her mother began walking rapidly down the street towards the market-square, with Madame Kong talking quite animatedly. Jade Moon struggled to catch her words.

"....and Tea Inspector Fang has heard much about our new Magistrate in Chengdu," said Madame Kong. "He says Prefect Kang is frightened of him. And that the Magistrate is really clever. Our Magistrate passed the civil service examination at a really young age. He comes from a very important family in Kaifeng. But there is also a mystery about why he is here and has allowed himself to become a lowly district magistrate. Tea Inspector Fang wouldn't say much about this...you know he can be secretive at times, Madame Tang...but I know he suspects much."

"But what does it all mean?" asked Madame Tang.

"I believe it to be good news. This is why the Magistrate has not met with the Patriarchs yet. He isn't afraid of them, Madame Tang. He isn't afraid of Patriarch Zhou! Tea Inspector Fang believes he and Magistrate Zhu will become the best of friends. Oh, I hope this is so, Madame Tang. Tea Inspector Fang may yet choose to put in a good word for Jade Moon."

They both looked up and were surprised then to find they had arrived at the forecourt of the jail already. The Deng brothers and Leaf were sitting on the front step, trays of food on their laps, staring at the three women open-mouthed.

Madame Tang, moved to bad temper as always when she saw the Deng brothers, said: "Get up out of the way you stupid boys. Can't you see we're here to visit the Magistrate? Think of your mother, if you can. She sits at home every day crying because she has delivered you into the world."

The Deng brothers and Leaf jumped up, almost spilling the food off their trays, and backed into the jail-room, but only so far. Madame Tang and Madame Kong marched into the jail, quickly followed by Jade Moon, who looked straight ahead, not wanting to exchange glances with the Deng brothers.

The reason for the Deng brothers and Leaf sitting on the front step, and being minded not to back too far into the jail-room then became suddenly apparent. Madame Wu was using her broom. Very little was escaping the violent motions she made, as she swept the broom back and forth without regard for any of the constables' possessions. Until she saw Madame Tang and Madame Kong, that is. She stopped her cleaning and spat on the floor in front of them, her face full of loathing. But then Madame Wu's face suddenly softened when her eyes focused on Jade Moon.

"At least there's one woman in this town with some metal in her," said

Madame Wu, her voice throaty and rasping. "The rest of you can burn in the deepest hell!"

Horse moved quickly. He had been eating his lunch with Little Ox in the cells, keeping well out of the way of Madame Wu. He put his tray down and came running out when he heard Madame Wu's voice. He did not know what to make of the animosity between the women – it was not men's business and so he didn't want to know – but he knew enough that he had to defuse the situation before something terrible happened. He ran forward, hustling Madame Kong and Madame Tang through the doorway into the corridor and then into the Magistrate's office, expecting Jade Moon to follow suit.

Horse had thought the Magistrate to be eating his lunch in the warmth of the garden, keeping out of Madame Wu's way also, but he was in fact standing at his desk, his back to them all, rearranging his papers.

"Magistrate!" exclaimed Horse, surprised. He bowed, hoping Madame Kong and Madame Tang and Jade Moon would do likewise, which fortunately they did. Except for Jade Moon, who somehow missed Horse's cue. She found herself staring into the piercing eyes of Magistrate Zhu, as he turned to find out just who had disturbed him.

~

M agistrate Zhu was uncertain how long the moment lasted. Later he would reflect on the encounter, and with some embarrassment, not knowing what emotions had appeared on his face, wondering how he had appeared to them – *how he had appeared to her*.

She was the tallest woman he had ever met, for her eyes were on a level with his own. And those eyes! He would later describe them to himself – inaccurately, of course – as being comparable in essence to Chef Mo's best broth: of a hundred subtle and remarkable flavours, all intermingling, forever moving and changing, infusing and over-loading the senses.

But such a comparison did not do her justice, could never do her justice. He had walked the myriad streets of Kaifeng, in every season. He had attended the best restaurants and the best parties, and seen dancers, singers and entertainers from every corner of the Empire – all talented, charming and alluring in their own right. And he had just walked and ridden more than a thousand miles from Kaifeng to the Fifth District, and had seen, he thought, all there was to see. But never had he met any such as her.

Fortunately, Jade Moon suddenly became aware of her situation, just who it was she was staring at. She gasped at her own impropriety and averted her eyes downwards, but not quite dropping into a bow.

Magistrate Zhu breathed in and out, conscious he was returning to the world and that time was, once more, progressing.

"Madame Kong and Madame Tang," Horse belatedly announced, uncomfortably conscious of how long the Magistrate and Jade Moon had stared at each other. He realised he should have spoken first, told her how to conduct herself in front of him. He hoped his mistake had not cost her dearly. Miserably, he shuffled behind them to take up station against the back wall.

"Magistrate, thank you for allowing us to deliver the contract today," said Madame Kong quickly. "Madame Tang and her daughter, Jade Moon, are with me."

Madame Kong feared the Magistrate had heard none of her words. He looked beyond her, toward Jade Moon, with a strange expression on his face.

"Magistrate! I am Madame Kong of the Inn of Perpetual Happiness," she said, more firmly this time. "I have brought with me Madame Tang and the contract as you requested."

"Madame Kong, my apologies," said Magistrate Zhu, partially regaining his senses. "You have taken me by surprise. My papers have become disordered, and I was trying to make things right. Though I do know your name. You are to be commended on your choice of chef. When I am less busy, I am to visit your fine establishment in the company of Senior Scribe Xu. He has given the Inn of Perpetual Happiness the best of recommendations."

"That would be my honour," she replied, bowing slightly.

Magistrate Zhu edged around his desk and took his seat, unhappy that Horse had not given him due notice of the women's arrival. With the agitation caused in his mind by his conversation with Sensible Zhou and Second Son Zhou, and the intrusion of Madame Wu to the jail to conduct her cleaning, he had quite forgotten he was expecting more visitors.

This was also his first look at Madame Tang, and he did not like what he saw. She was quite dissimilar to the diminutive and attractive Madame Kong. Madame Tang was a short, dumpy woman, with quite an evil cast in her eye, or so he thought. Could she really be mother to the tall young woman behind? This so disturbed his thinking that he wished he could order Madame Kong and Madame Tang to stand aside, to study Jade Moon again but more properly, and to understand the confusing thoughts now leaping about his mind.

"Madame Tang, thank you for attending this office," he said instead, trying to be polite, and not to judge the woman by her physical appearance.

Though, Madame Tang was not of a similar mind to withhold such judgement. She did not like his thin, pale and tired-looking face, or his sharp eyes, or the plainness of his black robe, despite many of the other women thinking his features fine, handsome even. And his fingers were too long and delicate – much like a woman's who had done no real work in her life. She shuddered at the thought of such a man holding the lives of her and Jade Moon in his hands. Madame Tang felt sweat breaking out across her back.

"Madame Kong, why are you here if you don't mind me asking?" asked Magistrate Zhu. "Is it some coincidence you are visiting me at the same time as Madame Tang?"

"Magistrate, it is not," replied Madame Kong, quickly. "Madame Tang is my particular friend. I am here to support her petition."

"Ah," replied Magistrate Zhu. "Is Madame Tang not able to speak on her own behalf? I expect my questions will be quite comprehensible."

"Oh yes, Magistrate, but I am Madame Tang's most special friend, and through the years she has performed such good service to this town. She and Jade Moon are making your constables' uniforms. They will all look very smart."

Magistrate Zhu glanced back at Horse, who nodded to confirm this was true. Then Magistrate Zhu remembered he knew this fact already and had already admonished Horse for making the contract. He breathed deeply, trying to clear the fog between his ears.

"Good, yes, I am sure the uniforms will be very practical. Now do you have the copy of this contract for me?"

Madame Kong nudged Madame Tang, frightened her friend would be confused by the presence of the Magistrate, and to have forgotten the contract within her sleeve. But Madame Tang was already moving. She stepped forward, extracted the rolled up document, slapped it down on the Magistrate's desk, and stepped back again with a speed which belied her great mass.

If Magistrate Zhu was surprised by Madame Tang's sudden movement he did not show it. He picked up the document, unrolled it and began to read, nodding as he did so. "Yes, this is it, good," he said, softly, to himself. Then to Madame Tang, he said: "I will need to retain this for a few days to compare it to the contract delivered by Sensible Zhou. I will give you a receipt so you should not be concerned."

"Jade Moon is so very young, Magistrate," whispered Madame Tang.

Magistrate Zhu looked up from the contract. Madame Kong put a hand to her mouth, quite shaken that her friend had just spoken without thinking.

"Madame Tang, did you say something?" asked Magistrate Zhu.

"Magistrate, forgive me, but my daughter is so very young," repeated Madame Tang, louder and more definite this time.

Momentarily taken aback, Magistrate Zhu strained in his chair to see past the two women to once more look upon Jade Moon. But neither woman moved, and Magistrate Zhu was forced to look back down at his notes. After a while he began to shake his head.

"Madame Tang, I believe you are mistaken. According to my records, your daughter is nineteen years of age. Most women of her age are already married. Are my records incorrect?"

Madame Tang placed a chubby hand to her mouth, unable to believe her own stupidity. She hoped Madame Kong would do her utmost to extricate them all from this disastrous and embarrassing situation.

"You are quite right, Magistrate," interrupted Madame Kong. "Children grow so quickly these days. Mothers tend not to realise this."

"Yes, of course, thank you, Madame Kong," replied Magistrate Zhu again looking down at his papers. After a short pause, he said: "Madame Tang, apart from the disputed contract, your daughter stands accused by the Family Zhou of threatening murder to Second Son Zhou. As this petition is of a criminal nature, I must inform you I shall be considering it before all other petitions."

"It is not true, Magistrate," said Madame Kong quickly, not trusting Madame Tang to speak any further.

Magistrate Zhu looked up. "What is not true, Madame Kong?"

"Jade Moon did not threaten murder, Magistrate. The petition is a ruse."

"Please refer to Madame Tang's daughter as Miss Tang, Madame Kong," said Magistrate Zhu, though not unkindly. "You must understand that this is a very serious allegation. However, you should know that any confession made to me before I have got to the truth of what happened that day would do much to mitigate any penalty to be incurred."

Magistrate Zhu looked from Madame Kong to Madame Tang, hoping they would comprehend the gravity of his words. It was only slowly that he realised that the criminal petition in question concerned the tall young woman standing behind Madame Kong and Madame Tang. And that it was she who was also responsible for the death of the bandit, Bad Teeth Tong – from a hundred paces, with a single arrow.

He shivered.

How was this possible?

If she had spoken to him and told him she had done no such thing, and though it was written in the file on the desk before him, he would have believed her....would have had no choice but to believe her. He began to wonder if he was losing his mind.

And this the same young woman who had created beauty with the touch of her fingers, with a simple needle and a measure of thread, the intricate embroidery of the magnolia plant, hanging in Senior Scribe Xu's hall.

How could this be?

Was it any wonder Magistrate Qian had found her so fascinating....that she possessed such artistic skill and yet such a propensity for violence? Here was a mystery to solve that would challenge the most incisive of investigators, the most thoughtful of philosophers, and perhaps even the most lyrical of poets.

Magistrate Zhu forced himself to take up his ink-brush, to dip it carefully in the ink, and to write out the receipt. After pausing to let the ink dry, he applied his personal seal and the seal of office, folded the document, and held it out for Madame Tang to take, which she did, again with surprising speed.

"If there is nothing else that you need to bring to my attention, then that will be all for now," said Magistrate Zhu. "There is no requirement for you to attend again, Madame Kong. I have grave doubts about allowing uninvolved parties into my examinations and deliberations. But I thank you for your assistance today."

Horse, knowing the interview was over, and concerned he may have earned a reproof for himself for not announcing the women first, was about to hustle the three women out of the Magistrate's office, when Magistrate Zhu said: "Senior Constable, please arrest Miss Tang. Place her in the cells to await examination and then escort Madame Tang and Madame Kong from the building."

There was then such a commotion from Madame Tang, such cries and screams and the tearing of her own fine dress, that Little Ox, the Deng brothers and Leaf all came running – Fast Deng being unfortunate enough to run into one of Madame Tang's flailing fists, knocking him senseless to the ground.

Using all of his great strength Horse propelled both Madame Tang and Madame Kong from the Magistrate's office, ordering Little Ox to lead Jade Moon to the cells – and leaving Slow Deng to care for his fallen brother. All this time,

Magistrate Zhu continued to examine papers on his desk, apparently unaware that anything unseemly had happened at all.

But Jade Moon chose not to leave.

Little Ox tugged gently at her arm, not wishing to hurt her, but undecided quite how to get her to the cells without force. If Jade Moon even noticed Little Ox's hand upon her, she did not show it. Her mind was solely on the Magistrate.

"Is this your law then…your Kaifeng law…that a daughter should be callously stripped away from her mother?"

Her voice was harsh, angry. Little Ox let go of her arm. Slow Deng stopped in his attempt to help his brother, wanting to be witness to all that was going to happen. Leaf stared up at Jade Moon in wonder, at the slight flush of her face and the dangerous light in her eyes.

Magistrate Zhu continued to examine his papers.

She spoke again, her tone more threatening, more insistent. "What kind of law is it that brings unhappiness to the people? Is this the reason you have come all this way from Kaifeng? Have you come here just to make me, my mother, and all the people of Tranquil Mountain, suffer?"

Magistrate Zhu felt the beating of his heart in his chest. He looked up. Her magnificent eyes burned into him – waiting for his answer. He stood, not wishing to be overawed by her, dominated by her.

"Miss Tang," he said, speaking slowly and calmly, forcing confidence and command into his voice, "as a magistrate, it is incumbent upon me that I never rush to judgement in regard to the people over which I preside. Though I cannot insist upon it, I would ask that you do not rush to judgement in regard to me."

She met his eyes for a short while longer. But, as he watched, fascinated, the fire within those eyes began to dwindle and die, to be replaced with mere curiosity. Then she dropped her head; and, with just a single glance back at him, her eyes still searching his face, she allowed Little Ox to lead her away.

"Magistrate, she is a heroine!" exclaimed Leaf, as if this explained everything.

Magistrate Zhu, his breathing shallow, his heart still thumping, knowing how close she had come to overwhelming him, found he had no words within him with which to reply.

~

"I'll wager Madame Wu could take Madame Tang any day," said Fast Deng, holding a cold compress to his swollen chin, hoping to inject some humour into the day.

"Only if she has her broom with her," replied Slow Deng.

Leaf almost cried with laughter, imagining such a fight in his mind. He could not wait to get back to the orphanage that night, and tell Miss Dai and all the other children just what he had seen. Miss Dai was especially proud of him for gaining employment at the jail, and working for the new magistrate. And she was just as pleased that he was able to bring back all the most important news. The work at the orphanage was difficult and exhausting, as well as the continual search for funds – but Miss Dai liked a good story as much as anyone.

The constables and Leaf were standing outside the jail, not wanting Jade Moon, who was sitting quietly in her cell, to overhear. Horse had left the main cell door unlocked and ajar, and Little Ox had placed a cup of tea by her side, for her comfort. Not that she had responded to their kindness. She would not even meet their eyes. She seemed not to be angry, but lost in her own thoughts.

"The people are going to hate us for this," said Little Ox. "I know what the Magistrate said about the law, and about the balance of Heaven and Earth, but surely to imprison Jade Moon is an offence against Heaven. Horse you must talk to him. This could be trouble for us."

"Definitely," said Fast Deng. "This looks very bad."

"Agreed," said Slow Deng. "Stupendously bad."

Horse nodded, already having made up his mind that that was exactly what he was going to do.

~

When Madame Tang arrived back home, she sat down at her table and began to cry, angry at her own stupidity for speaking up and saying idiotic things in front of the Magistrate. Madame Kong reached over, patted Madame Tang on the shoulder, and took the Magistrate's receipt off her. Madame Kong feared the document might get wet from Madame Tang's tears, or that Madame Tang might spill her tea across the table in her distress.

"Oh, Madame Kong, thank the Lord Buddha and the spirit of my departed father you were with me. I swear his eyes were as cold as ice. He looked right through me as if I was a ghost. What hope have I with such a man? What hope has Jade Moon? He will have Jade Moon strangled for what she did to Second Son Zhou, or sent to the Zhou residence without delay."

"Madame Tang, don't be concerned. It went much better than even I expected. I believe this Magistrate will listen to you and be fair. Just remember he is obviously very concerned about propriety. He is not like Tea Inspector Fang in that regard."

"Then you think all is not lost?"

"Nothing is lost, Madame Tang. Don't give up hope before the Magistrate has even begun his considerations. Remember what I said. He is not afraid of the Patriarchs, and I am certain he will not be unduly influenced by the words of that snake, Second Son Zhou. Now, I must return to the inn. My customers will be expecting me."

It was only after Madame Kong had gone that Madame Tang noticed Golden Orchid sitting in the corner, in Jade Moon's sewing chair, fear etched all over her face. Initially moved to send the girl on her way, back to the orphanage, Madame Tang felt suddenly glad of the company.

"Well, child, we must listen to Madame Kong and be optimistic. While we wait for Jade Moon to be returned to us, I will teach you your first stitches. Orphan or not, if you can sew you will always be useful to someone."

CHAPTER 32

MIDDAY, 21ST DAY OF THE 1ST MOON

*M*any people tried to obstruct their progress across the market-square, shouting questions or even obscenities, so much so that Senior Scribe Xu feared a riot – which in the market-square was a very serious matter, indeed a terrible crime. It would certainly bring Sergeant Kang running and his ruffian militia with him, to knock a few heads together, which would probably incite further trouble among the people. And what would the Magistrate say then?

But as it was, nearer to the jail, the crowd thinned to nothing – the aura of the Magistrate working its wonders. Senior Scribe Xu, together with Junior Scribe Li, thankfully entered unmolested into the jail.

Senior Scribe Xu had given strict instructions to Junior Scribe Li not to even glance in the direction of the cells, where *she* was being held. They were to march in line, directly into the office of Magistrate Zhu. This was not exactly protocol – they should have waited to be summoned – but Senior Scribe Xu did not want to hang about in the jail-room, and when they got to the office the Magistrate seemed grateful for the distraction. Horse was in there and from the tension in the air, and from Horse's chastened expression, Senior Scribe Xu felt that harsh words had been spoken.

"Senior Scribe Xu, have you important news for me?"

"I have the best of news, Magistrate," he replied, proudly. "I have a file...a legal record...proof that the murderer of Mister Gong is indeed a ghost."

"Senior Scribe Xu, what nonsense is this?"

Magistrate Zhu's mood had darkened in a blink of an eye, from congenial welcome to distinct antagonism. And Junior Scribe Li, wishing to save Senior Scribe Xu from any further public admonishment, was moved to act quickly.

"Magistrate, I am responsible for this nonsensical proof," he said.

Magistrate Zhu considered Junior Scribe Li with baleful eyes, extending his hand to receive the file from Senior Scribe Xu. "Junior Scribe Li, please explain how you came to find this file."

Junior Scribe Li knew his career was over – before it had really begun. He had forgotten the most basic rule of clerical practice: *Never use your initiative unless you are in the most extreme danger.*

"Magistrate, I realised that if this man Scary Face Fu, was responsible for the death of Mister Gong, then he must be a bad man. And that if he was a bad man, then he would have done other bad things and there might be a pertinent legal file. There are a great many files, some going back fifty years and more, but I did not get to these. I went back in time from this year, and by luck, just before dawn, I came upon a file from 1072. Magistrate Qian had written it up with help from a clerk who is sadly now deceased."

Magistrate Zhu turned to Senior Scribe Xu, who explained: "Junior Scribe Lu died in 1076. Physician Ji said he had a weak heart, and had possessed such since he was a baby. It was a great pity. He was a very good clerk and had a promising career ahead of him."

Magistrate Zhu returned his concentration to Junior Scribe Li, and indicated he should proceed.

"Magistrate, this file interested me. On reading the front sheet I saw it involved Tea Inspector Fang who, before the creation of the Tea and Horse Agency, was known then as Tea Merchant Fang. I was only a boy at the time, and living in Chengdu, so I have no memory of this. Well, in the file, it said that Tea Merchant Fang and Tea Merchant Wen were caught fighting in the street by Constable Wei, both very drunk."

Magistrate Zhu opened the file and read the first page quickly. "In the first moon, 1072?"

"Yes, Magistrate. The fifteenth day of the first moon. Magistrate Qian recorded all dates scrupulously."

"Good, please go on."

"Well, I read through the file, and I found that Junior Scribe Lu had recorded in the additional notes that Tea Merchant Wen had an alias, which was Scary Face Fu. Magistrate, I nearly fainted with relief when I saw this. But then I got scared. I realised that Mister Gong must have been attacked by a ghost, because there is also a death certificate in the property file—"

"Junior Scribe Li, please slow down, you get beyond yourself," advised Magistrate Zhu. "Give me some moments to read this file for myself. There is little enough of it here anyway."

There was hardly a sound to be heard in the Magistrate's office then, while the Magistrate read.

"Now I understand from the file," began Magistrate Zhu after that short hiatus, "that Tea Merchant Fang, as was, and Tea Merchant Wen, were fighting over lucrative tea contracts. Is this correct?"

"Oh, yes, Magistrate," replied Junior Scribe Li, "before the Tea and Horse Agency was created to buy up all of the tea, the Patriarchs bargained to get the best prices from the tea merchants. And the tea merchants had to compete to get the best contracts. It was very cut-throat. At that time only the Patriarchs were happy. They made a lot of cash."

"This is all true, Magistrate," agreed Senior Scribe Xu, "as I explained last evening."

"Yes, I think I understand this," replied Magistrate Zhu. "Please go on, Junior Scribe Li – explain Tea Merchant Wen's alias."

"Magistrate, I cannot," said Junior Scribe Li, dismayed by the Magistrate's request.

"You have read nothing to understand why Tea Merchant Wen was referred to by some as Scary Face Fu?"

"No, Magistrate, and we have not come across that alias anywhere else so far."

Magistrate Zhu nodded, thinking deeply. "Junior Scribe Li, you were going to mention a death certificate. This exists in another file?"

"Yes, Magistrate, Magistrate Qian writes on the last page in the legal file....yes, that is the note there, Magistrate....that, at certain times of the year, Tea Merchant Wen was lodged in a house not far from where the Gong brothers live now. I thought this might be significant. I have heard ghosts do not like to stray far from places they know well. I found the census files on that house and confirmed that in 1072 the house was leased from Patriarch Sun by Tea Merchant Wen. Then I retrieved the tenancy contract. I found that the contract between Tea Merchant Wen and Patriarch Sun had been terminated only after a death certificate had been received from Chengdu, with Tea Merchant Wen still owing cash. The house was rented out to another family soon after. I have found the copy of this death certificate and it is true that in Chengdu, in 1077, a man known as Tea Merchant Wen died from a fall. I am certain Tea Merchant Wen is now a ghost though I cannot say why he haunts the Gong family."

"I disagree," said Magistrate Zhu, shaking his head. "There are many known instances of death certificates being falsified by unscrupulous clerks in exchange for cash or favours. Have you told anyone else of your findings?"

Feeling less than confident now, Junior Scribe Li looked to Senior Scribe Xu to answer that most difficult of questions.

"Magistrate, all the clerks are aware of what Junior Scribe Li has discovered," said Senior Scribe Xu. "We thought it a most exciting development. I accept now that in this we were in error."

"Senior Scribe Xu, I wish any rumours of ghosts and such-like to be immediately quashed," said Magistrate Zhu, firmly. "The Gong family, and the people of this town are frightened enough already. Mister Gong was killed by a man. I am sure of it. Perhaps Mister Gong, as he lay dying, merely spoke of a memory and was not actually identifying his attacker."

"Then do you have more work for us, Magistrate?" asked Senior Scribe Xu.

Magistrate Zhu, thinking on the problem, nodded. "Yes, before I speak to Tea Inspector Fang about this, I would like to know more of Tea Merchant Wen. It should be possible to examine copies of all the contracts he was a signatory to. We can also now narrow the years to search to 1072 and 1073 – before the advent of the Tea and Horse Agency in 1074. Please examine these documents for me, and see if the name Scary Face Fu appears again. I have seen many aliases before but usually even the worst of criminals do not choose to alter their family names. There must be a reason for it."

"Yes, Magistrate," replied Senior Scribe Xu, appalled at the prospect of all the work that lay in front of them.

"Good, please start immediately. I would like a verbal report on your progress in the morning," said Magistrate Zhu. "That will be all."

"Yes, Magistrate."

"Oh, and have Junior Scribe Li clear his desk in the August Hall of Historical Records."

Senior Scribe Xu blanched. Junior Scribe Li felt his knees go, and steadied himself against the wall of the office.

"Magistrate, please...." Senior Scribe Xu's words dried up in his throat, as he saw the Magistrate smile, the first evidence of a sense of humour – though one that was cruel in the utmost.

"Senior Scribe Xu, I must have Junior Scribe Li working for me from this afternoon as a trainee legal secretary. I cannot function properly alone. I am to conduct the examination of Miss Tang this evening, and Junior Scribe Li will prove more than useful. A desk shall be set up for him in this office."

Lord Buddha, no! thought Junior Scribe Li. He knew Heaven would never forget or forgive his role in the examination of Jade Moon, that he may never, ever, see the streets and great parks and magnificent gardens of Chengdu again.

CHAPTER 33

"*B*arbarians do not always live in tents!"

This had been one of his father's favourite expressions – the implication being that many of the officials and clerks he had been required to work with at the Ministry of State, though they were all very Chinese, had the manners befitting the most uncivilised.

The Minister Zhu would arrive home, and if his day had been more frustrating than usual, he would repeat the words again and again at the dinner table. Then, as if suddenly remembering his son's studies, he would turn to him and ask: "Why should a barbarian, living among us and enjoying the benefits of our civilisation, find more lenient treatment under the law?"

Magistrate Zhu, as a young man and before he was a graduate of the civil service exam, would answer: "If a barbarian does not possess our capacity for morality, how can the same moral tests be applied to him?"

The Minister Zhu would point his finger, almost shaking with anger, and say: "You should not answer a question with another question. It is not clever. You should reply to me with respect, because I am your father. Your answer should be immediate, clear, concise and correct. How else will you be understood and be recognised as a great man?"

But the question his father had asked was not so simple, and Magistrate Zhu, in all the years since, had not been able to better his own question offered in reply.

The law, as it was written, was meant equally for Chinese and for any barbarians living or trading within the empire. This was simple enough for any to understand. But it was also true that the law was not *applied* equally. For the lesser

153

crimes, judges and magistrates tended to penalise the barbarians more leniently, often with fines rather than beatings.

As Magistrate Zhu had already explained to the constables, there were two reasons for this: the first, that barbarian though these people may be, it did no good to antagonise them or foment trouble in neighbouring barbarian lands by their harsh treatment; and the second, that as these people *were* barbarians, and therefore had no capacity for moral understanding, there was no hope of correcting their behaviour through the issuing of a harsh penalty.

"Just fine them, and send them on their way," said Judge Pei, his great mentor. *"What more can be done? You might as well beat a dog for walking on the wrong side of the street. Do you think after this beating, the dog would now know what to do?"*

Which was all well and good, but in Magistrate Zhu's mind – fifteen years on from taking dinner with his father, and almost ten years on from studying under Judge Pei – questions still remained. As his father's favourite expression implied, there were many born in China, who lived as aristocrats and worked as officials and clerks, and yet had the manners and comprehension of barbarians. Many even had the facial features of the barbaric. Tea Inspector Fang and Sergeant Kang of the local militia suddenly sprang to mind.

Could the rude Tea Inspector Fang be called any less a barbarian than a smiling and happy Tibetan merchant who set up his goods in the market-square, causing no problem to his fellow traders?

This question was troubling to Magistrate Zhu.

And there were other philosophical issues. Barbarian blood could not be so easily established. There were many Chinese in the north, even in Kaifeng, who had married barbarians quite happily. What was to be said of their children? Were these children closer to barbarians, to animals, than to civilised people? Or did the Chinese father or mother transmit the desired moral capacity to the child despite the barbarian blood running in its veins?

And what could be said of the disgusting practice of the Imperial Family, who for many years had married off imperial princesses – sending them into the tents of the barbarian warlords with chests of jade, silver and gold – in the often futile hope the barbarians would cease from crossing the frontiers to plunder and pillage at will? What then could be said of the children of these poor women? Magistrate Zhu shook his head, trying to rid the unhappy question from his mind.

In the literature there were tried and tested ways of recognising a barbarian – a true barbarian, that is, rather than a Chinese acting in a rude and boorish manner. Not only did barbarians live in tents, behave like animals, and practise all manner of perverted so-called rituals, but they *looked* different.

Magistrate Zhu had read that barbarians had *'deep set eyes and large noses'*. Sometimes these eyes could be coloured blue or green. Sometimes the skin was a dark copper colour, or so covered with wild hair and whiskers that the shape of the face could not be discerned at all. But, again, what did that say about men such as Sergeant Kang, who wore a profusion of hair and whiskers, as did many other soldiers and in the barbarian fashion? Did that make Sergeant Kang a barbarian?

And what did it say for Jade Moon who sat silently before him now, patiently waiting for him to begin his examination – more patient than any *Chinese* woman he had ever known? And how could he explain the presence of *this* young woman, so different from the young woman who had earlier spoken so brazenly to him, so rudely – an outburst that from many other magistrates would have attracted an immediate beating? Was he seeing the two faces of the struggle within her, the struggle for her soul? Was she one moment Chinese, the next barbarian? He knew he should pity her for having such inner conflict, show some compassion. But compassion was not uppermost in his mind. Hadn't Magistrate Qian written to say that he would find her 'fascinating'? Though 'fascination' was too feeble a word for what he truly felt. A spell had been cast over him. A spell of such subtlety and complexity and power that the most enchanting day he had ever spent in Kaifeng had now entirely faded from view.

∾

E arlier, at dusk, after a light dinner – the majority of which Magistrate Zhu had again pushed to the side of his plate – he ordered Horse to go quickly and bring Jade Moon to his office so he could complete her examination in regard to the assault upon Second Son Zhou. Junior Scribe Li, now known by all as Trainee Legal Secretary Li, prepared paper and writing materials.

"Magistrate, I am very nervous. My calligraphy will not have its usual excellence."

"I will make allowances, Trainee Legal Secretary Li. Breathe deeply, and do not let yourself be affected by what is about to happen. Just record exactly what she says."

Which Trainee Legal Secretary Li thought was fine for the Magistrate to say, whom he assumed to have had the appropriate training to deal with the most difficult of examinees and not become flustered in the presence of those who were criminal, potentially violent and almost certainly supernatural.

Horse brought Jade Moon in and guided her to the single chair placed before Magistrate Zhu's desk, and then took up station at the back wall. Trainee Legal Secretary Li avoided her eyes, feeling a deep and terrible shame rising in his chest. He could not explain it, but the fact that she was now before them, awaiting examination and judgement, felt the deepest of wrongs. He was certain Heaven would not be amused.

"Please sit down, Miss Tang, and do not be frightened. This should not take long," said Magistrate Zhu.

But Magistrate Zhu had lied. Much time had passed since then and Magistrate Zhu had yet to begin the questioning. His mind was so taken up with the past, his father, the wisdom of Judge Pei, the question of Jade Moon's barbarian ancestry, her beauty – exotic though it was – and her reserved demeanour.

He had hoped, upon closer examination, with his own emotions under control, to know instantly if Jade Moon was barbarian. This so he would at least know how to fix the penalty should he find her guilty.

He had already come to the belief that Jade Moon's mother, Madame Tang – after his encounter with her that morning – could not transmit any worthwhile

155

learning, let alone a capacity for morality. It probably should be therefore correct to conclude morality would descend through the father's line; but, as he was barbarian, this would leave her with no morality at all. Which could not be true. If she had no morality, where then did she get the courage and sensibility to protect the people, and to kill Bad Teeth Tong with her arrows? She was a conundrum. She confused the eyes and all the other senses. He did not know what to make of her – not at all.

Worse still, she was not dressed as the common girl he remembered from the morning. He had acquiesced to Horse's odd request that Madame Kong be allowed to visit Jade Moon in the afternoon, to take care of her appearance. How could he be called humane and refuse? But Madame Kong, with the skill that some women have, had wrought a remarkable change. If Jade Moon had been a feast for the eyes before, what could be said about her now?

Jade Moon's hair was still worn long, but tied behind her neck in a pony-tail, revealing the fine bone-structure of her face, and the pale, slender line of her neck. And that was not all. Jade Moon now wore an exquisite silk dress, peach in hue, which Magistrate Zhu thought did much to contrast with the very deep lustrous black of her hair. And a pale tint had been applied to her nails, easily visible as she rested her hands together on her lap, waiting patiently for him to begin.

It would be no lie to say she could have sat in one of the finest salons, next to his sister even, and not seemed out of place. No, not Chinese – but a barbarian princess, Mistress of the Steppe and the Thunderstorm, who had perhaps wandered south by mistake.

'*There are great contrasts within this young woman,*' he wrote quickly on his own paper, despite the presence of Trainee Legal Secretary Li, desperate in front of her to be seen to be doing something, and not to appear simple-minded.

'*This should be expected of the product of a marriage between a barbarian and a Chinese,*" he continued. He then crossed out the last comment and wrote: '*There is a strangeness about Miss Tang I cannot quite fathom. She is not like a normal woman, a Chinese woman. I have asked her to sit, and she has sat with her eyes downcast, as any man should expect. But I have the distinct impression she is studying me as I am studying her.*'

Magistrate Zhu crossed this last comment out as well, thinking, if his notes were to be reviewed at a later date by the judicial intendant, he may be thought of as an imbecile. He stuck to a basic description, thinking it important to record.

'*Her features are not obviously barbarian, in that her nose is small and well shaped and her eyes are very dark with an unusual lustre to them.*' He thought that to offer up a comparison for Jade Moon's eyes with Chef Mo's 'broth of a hundred flavours' not appropriate to a formal report. '*However, there are marked differences from the norm. She is of exceptional height for a woman. Also, though she is slim, she must be of exceptional strength. I have tested her confiscated bow* (he had asked Horse to open the jail storeroom and show it to him) *and found the draw to be difficult. However, it should be realised I am still recovering from an exhaustion of the mind and body, so such comparisons are perhaps unhelpful. Her cheekbones are pronounced, but not overly so, and her complexion is fair, if a little pale – no doubt due to the practice of her profession as a seamstress. Her lips are thin but well formed. I should say she is somewhat exotic-looking rather than classically beautiful in the Chinese style.'*

Magistrate Zhu placed his ink-brush down on his desk, not trusting himself to write further until his thoughts were properly composed. He wished also to say that there was a scent about her, as if he was in fact walking through a garden of flowers after the rain had fallen. He wished to say he felt obscured by her presence in his own office. He wished to say he could *feel* the great conflict within her – civilisation versus barbarity – and that there was something fundamentally disturbing about her. But how could he write any such things in his notes?

Instead he wrote: *'Though I have had little contact with the barbarian races, or with the products of Chinese-barbarian conjugations, I can confirm that—'*

Magistrate Zhu shook his head, sighed, and passed a line through this last section of text, thinking it best if he provided no description of Jade Moon at all. He would let Trainee Legal Secretary Li make all of the evening's record. And, if the clerk wanted to describe her, then good luck to him.

I have been three years out of practice, he mused, so perhaps I should stick to a rational line of questioning rather than attempting to see into the mind of this young woman using only my eyes. He also realised that to concentrate on Jade Moon's appearance would not do. It was evidence he was after, and a confession.

He shook his head again, trying to clear his mind, determined he had to begin. He coughed, cleared his throat, and looked very deep within to find his courage.

"Miss Tang, you must answer my questions truthfully. You must speak clearly so my secretary can write your words down. You have been accused of a very serious crime. But know that until I have written my judgement, you are neither innocent nor guilty. The truth of the crime…if it is a crime…is yet to be established. Do you understand?"

There was an almost imperceptible nod of her head. Magistrate Zhu wondered again whether he should dismiss all decorum and ask her to look up and open her eyes to him, so he could see the truth of her words. But he discarded the idea quickly, not wanting her gaze to ruin his concentration again. He condemned himself for his indecision and weakness in front of a simple seamstress – and a barbarian seamstress at that.

"You have been accused of threatening murder to Second Son Zhou, or at the very least wounding him with a knife," continued Magistrate Zhu, carefully. "If you wish to make a confession to this accusation, now is the time. Such a confession would reduce any punishment."

Jade Moon remained silent. Magistrate Zhu noticed she moved only to intertwine her fingers. Magistrate Zhu pondered this. He thought he would do the same if nervous, to prevent any outward show of fear. Was she nervous? She made no other outward signs of fear. There had been no tears or shaking or trembling of the limbs as was usual in the common people. And, most unusually for a woman, no heart-rending pleas for mercy or astonishing attempts at speaking convoluted untruths.

"Your failure to confess is noted, Miss Tang," Magistrate Zhu continued, with a sigh. "I will now ask you a series of questions. I ask you to be truthful, as you will be caught out in a lie. Did Second Son Zhou come to the door of your mother's house when your mother was out?"

Again, an almost imperceptible nod of her head. Good, thought Magistrate Zhu, that at least is progress.

"Did he open the door and enter your mother's house without knocking?"

Jade Moon nodded again, more pronounced this time.

"Had he come to collect the rent?"

Jade Moon lifted her head with a start, eyes dark and wide and angry. Magistrate Zhu, shocked by her unexpected movement and the ferocity of her emotion, sat back in his seat. She opened her mouth as if to speak, but then, with no words emerging, closed her mouth, and dropped her eyes to her lap once more.

Understanding instantly the meaning of this, Magistrate Zhu found a smile come to his lips, but a smile he was quick to dismiss. There was no humour at all in the tragic situation before him. He could well imagine the fear she had felt.

"Miss Tang, did you recognise this man?"

Again a slight nod.

"And did you take a knife to him, and cut him below his right eye?"

"Yes, Magistrate," she whispered, speaking in his presence for the very first time, her voice soft, controlled, *almost Chinese.*

"Good, this is progress," he replied. "So you felt threatened by him?"

"Yes, Magistrate."

"And you took this knife up because he hurt you?"

Jade Moon shook her head.

"Because you assumed he meant to hurt you?"

She nodded, raised her eyes momentarily as if wanting to speak more, and then dropped her head again.

"Then you screamed at him that you would kill him?"

She shook her head vigorously, and Magistrate Zhu noticed her long fingers curling and uncurling in her lap.

"Sometimes, Trainee Judge Zhu, a sudden shock or sudden question to the suspect will summon the truth," Judge Pei, his mentor, had instructed once. *"When you do this, be bold and do not contemplate failure!"*

Magistrate Zhu raised his voice to fill the office, and tried his hardest to speak harshly to Jade Moon. "Second Son Zhou said you threatened him with murder, Miss Tang. How can that be a lie? He is a nobleman and noblemen do not lie. Speak! I would have the truth of this!"

She raised her head, nostrils flaring, eyes burning bright as a thousand fires. "If I wished him dead, Magistrate, he would be dead! I do not waste words on such as him!"

This then was the young woman from earlier, who had nearly consumed him, dominated him. And this was the young woman who Second Son Zhou had been so unfortunate to meet that day. Magistrate Zhu met her stare, pushing aside his fear of the unknown, waiting patiently for her anger to subside, for her to remember where she was. As realisation eventually came to her, and she understood what she had done, she dropped her head once more, lips moving but no more words coming forth.

Magistrate Zhu smiled, relieved – but then a contrary feeling arose within him, that of loss. By all the rules of decorum, no woman should ever express herself so – so passionately, so profoundly. But when she had become quiet and withdrawn, he sensed she was no longer as she was meant to be. And that, for him, was, for some reason, a matter of regret.

This moment of self-awareness shook him to the core. He looked down at his hands, focusing his mind on his body, slowly returning to himself and to what he was there to do. He then spoke without emotion, seemingly without concern.

"Miss Tang, I have heard there is a tradition here that all judgements are read out to the people in the Temple in the presence of the accused. At the risk of attracting criticism I will not subject you to that. But I do find you guilty...of common battery, though, rather than of attempted murder. The circumstances of what happened that sad day are too obscure for me to rule otherwise. You will be punished immediately. I will have notice of my verdict and of your punishment posted by the constables on the door of the August Hall of Historical Records for the people to read."

Magistrate Zhu then paused, gathering his thoughts, and beginning to address Horse more than Jade Moon. "There are five punishments, of varying severity: death, exile, penal servitude, strokes of the heavy rod, and strokes of the light rod. Fines can also be issued if more appropriate and if the circumstances and nature of the crime allow. The crime committed by Miss Tang should normally attract many strokes of the heavy rod. But I am minded to consider her previous good character and service to this district through the killing of the bandit, Bad Teeth Tong. I note she has never been rewarded for this. And I must also take into account Miss Tang's barbarian nature, and—"

"I am not barbarian," she interrupted, her voice icy.

He looked towards her, unable to forgive this interruption when he was speaking to his senior constable.

"Miss Tang – control yourself! I am only speaking what is true."

She shook her head vigorously.

Magistrate Zhu willed himself to ignore her displeasure. He turned to Trainee Legal Secretary Li, and said: "Strike her last words from your record of examination."

"I am not barbarian!" Jade Moon repeated, more insistent this time, her fine white teeth bared.

"Miss Tang – you must control yourself!" Magistrate Zhu repeated, infuriated that she could not see he was doing his utmost to help her. "Your very rudeness lays bare your barbarian nature. And it is widely known that your father was some barbarian vagrant from the north who...."

His words trailed off as she rose from her chair. The room took on a sudden chill. Horse stepped forward from the back wall to restrain her. Magistrate Zhu shook his head, not wanting her further provoked, regretting his words spoken in anger – he had no evidence that her father was a vagrant. He had no true knowledge of her father at all.

"My father was perfect in every way," she said.

Each word was spoken with absolute clarity, each word carrying with it an immense burden of emotion.

Icy though her demeanour was, Magistrate Zhu could see the tears that were not far from her eyes. He cursed himself. What was it to live with such inner conflict, between the civilised and the barbaric? He could not know. He could only thank Heaven he had been born a man, rather than a woman or a barbarian. He was a magistrate: in post to judge, yes, but also to treat the people with kindness and compassion, whatever their birth – never to taunt or to ridicule.

He stayed silent for a while, waiting once more for the emotion to drain from her and for her to recall just where she was. Her recovery was much swifter this time. Soon she dropped her head. Magistrate Zhu indicated with a movement with his hand that she should retake her seat, which she did.

"My apologies, Miss Tang – I spoke inconsiderately and without knowledge. If your father was perfect, then I acknowledge that, for I have no evidence that he was other than that. And I acknowledge too that you have the advantage of me, for though my father was a great man – a famous minister in his time – he was far from perfect; and I, unfortunately, not the son he would have wished. Understand how it grieves me to reveal this to you, and how sad I am for you that your perfect father is no longer in the world of the living, and that you only have your mother for your protection. I am quite sure if your father had still been alive then this crime you have just been found guilty of would never have been committed, and the other legal dispute you are wrapped up in, never have been allowed to develop."

He then addressed Horse. "She is to have ten strokes of the light rod…but she is not to be hurt in any way."

Horse took hold of Jade Moon's arm, finding he had to help her up from the seat. Her attention was on the Magistrate, who would not look at her, preferring instead to focus on his hands. Horse pulled her to her feet gently, and she suddenly glanced at him, as if surprised he was there. There were real tears in her eyes, tears Horse could never ever remember seeing there before.

"Think carefully on my words, Senior Constable – that she is not to be hurt in any way." added Magistrate Zhu, still staring at his hands. "Conduct the punishment in the rear garden of this jail, out of the sight of the people. Neither I nor Trainee Legal Secretary Li are required to witness the punishment."

There arose in Horse then a great warmth. In that moment he felt he got the true measure of Magistrate Zhu. He nodded towards the Magistrate and also to Trainee Legal Secretary Li, whose face demonstrated an equal mixture of bemusement and relief. Horse took Jade Moon out into the garden, his heart lighter than it had been for many, many months. Then he gave her a small handkerchief with which she could dab her eyes.

"Oh Horse, I am an ignorant fool," she said.

And Horse, who made no move to retrieve the light rod from the storage cupboard, or to summon the other constables to assist, replied: "Our magistrate is wise enough and kind enough to know that that is not true."

"I am a criminal and he must hate me for my evil tongue."

Horse smiled, having seen much in that room between the Magistrate and Jade

Moon, much that he did not quite understand. But some things were clear, even for the stupid and clumsy third son of a blacksmith that he was.

Nothing else was spoken between them for some time.

And Jade Moon, struggling to understand herself what had just gone on between her and the Magistrate, and why Horse was smiling so, began to wonder when, and if, her punishment was going to start.

CHAPTER 34

DAWN, 22ND DAY OF THE 1ST MOON

There was not a moment during the day when Madame Wu, infirm and in constant pain, was not in motion. She knew, having seen it in others, that sitting still and letting illness and old age take over, meant death. And death was to be avoided, at all costs. Madame Wu was in no hurry to meet the host of departed relatives, most of whom she hated. The day of crossing over to the afterlife could be put off indefinitely as far as she was concerned. She would put up with the pain, the stupidity of the people around town, and the struggle to make ends meet, just to stay alive.

'Death will never take me napping,' was her favourite saying to herself. Consequently, she kept working, only sleeping lightly in her best chair with a blanket wrapped around her legs, and was up well before dawn. This was the time she made breakfast for the Magistrate and for the good-for-nothing boys who pretended to be constables. Madame Wu knew, through long years of experience, that the only security for people was not young men armed with swords, but the will to survive, no matter what.

However, she did not begrudge the work. Cleaning and cooking for the Magistrate paid well, and she worked hard at both. She was determined the Magistrate – about whom she was still to form a fixed opinion – would notice her effort and choose to maintain her employment indefinitely. Each month she was able to put some cash aside from what she earned. One day she knew she would no longer be able to cook and clean so well, and she needed to save for that time. Foolish people said that Tranquil Mountain was paradise, but Madame Wu knew better. For the old or the infirm or the poor, there was no place under Heaven that was paradise.

So well before dawn, Madame Wu had pots hung over her large cooking fire, preparing the breakfast for the Magistrate and the four constables. She always prepared plenty of food. She knew from long experience that for men or boys to do anything useful in a day, they had to be fed well. She was always pleased when there was food left over after they had eaten their fill. It proved she was giving them more than enough.

She stirred the rice and the meat vigorously, not minding the heat of the cooking-fire. Her wrinkled skin was tough as leather. And as she stirred she sang to herself:

"Food for the clever Magistrate with the dangerous eyes,
Food for Horse, who's big and strong and good,
Food for the demon Dengs, who deserve to be run out of town,
And food for Little Ox who braved the great forest, and walked home all alone!"

A cool breeze touched the back of her neck. She froze, thinking that, at a time so unexpected, death had finally come to her. She turned in terror, to face the demon. Instead she was horrified to see two men standing in her doorway, dressed as Tibetans, with scarves wrapped around their heads and faces. Only their eyes could be seen. One held a long knife in his hand. The other held a scroll out to her.

"You are Madame Wu?" asked the man with the scroll.

She understood him very well. He didn't speak in the babbling nonsense of the Tibetans. The dialect and tone of his voice was more reminiscent of the streets of Chengdu that she had graced as a girl.

"Are you Madame Wu?" the man with the scroll demanded again.

She nodded, but felt the hatred rise up in her for these men. They had invaded her house as if she was nothing but a common courtesan, happy to welcome any scum to her home.

"Put this scroll with the breakfast trays, old woman, and see the Magistrate gets it. Or else we'll return tonight and cut your throat like the scrawny chicken you are. Do you understand?"

But Madame Wu was not listening. Her eyes were fixated on the knife. She knew men, and knew they all lied. She knew they would not leave her house and let her live. Caught up in her terror, and believing that her death was but an instant away, she screamed at the top of her lungs, grabbed up her sharpest cooking knife, ran forward and plunged it with all her strength into the belly of the man holding out the scroll. So unexpected was her movement, that he clung onto the scroll still while looking down at the knife protruding from him. The other intruder looked on too, motionless, momentarily stunned by this unexpected event.

"Thieves! Murderers!" screamed Madame Wu. She ran behind her cooking fire, putting it between her and the intruders. She could not believe the man she had stabbed was still standing. Instead, she watched terrified as he pulled the knife out of his belly, incredulous at the sight of his own blood on the knife and on his hands.

"You old bitch, you will die for this!" he wailed, suddenly awake to the extent of his injury.

163

"Thieves! Murderers!" Madame Wu screamed again, but she knew, this time, that death was truly upon her and there was nothing to be done.

∾

L ittle Ox was tired. The Magistrate had said he was happy for them to catch sleep when they could during the day, but it seemed with so much going on there was too little time to sleep. Exhaustion was taking its toll on all of them. He had spent much of the night walking around town, on patrol with Horse, talking of Jade Moon, impressed with the Magistrate's obvious compassion for her.

"I'm going to get the breakfast," he had said, just after dawn, ignoring the snores from the Deng brothers still in their cots, the yawn of acknowledgement from Horse and the cry from Leaf, who wanted him to wait. Leaf had first to run an errand for the Magistrate, to the August Hall of Historical Records, to see if there was any new correspondence to pick up.

But Little Ox did not wait. In no time at all he was out of the jail forecourt, and turning into the narrow alley that led into the maze of streets behind the jail and to the Street of Great Good Fortune, where Madame Wu lived alone in her little house.

Little Ox knew that memory was a poor tool, not to be trusted. Children would come up to him in the street, and ask him to tell them the story of his long and lonely walk through the forest back from Chengdu. They wanted him to tell them the names of the ghosts and demons he had seen on the way, and describe how he had outwitted them, and lived. In truth he could not remember. Sometimes in his dreams he would remember the forest, the smell of dank vegetation, and the darkness of the night. But most of all he could recall only the fear: something he could not truly describe, or would not want to describe, to the children.

And so it was for him that day too. He would say later, that as he approached Madame Wu's house, he heard her screams and felt afraid – that he remembered not much else afterward.

But there were others in that street at dawn, who would later testify to their friends and neighbours that Little Ox started bellowing and took off running towards Madame Wu's house like a man possessed by the spirit of Guan Yu, Lord of War. And then to those few whom she spoke to, and to the Magistrate, Madame Wu would describe how she thought death had come to her, until with a great roar Little Ox came crashing through her doorway colliding with the intruder who had just that moment pulled the knife from his belly, forcing him into the wall – denting the wall badly, almost breaking into the house next door – and knocking the man stone cold unconscious.

Then, Madame Wu would tell that, as she ran around to pick her discarded cooking knife up from the floor, the other intruder fell on Little Ox, finding a knife from somewhere and trying to plunge it into Little Ox's heart. And how with lightning speed Little Ox had grasped the man's wrist and, still bellowing, heaved him with incredible strength into her opposing wall, badly denting that too, and began to pound his free fist against the intruder's chest and face.

"Thieves! Murderers!" screamed Madame Wu again, unable to use her cooking knife against the intruder as he grappled with Little Ox.

"You will all die!" the intruder shouted, trying to wrestle his wrist free from Little Ox's vice-like grip. But he felt himself weaken against the youth's surprising strength and began to panic. Again and again Little Ox pummelled him, and the intruder knew he must extricate himself or he would die in that pokey little house, full of the smell and steam of cooking, without the riches he had been promised.

He tried to spin out of Little Ox's grip. Using the wall behind him as leverage, and letting Little Ox's forward energy take him into the wall, he managed to reverse their positions. But Little Ox's grip on his wrist was so strong and the pain so excruciating that he dropped the knife from his grasp. In seeing the knife fall, Little Ox let him go, and with the sudden release, the intruder tripped over the sprawled legs of his fallen comrade, and fell to the floor, stunning himself.

Before he could waken, and save himself, Madame Wu was on him with her knife, slicing his throat from ear to ear, screaming: "That is how you kill a chicken!"

And then she did the same for the other, but laughing this time, revelling in her cheating of death, her rebirth.

Later, the Magistrate would ask Madame Wu why she had then gone to her doorway and shouted at the people in the street, saying they were all "scoundrels" and "fools" and "cowards" and waving her bloody knife in the air. With great honesty she replied – and because the Magistrate had asked her nicely – that her neighbours, not one of whom had lifted a finger to save her, were in her mind not much better than the dirt on the soles of her feet.

CHAPTER 35

"*S*ergeant Kang! Sergeant Kang!"

"What is it? What is it?" he spluttered, trying to appear bad tempered, but glad to be woken from the dream.

He had been in the southern forests again, fighting the heat, the insects, the rains, the mists, the pestilences and the fevers, as well as the savages who lived there. He still considered it a miracle, a blessing from Heaven, that he had been transferred just when he had given up all hope of living even to his middle years. He had been sent to Chengdu Prefecture, to lead a rag-tag militia in defence of the Fifth District and of the trade caravans that plied back and forth to Chengdu. It was true there were only twenty of them, mostly young lads at that, and they were not proper soldiers, not proper Imperial Army such as he, but Sergeant Kang could not be happier with how his life had finally turned out.

Except of course he had little cash, no wife, concubines or children, no further prospects of promotion, and the common people of Tranquil Mountain – the good, fine, decent people – hated them, and the slice of their taxes that went to the upkeep and out-fitting of his men.

He opened his eyes. Sunlight streamed through the torn paper on the barracks window and through the large holes in the roof through which water would pour when it rained. The morning mist had been burned off early by the sun, or he had slept later than he thought. He sat up, scratching at his beard and hair, trying to focus on the young soldier leaning over him.

"Well, speak up, Du! You must have some very good reason for waking up your sergeant."

"Sergeant, there is trouble across the bridge, near to the market-square."

"What are you talking about, boy? There's never ever any trouble in town, except for daft fights between the market-traders."

"No, it's true, Sergeant. One of the young priests from the Temple is here. He says we should hurry. He said that people have already been killed."

Sergeant Kang saw the young priest hovering in the doorway, noticeably shaking with fear. He then inspected his men, most of whom were still in bed and fast asleep.

Sergeant Kang rubbed his bleary eyes. He knew from bitter experience that the first reports of an incident were invariably wrong, either exaggerated beyond belief, or the exact opposite, hardly representing the true scale of the disaster. He had seen both in his time, in the southern forests: hearing of slight altercations on the road ahead, only to find when he had reached the scene that a whole patrol had been wiped out, lying dead in the road, shot through with arrows; or alternatively, when a great battle had been reported, he had hurried to the rescue with hundreds of men and found but a single soldier had stubbed his toe and fallen, creating panic all around. In China, you never knew what was happening until having seen it with your own eyes.

He jumped out of bed, pulled on his trousers, and still only in his night-shirt, grabbed his sword and made for the door. He lingered only to shout back in the direction of Soldier Du to: "Get those other lazy bastards up and follow me to the market-square!"

But when he had run across the Bridge of Eternal Union and reached the market-square, he found nothing amiss – nothing, except for people running this way and that. There were no bandits to be seen. There was panic though, and many of the market-traders were trying to pack up there goods, and with some urgency.

"Where are they? Where are the bandits?" he asked, trying to raise his voice above the hubbub and the panicked cries of the people.

Eventually those that still had some semblance of their minds intact pointed across the square, to the dark and dingy street leading behind the jail. He ran as fast as he could, recognising it to be the Street of Great Good Fortune, but leading where he did not know. He couldn't remember ever exploring it before. But soon enough, as the people scattered out of his path, he understood he was in the right place. A silent crowd had gathered around a house – a sure sign there had been trouble, but trouble long since over. He slowed into a trot, and then into a walk. There was no reason to hurry. He even sheathed his sword, lamenting the fact he could have spent longer in bed.

The Deng brothers were crouched next to Little Ox, who was sitting on the ground, looking shocked, pale and disorientated. The Magistrate stood in the doorway of the house looking inside, still as a statue. A young boy stood next to him doing exactly the same.

"What in the name of every fornicating sage has happened here?" asked Sergeant Kang of the Deng brothers. "Where's Horse?"

Fast Deng and Slow Deng stood, faces grim, but Sergeant Kang noted the spark of excitement in their eyes.

"Horse has taken Madame Wu to the jail," said Fast Deng. "This is her house."

Slow Deng added: "She's the Magistrate's cook, and she cleans the jail—"

"I know who she is, Slow Deng – you daft bunny!" replied Sergeant Kang, with a sneer. "What did she do?"

"Nothing," replied Fast Deng, "well, that may not quite be true. We think she cut some throats. There are two dead bandits in her house. We found her standing in the street threatening everybody with a knife. The Magistrate thought it best for her own safety she be taken to the jail. Horse volunteered. Neither of us wanted to go near the mad bitch. Not when she had that knife in her hands."

"What about Little Ox, what happened to him?" asked Sergeant Kang, scratching his beard.

Fast Deng and Slow Deng both shrugged.

"We think he helped her kill the bandits," said Fast Deng.

"Leaf got here just a little bit too late to see it all happen. But if you look in there," said Slow Deng, pointing into the doorway where the Magistrate and Leaf were standing, "you'll see the bodies."

Puzzled and disbelieving, Sergeant Kang wandered over to the doorway to look in. The Magistrate turned toward him when he sensed his presence.

"Ah, Sergeant Kang, I am glad you are here. There is a lot of blood, a lot of blood. I have summoned Physician Ji and Apothecary Hong but I am sure your experience and perspective would be most welcome."

Sergeant Kang thought the Magistrate did not look at all right. His face was drawn and pinched, and there were exaggerated dark circles around the eyes. From the house Sergeant Kang quickly caught the nauseating smell of cooking, and of blood, which, the Magistrate was right to point out, was everywhere.

"Buddha's Bones! Who are these young men, Magistrate? They don't look like half-starved bandits to me."

"That is what I hope to find out, Sergeant. My initial understanding from some of the people standing around here…I hope to examine some as witnesses in more detail later…is that these two men forced their way into Madame Wu's house. I don't know why. They may have been trying to rob and murder her. I understand she has very few friends and no surviving relations. Bandits might have thought her vulnerable. But the dawn is a strange time to rob a house, I think, when people are out of their beds and about their work. Whatever the truth of this, there was an altercation of some sort. Madame Wu was attacked. There is blood on her, but Senior Constable He has told me she is uninjured and the blood is not hers. By all accounts, Constable Wu – who had arrived to collect the breakfast – came to her rescue and fought with the two men. He has not spoken to me yet. His mind seems to be deeply affected. It is all still a mystery."

"Magistrate, I think Little Ox should be taken away from here," said Sergeant Kang. "It can't be good for him with the crowd gawping at him. This was his first battle. Wine, many cups of tea, and rest are the only remedy."

"You are certain he will recover then? I have been fearing his mind to be permanently damaged," replied Magistrate Zhu, frowning.

Sergeant Kang smiled. "Magistrate, Little Ox is young, and he survived. Which is more than you can say for the poor bastards in the house…ah, please excuse my soldier's language. He'll have a few bad dreams from time to time, but don't we all."

Magistrate Zhu nodded. "Thank you, Sergeant. That is comforting to know."

There was then an uncomfortable moment of silence between Magistrate Zhu and Sergeant Kang, until Leaf, much to the surprise of both of them, darted into Madame Wu's house, carefully side-stepping the pools of blood and retrieved a scroll he had spotted lying next to one of Madame Wu's cooking pots.

"Magistrate, this must belong to the bandits," said Leaf, with a grin, apparently unaffected by the scenes of gore in the house. He passed the scroll to Magistrate Zhu. Sergeant Kang scratched at his whiskers, peering carefully at the boy, trying to estimate his age, wondering when he would become available for recruitment to the militia.

Magistrate Zhu unfurled the scroll and read quickly. Sergeant Kang did not believe he could grow even paler but, before his very eyes, Magistrate Zhu did just that.

"Constables Deng and Deng, leave Constable Wu to my care," said Magistrate Zhu, his voice cracked and strained. "Please go quickly to the Inn of Perpetual Happiness. Ascertain the whereabouts and health of Tea Inspector Fang at once."

The Deng brothers, hesitant to leave Little Ox, did not instantly obey.

"Run, you monkeys! The Magistrate has just given you an order!" bellowed Sergeant Kang in his best parade-ground voice. The Deng brothers vanished down the street, as if a thousand bandits were after them.

Seeing the shock in Magistrate Zhu's face at his tone of voice, Sergeant Kang explained: "Magistrate, it is best to be firm with young men. Do not give them time to think...especially those two rascals."

CHAPTER 36

MORNING, 22ND DAY OF THE 1ST MOON

"Things aren't going so well," said Fast Deng, wheezing as they ran across the market-square, scattering the people as they went.

"The Magistrate is jinxed," replied Slow Deng, thinking of all that had happened since the Magistrate had arrived. "I reckon we'll both be dead before the end of the month."

But still they carried on to the Inn of Perpetual Happiness, avoiding the main entrance at the front, running down the side of the building to reach the private apartments of Madame Kong – where everyone knew Tea Inspector Fang was staying – at the back of the inn. However, once behind the main buildings they had to be careful. The inn, just like the Temple next to it, backed onto the high banks of White Dragon River. And though some years previously Madame Kong had commissioned Master Carpenter An and his sons to build a fence (one too many of the patrons had wandered out into the night looking for the privy and had never been seen again) the Deng brothers knew they still had to watch their footing. The fence was perhaps not as high as it should have been, and there were many gaps in its panels to slip through. As it was they almost tripped over the kneeling form of Chef Mo, who was crying profusely, his head poking between some of the wooden panels of the fence, looking down at the grey, rushing water below.

"Chef Mo, what is wrong?" asked Fast Deng.

"We are looking for Tea Inspector Fang...on the orders of the Magistrate," added Slow Deng.

Chef Mo pointed out a dark stain on the ground not far from him, between the entrance to Madame Kong's apartments and the fence. He then brushed away the tears from his eyes, and stared up at the Deng brothers, as if he could not remember who they were.

"Tell the Magistrate that Tea Inspector Fang is murdered," Chef Mo, cried. "Tell the Magistrate that the people have finally got their revenge on him and thrown his body to the fishes. Tell the Magistrate that Madame Kong is distraught, not to be consoled. And tell the Magistrate that the people can stuff their precious tea up their back-sides for all I care!"

Fast Deng and Slow Deng shook their heads at all this emotional nonsense. They wandered over to the dark stain that Chef Mo had pointed out, leaving him to wallow in his grief. Bending down, they studied the ground closely. It was not exactly a pool of bright red liquid, more a sticky black discolouration on the hard-packed soil. They touched their fingers to the dark patch, and brought their fingers to their noses.

"It's blood alright, but not fresh," said Fast Deng.

"Animal or human?" asked Slow Deng.

Fast Deng shrugged. Both had been around spilled blood all their lives, often helping their father, Butcher Deng, and their elder brother, Pork Chop, in slaughtering the animals for market. But how to tell the difference between animal blood and human blood?

"Physician Ji would know," said Fast Deng.

"Dad says there's no difference. He says it smells the same, tastes the same, is the same," said Slow Deng.

"Maybe – but there doesn't look enough to be one person's blood, and certainly not all the blood in Tea Inspector Fang and the Bian brothers," said Fast Deng. "Think about how much blood comes out of one pig when it's butchered."

"What if those Bian brothers finally got fed up of guarding Tea Inspector Fang and took his gambling winnings from him last night and ran for it?" asked Slow Deng.

It was well known that though gambling was proscribed by law, and was therefore forbidden by Madame Kong on the premises of the Inn of Perpetual Happiness, Tea Inspector Fang was an ardent gambler. He spent his evenings, when in town, locked in this pursuit, in the backrooms of the Inn of Harmonious Friendship – a rough establishment, beloved by Sergeant Kang and the militia as well as the more uncouth elements of the town – where the proprietor was not so fussy.

"Yeah, but you saw the bodies at Madame Wu's. They were not the Bian brothers."

"They could have been in league with them," argued Slow Deng.

Fast Deng shook his head. "I'm not convinced this is Tea Inspector Fang's blood. There's not enough. I've seen more blood come out of a big chicken, and Tea Inspector Fang's not a small man. I reckon he has as much blood as we have put together."

"Yeah, it doesn't make sense," agreed Slow Deng.

They both looked around them, and then, as if with one mind, focused on the fence built by Master Carpenter An. Skirting the still blubbering form of Chef Mo, they walked over to the fence to examine it carefully.

"Pig on a stick!" exclaimed Fast Deng, touching his finger to the congealed blood on the highest horizontal beam.

"Three pigs on a stick!" said his brother, looking over the fence, and down at the river below.

"Yeah, no wonder there's not much blood," said Fast Deng. "Chef Mo is right. They just threw Tea Inspector Fang over the fence after they stabbed him, or knocked him on the head. He's already reached the Great Yangzi by now."

Fast Deng made a sign to ward off evil. Slow Deng began to mutter a prayer their mother had once taught them.

"Was that for Tea Inspector Fang or for us?" asked Fast Deng.

Slow Deng shrugged. "Does it matter? The Magistrate's going to be in trouble for being the magistrate of the district where Tea Inspector Fang was murdered. And we're going to be in trouble because we were the constables on duty when it happened. That blood's been drying for some time. What do you think are the odds that Tea Inspector Fang was being murdered when we were asleep in our cots?"

Fast Deng whistled. "Yeah, but Horse and Little Ox were on patrol. We could blame them."

"This town is cursed. We should've run when Magistrate Qian died. We could have made our fortune in Chengdu by now," said Slow Deng.

Fast Deng sighed. "Who'd kill Tea Inspector Fang? I can't believe the Bian brothers did it, or they conspired with bandits. Everyone else was frightened of Tea Inspector Fang, including the Patriarchs. And don't forget, Tea Inspector Fang was no weakling. It doesn't make sense."

Slow Deng did not have an answer. He looked over the fence and down at the river again. Not that there was anything to see. Together they lifted Chef Mo off the ground, and for his own safety returned him to his kitchen and to the place where he was happiest, where the junior cooks promised to take care of him.

⌇

"Y-you cannot come in," stammered Peach, standing shoulder to shoulder with her younger sister, Pearl, holding hands, attempting to block the doorway to Madame Kong's apartments.

"Hey, you maids! Out of the way! We're constables!" shouted Fast Deng, trying to pretend he was angry.

"Yes, we are very important men," said Slow Deng, trying to get a look at the maid's faces.

Peach and Pearl were reputed to be very pretty, but were at that moment looking down at the floor trying to avoid the Deng brothers' eyes. The maids had been doing what they could to protect Madame Kong from visitors. They were dressed in their oldest clothes, with black headscarves wrapped around their heads, a legacy of the cleaning they had been doing before it had been discovered that Tea Inspector Fang had never returned. They had been sitting together, bereft of orders and direction, until they had seen the Deng brothers wandering around. They had run to defend Madame Kong's apartments, understanding she would not want to be disturbed in this time of mourning, but only too aware themselves that they did not quite look their best to meet young men – especially young men who were constables.

"We can go anywhere we want to investigate a crime. The Magistrate says so," said Fast Deng.

"Anywhere we want," agreed his brother. "It is the law."

"Y-you cannot enter Madame Kong's apartments, they are private," insisted Peach, wishing her sister would speak up and help, instead of just shaking with fear.

"We don't want to hurt you, but we will if we have to," said Fast Deng.

"Yes, we will hurt you if we have to," agreed Slow Deng. "We are investigating a serious crime. And everyone knows that it's a crime to stop us investigating a crime. You won't like it if we have to give you a slap."

Fast Deng, frustrated and yet excited by the situation, advanced on the two maids, who, seeing they had done all they could to protect Madame Kong's honour and privacy, backed away, and held each other closely, overcome with the emotion of the day.

"Hey, there's no need to cry," said Fast Deng.

"Yeah, don't listen to what they say about us, we're really nice guys," added Slow Deng. "We're only here because the Magistrate ordered it."

"You look around, and I'll question the maids," said Fast Deng, pushing his brother forward into Madame Kong's apartments.

Furious that he had been out-manoeuvred, Slow Deng stomped off to explore, hoping to find some evidence for the Magistrate. But soon he was lost in fascination of the riches that surrounded him. He knew that Madame Kong was wealthy – possibly even wealthier than the Patriarchs – but he had never seen such luxury, such exquisite lacquered furniture, such decorated screens depicting great mountains and trees and kingfishers flying over rivers, and curtains and drapes embroidered even in gold. It suddenly felt wrong for him to be there, that he could be taken for a thief. He still had no uniform, and the Magistrate was far away over the other side of the market-square.

But he kept on, moving silently from room to room, memorizing what he was seeing, so he could tell Horse and Little Ox all about it. Eventually he found Madame Kong's bedroom. She was sitting within, her mature but still attractive face dark with grief.

She did not admonish him for entering her apartments uninvited. Instead, she said: "Young man, go tell the Magistrate that the people have finally killed him. They have hated him for so long. It was only a matter of time. Go tell the Magistrate that I curse the people of this town…that I no longer want to live anymore… that they have taken from me one of the best men who has ever lived."

Slow Deng bowed, then turned and ran, cold chills chasing up and down his spine. He found his brother still speaking to the maids.

"Their names are Peach and Pearl, and they are sisters. Peach is seventeen years old and Pearl is sixteen," said Fast Deng. "I've told them we're twins, but I came out of our mother first, so I'm cleverer and stronger than you."

"Do they know anything useful?" asked Slow Deng, irritated with his brother's stupidity, but very impressed with the maids, who had now raised their faces to them, and were prettier than he had could ever have hoped.

"They didn't see a thing," said Fast Deng. "They said it was quiet last night."

"Is that it?"

"Not quite – they've heard of us," replied Fast Deng, looking proud.

"Oh yes, we have heard of you," said Peach, feeling more confident now, liking the two brothers a lot. "Madame Kong says we must on no account talk to you."

"Oh yes," agreed Pearl. "You have a bad reputation."

Then both girls, having forgotten their tears and the sadness of the day, began to giggle.

Fast Deng and Slow Deng exchanged a glance, in silent agreement that not quite everything was going wrong in Tranquil Mountain.

"We've got to report back to the Magistrate," said Fast Deng.

"Yeah, he relies on us," said Slow Deng.

"But don't you girls leave town."

"You could be suspects."

"And we may have to talk to you again."

Peach and Pearl nodded solemnly, worried again, until the Deng brothers grinned and they realised the constables were just teasing them.

CHAPTER 37

"*It should not be underestimated the damage that can be caused by the commission of just one terrible crime. This damage can cascade down the generations like a waterfall.*"

So had spoken Judge Pei.

Magistrate Zhu sat in the garden of the jail, these words so clear in his mind they might have been spoken only the day before, rather than the ten years past it had really been. He wished the old jurist was sitting with him now, so he could ask for an opinion of what he should do – not that he had an extensive range of options.

"It should not be underestimated how much a woman can befuddle the mind, how much damage she can do," Magistrate Zhu said, out loud, speaking a tragic parody of Judge Pei's words.

For that had been the real problem. He had become distracted by Jade Moon, by her situation, by her exotic beauty and by her fascinating nature. He should have acted sooner. He should have acted immediately after Trainee Legal Secretary Li had discovered a link – no matter how tenuous – between the murder of Mister Gong and the past of Tea Inspector Fang. He should have visited Tea Inspector Fang. He should have questioned him about Tea Merchant Wen, who was Scary Face Fu. Maybe then, this one terrible crime could have been avoided.

In his hand he held the scroll found in the house of Madame Wu, no doubt delivered by the two bandits who had been killed there, and intended for him anyway. Magistrate Zhu opened the scroll and read the words written there for what probably was the hundredth time that day.

175

Magistrate

In return for Tea Inspector Fang's life, please deliver to me ten thousand strings of cash in coin, gold or silver. You must come alone. I will meet you on the trail up the valley, leading to Serene Tiger Monastery, an hour after midnight.

You may use a lantern to light your way, but do not think to bring your constables with you or the militia. If you do then Tea Inspector Fang's blood will be on your hands.

The Ghost of Scary Face Fu

I t was a simple letter, the characters written childishly – sign of some basic education, but no more that that. The letter was also proof of the link between the murder of Mister Gong and Tea Inspector Fang – not that he would have needed it. Two crimes, happening so close together. Even he, with his mind so confused by Jade Moon, would have been hard pressed not to eventually see the connection, even without the ransom letter.

"I have once more been proved to be lacking," he mused, wishing his sister had not come to him and persuaded him to seek office.

He saw it in his mind now, all that had happened.

Tea Merchant Wen, whose alias had been Scary Face Fu, who was hardly remembered around town and who had fought with Tea Inspector Fang in the street over the precious tea contracts all those years ago, had returned. A fabricated death certificate – created by a clerk in Chengdu only too willing to accept a bribe – had been enough to convince the bureaucracy that was China that a man was dead and gone. Mister Gong had died because he had encountered this man, by chance, by misfortune, who was no longer supposed to be alive. Mister Gong had died because the man had not wanted to reveal himself and his true intentions too soon – that the real crime he was to commit, the crime that would cascade down the generations, was in fact the kidnap of Tea Inspector Fang.

But there were still questions.

What had this Scary Face Fu, who was Tea Merchant Wen, been doing out on the street, in the rain and the fog? As a former tea merchant he would have known Patriarch Sun well. Had he been visiting the Sun residence then, when he had bumped into Mister Gong? But if Mister Gong had known his alias, how was it that the sons of Mister Gong did not?

He kept these thoughts to himself. He did not want to confuse the constables, and certainly did not want to spread suspicions about Patriarch Sun, the head of a noble family. He had already confused his constables enough letting them think for a time that Tea Inspector Fang had been murdered, the Deng brothers returning from the Inn of Perpetual Happiness full of stories of bodies cast into White Dragon River.

And he did not need any remembered words of Judge Pei to remind him of the difficulties involved in the investigation of rich and powerful men. He had investigated far too many himself, while appointed to the Censorate, before his meteoric fall from grace. Powerful men surrounded themselves with high walls, in more than one sense. Powerful men had many friends willing to lie on their behalf. Powerful men had political connections that could lead to an investigation being ended before it had even begun.

He would need evidence, the best evidence, before moving his investigation along that track. Best to forget Patriarch Sun for now. Anyway, he needed to concentrate on the ransom letter, and find a way, any way, to get Tea Inspector Fang back safe and sound.

Naturally, on discovering the common understanding of his constables, and therefore the people, that Tea Inspector Fang had been thought to be dead, murdered, he had gone without delay to visit with Madame Kong. Her relationship with Tea Inspector Fang, though not to be condoned – she being a widow (and his familial situation unknown) – still had to be acknowledged and sympathized with.

He had reassured her and Chef Mo, who had come at once from his kitchen to Madame Kong's private apartments to listen, that though Tea Inspector Fang had been kidnapped, which was a very serious matter, there was still hope. And as magistrate, he would be bending both his mind and his will to Tea Inspector Fang's safe return.

Madame Kong, though slight even for a woman, had touched him quite unexpectedly and forcefully, gripping him by the hand. She said that she could offer a thousand strings of cash in silver ingots immediately. And, if the bandits would wait, she could raise further cash. Magistrate Zhu had thanked her for her offer, but wanted time to think of how to proceed.

What he could not bring himself to tell Madame Kong, Chef Mo, or the constables was that this was no normal kidnap for cash. There was history between this Tea Merchant Wen and Tea Inspector Fang. He was sure of it. Much more history than a simple fight about tea contracts in the street. What had Senior Scribe Xu said: that many tea merchants were ruined after the creation of the Tea and Horse Agency? And that Tea Inspector Fang had been one of the few lucky enough, or well connected enough, to be given a post (and no doubt a very lucrative post) in the new agency.

This then could be less about cash than vengeance…the righting of a perceived wrong. And, if this reasoning was correct, then even ten thousand strings of cash – a monstrous sum – might not buy the freedom and the life of Tea Inspector Fang. The ransom could be accepted and still Tea Inspector Fang never seen again.

Was he still alive now?

Magistrate Zhu thought so, hoped so.

But for how long?

Even if he paid the cash, if such a sum could be raised in a very few hours – he only had the equivalent of one hundred strings of cash in his travelling luggage, and to get more would have to write to Chengdu to set up a line of credit – he could readily imagine Tea Inspector Fang being killed in front of him, or being dragged away, over the mountains to the west, to be cast down into some terrible crevasse, or given over to the barbarians for use in one of their ghoulish rituals as a human sacrifice.

And this would not just be a personal tragedy for Tea Inspector Fang or his family, or for his friend Madame Kong, whose obvious grief had been terrible to behold. The death of a government official would bring repercussions – severe repercussions – to the district.

As for himself, his dream of renewal, of atonement, of family honour regained, lay shattered all around him. And all because he had missed a vital clue, and had failed to speak to and warn Tea Inspector Fang. He had had thoughts only of Jade Moon. Even the last night, when he could sleep, he had dreamed only of her.

"Ah, sister, what would you say of me now?"

Magistrate Zhu shivered in the warmth of the afternoon sun.

CHAPTER 38

"You've got to do something Horse," said Sergeant Kang. "You wanted to be a constable. And as you're senior it's your job to speak to him. It's getting late. The day is almost over. The Magistrate must do something…decide something…even if he announces that Tranquil Mountain is under martial law. Not that he ever would because I think he's got more sense."

It was indeed getting late, and the sun was sinking low in the sky. They were all sitting in the forecourt of the jail, not wanting to disturb Little Ox, who was in the jail-room, sleeping off the shock of the morning and a special draught prescribed by Physician Ji, fetched at lightning speed by Leaf from Apothecary Hong's shop. Chairs had been brought out of the jail, and now Sergeant Kang, Horse, the Deng brothers, Leaf, and even Trainee Legal Secretary Li sat together, taking the air. Many of Sergeant Kang's militia had appeared to have transferred their duties from the barracks to the jail, and were now slumped in various positions on the ground, snoozing the day away.

Sergeant Kang pointed out of the gate, at the people in the market-square, still full with late shoppers and curiosity seekers.

"Look at them, Horse. The common people are nervous. They are waiting for the Magistrate to do something…anything. He's got to demonstrate he is in charge and dealing with the problem. Nervous people do stupid things, and we have enough problems in this town without the people rioting and fighting in the streets. Physician Ji can only prescribe so many sedatives. I know you have only been a constable for a year, and are still young and know little of people, but you must understand us Chinese. We are not like the barbarians who are used to leaders being killed or assassinated, and who just elect a new leader and carry on

179

as if nothing has happened. We don't do that. We seek for answers from Heaven. We wring our hands and pull our hair out. And if we can't take vengeance on those who have harmed us, we take vengeance on ourselves.

"Listen, years ago, when I was stationed in the southern forests, a young official came out from Luzhou. He was working for the Ministry of State or maybe it was the Ministry of Works, or...well, it doesn't really matter. He was young, like Magistrate Zhu, but full of mad ideas. He thought he could sit down with the savages, live with them in their miserable villages, and could civilise them just by speaking to them. Have you heard of anything so daft? Well, one night this idiot official says something wrong. I don't know what. Maybe he said that one of the chief's daughters was ugly. Well, the savages just set on him and killed him, without a second thought. They put him in a pot and—"

"Pig on a stick!" exclaimed Leaf, his mouth dropping open.

"They cooked him?" Fast Deng, horrified, tried desperately to stifle a laugh.

"And ate him?" Slow Deng put his hands over his face, but was memorizing every part of the story. He was certain the maids would love it.

"Maybe they ate him, or maybe they strung him up from the nearest tree for the crows to peck at," replied Sergeant Kang. "It doesn't really matter. The point of the story is this: the local prefect went crazy and sent in the army. And General Chu, who was in charge then and known to us as Mad Chu, ordered that we wipe the savages' village off the face of the Earth – and every other village within a day's walk. Which we did. Then there was much soul searching and back-stabbing in Luzhou. Magistrates and sheriffs and clerks lost their jobs. And I heard that even the young official's father committed suicide. Do you understand? We couldn't just write a report to say the young official lacked the brains he was born with. Someone else had to be to blame."

Horse had tried to follow every word, and consider carefully every nuance of Sergeant Kang's story. But still he felt he lacked the essential point. "Sergeant, the Tibetans don't make trouble here or cook people."

"No, you dummy, I'm talking about us...us Chinese. We may be civilised but we're daft. The Magistrate is deep in the manure, and he knows it. The Tea and Horse Agency is important here. It doesn't matter that Tea Inspector Fang was an arrogant bastard, who liked to throw his weight and his cash around town. He was a government official and important."

"But Sergeant, the note from Madame Wu's said he was only kidnapped and not murdered, and that if cash is paid over, then—"

Sergeant Kang roared with laughter. "What's the difference? Magistrate Zhu has still lost an important official. He is the presiding magistrate. His career, such as it was, is over. And though the Patriarchs may be laughing into their teacups, because they hated Tea Inspector Fang so much, they won't be laughing when Prefect Kang panics in Chengdu, and sends in the army to knock a few heads together. That's what soldiers do. That's what we're good at."

"As well as sleeping?" Fast Deng pointed at the militia lying on the ground, eyes closed, oblivious to everything.

Sergeant Kang was quick to anger. "Hey, if you and your turnip of a brother would think more about helping your magistrate than in how you're going to impress those maids then we'd all be better off!"

Horse was irritated by the distraction. "Sergeant, are you saying there is trouble coming to the Fifth District?"

"Big trouble, Horse...haven't you been listening? That's why the Magistrate is sitting in the garden of this jail refusing to speak to anyone. He knows what's going to happen and he is trying to think of a way out of the mess. But what he doesn't realize is that he doesn't have long to think."

"So he needs to rescue Tea Inspector Fang," said Fast Deng.

"Absolutely," said Slow Deng.

Sergeant Kang roared with laughter again. "I thought you two were supposed to be bright. Tea Inspector Fang is as good as dead – ransom or no ransom. We will be lucky if the bandits return the body to the family in return for the cash."

Horse turned to Trainee Legal Secretary Li, who so far had refused to comment. The young clerk though was looking miserable as well as unwell, having had to take copious notes when Physician Ji and Apothecary Hong conducted the examination of the bodies of the bandits killed by Madame Wu. Horse saw by the sorrow in his eyes that Sergeant Kang was not making stuff up.

Horse thought some more and nodded, his mind decided. "I will go to Magistrate Zhu and apologise. It was my fault that Tea Inspector Fang was taken in the night by bandits. I was senior constable. I should have been keeping the peace. I will then go to Chengdu and tell Prefect Kang the truth of what has happened. I will ask him not to send soldiers here."

Sergeant Kang began to laugh...a laugh that quickly died when he realised that Horse was being sincere. Sergeant Kang became so angry, he jumped up out of his chair, leaned over to Horse and punched him none too gently on the side of the head, with a speed that surprised them all.

Fast Deng and Slow Deng had never, ever seen the look that then crossed Horse's face. It was a combination of fury and amazement. And they grew very afraid. By all rights Horse, who was almost twice the size of Sergeant Kang, should have been able to pummel the old soldier into the ground. But Sergeant Kang had a reputation for being a dirty fighter. And none of them wanted Horse to try.

But Sergeant Kang knew his man. Horse did not move. He was frozen to his chair.

"Horse," said Sergeant Kang, firmly, "you are a good boy, but you must start thinking sensibly. To officials, we constables and soldiers are like dust in the wind – meaningless. Even if Prefect Kang granted you an audience, he would not listen. He would just order your head to be removed from your shoulders as an example to others. And *then* he would send the soldiers here. Don't be a dummy. Go see your magistrate, and tell him that the people expect him to do something... anything. It's not enough that he can order the beating of a defenceless girl. He has to be seen to order the hard stuff too."

"But we didn't beat Jade Moon!" blurted out Fast Deng.

"Just pretended to," added Slow Deng.

There was a terrible silence for a moment, when Horse turned his newly-discovered rage in the direction of the Deng brothers, who both realised too late their mistake.

However, Sergeant Kang merely scratched his whiskers, began to grin, and then to laugh yet again. "You know, I'm beginning to like this magistrate. I think he has a modicum of sense. I wouldn't lay a finger on that she-wolf even if the Emperor himself ordered it. Sure she is easy on the eye, even if she is too tall for my tastes. But you have to remember that she did for Bad Teeth Tong at a hundred paces with her bow and arrows. And she ran Second Son Zhou out of her house with a kitchen knife. Women are hard to figure out at the best of times, but barbarian women are known for their bad tempers. I knew a soldier once who married a barbarian woman, and he...."

Horse let himself drift away from Sergeant Kang's story, praying for calm to once more enter into his body and his mind. Yes, Sergeant Kang had said some terrible things, and had hit him, but it was more than that. He was senior constable, and Sergeant Kang was right: something had to be done. He must speak to the Magistrate. They must do something to rescue Tea Inspector Fang.

CHAPTER 39

"*I* do not begrudge any woman her happiness, especially a widow. But I think she is well rid of him. He didn't even wear a hat. And he had the worst manners of any man I have ever met. So what if he was rich and well-connected? Good manners have to mean something, don't they? But would she listen to me? I am her friend – her only true friend in this miserable town – but she would not listen. She spoke only of trying to ransom him with her own savings. She would rather waste her own hard-earned cash than see sense. She should give him up as lost and move on with her life. I told her, men come and go – it is just a fact of life. But I might well have been speaking to the wall."

Madame Tang concentrated on her sewing for a while, letting her daughter, who had been in the foulest of moods all day, and Golden Orchid, the orphan girl, reflect well on her words. She then glanced up at Jade Moon, who refused even to acknowledge her mother with a smile. Jade Moon's face may well have been made of stone.

"Well, what else am I to say, Daughter? Should I lie and say that Tea Inspector Fang was a good man? He wasn't, and everybody knows it. And it is time that Madame Kong saw the truth. She is the wisest of all in matters of business, but she has no sense at all when it comes to men."

Jade Moon did not reply. Instead, Madame Tang looked to Golden Orchid for a response, which the young girl duly supplied.

"Madame Tang, is it true that the bandits have probably killed Tea Inspector Fang already, like they already did for Mister Gong? That is what Leaf says."

Madame Tang snorted with derision. "Leaf! What does that young boy know? Miss Dai should keep him locked up in the orphanage. It is a scandal that the

183

Magistrate is using him as a runner. This shows how thoughtless this young Magistrate is, and irresponsible. But dead or kidnapped, it's all the same. What's important is that Tea Inspector Fang is gone. And this town, and Madame Kong, are well rid of him."

Madame Tang stopped her sewing, wanting to concentrate, to remember properly what she had been told, so her words had the best effect.

"And I have learned that we are soon going to lose Magistrate Zhu too. I have heard that the Magistrate's career is finished. He will be removed, probably in a few days." Madame Tang looked to Jade Moon. "Isn't that the best of news, Daughter? With no magistrate, there will be no legal decision. And then you won't be sent to the Family Zhou as a concubine. With good fortune Second Son Zhou will be dead of some plague before we get another magistrate. Or perhaps Second Son Zhou will have lost interest in you. Though what that unnatural man sees in you anyway I do not know."

Jade Moon would not be drawn, not even giving her mother the benefit of her eyes.

"Why is the Magistrate finished, Madame Tang?" asked Golden Orchid, happy to learn everything she could from a woman so confident in her opinions.

"Child, there are things you should know about officials," replied Madame Tang. "They may look glorious in all their finery, and be more arrogant than a box of snakes, but their careers are often over just as quickly as they've begun. In fact, Magistrate Zhu will be lucky to keep his head for being in charge when Tea Inspector Fang was made to disappear."

Jade Moon slipped with her needle, barely missing her thumb. She bit her lip, struggling to concentrate, wishing her mother would, for once, shut her big mouth.

"I have heard that at the very least he will be criticised," continued Madame Tang, "which is a serious matter."

"Criticised." Golden Orchid repeated the word, marvelling at the sound and feel of it on her tongue.

"Oh, yes, child. It is a most terrible punishment for an official. But I don't want to go into details. It is not something for young ears. But he could be stripped of his hat and robes, beaten until he no longer has any sense in him, and then shipped off to exile on some desolate island to reflect on his mistakes and die in dreadful pain from some fever."

Madame Tang noticed that Jade Moon was staring at her again, eyes blazing this time. But Madame Tang was unafraid, well used to her daughter's unbridled emotions and unpredictable temper – the ghastly inheritance of the father. Madame Tang pointed a chubby finger almost in Jade Moon's face.

"Don't you look at me like that, Jade Moon! I am not stupid. I know you have taken a liking to that young magistrate, ever since he let you off with just a simple beating for sticking a knife in Second Son Zhou's face. I saw you return home in a dream. But you are like Madame Kong. You have no sense about men. Did you know the Magistrate wrote a notice of your punishment and had those fool constables nail it to the door of the August Hall of Historical Records to read? Everyone now knows you are a criminal. I should have drowned you in a bucket at birth for all the trouble you have caused me!"

Golden Orchid gasped, putting her hand to her mouth, never hearing such words before. But Madame Tang was not finished, not finished at all.

"Daughter, you think just because you are tall, and wear your hair long like a wild woman, and stick your nose in the air, he would notice you and remember you. Well, he won't. To him you are nothing, just a seamstress, just an ugly barbarian girl! The best you can ever hope for from such a man is charity. And he has none to give. I can assure you of that."

"I was not beaten." Jade Moon's voice was soft, almost a whisper, but full of vehemence.

"You would lie to your own mother in her own house? Everyone knows you were beaten. The Magistrate wrote your punishment down on the paper. Are you calling him a liar? Lord Buddha, help me! What am I to do with you?"

But it was true. Jade Moon had not been beaten. She was resolved to remember Magistrate Zhu and his kindness until the end of her days.

Jade Moon put down her sewing, trying to recall how many coins she had left in her purse. She stood up and reached for her jacket.

"What is it, Daughter?" asked Madame Tang, suddenly nervous. "Where are you going? You should not be going out. You should be hiding your face in shame."

Jade Moon was not to be dissuaded. She held her hand out to Golden Orchid, who gladly took it, and said: "I am going to the Temple to make an offering for the soul of Tea Inspector Fang."

"Then you have more cash than sense, you stupid girl!"

"And then, Mother, I am going to pray for the safety of Magistrate Zhu and for his career."

Jade Moon left their door open as she walked out onto the street, dragging an excited and giggling Golden Orchid behind her. Madame Tang's bemusement did not last long. She was not one to be left behind. She reached for her shawl and waddled after them, determined that despite the shame of Jade Moon's punishment, the common people should see the Tang women together, unbroken and unbowed.

CHAPTER 40

*H*orse approached the Magistrate, still sitting alone on the stone bench in the garden of the jail. Horse had some words, words that needed to be said. Sergeant Kang was right. The people were getting nervous. Something needed to be done. But hardly had he completed his bow, when those prepared words just evaporated from his mind.

It was the Magistrate's expression that had done it. Horse had never seen such sadness and defeat in any person, not even in Little Ox when he had sat on the doorstep of his house, after the death of his parents, waiting for something to happen.

"Magistrate, I—"

"Senior Constable, don't speak," said Magistrate Zhu, his voice slow and tired. "I need to confess to you that I am not worthy to be your magistrate. I have made mistakes, both here and far behind me, in Kaifeng. I have brought a dark shadow to this district. I am responsible for all that has come to pass."

"Magistrate, I do not understand your words."

"Senior Constable, I have spoken to you about the balance of Heaven and Earth, about how important it is for this balance to be maintained. But I think I have come to understand now that a man cannot take responsibility for this balance if his soul is not clean. I am talking of magistrates and judges now, and not the common people. You should know that there is a residue on my conscience. Years ago I committed a great crime. And I did not make proper amends. Instead I sat alone in my study on my great estate wondering how all the sadness of my life had come to pass. Then I came here, thinking my service to the people would atone for these past mistakes. But instead I have brought evil with

186

me, to this town. It is no coincidence that Mister Gong's murder and Tea Inspector Fang's kidnap happened the moment I stepped foot in this district. This is no simple arrogance, Senior Constable. I take full responsibility."

"Magistrate, I—"

"No, Senior Constable, I wish no argument on this matter. I have argued enough with myself all day. I have sought to blame Tea Inspector Fang's disappearance on another…on Miss Tang, blaming her for entrancing me, for distracting me from the evidence that had been placed before me. Do you see how little I have become? Only a weak man would blame a woman for his mistakes. Only a weak man would allow himself to become so distracted in the first instance. And I have the nerve to sit in judgement of her. She has done nothing to deserve my censure and certainly nothing to deserve her sad fate. If she knew what I had done, or knew the kind of man that I am, then she would look at me with nothing but contempt. In her eyes, I am sure I would be the lowest of the low. It was a foul day for the common people of this district when I was sent here, and fouler still for you and the other constables. I can educate you in the words of the law, but I cannot educate you in what it means to be humane."

Horse understood nothing of this. And though he knew that he had learned very little about crime and criminals, and about the balance of Heaven and Earth, he was certain that Magistrate Zhu was beyond reproach. Suddenly words came to his mind, words from the past, words that could help.

"Magistrate, my mother told me that if it is always my intention to do good, then I will never bring evil on myself or on others. You did not bring evil to this town, evil men brought it."

Magistrate Zhu contemplated this for some time, wanting his response to be prepared and very gentle. "Senior Constable, I know nothing of the wisdom of mothers. Mine was lost giving birth to my sister. I hardly remember her. But I fear your mother is sadly mistaken. There are times when the intention to do good can attract the greatest evil. Good intentions must always be tempered with wisdom, with good sense."

Horse felt himself redden, appalled at what he had done, trying to be clever to the Magistrate.

"No, Senior Constable, don't be embarrassed. You have listened and you have begun to think. That is enough for now. One day, if Heaven allows it, perhaps in the afterlife, I will speak to you further about this, about what I myself have learned. But for now I am sure you wish me to act. I see it in your face. There is no time to summon another magistrate from Chengdu to bring true justice to the people. So I have decided to do what I can, to make amends in this life in just a small way. Please go in person to Senior Scribe Xu. I do not want the boy, Leaf, involved in this. Tell the senior clerk I wish to summon a meeting of the Patriarchs, this evening. I do not believe it will do any good. I think my path is set in stone. But I have to ask them, I think."

CHAPTER 41

"Magistrate, you don't fully appreciate this town or its concerns," said Patriarch Yang. "But then, how could you? You have been here but a few days, and by all accounts have spent much of this time asleep. Yes, truly it is sad for Tea Inspector Fang and his family, but you must understand he was not liked."

Senior Scribe Xu looked down into his wine cup, keeping his thoughts to himself. This was not the whole truth. Madame Kong and Chef Mo were both distraught.

"Magistrate," spoke up Patriarch Zhou, "you must always have the welfare of the people uppermost in your mind. In view of this, you must understand that the Tea and Horse Agency are slowly bankrupting us, preventing us from harvesting the tea more than twice yearly and paying far too little for what is harvested."

"Yes, so don't judge us harshly for not wanting to throw cash away in trying to release Tea Inspector Fang from the hands of bandits," added Patriarch Sun. "Tea Inspector Fang has been enriching himself on the back of our sweat for more than ten years now. He is little more than a bandit himself, and not worthy of being saved."

Senior Scribe Xu pursed his lips. He was there ostensibly to make notes of what was said, to make a record of the first meeting of Magistrate Zhu and the three Patriarchs. So far he had written nothing – the words spoken not a creditable record for any of them.

Of course, there might never have been a meeting at all. When Magistrate Zhu had asked for the meeting to be convened for the early evening, Senior Scribe Xu had first been seized by a terrible panic. What if the Patriarchs refused, citing

188

other commitments, or the pressures or work in the days leading up to the first harvest? Would they not have been within their rights to find such excuses? After all, it would have been polite and politic for the Magistrate to call upon them prior to a time of great emergency, as Patriarch Yang had none too subtly pointed out.

Surprisingly, each of the Patriarchs had agreed to the immediate meeting, driven most likely by their curiosity to see for themselves the new magistrate rather than any concern over Tea Inspector Fang.

"Senior Scribe Xu, you must not let the Patriarchs bully Magistrate Zhu," had said Rose, his house-keeper, earlier that evening, laying the small fish and accompanying vegetables down in front of him. "I have been hearing good things about that young man today. When I met him I wasn't so sure. It is not every day that you open a door to a magistrate. I was so taken with fright I didn't take a good look at him. But I have been hearing rumours...about Jade Moon."

Senior Scribe Xu had looked up from his food. "What rumours, Rose? Magistrate Zhu had her beaten, that is all there is to know."

Rose laughed mischievously, her manner almost girlish. "Maybe...maybe not."

Senior Scribe Xu had then become irritated, not wanting to be distracted from the problem of the upcoming meeting. "Rose, don't speak in riddles. If you have something to say, then say it."

Rose's became irritated in turn. "All I am saying, Senior Scribe Xu, is that the Magistrate has something about him...perhaps more good sense than a young man is supposed to have. You must not let the Patriarchs bully him or frighten him away back to Kaifeng. He has only just got here, and we need a magistrate. It's not his fault that bandits have come to town now. And, from what I hear, the rest of China is infested with bandits. So don't let them bully him. If I know those miserable old men, all they will do is gloat over Tea Inspector Fang's disappearance and give Magistrate Zhu no help at all."

And so it proved.

"Magistrate, forgive me for being so blunt," growled Patriarch Yang. "But you have been blunt yourself in coming to my house, ignoring all good civilised custom, refusing to make proper introductions and instead merely reading to us a note purporting to have come from bandits, who have supposedly taken our beloved tea inspector away." Patriarch Yang rudely pointed at the Magistrate, only sitting a few paces from him. "You are a young man...supposedly educated. But you expect the three of us, charged by Heaven with the protection of our estates, our families and the common people of this district, to suddenly show concern for the health of Tea Inspector Fang. What kind of nonsense is this? Why should we find ten thousand strings of cash to ransom him back to us when all he has brought this district is poverty and misery?"

"Yes, you are a fool, Magistrate, if you think this," said Patriarch Zhou, who now harboured an extra, special resentment for Magistrate Zhu for the way his son, Second Son Zhou, had been summoned to give evidence in the matter of the she-wolf, Jade Moon.

And Patriarch Sun was even more pointed. "We hear you are a rich man, Magistrate. If you wish your friend, Tea Inspector Fang, to be returned, put up your own cash. But before you do, Magistrate, think whether this is even worth your while. He is probably dead already. And no one at the Agency will care. They will send another just like him, to continue their torment of us." Patriarch Sun's smile was cold, dangerous.

Senior Scribe Xu had to remind himself to breathe. He knew Magistrate Zhu had a temper, and expected then the most terrible things to come out of his mouth – perhaps even a revealing of a hidden purpose for his coming to the Fifth District. But Magistrate Zhu said nothing of the sort. His face was impassive; a little colour came to his cheeks, but that was all. It was as if all the words spoken to him by the Patriarchs had been expected, and that his refusal to engage in the proper courtesies, and in the quick reading of the ransom letter, had been a way of getting the meeting over with.

Senior Scribe Xu knew he could not sit by. "Patriarchs, it should be remembered that though Tea Inspector Fang is unloved in this district, he remains a government official, and so his loss could have terrible repercussions to—"

"Senior Scribe Xu, don't waste words," interrupted Magistrate Zhu. "Nobody around this table is stupid. The Patriarchs know full well the consequences of Tea Inspector Fang's disappearance. But they choose to believe that they are already suffering evil enough at the hands of the Agency, that no further evil can befall them or this district. I am not here to convince them otherwise. I am merely asking for help in saving the life of a man."

"He is dead already," said Patriarch Yang, looking away from the Magistrate's gaze, fingering the sword at his side. "And the Agency won't want to make trouble, not at this time of year, not when the first harvest of the tea is due."

"I agree," said Patriarch Zhou, gruffly. "Tea Inspector Fang had so many enemies it was only a matter of time. Unfortunate for you, Magistrate, that it happened in the time of your magistracy, but such things are in the lap of the gods. Write to Prefect Kang and make your apology. You should know there was no love lost between Prefect Kang and Tea Inspector Fang, so Chengdu won't mourn him either. Then, if you are not removed from post, concentrate on petty criminalities of the common people and most of all on the ruling you must make on the dispute between me and Madame Tang. I have waited two years already. How much longer should I wait?"

Patriarch Sun was amused by Patriarch Zhou's words. But Patriarch Yang was tired of hearing Patriarch Zhou's problem with Madame Tang and that barbarian daughter of hers. Anyone would think that the life of a common young woman was of some importance.

"Magistrate, before this meeting is over, there should be perfect clarity between us all," said Patriarch Yang. "You should know that there is only one thing of importance in this district, and that is the tea. Everything else, even the kidnap or murder of a government official, is an irrelevance."

"And you all should know," replied Magistrate Zhu, "so there is perfect clarity between us, that I consider the murder of Mister Gong – an old man, and a common person – more important than all of the tea in China. Without justice, everything else is an irrelevance."

Magistrate Zhu got up from around the table, never once having taken a sip of wine from his cup. And, with barely a nod of acknowledgment to Senior Scribe Xu, he left the room.

"He is a young fool," said Patriarch Zhou. "Idealistic. It is no wonder Kaifeng wanted rid of him."

"I agree," said Patriarch Sun, indicating to a servant that his cup should be replenished.

Senior Scribe Xu, feeling glum and without hope for the future, turned to Patriarch Yang, expecting further meaningless comment. Instead he was surprised. Patriarch Yang almost snarled with rage, addressing both Patriarch Zhou and Patriarch Sun.

"If I find either of you to be responsible for the kidnap of Tea Inspector Fang you will have me to deal with, and not that young magistrate! I have never heard of anything so foolish...so dangerous. This may be the excuse the Agency needs to send soldiers to seize our tea gardens from us, saying that we can no longer guarantee the security of the tea!"

Senior Scribe Xu left the Yang residence with those words, and the denials of the other Patriarchs ringing in his ears.

CHAPTER 42

EVENING, 22ND DAY OF THE 1ST MOON

The past was gone. What could be done about it? Her husband was long dead. And her son was now gone, disappeared these last three years, but known to have gone to Chengdu, to seek a new life, unhappy with his prospects in Tranquil Mountain. She had mourned, and coped, and moved on. But Tea Inspector Fang, a good man though a tough man – how would she replace him in her life? She could not.

She sat before the Magistrate's desk with Chef Mo. Her friend, and the greatest cook she had ever known, had selflessly offered his own saved cash – as she knew he would. They both waited for Magistrate Zhu to speak.

"Madame Kong, Chef Mo, I have just visited with the Patriarchs. It is as I expected. They are fixated on their own problems...the tea. They will not put the cash up to save the life of one man. Even if we knocked on every door in town, and they were kind enough to give, we would still not raise that much cash."

A hollowness formed in Madame Kong's heart. She sensed rather than saw Chef Mo put his handkerchief to his eyes. There was nothing to be done. Nothing could be done. If they had been given more time, assets elsewhere could have been liquidated, the Agency could have been written to....

"Madame Kong, are you listening to me?"

"Magistrate, forgive me – I am overcome with grief."

"Madame Kong, do not give up hope," said Magistrate Zhu. "There is another way. I am a magistrate, a scholar, a scion of a very rich and famous family in Kaifeng. My value to these criminals is a thousand times more than Tea Inspector Fang. I will answer the call of their ransom note. I will meet with them this night, and offer to exchange myself for him. These criminals will have to be patient, of course, and hold me in the mountains for many months to get their cash, but they will get their cash eventually. I am not afraid. Not any more. What remains of my conscience has decided for me, and...."

Madame Kong did not hear the rest of his words. Sudden joy and love for the young magistrate overwhelmed her. Later, walking back across the market-square to the inn, as if floating on the clouds themselves, she marvelled at what Magistrate Zhu had done for them.

"It is as if Heaven itself brought him here, just in time," said Chef Mo.

Madame Kong nodded, in satisfied, silent, agreement.

CHAPTER 43

"*I*t is as if a great pile of manure has fallen out of the skies and landed on our heads," said Fast Deng.

"Absolutely," said Slow Deng.

Leaf laughed, picturing this in his mind. Little Ox turned his sad eyes toward Horse. Little Ox had woken, and had taken some tea, but he had still not gained his voice, or spoken of what he had seen and done in the house of Madame Wu.

"We will be the laughing stocks of all China," said Fast Deng.

"The first constables ever to lose their magistrate," said Slow Deng.

"Enough!" insisted Horse. "I am trying to think."

The Deng brothers closed their mouths, for the moment, giving Horse some much-needed respite. His head pounded. He had told them of what he had heard in the Magistrate's office, of how the Magistrate had promised Madame Kong and Chef Mo that he would meet with the bandits, and attempt to exchange himself. At first he thought he had been hearing things, that it was all a bad dream. But then, after Madame Kong and Chef Mo had left the jail, to return to the Inn of Perpetual Happiness and await developments, Magistrate Zhu had spoken to him directly.

"Senior Constable, I wish you to leave me for the moment. I have to compose a letter. Then I wish you to accompany me to the house of Senior Scribe Xu. He deserves an explanation for what I am about to do."

Horse thought then his heart might burst. "Magistrate, you cannot go. The people cannot do without a magistrate." He bowed deeply after saying these words, thinking he might have spoken out of turn.

But Magistrate Zhu had been moved. "I thank you for that sentiment, Senior Constable. But there are better magistrates than I in China. Another one will

194

arrive here, eventually. I cannot remain behind my desk when there is something I can do. I have an opportunity to atone for past mistakes and to prevent future evils. If Tea Inspector Fang is not returned then I think it will not go well for this district."

Horse understood this. He remembered Sergeant Kang's thoughts on the subject. Still, it did not feel right to let the Magistrate go off alone into the night.

"Magistrate, I shall come with you."

"No, that is forbidden. If the bandits spot you they may kill Tea Inspector Fang instead of releasing him. You will remain here, in town, with the others."

"Magistrate, you have not decided about Jade Moon's contract. You cannot go until—"

"Senior Constable," interrupted Magistrate Zhu, firmly, "I have not forgotten about Miss Tang. She is never far from my thoughts. You should know, it is her courageous image that inspires me to go meet with these bandits, and do what is right. And perhaps it would be better for her if I was not here. Sometimes it is best that some judgements are not made at all."

Horse was dismissed then. He explained to the horror of the others what the Magistrate had in mind to do that night. Even Little Ox awoke from his deep sleep to listen, and none of them had the heart to send Leaf home, back to the orphanage.

"Horse, you should go speak to Sergeant Kang," suggested Fast Deng, in a whisper.

"Yeah, he won't be frightened of telling the Magistrate he's being daft," agreed Slow Deng.

But Horse had already thought of this and dismissed the idea. The soldiers had all vanished when the sun had gone down, not even staying for dinner. It seemed there was a special night planned at the Inn of Harmonious Friendship, though the reason for the occasion remained a mystery to Horse.

"There's nothing to be done," he said, simply.

But Fast Deng was not about to give up. "Horse, what about the balance of Heaven and Earth?"

"Yeah, Horse, what about that? Surely, us losing a magistrate is going to break the whole world apart," said Slow Deng.

Horse shook his head. He had not had the heart to tell them all that the Magistrate had spoken of earlier, about how the Magistrate believed he was responsible for bringing evil to town, because of mistakes in the past, made far away, in Kaifeng. They would not understand. He did not understand.

Horse wandered over to the doorway, looking out into the night. The market-square was quiet. Through the mist he could see the lanterns glowing brightly outside the Inn of Perpetual Happiness. At least Madame Kong and Chef Mo will be happy this night, he thought.

"We should fight and kill those bastard bandits!" shouted Leaf, banging his little fists on the table. He was worried that an eventful day may be grinding to a miserable halt.

The Deng brothers laughed. Little Ox shook his head, having done enough fighting already that day.

"Leaf," said Horse, patiently, "we do not have swords. We do not even have uniforms."

"But he does have a point," said Fast Deng.

"Absolutely," agreed Slow Deng.

Horse sighed, knowing he should not give up. "I will speak to the Magistrate again," he said.

CHAPTER 44

LATE EVENING, 22ND DAY OF THE 1ST MOON

The banging on the door, so very late in the evening, was as unexpected as it was shocking. Madame Tang, never one normally to shirk a fight to defend her home or family – such as it was – was momentarily paralysed with fear. By sheer force of will she took back possession of her faculties, remembering the deep knowledge that action is always better than inaction. She struggled out of her chair, moved herself into the backroom with remarkable speed and headed for the tray placed near to the stove. On it was her cherished set of kitchen knives.

Jade Moon lifted Golden Orchid, who had been allowed to fall asleep curled up on the floor. She followed her mother into the backroom, carrying the young girl in her arms. She placed her down in a dark corner and covered her with a blanket, hoping against hope that she would be missed in any commotion that was to come. Jade Moon regretted persuading her mother to let Golden Orchid stay the night, to not return to the orphanage, for selfish reasons. For Jade Moon had noticed that Golden Orchid had lightened the atmosphere of the house and diverted her mother's too acute observations.

Madame Tang passed her longest and best meat-cutting knife to Jade Moon, who would make the better use of it.

"Daughter, it is better to be dead than to be carried off to the mountains by bandits."

"I agree," replied Jade Moon, all animosity between them forgotten in that moment.

But then came more banging at the door, and a faint female voice – a voice struggling to be heard but not so loud as to waken all who lived on the street.

"Madame Tang! Madame Tang!"

197

Fear dissolved into faint smiles. Another shared experience survived. Knives were placed back on the tray. Quickly the coldness and trouble that had developed over the years, between mother and daughter, was restored.

"Go open the door, you stupid girl! It is Madame Kong."

Jade Moon went quickly to the door and unlatched it. Madame Kong scurried into the house, her face wet with tears. Still suspicious of what lay out in the dark, Jade Moon sniffed the air, looking up and down the street. The mist had come down, as was usual for the hour. Nothing moved, nothing stirred. She shut the door, telling herself that the foreboding that had been growing within her all evening meant nothing.

Madame Kong embraced Madame Tang, not that this expression of affection made Madame Tang content about the surprise visit.

"Madame Kong, you should not be out at this hour," she chided. "Do you not know there are murderers and bandits about? Wasn't your beloved Tea Inspector Fang taken off the street with absurd ease in the dark? And he was a big man, quite used to threatening people with his fists."

"Oh, Madame Tang, these are not tears of fright you see on my face, but tears of happiness. I went this very evening to see the Magistrate. He is such a fine man – a true gentleman. Not once when I was speaking to him did he censure my womanly emotions. I offered him all the cash I had to hand. Chef Mo did too, for he accompanied me to the jail. I said to the Magistrate: 'Please give my cash to the bandits, though I know it's not nearly enough.'"

Madame Tang guided her friend to her own chair, wondering why Madame Kong could not accept the truth of the situation that, despite what was written in the ransom note, Tea Inspector Fang was already dead, murdered, and that life must go on.

"Madame Kong, I am your particular friend, and—"

"Madame Tang, please listen. I have come to tell you the greatest, most wonderful, news. I could not stay at the inn. I had to share my joy. I had to tell you and Jade Moon what sort of man he is."

"Which man?" asked Madame Tang, confused. She feared her friend might be succumbing to the madness of grief, never to return. Madame Tang had seen before it in others, so affected by grief their minds and bodies had become separated.

"Madame Tang, I am talking of Magistrate Zhu, of course. I can only think that we are all blessed by Heaven that he has come to us now, at this time. You cannot imagine—"

"Madame Kong, please slow down," interrupted Madame Tang. "Would you like some tea? It will calm your mind. Magistrate Zhu should be ashamed that he has you so worked up."

"Oh, Madame Tang, it is not what he has done but what he is going to do that has filled me with so much excitement. He is going to sacrifice himself for the good of Tea Inspector Fang, for the good of all of us. He is going to offer himself to the bandits in exchange. As a magistrate he can be ransomed for a much greater price and...."

Madame Tang did not need to hear more. Her mind was already calculating the odds of the Magistrate's return, thinking them weighted well against the Magistrate's favour. He would be carried off to the mountains, wait for many months to be ransomed to Kaifeng, and return to his home estate dishevelled, just skin and bone, old before his time.

But what an unlooked for boon this was. If there was no magistrate there could be no judgement made against her. And no judgement meant that Jade Moon would not be taken away, would not be forced into the bed of that freak of nature, Second Son Zhou. She felt the happiness explode out of her chest. She had not been so happy since the day of Magistrate Qian's death, kind man though he had been.

"Oh, Madame Kong, I can't remember ever hearing such wonderful news!" she exclaimed, meaning it.

Then, wanting to share her new-found joy with her daughter, she turned her round and gleeful face to Jade Moon. But Jade Moon's expression was one of grim, grey stone, her lips taut and thin, her eyes like black jewels, moist and glistening – full of pain.

"Oh, you stupid girl!" snapped Madame Tang, furious with her daughter's lack of vision. "Don't you see what this means for us and for Madame Kong?"

Jade Moon did not reply. Neither did she speak when Madame Kong, happy to have delivered her message of salvation, left to return to the inn, despite Madame Tang's entreaties to stay the night.

Sometime later, sitting in her chair, angered beyond all reason by her daughter's incredible attitude, Madame Tang found she could no longer control her tongue.

"Are you so self-centred you do not think of the good that this will do us, that we will stay together, mother and daughter, for all the years to come? Are you so caught up in your stupid girlish dreams of a man you could never hope to possess? You are too tall, too strange looking, too barbarian, for him to even consider you even as a mistress or concubine – let alone as a wife. Do you think Heaven sent him here for you? Do you really believe that you would ever cross his arrogant and officious mind? You do not even know how to dress as a lady. Even Madame Kong's wanton maids don't let their hair down like you and wear such plain clothes. And you then have the nerve to walk around with your nose in the air thinking a man such as Magistrate Zhu would think well of you. I swear I must have dropped you on your head as a baby."

Jade Moon, who in her distress had begun working feverishly on the constables' uniforms, kept her mouth shut, returning her mother only a look that was vile and ill-tempered – a look that Madame Tang had seen too often before, though maybe never so intense. Madame Tang shook a chubby fist in her daughter's direction, refusing to be undermined or her new-found joy lessened by Jade Moon's barbarian melancholy.

CHAPTER 45

LATE EVENING, 22ND DAY OF THE 1ST MOON

Honoured Sister

Please pass along my sincerest regards to the Minister Yu and to your husband. I hope this letter finds you and your children in good health, and you do not become debilitated by its content.

A great evil has befallen the town of Tranquil Mountain and the Fifth District. I have received a note from a bandit, who claims to be holding Tea Inspector Fang captive. I have not spoken of Tea Inspector Fang before, but he is a minor official employed by the Tea and Horse Agency – a government department created by imperial edict to regulate the growing and selling of tea in this province. Though you might not comprehend the rank, Tea Inspector Fang is very important in Chengdu Prefecture, and his kidnap is for the district a local disaster.

I believe I have no choice but to attempt to exchange myself for the Tea Inspector, and convince the bandits that my life – in cash terms, at least – has the greater value.

You must understand, little sister, that I have been expecting for three years just such a calamity to swallow me up whole. It is no more than I deserve. Remember that before I left the Zhu family estate, I saw an owl perched on a gatepost, staring at me. I took it then to be a portent of my impending death, that I would not return to Kaifeng and to the Zhu estates. I do not doubt that the Minister Yu will spare no effort in arranging a ransom for me, and you will be unceasing in your efforts to assist, but I suspect my health will not withstand a prolonged stay in the mountains and wild forests of this region.

I am convinced there is no military solution to this problem. The local militia are second-rate at best and it is well known that the bandits are able to disappear at will at night. I can find no other path that befits my conscience. My mind is made up. So this could be my last letter to you.

I will travel up the valley this night. If the ransom is a trick, and Tea Inspector Fang already dead, or if the bandits do not accept my proposition then I do not hope to survive. I do not want you to worry for me. If I am killed then I will find my own way to recover my honour in the afterlife, or, if the Buddhists are correct and I am to be reborn, then perhaps I will be the son of one of your sons, and can make amends for the foolishness of my life and the shame I have brought upon the name of Zhu. You are now in the bosom of the great and distinguished Yu family. I am glad at least for that.

Minister Yu holds a copy of my last will and testament. Your sons will inherit a third of the Zhu estate each of what is remaining of the estate after the third taken for your dowry is considered – to be managed in trust for them by Minister Yu until they have reached the age of twenty-one. The other third is to be given up to Sheriff Min of Kaifeng, as I have previously discussed with you. This is my recognition in this life for the courage and correctness of his actions when three years ago I was found wanting. I wish you to explain this to your sons when they are older, so they come to understand why the Zhu estate was broken up, and why, when they come to sit the civil service examinations, they should go and seek out Sheriff Min and come to understand what is required to truly bring justice to the people.

Little sister, do not think my constables are failing me in letting me go alone to meet with the bandits. My senior constable has come to me on at least five occasions this evening and tried to change my mind. On the last occasion I confess I lost my temper with him. I shouted, saying: "Two years ago Miss Tang shot and killed a bandit-leader with an arrow, standing firm and alone when there was confusion and panic in the market-square. As a magistrate, do you think I am any less capable?"

I know I have not written to you of this Miss Tang. This has been remiss of me. I dearly wish I had the time to describe and discuss her with you. Suffice to say she is a young seamstress, unfortunately contracted to be a concubine, who two years prior to my coming here demonstrated uncommon presence of mind and bravery. My meeting with her has left an indelible impression in my mind, and she is now never far from my thoughts.

I regretted my words instantly to my senior constable, for quite correctly he was upset. I knew he had been only trying to do his duty. I told him then not to worry, that if it was my time to die then it had already been foretold, and that his greater duty was to the defence of the people and not to me.

Now, as I sit alone in my office and write to you, I wish my senior constable was indeed coming with me. I hope my fear does not get the better of me this night. I will be holding an image of Miss Tang in my mind as I walk up the valley, hoping her proven courage can inspire me to do my duty. The irony is not lost on me. How can a simple seamstress, contracted to be a concubine, inspire a scholar who is a former judge and is now a rural magistrate? I do not know the answer to this, but it is true.

Please do not forget that in the last hours of my life I finally had the courage to do what was right.

I wish you a long and happy life.

Your brother
  Magistrate Zhu
  Fifth District, Chengdu Prefecture

Magistrate Zhu put down his ink-brush satisfied. He would now go see Senior Scribe Xu and explain himself, so it would be seen in the local histories to be written, that his actions to come that night were rational, considered and necessary. It was a pity about the porterage list, but not so about the awaited decision in the matter of Jade Moon. Yes, better there is no decision there at all, he thought again, for the thousandth time that evening. Like Magistrate Qian he had destroyed his own thoughts about that dispute, in the flame of an oil-lamp. He wondered if Magistrate Qian had smiled then, as he had done.

"*The belief in true justice under Heaven is a chimera – a passing fancy only,*" had said Judge Pei. "*As judges and magistrates, we must all just do the best we can.*"

CHAPTER 46

Senior Scribe Xu's thoughts had just turned to bed, hoping that he might achieve the miraculous that night and sleep. But, before he could step out of his study, Rose, his maid, whom he had forgotten to dismiss that evening, came to him in some agitation.

"Senior Scribe Xu! Senior Scribe Xu! The Magistrate and Horse have come again," she wailed.

He urged her to calm herself, to show the Magistrate into the main reception room, and then to prepare tea.

"Rose, you must understand that as the people depend on the Magistrate to show serenity in the face of great danger, the Magistrate also has the right to expect the same from the people."

"Senior Scribe Xu, it is no time to tell jokes," she replied, hurrying back to the hall where she had left the Magistrate closely studying the embroidery of the magnolia created by Jade Moon. She felt a great sadness with him, and with Horse, whose face was a picture of abject misery. The trouble men get themselves into when they don't have a sensible woman to guide them, she thought, as she led the Magistrate through to the reception room, indicating Horse should remain in the hall. She would bring him tea separately and try to learn from him all that had been going on.

Senior Scribe Xu breathed deeply, willing himself to relax, wanting to show the Magistrate that as senior clerk in the Fifth District he remained in charge of all of his faculties, regardless of the terrible times they were all living in. He walked into the reception room slowly, and bowed deeply.

Senior Scribe Xu then turned to Rose, who was still hovering in the doorway.

He requested that she bring wine as well as tea immediately. He then invited the Magistrate to sit at the long table in the middle of the room.

"Thank you, Senior Scribe Xu. Please forgive this late visit, but there are matters I would discuss with you which cannot wait."

"Yes, of course, Magistrate, but you should not apologise. My house is open to you even if it is the middle of the night. I was actually just working myself."

"Firstly, Senior Scribe Xu, I have to confess the porterage list is still incomplete. I have studied the document and found it beyond my powers this evening. There are so many names to verify. Even if I worked all night, and all my constables could read and write, we could not get around to all the houses and complete it. I noted that some of the people listed live on the farms in the south of the valley. I am afraid it is one more failure on my part."

Senior Scribe Xu was confused – there were days yet for the list to be completed. "Magistrate, don't be concerned. My junior clerks can assist and go through the list quickly deleting the known sick and the dead. As long as there are enough people to carry the tea to Chengdu, the Patriarchs and the Tea and Horse Agency won't care and your duty will have been fulfilled."

"Thank you, Senior Scribe Xu, I am grateful."

"Tea is life itself in this district, Magistrate," said Senior Scribe Xu, with a gentle laugh.

"I disagree."

"Excuse me, Magistrate, I did not—"

"No, Senior Scribe Xu, I meant no criticism of you, of the people here or even of the Patriarchs. But I find it hard to equate the value of tea with the life of even one man."

"Magistrate, even Tea Inspector Fang would understand. Many people have died over the years transporting the tea over the dangerous trail to market in Chengdu. It is just the worst luck that he has been taken from us right in the centre of town."

"Yes, I appreciate that, Senior Scribe Xu. But I failed to construct even one good argument for the Patriarchs this evening in regard to the value of a single life, and I have none for you now. But I know what I feel in my heart."

"Magistrate, I am sure the gods all sympathise with our plight and that of Tea Inspector Fang. No matter which way we turn in life there is often evil."

They paused as Rose placed a tray of tea on the table, and poured a cup for both of them. Then she hurried out and returned with flasks of wine and a plate of small cakes she had cooked, which Senior Scribe Xu sadly noted he had been going to eat for his breakfast.

"Rose, you must go to your home and your husband," Senior Scribe Xu said, more sharply than he intended.

Rose bowed, but before she left the room, to Senior Scribe Xu's horror, she addressed Magistrate Zhu, forgetting in the emotion of the moment her manners and her usual fear of authority.

"Magistrate, you must eat one of these cakes, and keep up your strength. I am sorry I am not a good cook. I am sure they would not be as good as she would cook them."

"She?"

"Jade Moon is a very fine cook I hear, and the most talented of seamstresses and embroiderers. She can also plug a bandit at a hundred paces with an arrow. What more could a man ask for in a—"

"Rose!" exclaimed Senior Scribe Xu, horrified. Rose vanished abruptly through the doorway before he could chastise her further.

"Senior Scribe Xu, I did not understand your maid's meaning," said Magistrate Zhu, confused. "Why was she speaking of Miss Tang?"

"The people are so frightened of the bandits, Magistrate, that the women are talking more nonsense than is usual. People forget their manners completely in evil times."

"Ah, of course – it is understandable."

"I apologise, Magistrate."

"There is no need, Senior Scribe Xu. She meant no harm, I think. Did you know I have received a visit from Madame Kong this evening?"

"Madame Kong?"

"Yes, and Chef Mo also. They knew the Patriarchs would not give over the ransom. They came to me to offer all the cash they had. It was very moving. I was so ashamed at what I had allowed to come to pass in this district I could hardly look either of them in the eye."

"Magistrate, you should not berate yourself. It is not your fault Tea Inspector Fang was taken. If you—"

"Why did you leave Chengdu?" asked Magistrate Zhu, suddenly. "I understand you were not born here."

"Magistrate, I w-was off-offered this position," stuttered Senior Scribe Xu, surprised by the personal nature of the question.

"Forgive me, Senior Scribe Xu, I thought possibly you had come here to escape the politics of a prefectural capital. I am sure they are not to every man's taste."

"Magistrate, I accepted this post on the advice of my wife. My health was too delicate for Chengdu. The air in the Fifth District is very clear."

"Ah, I understand, Senior Scribe Xu. I thought perhaps you might have been shocked at what you discovered in the palaces...in the behaviour of those who should know better."

"Magistrate?"

"In Kaifeng, when I had passed the civil service examination – did you know I came third that year and was given a commemorative seal for my personal use? – I entered public service immediately, destined for high office. The men who came first and second that year were rewarded immediately with responsible posts, and deservedly so, for I, like many others, thought them the best of men. I was proud to consider them my friends."

"Ah," replied Senior Scribe Xu, for want of something better to say. He tried to imagine what it must have been like for the Magistrate to be known as the third cleverest man in all China for that one year. He was sure he would have fainted with the pride.

"I commenced my specialisation in law then, Senior Scribe Xu, and after passing more examinations, took a post in the Ministry of Justice, under the tutelage of Judge Pei, a quite brilliant jurist – also a humane and deeply compassionate man. He has been dead these last five years now."

Magistrate Zhu looked very sad, and Senior Scribe Xu took the opportunity to pour more tea. When the Magistrate said nothing further, Senior Scribe Xu commented: "Magistrate, I have heard that in China one should not mourn when a great man passes, for it is certain that another is born in his place."

Magistrate Zhu nodded. "I have heard that too, Senior Scribe Xu. But I cannot vouch for its truth. I fear I will never meet another such man as Judge Pei. I learned as much as I could from him. Then I was offered a post as a Censor – working in the Censorate to uncover the crimes of clerks and officials. I was ambitious, you see, which I now regret. I should have remained with Judge Pei longer and comprehended more to counter my own failings. I had passed all my examinations with ease, and thought myself the most learned and moral of men, that I could trust my own instincts in all matters. You see, I thought the practice of law to be a simple thing – a matter of deciding between right and wrong. I also thought the clarity and content of my memorials and judgements would echo down the ages. I could not have been more wrong. I saw terrible things done by men... incomprehensible things. And I found that, for all of my education, I myself was not the man I thought myself to be."

"I understand, Magistrate," said Senior Scribe Xu, as Magistrate Zhu stopped talking, pausing for breath.

"I am not sure you do, Senior Scribe Xu. I need to tell you a story, so you shall understand what I am to do this night and why."

Senior Scribe Xu kept his silence, his interest more than aroused.

"Just over three years ago, a man came to me, a common man – a shop-keeper I think. This was in Kaifeng. He was in great emotional distress, and could not restrain his speech. He was brought to me by a constable whom I had come to know and trust. This common man had a daughter, who, when shopping in the market, had been taken by traffickers in young women. She was, I understand, quite beautiful. We could say the father should have taken greater care of her, but you should know, Senior Scribe Xu, that there are people-traffickers who will even break into a house to steal a boy or a girl or a baby still in its crib. These people are so evil I find it hard to imagine the sages could have known of their existence or they would have written more extensively on their crimes. Now this bereft father was brought before me so I could examine him. I wished to understand why he had come to me at the Censorate rather than approach his local sheriff."

Magistrate Zhu paused, looking down at his wine, touching his fingers delicately to the rim of the cup.

"Magistrate, are you alright?"

"Yes, Senior Scribe Xu, forgive me. I was travelling in the past. The father of this young woman, this common man, explained himself, and accused two men – both in high office, you understand – as being those running this gang of people traffickers and profiting from their crimes."

"It is quite unbelievable, Magistrate."

"I thought so too, Senior Scribe Xu. For these men he named were known to me. They were my friends. I would eat and drink with them at the best restaurants many times a month. They were the two who had come first and second in the civil service examinations when I had come a distant third. Never had I known better or cleverer men. And to think they had been accused was more than my emotions could bear."

"This is quite understandable, Magistrate."

"No, Senior Scribe Xu, you are not listening to what I am saying. I was so offended by the accusation that I lost my temper completely. I think my voice carried into every room of the Censorate offices in Kaifeng. You see, I was younger then and more prone to outbursts. I berated the constable who had brought this man to me, and then ordered this man to be beaten for what had come out of his mouth. This my constables did, severely, knowing my incensed feelings on the matter.

"You must understand, Senior Scribe Xu, the law says that for those who accuse falsely, they should receive the same punishment as if they had committed the crime themselves. This man had risked much in coming forward and saying what he had. But I did not wait to think, or investigate further, or write a considered judgement against him. And it is to my everlasting regret and sorrow that this man, this father who had lost his daughter, died from the injuries received from my constables that very night."

Magistrate Zhu paused. Senior Scribe Xu, concerned that the Magistrate might be too exhausted to continue, and wanting to spur him on, asked. "What happened then, Magistrate?"

"You must understand that though I was appalled by his accusations against my friends, I intended him a simple beating only. I severely chastised my constables. But I believed them when they had said they had not meant to kill the man… that he must have had a weak heart. I fined the constables, of course, but felt somehow that justice had been served. To accuse educated and moral men of heinous crimes should inspire terrible repercussions. But you must know, Senior Scribe Xu, that in the depths of the nights that followed, I very much regretted the death of this man, coming to believe that perhaps he had been so deranged by his loss of his daughter he was deserving more of compassion and sympathy rather than punishment."

"Yes, I see that, Magistrate. When things go wrong we all look around to blame someone."

"Exactly, Senior Scribe Xu, which was my thinking. An apology was issued to the family, and his funeral paid for, though my supervisor did not find fault with me for my actions. And neither did my father. Have I ever spoken of him and his accomplishments?"

"No, Magistrate."

"Perhaps another time. My story has not finished. Months later, as I was investigating the bribing of a clerk, a district sheriff came to me – a man I did not know well, but for whom I have since developed an undying respect. Sheriff Min is not well educated, and his calligraphy is abominable, but he had served as a sheriff for some years, and had a reputation for honesty and integrity. This is why I chose to listen to him. He asked me to examine a man he had recently arrested, who was willing to speak on his knowledge of other more serious crimes in exchange for a lesser sentence. Sheriff Min requested to sit in on my examination of the man and that I should not beat him regardless of what he might say. Intrigued, I agreed, and listened to this criminal's story. His name is not important but he said he was a smuggler of goods – mainly wine and salt – and named to me others he associated with, and that he greatly regretted his crimes. He also named officials, important men who had offered protection to him and his associates, and protection also to another gang involved in the greater crime of the smuggling of people. This man said these officials had profited tremendously from their criminality."

"Ah," said Senior Scribe Xu.

"Senior Scribe Xu, I swear Sheriff Min had to physically restrain me. My two friends had been named once more. I fear if Sheriff Min had not done so, I would have beaten this petty criminal senseless with my bare fists. And for what? For telling the truth?"

Magistrate Zhu shook his head at the memory.

"How could this be, Magistrate?" asked Senior Scribe Xu.

"I did not know, but perhaps should have known. In the days that followed Sheriff Min took me to see further witnesses, to speak with some of the trafficked people he had recovered. More criminals confessed to their crimes and in turn accused my friends – these high officials, these most moral of men – of taking cash in exchange for protection and favours. It took an age, and I barely slept or ate or drank in that time, but eventually I was convinced and did what was right and took Sheriff Min to my supervisor. I then retreated to the estates of my father.

"What followed did not take long. My father was informed at his desk that not only had I covered up a serious crime by the beating to death of the father of a kidnapped young woman – intended or not, what did it matter? – but that I also had consorted regularly with these men, supposedly my friends, and allowed them to buy me drinks and food with the profits of their crimes. My father was told that, for reasons unknown, I was blind to their pervasive and corrosive immorality.

"The investigating judge – Judge Pan, a great man – said of me: 'Only a child could have seen less than Judge Zhu.' And he was right. My father died soon after from shame. Others wrote my father's eulogy and officiated at his funeral rites. I did not leave my study to attend the funeral. I did not want to dishonour my family any further."

"Magistrate, I—"

"Please, let me finish, Senior Scribe Xu. There is more you should know. Because of our high position, my friends and I were therefore worthy of the eight deliberations. I will not go into legal detail, but understand that because of our rank we were given special treatment under the law; our punishments not what they might have been. A common person would have been strangled for people-trafficking, but my friends were allowed to pay large fines – though they were removed from office and lost their noble rank. Where they are now, I do not know. Perhaps they were sent into exile."

"But Magistrate, you had not been involved in the trafficking of people," interrupted Senior Scribe Xu. "You were not as guilty."

"That is true, Senior Scribe Xu. And Sheriff Min spoke to the truth of that in front of Judge Pan. But my failure to act months before when the father of this kidnapped young woman had accused my friends, not to mention his death at my hands, and the lack of wisdom in my associations and my lack of insight into their true characters spoke against me. I could not continue at the Censorate. I was removed from office, though found neither guilty nor innocent. Judge Pan could only find me stupid, lacking talent and composure, and not worthy of the least respect. Few know of this judgement. The Censorate protects its own secrets. My file is closed to any who would seek to look at it.

"For three years I rotted away on the estate, Senior Scribe Xu, reflecting on what I had done. A braver man than I would have taken his own life. Then Emperor Shenzong died, and my sister came to see me. She was sensitive to the winds of change blowing through the streets of Kaifeng. She convinced me to call upon the Minister Yu. He is very senior in the Ministry of State. My sister is fortunate enough to be married to his son even though I think him a very dull fellow.

"I knew Minister Yu to be a decent man, who had been good to my sister and had not thrown her out of his family when he discovered my shame. He spoke to me with great kindness, and we reflected together on the achievements of my father – which I might add were considerable. He then said there had been changes already in the palaces in Kaifeng, and that some whose careers had been successful were now in retirement, and some who had fallen out of favour were now being reinstated. He said…and I shall never forget these words all my life… that atonement is achieved only through good works, in the service of the people, and not through the constant reflection on mistakes.

"In that moment, Senior Scribe Xu, I was persuaded. The Minister Yu said that I should take whatever post was offered me, no matter how lowly, and do what I could for the people. I have to confess I wept for some time after that meeting. He recommended me to Prefect Kang in Chengdu…who does not know my unsavoury past except that I was once of the Censorate and Ministry of Justice… and to take any post, and to disregard the more venal aspects of Prefect Kang's conduct."

"I have heard many stories, Magistrate," said Senior Scribe Xu.

"Yes, I have heard these also, but I am not with the Censorate now."

"But why have you told me all about your past, Magistrate? This is personal to you and not for my ears."

"I want you to understand what I am about to do and to apologise."

"Apologise? For what, Magistrate?"

"For bringing evil with me."

"Magistrate, please, you should not say such things. You—"

"An injustice cannot be allowed to go unanswered, otherwise disaster and further evil will follow. You should understand this, Senior Scribe Xu, that any injustice, great or small, moves Heaven and Earth out of balance."

"Yes, Magistrate, it makes sense, but—"

"Good, then you should also understand I might have brought all this evil upon this district by accepting the magistracy here, thinking to begin my career again. My arrogance knows no bounds, Senior Scribe Xu. The people have suffered for it: Mister Gong has been murdered and Tea Inspector Fang has been kidnapped. Do you not see the coincidence, Senior Scribe Xu?"

"Magistrate, I—"

"Senior Scribe Xu, my career is long over and should have never been restarted. How can I begin my life again when I have not atoned for the harm that I have already done?"

"Magistrate—"

"You will not dissuade me, Senior Scribe Xu. I am going to meet with the bandits this night, and offer myself to them in exchange for Tea Inspector Fang. It should be no matter to convince them of my greater importance and considerably greater value."

"Magistrate, you should not—"

"Please, don't protest, Senior Scribe Xu, my mind is made up." Magistrate Zhu reached into the sleeve of his robe and took out a folded paper. "I have a letter for my sister in Kaifeng. Would you send it on for me?"

"Of course, Magistrate, anything you may wish, but—"

"Senior Scribe Xu, you must understand my reasons, why I think Heaven brought me here. I am not worthy to be your magistrate, but I can seek my lost humanity and restore honour to the name of my family."

"Magistrate, with respect I must disagree," said Senior Scribe Xu, starting to panic. He knew the Fifth District could get along quite nicely without Tea Inspector Fang but not without a magistrate, and certainly not with all the trouble that was soon to arrive from Chengdu.

"Senior Scribe Xu, if I can exchange my life for Tea Inspector Fang, then perhaps the balance between Heaven and Earth will be restored."

Magistrate Zhu then stood up from his seat, looking to Senior Scribe Xu as a man already dead.

"Magistrate, please reconsider. Tea Inspector Fang may not be still alive to be exchanged with your person."

"Even so, I must try, Senior Scribe Xu."

Senior Scribe Xu stood also, seeing that the Magistrate, for good or ill, was set upon his course. A million thoughts raced about his mind, first and foremost that he himself was sure to be criticised, by the people as well as Prefect Kang, for allowing Magistrate Zhu to do something so reckless and foolhardy, as well as for losing a magistrate after only a few days.

However, there was one thing he could ask, so he could better tell the Magistrate's story if any should ask.

"Magistrate, before you leave I would like to know what happened to the girl, the one who was taken by the people traffickers. Was she ever found?"

Magistrate Zhu sighed. He looked down and studied the back of his hands, and did not speak for some time. Senior Scribe Xu wondered if he should repeat the question when Magistrate Zhu suddenly opened his mouth.

"I should have gone looking for her instead of brooding on my estates. Sheriff Min did so. He spent months searching for this girl even after his tenure had come to an end. He eventually found her – I don't know how – in a neighbouring province, serving as a slave to a rich merchant. He brought her home to her family. He did what I could not do. Is it not a relief that even when evil permeates our society at every level, China still produces heroes such as Sheriff Min?"

"I am glad for the girl and her family," said Senior Scribe Xu, sincerely.

"But what she thought when she found her father dead I do not know," said Magistrate Zhu, sadly. "I sent them cash, of course, to be a dowry for the girl. And I sent cash as a reward to Sheriff Min. You see he gained no recognition from the authorities for what he had done. The scandal of high officials involved in people-trafficking had caused many important men to look the other away. I am pleased to say Sheriff Min has found tenure again. I have left him a full third of the Zhu estates in my will for his heroism and devotion to the law – though he does not yet know it yet. It is the least I can do for him. Though not an educated man, he knew enough not to let an injustice stand. Now, this night, I will follow his guide and do what I can for Tea Inspector Fang."

Senior Scribe Xu nodded, greatly moved by the story, and by the Magistrate's decision. He walked the Magistrate to his door and bade him goodbye with a heavy heart. It was well after midnight when he sat up in bed, shocked by the sudden and belated realisation that yet another magistrate had left the matter of Jade Moon and her concubinage quite unresolved.

CHAPTER 47

"Senior Constable He, it is a curious thing but it seems to me that in life we are granted so much time for trivialities but so little for those matters of the greatest importance. I have no words to explain this, but I wish I could have stayed with you longer and spoken to you more of the importance of the law."

Magistrate Zhu hesitated then, and Horse thought his courage was going to fail, that the Magistrate would change his mind, accept that Tea Inspector Fang was lost, and continue to lead them.

"Magistrate, I—"

"You must always remember what it is to be a constable, Senior Constable He. You are here to serve the people. Nothing else matters; nothing else is important. Remember this and all the other things...all the other concerns...will find their natural place."

These were the last words spoken by Magistrate Zhu. He had not even said farewell.

They had been standing alone, at the north gate, all other accompaniment forbidden. The Magistrate had been dressed in his finest robes of vermillion, and carrying nothing more than a lantern accepted off Sergeant Kang – a sword was refused – and a small book. "A gift from my sister, the Lady Yu," he said, noting Horse's interest. "A volume of poetry of the great Master Du Fu. I understand he lived for some years in Chengdu, in the time of the Tang Dynasty. I have never been a great lover of literature, memorizing just what was needed to pass my examinations. I much prefer to read legal precedents. But my sister is insistent that his words have much value. Perhaps, in the mountains, I may discover this value for myself."

Back at the jail, the Magistrate had also placed a few small ingots of silver within his girdle. "These may ease my passage with the bandits. There are some others in my travelling luggage. If you or the constables need cash for anything of importance then speak to Senior Scribe Xu, who can convert the silver to strings of cash coin."

After the Magistrate had said he was ready, he had cast one last look around his apartment and office, had said goodbye to the Deng brothers, Little Ox and Leaf, and finally to Sergeant Kang and his militia, who had just stumbled out of the Inn of Harmonious Friendship to see what was to happen. All had bowed to Magistrate Zhu, deeply and with the greatest respect, but some of the militia, worse for the wine and their great emotion, fell down as they did so.

Horse had then walked with Magistrate Zhu in silence along North Gate Street. They passed within a stone's throw of Senior Scribe Xu's house again, and of the great residence belonging to Patriarch Yang. Horse felt great bitterness then, that no one in the district had offered the help that they could, and that there were so many questions left outstanding as to who had helped the bandits kidnap Tea Inspector Fang. Not that he felt he could raise the matter with the Magistrate, not now. It was too late, far too late for such considerations.

The North Gate was unguarded as usual, not really a gate but a great opening in the wall where large wooden doors used to hang. The doors were long gone, except for their hinges and the remnants of their frames. There was no cash in the town to replace them, and – as the Patriarchs argued – the town walls were so low, so eroded in many places, and so easy to climb over, there was no sense in doing so.

Horse pointed the trail out to Magistrate Zhu, a dirt track, the beginnings of which were just visible in the mist. "Take care of your footing, Magistrate. It climbs steeply in places, and always follows the course of the river. The fishermen who live on the shores of the Lake of Clouds, beyond Dancing Tiger Pass, use it all the time to bring fish to town, but they know it well, are sure-footed and never use it at night."

Magistrate Zhu had nodded, and smiled. Then he was gone, swinging his lantern before him, the warm glow of the light soon swallowed up by the darkness and the mist.

Horse stayed standing at the gate, despite the chill of the night, for the longest time. He knew he should have not abandoned Magistrate Zhu, regardless of all the arguments put forward in private by Sergeant Kang that his presence, and the presence of any other constables or militia, would serve only to endanger the Magistrate further.

"Listen Horse, it's best not to interfere in the lives of officials," had said Sergeant Kang. "They are not like the common people. Sometimes they do and say the daftest things."

As he stood at the gate, Horse thought of Sergeant Kang's words, believing he had been trying to bring humour to a difficult time.

Finally, sadly, he turned away, and cast his mind back to the troubles of the town. Though it was now well after midnight he ought to go out on the streets with the Deng brothers and Little Ox. They must do what Magistrate Zhu would have expected of them and keep the peace. After all, as Sergeant Kang had also pointed out, without a magistrate again, some of the people were bound to misbehave.

Horse walked slowly back down North Gate Street, finding some solace in the silence of the town, that all the decent people were locked safely in their houses, sleeping or, as he would wish, kneeling at their family shrines, praying for the soul of Magistrate Zhu. Then he noticed that the street was lighter than it should be, despite that many of the lanterns hung over the doorways had already burned out.

He stopped and looked up. A large half-moon had broken through the mist and the clouds, casting a silvery light all around. Was this rare event a good omen? Could the Magistrate see the moon from further up the valley? Would its light keep his feet safely on the trail? Horse certainly hoped so.

He stared at the moon for some time, recalling the early years of his childhood, how his mother had told him the story of the hare and a beautiful lady, a great Queen, who lived on the moon in an incredible castle. He had often stayed up late afterward, and crept out of the house on the few nights the sky was clear. He had stared for hours and hours, hoping just once to see the hare and the beautiful lady.

Then, a few years later, Jade Moon and her mother had come to town. Horse had looked on the tall, impressive girl for the first time and learned her name. He had gone to his mother, saying surely this Jade Moon was a daughter of the Lady of the Moon, that perhaps that she had fallen to the Earth or that Madame Tang had stolen her away. After all Jade Moon did not resemble her mother in any way and there was a sadness about her that he could almost feel.

"Horse, I cannot say anything for sure. I am the simple wife of a blacksmith," his mother had replied, laughing. "But unusual people, even unusual girls, will most likely do unusual things."

But nothing had happened, and Horse had eventually forgotten the thought he had had of the Lady of the Moon, and of Jade Moon possibly being her daughter. In the years that came after, Jade Moon had smiled at him, and spoken kindly to him on her visits to the smithy with her mother. And sometimes she even brought cakes and sweets, offered in friendship.

But everything changed one day.

Bad Teeth Tong had come to town, and Jade Moon had shot her arrow – just one arrow – and nothing had been the same again. Jade Moon hardly ever left her house, and certainly did not come to the smithy. And his own mother and father had argued, which happened only once, his mother usually accepting of all that was said in the house.

"That she-wolf and her mother should be run out of town," his father, Blacksmith He, had grumbled at the table. "She will bring disaster on all of us."

His mother had pushed her dinner aside, got up from the table and said: "That you are my husband I would not change, for you are a fine worker and have given me three strong and healthy sons. But you are often a stupid and foolish man, who does not see the value of things before your very eyes. I have thought on this all day, and now know that Jade Moon is a heroine reborn. And if she is here, then Heaven has said it is to be so, and one day I think she will do even greater things than she has already done."

214

His father had shrugged, and nothing more had been said by his parents concerning Jade Moon that day or any following day.

Horse stared up at the moon. Was it coincidence this moon should appear now, reminding him of his mother's words?

He knew he had no right to ask. She owed him nothing. She owed Tranquil Mountain nothing. And Horse realised he knew nothing about heroes or heroines, or the will of Heaven. He was but a stupid and clumsy son of a blacksmith. But was this moon not trying to communicate something to him, appearing to him as it had just done? And could he not promise her something in return, that he would never allow her to go to the house of Patriarch Zhou, and the bed of Second Son Zhou; that he and the other constables could hide her, or help her escape from that fate? The Deng brothers were tricky. They could think of something. Surely, their cleverness *must* be good for something. He could personally even strangle that monster Second Son Zhou in the street. His strong hands could do that, he knew. The punishment would be worth it, death or exile; but what did it matter? At least he would have done one good thing in return, for her.

Horse began to run, his long legs pumping hard, back to the jail. He thought ahead. In the storeroom were her bow and arrows. The storeroom was locked, and the key, now where was that? Did the Magistrate still have it? Horse wasn't sure, but he knew if needs be he could break it open with his bare hands.

"I will not stand by and do nothing!" he shouted as he ran, not caring whom he woke, or about the barking of dogs that erupted all around him.

CHAPTER 48

*H*ardly a night went by for her without a memory of standing over the body of Bad Teeth Tong, his eyes staring up to Heaven, his hands still grasped around the shaft of the arrow, blood oozing from where it pierced his chest. Up close, he had not looked much: a dark, emaciated face, filthy unkempt hair and beard, and ragged clothes covering his body. But she had done this thing. She had killed this man. And in the hush of the market-square – the other bandits chased off by some of the people – she had learned something her father had not taught her, something no one could teach her.

"*Once the arrow is gone, ready another immediately in its place,*" he had said. "*The first arrow is already past, and needs no further consideration. Empty your mind. Be receptive to what comes next.*"

But what came next was silence, and Bad Teeth Tong breathing his last. What came next was the cold north wind stinging her face, bringing tears to her eyes. What came next was a feeling of darkness emerging from the depths of her heart, smothering the light of the world.

"It is a miracle! A miracle!" exclaimed Mister Peng, struggling to his feet. "My life has been saved."

Mister Peng offered her some of the produce from his stall which had collapsed to the ground. "It's not much, but it's all I have," he had said, holding the goods out to her.

Jade Moon had shaken her head, and turned away from him. Without speaking she had allowed Physician Ji, who had appeared from nowhere, to walk her slowly home. She had lain down on her bed, ignoring the questions from her mother, or the neighbours coming round to call. Physician Ji had stayed some time, speaking words of reassurance to her mother.

"Oh, Physician Ji, what am I to do?" her mother had cried. "My daughter has lost her mind."

"Madame Tang, her spirit has left her body for a short time – that is all. Have faith, her spirit will return. Her body is strong, and young people are not like the old; they can absorb many shocks."

Then Apothecary Hong and his smiling son, Wondrous Boy, had arrived. Apothecary Hong had opened up a small box full of roots and powders, and, after a short but intense discussion with Physician Ji, and some comment from Wondrous Boy, who was listened to though barely a man, the appropriate powder was chosen.

"But I do not have the cash for such a rare medicine!" Madame Tang had protested.

Physician Ji didn't listen, taken up as he was in pouring out the powder and stirring it into Jade Moon's tea. It was left up to Apothecary Hong to answer.

"Madame Tang, it is but a dried extract of a rare plant that took me many adventures and many days to find in the unexplored lands far south of here. It is a soporific only, but gentle, allowing a healing to take its course, uninterrupted by the concerns of the mind. I offer it to you freely, glad now that I took the trouble to find it. Surely it is the least that any of us can do."

In the days that followed, her mother would sit next to her, and prop up her head and force her to drink the tea, made bitter by Apothecary Hong's powder. Her mother would talk softly to her, about the many gifts the people had left at the door, and how through what she had done, an opportunity for a different future had been presented to them.

"Jade Moon, don't worry. The people believe you are special…supernatural… a great heroine reborn. Let Patriarch Zhou and his sons try to take you now. Let them come. The people will defend us."

Then a full month later, when her recovery was seen to be complete, Constable Wei had come to the house, and escorted her to the jail. Her bow and arrows were confiscated, and she had been made to sit before Magistrate Qian. The kind old man had stared at her for the longest time. Finally he had spoken to her.

"Miss Tang, I am not a real magistrate. I was once a sheriff who did his duty, and for that, and against my will, I was promoted and sent here. I have not had the benefit of a proper education. I have not had the benefit of learned men around me. So forgive me if I say that I do not know what to make of you or what should be done."

Constable Wei had afterward returned her to her mother. Then, on the day of her birthday, men came from the Zhou residence, led by the beast, Second Son Zhou, to take her away. Her mother had screamed and screamed and the people had come, as promised, throwing stones, shouting, and making such a commotion that Second Son Zhou and his men had actually run for their lives.

Two years had passed since then, but nothing really had changed because nothing had been resolved, and the fear of the future had never gone away. And now, with Magistrate Zhu gone, nothing would be resolved – for good or ill. Jade

Moon wondered where he was, whether he was still alive and, if so, what clever words, what intelligent words, he was speaking. She hoped – she prayed – the bandits would spare his life and listen, as she had listened, to be entranced by him, as she had been entranced.

Her mother was wrong. Another magistrate would come, but not as clever this time. Not as young and handsome. Not as caring and compassionate. And she would be sent to the Zhou residence without delay, and Second Son Zhou would come to her, and she would kill him with a hidden knife when he tried to touch her, and then she would cut her own throat and the pain of life would be over. Then, in the afterlife, she would look for her father, and ask him why he left her when he had, and why all of this sadness had had to come to pass.

She sat alone in the room, her mother long since retired to bed. She had tired of the sewing of the constables' uniforms, her heart no longer in it.

There was a tap on the door – hardly a knock – but there just the same. She threw her sewing to one side, having the most extraordinary thought that he had returned to town, or had not gone at all, and Magistrate Zhu had come to ask her to go with him, into the mountains, away from all the trouble in the world.

Stupidly, and without further consideration, she unlatched the door and opened it to an incredible sight. The street was full of soldiers – Sergeant Kang's soldiers – and Little Ox and the Deng brothers, and Golden Orchid's little friend, Leaf, and Trainee Legal Secretary Li, whom she did not really know but who had been at her examination by the Magistrate, and Horse standing before them all, his mouth open, holding out a long bundle wrapped in coarse cloth, hiding things that she knew very well.

"Where is he?" she cried, snatching the bundle out of Horse's hands, letting the cloth fall to the ground, revealing her bow and quiver of arrows.

She did not know who told her – she thought not Horse, who seemed unable to speak anything at all – but when she knew, she ran, down the street, into the market-square, then north, past the jail, into North Gate Street, not stopping to catch her breath, not stopping to worry about the future, not stopping to think at all.

CHAPTER 49

$\mathcal{A}$s he was swallowed up by the darkness and struggled up the trail made slick and dangerous by the condensed mist, he thought how fitting it was that his life should have brought him to this place. Here he was, on the edge of a raging river, imperilled not just by nature but bandits too, at the farthest reaches of the Empire and civilisation, determined to bring justice where there was none and to find release for a man who, if not completely innocent, was certainly not deserving of kidnap or murder.

He hoped that the spirit of Judge Pei walked with him, and that his father was at peace at last with his son's life. And he hoped that even if his mission proved to be unsuccessful, the act of sacrifice would be enough for him to mount the benches of the judiciary in the afterlife, to be welcomed by the magistrates and judges of the olden days – even of the Golden Age, if there was really ever such a time – and be allowed to continue to practice law. Surely this last act should be enough to guarantee that simple wish.

Occasionally, he stopped to listen, half-hoping he would hear Horse running up behind him, having found some pressing reason for him not to carry on, that Tea Inspector Fang had turned up safe and sound after all, and the ransom note just a bad joke. But when he strained his ears, he heard only the torrent that was White Dragon River. There was not even the howl of a distant wolf or the eerie barking of foxes. But then he did not know whether foxes lived this far into the mountains, and thought it just as likely he would encounter a tiger on the trail.

He carried on, further up the valley, unable to determine his progress. Horse had told him the path would eventually take him to the head of the valley, where he could cross a rickety bridge to the other side of the river, over to the Serene

Tiger Monastery, or choose to continue over Dancing Tiger Pass, skirt the edges of the Lake of Clouds and the huts of the Happy Fishing Village, and lose oneself in the mountains, beyond which lay Tibet.

When would the bandits intercept him? Before the bridge? Beyond the pass? Horse had said that in daylight the bridge was half a morning's stiff walk. He hoped the bandits would find him before then. And what if he met no bandits at all, and was forced to walk and walk and walk until he dropped down on the trail from exhaustion? And there was also the possibility, not mentioned to the constables, that the bandits killed in the home of Madame Wu were all there ever had been. Tea Inspector Fang could now be trussed up somewhere, hidden, dying of thirst, hunger and the cold, not knowing why he had been abandoned, never to be found.

Magistrate Zhu put such unhelpful thoughts out of his mind, and concentrated on putting one foot after the other, holding the lantern as far out in front of him as he could, trying to keep Jade Moon's face in his mind – a cherished memory for him of supreme courage, to inspire him in this his darkest hour.

"She would not wish me to give up," he said to himself. "She would wish me to continue, to save Tea Inspector Fang. She would wish me to atone for the things that I have done."

Then he shuddered at the thought of Jade Moon ever learning what kind of man he had been, how a man already wronged through the loss of a daughter had been beaten to death through his temper and mistake – and how he had retreated to his estates like a coward rather than do everything he could to put things right.

He slipped as he thought of this. He ended up on his knees, dropping the lantern, fortunate only in that the lantern stayed lit. He marvelled at how the fishermen must run up and down the narrow trail, admittedly during the day, carrying their catches of fish to market; and the monks, coming to town to beg alms and to instruct the people in their homes on the requisites of a virtuous life. He struggled back to his feet, wiping dirt off his robes, conscious he was making the slowest of progress.

Finally he came to a widening in the trail. There he discovered a large rock jutting out from the forest to the side, flat enough for him to sit upon and to rest. He placed the lantern to one side of him on the rock, and sat, catching his breath.

A haunting melody came to mind, and an image from the past, of him returning to the Zhu estate, confident then in the future. He had just returned from a shared audience with the Emperor, his answers to his final examination – the Palace Examination – considered so meritorious they were read out by the Chief Examiner, as were nine others that day. The Emperor had placed him third, and he was so proud. The next day his name, along with the nine others, would be made public for all of Kaifeng to learn. Not for him to scrabble to see all the other names posted, the jostling and pushing, seeing those slink away whose dreams had come to nothing, or fighting off those fathers hoping to arrange an immediate marriage for their daughters, believing there to be no better prospect than a successful candidate.

He found Sparrow, his sister, in one of the gardens of the estate, sitting in the shade of a plum tree, singing that haunting melody.

"So brother, I see from your expression that you have exceeded yourself."

"I did not come first."

"Ah, father will be so disappointed."

"Third."

"Ah, enough for your name to be written onto the golden placard and carried in honour all over Kaifeng."

"Yes."

"Then that will have to do."

"What was that song you were singing? It is new, is it not?"

She nodded, a cloud crossing her face. "I felt restless waiting for you to return. I went down into the market. There was an old barbarian woman there selling singing-birds. She was singing the melody to them."

Sparrow had the remarkable gift of being able to reproduce perfectly any song that she heard.

"What is it about?"

"Oh, brother, I don't know. The words were strange…foreign…barbarian. It is a lament, I think. I chided the woman. I said to her she would not sell many birds if all they could sing was a lament. But I came home, and could not get the melody from my mind. Forgive me, brother, I am not myself. Today, I regret that I am born a woman and not a man." She got up from her seat and quickly embraced him. "I am happy for you, brother, and for our father who raised us. He will be so proud."

And so he was, for a time.

And Sparrow had sung rightly that day, for his career – such as it was – was worthy only of such a song.

"Sing your lament for me now, Sparrow," he said out loud, over the sound of the rushing river water. "For I am—"

"So, Magistrate, you have granted us an audience after all! We have been exchanging wagers, thinking you may not come."

Startled, Magistrate Zhu slipped off the rock, realising too late he had been surrounded by a group of seven or eight rough-looking men – criminals obviously – holding swords or clubs or knives, as well as lanterns. How they had approached him unseen and unheard? He cursed himself for being, as always, lost in the past.

Taking courage, hoping they would not strike him down immediately, he said: "I am Magistrate Zhu."

"And I am The Ghost of Scary Face Fu," replied a young man, stepping forward out of the gloom. Unlike the others he was richly dressed, though the golden robes seemed too big for him, as if he had taken them from another man. But it was the man's face that attracted Magistrate Zhu's gaze. He was young, yes, and clean-shaven, but the face bore a curious deformity, as if one side had turned temporarily liquid, dragging the one eye down, before setting in place again. So this was what was meant by 'scary face'.

But something was wrong. What nonsense was this? The deformed young man was hardly older than his constables. And Tea Merchant Wen, whom he had convinced himself to be Scary Face Fu, had fought in the street over a tea contract with Tea Inspector Fang more than fourteen years before.

"You are not Tea Merchant Wen," said Magistrate Zhu.

"Ah, Magistrate, replied the man. "I am but a ghost."

"Don't lie to me, boy! You are no ghost," said Magistrate Zhu, irritated, his fear forgotten momentarily.

Rage filled the young man. A knife appeared in his hand, and he instantly pressed it to Magistrate Zhu's neck.

"An arrogant magistrate's throat is as easily slit as any other's," he hissed.

~

Tranquil Mountain was now behind her. She was already upon the slippery trail running hard up the valley, refusing to feel the tiredness of her limbs or the pain of her breaths rushing in and out of her lungs. She concentrated only on her footing, not wanting to slip off the trail and into the river. Her mind was only of one thought: that he could not be allowed to die.

Still, as she ran she cursed herself for not acting earlier, when Madame Kong had come to the house and explained what the Magistrate in his stupid wisdom and misplaced courageousness had decided to do. Why had she not acted then? Why had she waited until the constables and the soldiers had knocked on her door to persuade her to do what only she could do?

"Oh, I am such a fool," she shouted out loud.

She kept on running, though the going was hard and perilous. The mists swirled all about her, confusing her, blinding her. She was relying on her instincts and her speed to keep her safe, and the occasional silvery beam of moonlight that broke through the clouds and the mist, lighting the trail a short way, before the moon was once again obscured.

She hurried on, wondering how far she would have to go, hoping she was not too late. Terrible thoughts came into her mind, of him lying dead and murdered further up the trail, his life-blood leaking out onto the ground, or him bound and gagged, and being carried off into the mountains, never to be seen again. She had heard stories of the barbarians who lived over the mountains. Not all were as friendly as the Tibetans who came into town. There were some valleys it was said, where the dark arts were practised, where people were sacrificed to demons, their heads cut off or their hearts cut out, the remains thrown away to be feasted on by great ravenous vultures.

"I will not allow it!" she spoke to herself, resolute, so that all of Heaven and Earth would understand her intention.

The trail grew steeper now. She felt the muscles in her legs burning, her strength beginning to fail. But he was close. She did not know how she knew, but she could sense his presence. She was sure of it. And he was still alive!

She slowed her pace, finally stopping, straining her ears to listen to what lay on the trail above her. She could hear the torrent of river water rushing by her, and the muffled curses of the soldiers doing their best to follow up behind her, but up in front...no, there was something...definitely voices. But whose voices she could not tell. The mist was thicker here, and she could see nothing before her. She walked forward, bow at the ready, not wanting to blunder into the bandits and be captured like a simple fool.

Then, out of the gloom, she finally saw the faint yellow glow of lanterns, and the voices became much more distinct; so much so that she recognised one especially, its tone clear and cool – a kind voice that had forever impressed itself on her soul. And then there was another voice, but this harsh and cruel, full of hate and violence.

She stopped still, not knowing exactly how far they were ahead of her, not wanting to make a mistake, not wanting to precipitate a murderous act before she was ready herself.

For a brief moment the mists parted, and above on the trail, the form of Magistrate Zhu became clear to her, but also the forms of a number of men she did not know. Bandits! A cold hand touched her heart when she saw the glint of a knife at the Magistrate's neck. She lifted her bow and nocked an arrow to the string without a thought, but by then she was already too late. The mists closed in again, and the forms once more grew indistinct and then vanished.

Even she could not shoot on memory alone. Had she arrived in time, only to hear him murdered?

"Oh Father, help me!" she cried, silently, invoking his spirit, so the mists might clear and her arrow fly true.

But, if her father was nearby, he did not help. If anything the mists grew thicker, and the voices above her began to be drowned out by the shouts of the soldiers and constables coming up behind. Had the moment, that one moment, been missed?

~

F rozen to the spot, unable to move away from the knife, Magistrate Zhu was barely able to whisper: "I have come to offer myself in exchange for the life of Tea Inspector Fang."

The knife lifted away from him slightly, and the young man pressed his deformed face closer to the Magistrate's own.

"I told my men you would come, because magistrates are fools, and because I knew the Patriarchs would not give up their cash. You magistrates all believe that the people will do as you say, that we all can find renewal no matter what we have done. I have not made up my mind if I will kill you too…perhaps, perhaps not. If I did I would certainly be famous for all my days. But I really lured you here to bear witness, Magistrate; witness to the vengeance of the family Wen…vengeance for what has been done to us by men like you."

The young man turned away, beckoning for someone to be pushed forward into the sphere of light cast by the lanterns. It was Tea Inspector Fang, his arms roped tight behind his back, his mouth gagged with a silk handkerchief, supported on either side by bandits. His face was bruised, his eyes swollen shut, testament to the beating he had suffered.

"Behold the great tea inspector, Magistrate. He is not so rude and arrogant now, is he?"

"Young man, I do not know what you have suffered that has led you to this path of criminality. But I am of the family Zhu, and am worth much more—"

"I don't want cash, Magistrate! Do you think I could not ransom Tea Inspector Fang for a mountain of silver in Chengdu? Why would I keep you the long months it would take for an answer to return from Kaifeng? I am Chinese, not barbarian. I do not choose to hide out in the mountains and the forests. You have been lured here for one reason only: to see Tea Inspector Fang meet his death. And then I will return to Chengdu, and gather up the gold, silver and jewels that Tea Inspector Fang has accumulated all these years. A little beating and humiliation was all it took to reveal their hiding places. You must understand, Magistrate, that I am not a greedy man. I am just someone who wants what should have been his by right, not by your stupid law."

"Do not do this," pleaded Magistrate Zhu. "Whatever Tea Inspector Fang's crimes towards your family, I am sure compensation can be awarded."

"Compensation?" The young man laughed harshly. "His blood is my compensation. Blood is all I have ever wanted. Be my witness, Magistrate, and then I may let you go free."

But Magistrate Zhu ignored these last words, and addressed himself to Tea Inspector Fang, knowing in that moment all hope was lost. "Forgive me, Tea Inspector Fang – I have failed you."

Tea Inspector Fang showed no signs of hearing him, his head now bowed, his spirit surrendered to the inevitable. The deformed man raised his knife one more time, and Magistrate Zhu saw what was to come, the spurting of blood, Tea Inspector Fang's body tossed into the river, the family Fang forever having to bear the shame of a body not to be recovered.

Magistrate Zhu threw himself forward to grapple with the young man, to try to wrest the knife from him. So unexpected was this movement, the deformed man backed away, lost his footing and slipped to the ground, the knife spinning away out of his grasp to the ground. Magistrate Zhu pounced on it, his only hope before the deformed man and his bandit cohorts could recover their senses. But he had lost it somewhere in the dark, and when he looked up, bending over him with a short-sword was another of the bandits, murder in his eyes.

～

"Father, do not let him die!" she screamed inside.

A breeze suddenly touched her face. The moon appeared from behind the clouds casting a silvery radiance all around, giving depth and perspective where there had been none before, seemingly evaporating the mist with its light touch. The scene had changed. The knife was no longer at his neck, but Magistrate Zhu was on the ground, a bandit above him, sword raised to deliver a death blow.

This time she did not hesitate. This time she loosed her arrow, and then another, and then another, until the soldiers pushed past her, knocking her off balance, obscuring the view before her. Moonlight glinted off their swords and they entered the fray, whooping and shouting.

Then the Deng brothers rushed past her, and Sergeant Kang too. She wanted to follow them, to make sure *he* still lived, that her arrows had found their targets. But her energy, her *qi*, was totally spent now. She could not move. She dropped her bow to the ground and held her head in her hands, feeling that all of Heaven was spinning about her.

~

T he bandit standing above him was thrown backwards, an arrow impaled in his throat, sword lost, flying through the air. Then another arrow flew, and another bandit fell backwards, and another and another, until there were great cries all around and screams of panic and death. Overcome with all that happened about him, never having seen so much anguish and blood, Magistrate Zhu tore his eyes from the dead and the dying just in time to see Tea Inspector Fang topple forward – his bandit guards either dead or running – and fall toward the river. Magistrate Zhu reached out to him, unsteady himself on the slick trail, and pulled him away from danger.

Then, holding on to Tea Inspector Fang for all he was worth, Magistrate Zhu looked down the trail to see who had been his salvation. He saw soldiers, and his constables, and, in the light cast by the silvery half-moon breaking once more through the mist, he saw her. She was staring at him, the moonlight illuminating her face – a vision of determination and supernatural beauty, if ever there was one. Then she was gone, the mists swallowing her up.

"Ah, Magistrate, so you're still with us then?" asked Sergeant Kang. "So which one's Scary Face Fu?"

Magistrate Zhu, in shock, his throat dry, astonished by what *she* had done, looked around. Among the dead and the dying he couldn't see the deformed young man. He released the trussed Tea Inspector Fang into the care of Horse, who smiled at him, relieved. Magistrate Zhu walked up the trail with Sergeant Kang, looking into the faces of those bandits who had been captured. He did not see Scary Face Fu.

"Scary Face Fu is escaped," he said, softly, though his mind was truly on Jade Moon, who had come for him, who had rescued him, who had saved him for no reason at all.

"Ah, well – he won't last long in the forests here on his own," muttered Sergeant Kang. "Hunters will bring him in, or perhaps the Tibetans will find his rotting bones."

Magistrate Zhu once more sat down on the large rock. He glanced down the trail. She was gone. Only the militia soldiers and his constables remained. He shivered from the cold, or was it the shock of sudden violence? A she-wolf, Second Son Zhou had called her among other things. Yes, he had seen that just now in her eyes. But he had seen more; a whole life-time's more. In that moment he had known that his atonement still awaited him, that the rescue of Tea Inspector Fang was not it. Heaven had brought him here for another reason – to right a terrible wrong.

CHAPTER 50

"*T*rainee Legal Secretary Li, what are you writing?" asked Fast Deng.

The twins took their seats around the small table in the jail-room, quickly followed by Little Ox and Leaf. Little Ox seemed to all to be recovered from his battle with the bandits in Madame Wu's house, though he still would not speak of it. He would only speak about what the Magistrate had done, as if the events of that particular night had wiped away all that had happened before. Leaf was as he always had been, excited to be in the midst of great and important times.

Trainee Legal Secretary Li placed his ink-brush down on the table and gathered his papers together, very glad of the interruption. He, for one, had found the Deng brothers to be not as bad as he had been led to believe. He saw in them much potential for education – especially in the arts of reading and writing. He was determined, when the opportunity presented itself, to speak to the Magistrate about this. Surely to have constables who could read, write *and* keep the peace was an ambition worth achieving? Though Schoolmaster Chu's patience had been sorely tested by the twins, it was probable he had not tried to teach them as hard as he might.

He even found he enjoyed the company of the constables, and the atmosphere of the jail-room not as oppressive as he had once thought. This was especially so this morning, when the Magistrate had taken to sitting in the garden and was not in the mood to talk.

"I am writing a Recollection of Facts, young Constables," said Trainee Legal Secretary Li. "The Magistrate has charged me with this task so when he comes to consider the sequence of events, and where to apportion blame or praise, he can do so at his leisure."

"Ah," said Fast Deng, impressed.

"And do we figure strongly in this Recollection of Facts?" asked Slow Deng.

"Oh, yes, I have recorded all of our names – where we were and what we did – and even have from Sergeant Kang a full roll-call of the Fifth District militia for last night: who was on duty, who was not on duty but should have been, who was drunk on duty, who was not fit enough to run up the trail after the bandits, who nearly fell in the river and was just rescued in the nick of time, and so on and so on. The Imperial Army does have its faults, as we all know, but they do like to keep accurate records."

"And you've put in your Recollection of Facts all about Jade Moon?" asked Fast Deng.

"And how she did for the bandits with her arrows?" asked Slow Deng.

"And how we chased the remaining bandits up the trail until the mist got so thick we had to give up?"

"And how Horse carried the Tea Inspector Fang back to town?"

"And how Little Ox led Jade Moon back to her house and got an earful from her mother for his trouble?"

"And how, if Scary Face Fu and those bastard bandits come back, we will kill them all and chop up their bodies and feed them to the crows?"

The last question had been posed by Leaf, whom Trainee Legal Secretary Li was a mite wary of. For a very young boy, he seemed to relish the violence more than was natural. Not that the constables seemed to notice. Even Little Ox was forced to raise a smile by Leaf's uncouth language and uncommon exuberance.

"Yes, yes, I have included all that is necessary, Constables. But there is still some I have to write," said Trainee Legal Secretary Li. "But I find my calligraphy this morning is not what it should be, that my nerves are still....exhilarated and raw."

All the constables nodded, knowing exactly what the clerk meant. There had hardly ever been a night like it in the long and somewhat obscure history of Tranquil Mountain – a night that would be discussed and argued about for many months and many years to come.

"Trainee Legal Secretary Li, is it right to include what the Magistrate said to Horse?"

The question had come from Little Ox. When the Magistrate had learned that it had been Horse who had broken into the storeroom, given Jade Moon her bow and arrows, and thereby endangered her life in what Magistrate Zhu termed, '*the most foolish and irresponsible escapade I have ever heard of*', he had shouted awful abuse at Horse. And then, as if finding himself again a few moments later, the Magistrate had apologised, and commended Horse for his good sense. Horse had been left with the impression that he had done right and wrong at the same time.

Horse was now with Sergeant Kang at the barracks, where the few prisoners from the night's work had been taken, inspecting at the Magistrate's behest the condition in which they were being held. As they were to be transported to Chengdu sooner rather than later, and as the Magistrate's mood after his rescue had been more difficult to judge than usual, Sergeant Kang had taken it upon himself to look after the prisoners. The prisoners, hardly older than the constables, thought this a kindness. They feared summary execution at the hands of Magistrate Zhu for being present at, if not accessories to, his attempted murder – their uneducated minds having no appreciation for Magistrate Zhu's commitment to the administration of the law.

Trainee Legal Secretary Li thought carefully for a moment about Little Ox's most incisive and pertinent question. He did not know how much he should impart to the impressionable minds of the young constables, about the subtle art of writing reports. But he finally decided, as part of their education, that it was a day for truth.

"Constables, even though I am writing a Recollection of Facts, you should understand that there are some facts it is wise not to have recollected. In reading about themselves, officials expect to see that they have, at all times, exhibited a most reasonable and generous attitude...regardless of the provocation. Similarly, I will not record that young Leaf here was out late at night against the standing orders of the Magistrate, when he should have been safe in bed in the Always Smiling Orphanage, and how he should certainly not have been found kicking and verbally abusing the bodies of the dead bandits."

Trainee Legal Secretary Li said this last with a smile. It was true he was unsure of the boy's mental harmony, but there was no doubting that Leaf had gained great distinction that night, especially in the swift relaying of the message to Madame Kong of the most magnificent rescue of Tea Inspector Fang.

"So, young constables, it is always best to be selective when committing words to paper," continued Trainee Legal Secretary Li. "Horse does figure strongly in my Recollection of Facts but only as a constable who sought to do his duty. I will attach an addendum – an additional section – for the Magistrate also to consider. I will report the people now regard Horse not only as a young man of great initiative, but also a young man of exceptional common sense. I will see to it that the Magistrate considers this addendum most carefully. In fact, if necessary, I will read it out to him, again and again."

Little Ox was satisfied. There were smiles all round the table. Even Madame Wu's food that morning had tasted better than usual.

"I think there will be rewards," added Trainee Legal Secretary Li.

"Cash?" inquired Fast Deng, his eyes lighting up.

"How much?" asked Slow Deng, looking to his brother, thinking of Madame Kong's maids. He was sure both Peach and Pearl would be impressed with a gift or two.

"Well, there is an official scale of reward for the killing and capture of bandits...a quite generous scale, I can tell you," replied Trainee Legal Secretary Li. "But who can put a price on the rescue of a government official and a magistrate from certain death? I have never heard of such a thing. And then there is Jade Moon. How can she be seen to be rewarded when the Magistrate is still to rule on her contract to join the Family Zhou as concubine? There is quite a mess for the Magistrate to sort out.

"But, young Constables, there is more to rewards than simple cash. I will demonstrate this by the telling of a personal story. This very morning I went to call on Senior Scribe Xu, to brief him on all that has happened...just so the appropriate paperwork can be commenced in the August Hall of Historical Records. As I was returning across the market-square I happened to bump into Madame Xi, the match-maker, quite by chance. Now I have been considering for myself the advantages and disadvantages of marriage, and I spoke to her of this again. And do you know what she said to me?"

The constables shook their heads, hardly able to breathe, not wanting Trainee Legal Secretary Li to stop or become distracted from his fine story.

"Well, Madame Xi said: 'Trainee Legal Secretary Li, you have made a most auspicious move to work with Magistrate Zhu. Many eyes...many pretty eyes are upon you. And though your salary has not changed...which is always a factor, I am afraid...I can say, with complete conviction, that I can arrange a most perfect marriage for you when you are ready. And you should tell those constables to come see me too. I have already taken the names of ten fathers each interested in securing Horse as a son-in-law...and all this before sun-up!'"

In speaking the words of Madame Xi, who, by virtue of her profession, was very well known around town, Trainee Legal Secretary Li had cleverly and amusingly emulated the high pitch and speed of delivery of her words. Leaf almost fell off his stool with laughter. But the other constables, even Little Ox, were just as impressed with the meaning of the words.

"We were considering the maids," said Fast Deng.

"Yes, Madame Kong's very pretty maids," added Slow Deng.

Trainee Legal Secretary Li nodded, understanding, but thinking he should warn the Deng brothers of how things were. "Then you should both tread very carefully. Madame Kong does not like her maids to be married – for married women tend to be the most abusive of men, even if they are paying customers. If Madame Kong discovers your interest she may well obstruct your progress, or even send the maids back to Chengdu where she found them. If you are certain of this path then you must concoct the cleverest of plans, perhaps even save enough cash to offer Madame Kong compensation."

Fast Deng and Slow Deng looked at each other, very glad that Trainee Legal Secretary was now working with them in the jail and able to offer so much wisdom but dismayed at the same time about how complicated life was.

"You could dress up as bandits, and pretend to kidnap them," said Leaf, unhelpfully.

"It is best I don't write that down either," said Trainee Legal Secretary Li, smiling.

CHAPTER 51

MORNING, 25TH DAY OF THE 1ST MOON

*T*wo days had gone by since her daughter had vanished in the middle of the night. Two days had gone by since she had woken shivering from a bad dream, finding Jade Moon missing and the door to the house swinging on its latch. Two days since she had run out into the street, finding it empty of people, not knowing which way Jade Moon had gone.

Then, in the middle of the street, she had fallen to her knees, and prayed to the spirit of her dead husband – the first and only time – to keep her daughter safe. After all, as she vehemently reminded him, Jade Moon had been always more his than hers.

Hours had gone by. Madame Tang had never known such a vigil, had never known she could cry so much, suffer so much. But her prayers had finally been answered in the hour before dawn. Little Ox had brought her home, though a different girl, and Madame Tang had called Little Ox the most terrible names she could think of.

Jade Moon had collapsed into her arms. Madame Tang then had helped her to her bed. In all the commotion Golden Orchid had awoken, and not wanting the young girl to think or to hesitate, Madame Tang had ordered her to prepare tea on the instant. "Hurry up child, can't you see my daughter is in trouble!"

Madame Tang had covered Jade Moon, still fully clothed, with a quilt, and held her, trying to stop her shivering. Jade Moon spoke then, just once and had not done so since.

"Mother, I had to – I could not let him die."

Madame Tang had lifted Jade Moon's head so she could sip the scalding tea slowly, and stroked her forehead gently until she had drifted off into a troubled sleep.

Physician Ji had arrived before the dawn without needing to be summoned. He quickly went to Jade Moon's bedside, made a cursory examination, gently taking each wrist and listening to her pulses, and then nodded, satisfied, not wanting to disturb her sleep further.

"Madame Tang, I will return later in the morning with some medicine. She should sleep now. Make sure there are no loud noises in the house, and the people do not bother her."

Madame Tang wrung her hands. "Physician Ji, what has she done? What has been done to her?"

"Madame Tang, I cannot properly say for I was not there. But some of the soldiers tell me they have witnessed a miracle of archery: arrows shot on bad and rising ground, at distance and through the mist. They spoke of a moon breaking through the clouds when it was needed, of the Magistrate and Tea Inspector Fang rescued from certain death, and of bandits defeated, killed or sent fleeing into the mountains. The soldiers say, without a doubt, she is a heroine reborn. Perhaps this is true, Madame Tang – perhaps this is true."

After daybreak people began coming to the door. Furious, Madame Tang thought to give them the full force of her tongue. But these people, often people she did not know, bowed to her, left gifts of food and clothing and cheap jewellery, and above all kept a respectful silence. Madame Tang, for once, kept her mouth shut.

Madame Kong came at midday. She embraced Madame Tang as if she were a sister and not just a friend.

"Madame Tang, I cannot speak what I feel. But Jade Moon has returned to me Tea Inspector Fang, who even now recovers from his ordeal."

Madame Tang then took Madame Kong into the backroom, where Golden Orchid was sitting patiently next to Jade Moon's bed, watching her sleep.

"I know she is difficult, Madame Tang," said Madame Kong, in a whisper, "and she has caused you great trouble and many worries these last years, and does not always conduct herself as a young woman should. But you should know that to me she is beloved, and the daughter I have never had. Chef Mo is preparing food for you, so you will not have to cook these next few days."

Madame Kong then held up a small lacquered box. She opened the lid for Madame Tang to see its contents. Within lay a delicate pendant on a fine gold chain, made of the finest jade. Madame Tang gasped, understanding its great value.

"It is not an adequate compensation for what she has done," said Madame Kong. "Who can put a price on what has been returned to me? But it will suit her complexion and her great spirit. It was a gift to me from Tea Inspector Fang, never worn. I do not know where he got it. The pendant is ancient, I think. The carving on the jade is of two great dragons, intertwined. I was never comfortable with the fierce spirit that resides within it. I now know why. It was never meant for me. It is for her. She should wear it when she is summoned to the Temple, to hear the

Magistrate's ruling on her future. It will give her extra courage, and maybe give the hateful Family Zhou pause for thought."

Eventually, much later in that first day, Jade Moon woke up, and took some of Chef Mo's food. Physician Ji came and examined her again, and again later in the night, both times telling Madame Tang there was nothing to be concerned about.

"But Physician Ji, she does not speak!" hissed Madame Tang, concerned.

"Do not worry, Madame Tang – she will speak when she is ready. And do not forget there are many in town ready to speak for her. Do you know that Senior Scribe Xu is in possession of a great petition, which he is soon to hand over to the Magistrate?"

The next morning Madame Tang found out more. The kind and gentle and elegant and always compassionate Senior Scribe Xu came to call.

"Oh, Senior Scribe Xu, I am so worried. She still does not speak!"

Jade Moon would not leave the backroom, even though she was awake. She continued with the sewing of the constables' uniforms as if nothing untoward had happened.

Senior Scribe Xu had consoled her, saying: "Madame Tang, she will recover. And you must not worry about the future. It is true no one knows the law as well as Magistrate Zhu, and that he is a stickler for detail and procedure, but even he cannot but be moved by what she has done this time. The people are in awe of her. Surely that has to mean something."

Later that day, the second day, Jade Moon still would not speak, even though Madame Tang had gone to her, pinched her quite roughly, and spoken to her as you would a naughty child. Jade Moon did not respond or complain, but merely slapped her mother's hand away. Exasperated, Madame Tang concentrated on teaching more stitches that Golden Orchid could practise and sew, and was more than happy to be disturbed when Madame Deng came to call.

"Well, Madame Tang," said Madame Deng, "isn't it all a to-do? Some of the people are even saying kind things about my twin sons, who have become fine constables. Though I should inform you I have exchanged terrible words with your other friend, Madame Kong. I've told her to keep those grasping maids of hers away from my boys. A maid sees a constable as a fine catch, or so I have been told. Anyway, what I came to tell you was this: Sensible Zhou, elder brother to that monster Second Son Zhou, was overheard speaking to a worker in the Zhou tea gardens. He was quite overwrought. He said that if Jade Moon was now forced into the Zhou house, and taken to Second Son Zhou's bed then the Family Zhou would deserve to be swept up in a great whirlwind of destruction by the wrath of Heaven. Now, Madame Tang, what do you make of that?"

CHAPTER 52

"*M*agistrate, come in! Come in! Please sit with me. Eat if you wish. There is plenty of food. Chef Mo insists I recover my strength. Hardly an hour goes by without him putting another food tray in front of me."

Tea Inspector Fang was finally out of bed. He was sitting at a table in one of Madame Kong's private rooms in the Inn of Perpetual Happiness. Trays of food were laid before him. The aromas were intense, inviting. But Magistrate Zhu was not there to sample the food. He was there because of the man. He took a seat at the table, considering Tea Inspector Fang's appearance.

"Ah, don't look so alarmed, Magistrate. Physician Ji has pronounced me well on the road to recovery."

This was true to a point. However, Physician Ji had spoken to Magistrate Zhu, in confidence, saying: "The cuts are healing, the swelling is lessening, and the bruising will fade with time – but the man inside is not the same."

Magistrate Zhu could see for himself that this was true. Ignoring the brave words, before him sat a haunted, distracted man. Torture and kidnap would do that, supposed Magistrate Zhu, but he suspected a much deeper, much more personal problem.

"I am glad you are looking so well, Tea Inspector Fang. Please send me away though if I am disturbing the harmony of your meal."

"Nonsense, Magistrate – I am glad you have come. Both Madame Kong and Chef Mo tend to fuss. I could do with some sensible conversation."

"I came to apologise."

"Whatever for? Surely I should apologise to you, Magistrate, for causing you so much bother."

"I should have prevented your kidnap."

Tea Inspector Fang laughed, filling the small room with his voice. "How? Bandits come and go with the seasons. In China they are a fact of life."

Magistrate Zhu nodded at the truth of this. He chose not to reveal the connection he was already aware of between Tea Inspector Fang and these bandits, that the youth with the deformed face had been using the alias 'The Ghost of Scary Face Fu' – a name, in part, that should be known to Tea Inspector Fang through his old competitor Tea Merchant Wen. Everything pointed to the fact that this kidnap was much more than it seemed. The rage on the deformed youth's face had been personal. Was Tea Merchant Wen still alive, pulling the strings of these bandits in the background somewhere? Had Tea Inspector Fang offended this youth somehow in the past? Or was there something else going on, something as yet unseen?

"Please tell me what happened that night." Magistrate Zhu's question was quietly spoken but firmly put.

"Magistrate…I would rather forget."

"It is necessary – the Bian brothers?"

"My guards? Murdered, I think – their bodies tossed into the river. I cannot rightly say. I was returning to this inn late, after a night's carousing. I was knocked on the head. Next I awoke in the forest, bound hand and foot."

"Why did they beat you so badly?"

"Ah, you should know by now, Magistrate – tea inspectors are not the most well-loved men in China."

"Who was the youth with the deformed face?"

Tea Inspector Fang sighed. He put down his spoon and pushed his food tray away from him. "I do not know. He did not give his name."

"He wished you dead."

"So do many, Magistrate."

"The ransom was in my view immaterial – a bonus perhaps."

"Bandits always want cash or food, Magistrate."

"He wanted a witness to your murder."

"Ah – how strange. But when you came for me, Magistrate, I was no longer myself. I had not eaten or drunk any water, and my eyes and ears were swollen shut from the beatings."

"Does the name 'Scary Face Fu' mean anything to you? The youth with the deformed face used it."

Tea Inspector Fang refused to meet his gaze. "Should it? An odd name to be sure. But you know how it is with bandits; they give themselves these names to puff themselves up and to frighten old women and children."

Magistrate Zhu smiled and nodded in agreement, reflecting on the lie he had just been told. That path of enquiry would have to wait. He did not want to push the tea inspector, not yet. And there were other paths to try.

"I believe the bandits had help."

Tea Inspector Fang pondered this for some time. "Do you have proof?"

"No – suspicions only. I am certain the same bandits murdered the old man, Mister Gong. That killing took place not far from the Sun residence."

"Ah – but Magistrate this is China. Murders are not so uncommon."

"Before he died, Mister Gong spoke the name 'Scary Face Fu'."

For the first time Tea Inspector Fang looked truly shaken. "Magistrate, I had not heard that. I pay very little attention to local gossip. My mind is always on tea and how little I can pay the Patriarchs for it."

"I am interested in Patriarch Sun."

"Don't be, Magistrate. You will not profit by such interest. The Patriarchs have many faults, I can tell you – but they are clever men. They do not need to consort with bandits. Oh, I am sure they would like to be rid of me...but kidnap and murder...no, I don't think so."

"They have many fears, about the tea, about the Agency."

Tea Inspector Fang looked pensive. He touched his hand to his face, feeling the bumps and bruises. "Forget Patriarch Sun – you will find no proof there."

Magistrate Zhu did not disagree. He had already concluded that Patriarch Sun – even if guilty – would be hard to snare. The few bandits captured alive had confessed only to loitering in the woods. They had said they had known nothing other than a bad official was to be kidnapped, had never been to Tranquil Mountain before the taking of Tea Inspector Fang, and that they didn't know the true name of the deformed youth, who they admitted only as their chief. To them he was simply, 'The Ghost'. He was clever, they said – a born leader. They were simple youths, from Chengdu, and had been intent only on quick riches. They had explained only that on the night of the kidnap, 'The Ghost' had left them and gone into town as he had done before, only to return before dawn, pushing a trussed up Tea Inspector Fang in front of him. That had been the extent of their confessions. Truth or lies, who could tell? But the confessions had been made separately, and were, in most details, consistent – and to Magistrate Zhu's mind, quite believable. Nothing had been said to incriminate Patriarch Sun or any of his men.

"Some of the bandits are unaccounted for, Tea Inspector. The youth with the deformed face was not recovered. Your life could well be still in danger."

Tea Inspector Fang shook his head. "I do not think so, Magistrate. Bandits would be foolish to try again so soon. They are more likely away to the mountains, or to have scurried off back to Chengdu. Tibetans may find them begging for food on the trails and bring them in. And, don't worry, I will purchase better guards. The Bian brothers were dreadful, but cheap. I have only myself to blame."

The last was said with some emotion. It was the first truth about the kidnap that Tea Inspector Fang had spoken, thought Magistrate Zhu. He rose out of his chair. "You are tired, I will leave you now."

Tea Inspector Fang suddenly stood up and reached out and took his hand, shocking Magistrate Zhu somewhat. He tried to pull away but Tea Inspector Fang held him tight.

"Magistrate, I understand what you did in coming for me. Few would have done the same – not even my own family. I would like us to be friends. I do not make friends easily, and men such as us – men of power and influence – should be friends."

His hand no longer his own, Magistrate Zhu replied: "Yes, I would like that."

"And if there is any favour you would ask of me – anything – then please ask it. Whatever you need, it is yours."

Magistrate Zhu saw the offer was genuine, and heartfelt. Despite the lies and the rough bravado, Magistrate Zhu felt warmth and compassion for him. Regardless of what was to come, Magistrate Zhu understood that the kidnap and near brush with death would make Tea Inspector Fang a better man.

"Tea Inspector, there is one favour I would ask of you, though you must bear with me, for the favour is not so simple."

"Ah, Magistrate – with you, I would not expect otherwise."

CHAPTER 53

"*If we cast aside the law, then we may as well collapse our own houses and live in tents – for we would be no better than barbarians.*"

So had said Judge Pei, the wisest man Magistrate Zhu had ever known. And he did not disagree, for without the law, there would be chaos. The law was for the protection of all. To ignore the law, to do as everyone wanted him to do, to tear up Madame Tang's contract as if it had never existed, would create such a terrible precedent the ramifications of which could not be overstated. Even in the afterlife, the spirits of all the great judges and magistrates who had gone before him would raise great howls of protest, and rend their official robes in grief and shame at what he had done.

In breaking into the storeroom to retrieve Jade Moon's confiscated bow and arrows, Horse had stepped beyond the law and had been proved to be right. But Heaven loves, Magistrate Zhu thought, a guileless man – and there was no one more guileless than Horse. But he himself was different. He was educated, literate, and a magistrate, and in possession of a troubled conscience. He could not so easily step beyond the law. He was no hero, no instrument of Heaven. For him to ignore the law, which was his tool, would be to run counter to his very nature – and would invoke the severest of penalties.

But still he could not ignore the fullness of the mystery that threatened to envelop him: the unexpected and unlooked for relationship that had been formed in this remote district by Heaven, that had been made not by the deadly flight of the arrows that saved his life – as most would think – but in the instant that Madame Kong and Madame Tang bowed low in his office, and Jade Moon, left standing, had locked her eyes with his. In that instant, all law, all education, all learning, all memory, all earthly morality had been forgotten – had indeed become irrelevant. For him then, in that instant, Heaven and Earth had joined. How could he afford to ignore that?

But also how could he ignore that he was Chinese, an aristocrat, and of a family of the greatest lineage, and she just a commoner, a seamstress – and, worst of all, of barbarian blood? It did not make sense. Why would Heaven create such a connection, such a relationship? What was his duty now towards her because of that relationship? And how could he perform that duty without coming into conflict with the law?

There was no doubt in his mind that he had a debt of blood to Jade Moon – as did the whole of Tranquil Mountain and the Fifth District. But in his heart he knew Heaven required more from him. The mystery of that instant connection to her, that duty that went beyond the usual definitions of law, had to be honoured. He was sure that would be how Sheriff Min would advise him. And what—

"Magistrate?"

He looked up. Horse was there before him, bowing deeply. "Yes, what is it, Senior Constable?"

"Magistrate, I am about to go out on patrol with Constable Wu. Is there anything you need before we leave the jail? Constables Deng and Deng should return from their patrol within the hour."

Magistrate Zhu shook his head. He had drunk more than enough tea that evening, trying to fortify himself for the judgement that needed to be written. Horse nodded, and bowed again. He was almost out through the door when Magistrate Zhu called after him.

"Senior Constable!"

"Yes, Magistrate?"

"Thank you."

"For what, Magistrate?"

"For everything."

CHAPTER 54

"*M*agistrate Zhu, surely there is some obscure legal reference you can find, some clever solution."

"Senior Scribe Xu, I have reviewed the written contract. You prepared it yourself. Every term is clear. It is quite correct in law. What am I to do? Invent some nonsense to please the people? And what would happen if I did this? Patriarch Zhou would appeal to a higher court in Chengdu, perhaps even Prefect Kang himself, and my erroneous decision would be overturned and I would be labelled an idiot...which I am not. Every trader in this district, and maybe many other districts too, would ask me to tear up their own contracts because for whatever reason they have decided not to pay up or honour them. There are some in China who do business on just a handshake. How can a written contract be worth less than this?"

"But Magistrate—"

"Does Patriarch Zhou wish to rescind the contract, or negotiate a variation in the terms?"

"No, Magistrate, he is stubborn, he will not consider—"

"Then there is nothing to be done. The contract is simple...straight-forward. Magistrate Qian should have made a judgement on it years ago."

Senior Scribe Xu had slunk away, a picture of misery. Magistrate Zhu had glanced up at Horse then.

"Well?" he asked, angry with the insolent look on Horse's face.

"I have nothing to say, Magistrate."

"Senior Constable, she could be the daughter of the Jade Emperor himself – it does not make a difference! A contract is a contract!"

Then, a short while later, Senior Scribe Xu had returned to the jail. He had a whole posse of clerks in tow, and carried in his hands a piece of paper with many, many names on it. It was a petition, though not in any legal sense.

"M-Magistrate Zhu," Senior Scribe Xu began, his voice tremulous, "these people, listed here, are all of the same opinion."

"Is any of them a magistrate?"

The question caught Senior Scribe Xu off guard. He became confused and began to study the paper and the names written upon it, much to Magistrate Zhu's fury and frustration. Fortunately Trainee Legal Secretary Li was present, and much more attuned to Magistrate Zhu's recent moods. He was able to curtail the increasingly embarrassing moment with a few choice words.

"I believe there is only one magistrate in this district, Magistrate Zhu. And I do not remember you putting your name on such a paper."

Senior Scribe Xu and the clerks all filed out of his office quickly, though unhappily. It was then left up to Trainee Legal Secretary Li to instruct Magistrate Zhu on the proper procedure for the reading of judgements in the Fifth District.

"Magistrate, when it is time, and when you are ready, I will go to the Temple and confer with Head Priest Lü. He will open the Temple to the people. The evening was Magistrate Qian's preferred time, but may I suggest, to avoid drunkenness and trouble, this one occasion you read your judgement at midday."

"Agreed."

"Ah, I am so relieved, Magistrate. When the people have gathered...oh, and don't be concerned by the number of barbarians and their wives and children as they do like a good spectacle...you will enter, walk through a gap in the people sprawled all over the floor and take your seat upon the dais. Senior Scribe Xu will be seated nearby, as will I, to take notes. The Patriarchs will be seated at the front in great chairs, in places of honour." Trainee Legal Secretary Li paused. "Have you ever spoken in public, Magistrate? I know this tradition of public courts is considered even in Chengdu to be most bizarre."

"I have spoken in front of large groups...but groups of scholars, not the common people."

"Ah."

Trainee Legal Secretary Li considered this, thinking there should be not too much difference. In the past, he had read somewhere of fighting and awful slander between scholars. But the Magistrate was looking most nervous – he had surely not got over the closeness of death of a few nights before – and Trainee Legal Secretary Li thought it best to assuage his concerns.

"Magistrate, the constables will not leave your side. I have also been in communication with Sergeant Kang...to arrange additional security, you understand."

Magistrate Zhu nodded, smiling, more than pleased with this. "That is most considerate of you. But the soldiers should stand well back. They should preferably be outside of the Temple. The people must not feel oppressed by the law that I read to them. Instead they must believe that they are the beneficiaries of that law. The correctness of law should not have to be confirmed by the threat of arms."

"Ah, I am sure they will not be confused by your words, Magistrate. But, I asked Sergeant Kang to come to speak to you today so it will be clear in his mind what you expect of him."

"Trainee Legal Secretary Li, I am pleased...more than pleased."

Not that Sergeant Kang had any intention of listening to what Magistrate Zhu had to say about the ongoing, unhappy, distrustful, and troubled relationship between the Imperial Army and the people in China, or of the security arrangements required for the Temple. Sergeant Kang had gone into the garden, where Magistrate Zhu had been sitting at peace, had collapsed onto a chair without even a bow, and had proceeded, quite rudely and without invite, to revisit the events of a few nights before.

"Magistrate, I am forty years old...maybe forty-one or forty-two, I am not sure...but I can tell you now that in all my years of soldiering I have never seen anything like that girl, Jade Moon. And I have seen some incredible things."

"Her name is Miss Tang."

"Certainly, Magistrate. Now it is true there are some strange girls in the world, and there are wives and mistresses who follow armies to do the cooking and cleaning...in addition to all the slave women. It is true also that occasionally a girl will dress up like a man, and pretend to be a soldier. And I can tell you there are men who dress up as women to escape from being a soldier – but that is a different matter entirely. But Magistrate, you should know I have never seen anything like what I saw the other night...not even in the great southern forests. She flew up the trail after you like an avenging demoness. Ah, even the great sages would have stepped aside and let her through. Even Soldier Du, my fastest man, couldn't keep up with her. And she let fly her arrows uphill, at more than a hundred and twenty paces...in the fog, Magistrate, and in the dark! Not one arrow missed its target. Not one. And when Horse and I caught up with her we saw a wildness in her eyes, the like of which I have never seen in any woman...and never want to see again. It chilled my blood. She is no ordinary girl – and deserving, I think, of some extraordinary consideration."

Sergeant Kang scratched at his whiskers, feeling suddenly thirsty, wondering when he was going to be served something to drink. Little Ox had not even come running with some tea. He couldn't remember when he had said so many words at one time, the brains of his young soldiers preferring shorter, sharper sentences. He hoped he had said enough. Horse had pleaded with him to intervene. As had many other people too.

But Magistrate Zhu did not respond. He merely looked away. Sergeant Kang, uncomfortable always in the presence of authority – even civilian authority – decided not to out-stay his welcome. He got out of the chair, made a half-attempt at a shallow bow and returned to the safety of the jail-room.

The constables surrounded him and many of his own militia too. "Well, I certainly told him what was what," Sergeant Kang told them all.

But Horse wasn't fooled, and walked away, out of the jail, unhappy. Sergeant Kang did not bother to follow him, or make excuses. What else could be done?

Back in the garden, with the sun already sinking behind the mountains, the day of the reading of the judgement soon to come, Magistrate Zhu did not move. He was as fixed in his seat as he was in his mind.

The law was the law. And he for one – after all the mistakes he had made in the past and with the greatest respect to the memory of Judge Pei – was not going to cast it to one side.

CHAPTER 55

*T*rainee Legal Secretary Li believed that fortune was shining upon him, and most unexpectedly.

Not allowed to pursue his clerical career in Chengdu as he had wished, his father had sent him to the Fifth District. And then, again against his wishes, Senior Scribe Xu had done nothing to prevent his recruitment by Magistrate Zhu to be a legal secretary. Many of the other clerks had sympathised, saying that life surely could be cruel, to have to work in a smelly and musty jail, and be surrounded by constables who were not yet men, who could hardly dress themselves, and who could hardly read and write.

And that was not the half of it.

"I fear for you, Trainee Legal Secretary Li," said one of the other young clerks. "Magistrate Zhu has an inconsistent temper. Your days will be very stressful indeed."

Which was true.

That very morning Magistrate Zhu had sought to criticise his calligraphy, even though it was close to perfection, and his punctuality, even though he had arrived at the jail well before dawn, and even the poor state of his robes, though his tattered robes were, for a clerk, the norm and a genuine reflection of his poor salary.

"Trainee Legal Secretary Li, don't you realise we will be before all the people today…in the Temple? You must consider how you are to be perceived!"

Later, more than insightful, Horse had said, grimly and without humour: "His conscience is troubling him."

Madame Xi, the match-maker, had then visited the jail, and said: "Take my

243

advice, Trainee Legal Secretary Li, and attach your star to Magistrate Zhu. Things happen around that man, both good and bad. Look at what has happened here in town, in only the last few days; surely more than has happened in years. Not only will you attract a good wife, I am convinced you will never be bored."

Trainee Legal Secretary Li laughed, sitting in the Temple already at his desk next to the dais, remembering her words. Yes, it is a good thing never to be bored – a very good thing indeed.

He set out his writing materials, his ink-brush, his ink-stick, his ink-stone and water with which to prepare the ink, set sheets of fresh paper to one side, and waited patiently for the Magistrate to arrive.

The people had already gathered, and in great numbers. They filled the Temple, sprawling not only all over the great floor, but crammed into every nook and cranny. In fact so many people had left their houses, wanting to hear for themselves the fate of Jade Moon, not all could get into the Temple. To the consternation of the Temple priests, the people were trampling all over the garden, not minding if they sat on the rarest of mountain orchids or devastated great ornamental displays. Head Priest Lü was always asking for more people to attend the Temple but surely this was not quite what he had in mind.

The Patriarchs and their families were already in their seats of honour near to the dais. The constables, except for Horse, were standing before the dais, though looking opposite to most, out across the crowd, appearing to be terrified the people might rush them at any time. And Senior Scribe Xu was already on the dais, seated next to the Magistrate's chair, his expression troubled, supposedly there to offer instant advice on procedure. Not that – if the last few days were any proof of this – the Magistrate was one for taking advice, any advice at all.

Kneeling before the dais was Madame Tang, already in a state of distress, being offered comfort by Madame Kong. The people had given way, creating a great path in the Temple for them to walk down, a path that Madame Tang had barely stumbled down at the slowest of gaits, determined that the tragedy of her life was known to one and all.

"The Magistrate won't be impressed with that sort of scene," Trainee Legal Secretary Li had muttered to himself, hoping he was at last gaining some insight into the Magistrate's character.

But he was also sure the Magistrate could not fail to be impressed by what came next. For he certainly was. Jade Moon walked some distance behind her mother and Madame Kong, unassisted, head unbowed, tall and very, very proud. The people had looked on in silence, marking her progress. Her long skirts and blouse appeared new – a gift from Madame Kong? – the silk the colour of coral. Her hair had been put up for once and oiled, its deep blackness gleaming as it reflected all the light within the Temple, revealing a face of remarkably fine structure, upon which a slight dusting of rouge had been applied. And with her hair up and her blouse open wide at the neck, all the people looked for and could see a golden necklace, from which hung a most marvellous pendant made from the finest jade.

Even the Patriarchs were astonished, turning around in their seats. And when Jade Moon knelt down in front of the dais, just behind her mother and Madame

Kong, a great commotion arose among the people, and Trainee Legal Secretary Li heard not a few choice insults directed at Patriarch Zhou and Sensible Zhou – and, of course, that offspring of the unnatural coupling of a dog and a sow, Second Son Zhou.

Trainee Legal Secretary Li tested his ink and his ink-brush, taking up a piece of paper and writing: *We Chinese are a naturally calm, law-abiding and respectful people. But at certain times, under great provocation, great passions can arise within us and trouble can ensue.* He frowned, looking at what he had written, deciding not to continue that line of thought, not wishing to tempt fate.

Instead he wrote next: *It is said that there are off-shoots of the Imperial Family who have taken up residence in Chengdu. But in my years of living in that great city I never once saw an imperial princess. However today, in the remotest of districts and in the remotest of towns, I have seen genuine royalty, though of the most exotic and barbarian kind.*

He frowned again, thinking his words overblown. He decided it was not a good day for writing. His own emotions were getting the better of him. He put down his ink-brush and looked up, in time to see the Magistrate make his way through the people, with Horse at his side. He also noted the presence of Sergeant Kang, who took up station in the doorway, picking at his teeth, privately amused by the whole proceedings.

The Magistrate took his seat on the dais next to Senior Scribe Xu, and without once glancing at Jade Moon, or speaking any words of welcome to the people, or making a comment about the weather – as Magistrate Qian would always do – he unfurled a scroll, and coughed to clear his throat. And, with a face so white with nerves he looked like a ghost, he began to read.

Trainee Legal Secretary Li, pleased beyond measure to be present at this supreme locus of history – could it be described any other way? – took up his ink-brush enthusiastically, and began to make a full and accurate record of all that the Magistrate said.

"*Seven years ago Madame Tang came to this district and put her name to a contract with the noble family Zhou. The contract was written properly and witnessed correctly. The contract was signed without coercion and has been upheld by all the parties and the witnesses as a true document. The contract is therefore wholly lawful.*

"*The terms of the contract are very simple. Madame Tang was offered the lease of a house at a preferential rate where she could live and operate her business as a seamstress. She was also extended credit by the family Zhou so she could procure materials and tools for her trade. In exchange, Madame Tang was expected to deliver up her daughter, who was then twelve years old, to the family Zhou as a concubine. This was to happen on the child's seventeenth birthday.*

"*The contractual dispute has arisen because the child, whom I shall now refer to as Miss Tang, was not so delivered up. Instead, Madame Tang has argued, by way of petition, that her daughter is somehow no longer her daughter. She argues that since the day of the killing of the bandit Bad Teeth Tong, only shortly before Miss Tang's seventeenth birthday, a supernatural quality has descended upon her daughter – a quality she does not feel able to command or control. This quality, she says, can be attested to by many people. Because of this, because she now feels she cannot offend Heaven and send her daughter to be a concubine, she offers fifty strings of cash to the family Zhou in compensation and to fully discharge the terms of the contract.*

"The family Zhou have rejected this offer, and wish the original terms of the contract to be upheld – as is their right.

The Magistrate paused to get his breath. Trainee Legal Secretary Li massaged his wrist, finding it harder than he had guessed to write so quickly and still maintain the near-perfection of his calligraphy. However, he could hardly wait for the Magistrate to speak again, to discover what the Magistrate had decided should be the fate of Jade Moon. Wagers had being taken all over town. Most were gambling that if Jade Moon was forced to enter the Zhou residence, within a month a great storm would develop, lightning would strike its roof, and not one person inside would be recovered alive. Moreover the ghost of Second Son Zhou was expected then to wander the Earth, for all time, forever bemoaning its own stupidity.

Trainee Legal Secretary Li had refused to gamble, thinking his new post made such an act inappropriate. But only the evening before, late, in the drinking-room of the Inn of the Laughing Monk, where all the clerks – the ones allowed by their wives to go out – had gathered, he had said out loud, and to great applause: "Heroes and heroines are never of the people, but made for the people by Heaven! To interfere with the life of a hero or heroine is like grabbing hold of the tail of a tiger – to court the gravest of dangers. What sort of fool would do that?"

To which all the other clerks shouted out, in drunken glee: "Second Son Zhou!"

It was a very happy memory.

Magistrate Zhu coughed again, ready now to recommence the reading of his judgement.

"To illustrate my decision, I wish first to instruct you in my thinking by telling you all a story. A man owns but one rabbit. He then contracts with a noble family to provide them with this rabbit. The contract does not specify whether the rabbit is small or large, fat or skinny, black or brown, healthy or sick – just that this rabbit is to be provided to this noble family on a certain date. Now the evening before this day, the man is sitting down to dinner looking upon this rabbit, when the rabbit sits up and begins to talk, reciting the words of the sages themselves."

Laughter rang out across the hall. Trainee Legal Secretary Li was thankful for this, as the Magistrate was forced to pause, and he was able to rest his fingers. Slowly the people began to settle, but most kept smiles on their faces, desperate for the Magistrate to continue with his story. Trainee Legal Secretary Li noted Jade Moon also looked up, forgetting perhaps the story referred to her, no doubt also entranced by the Magistrate's fine words.

The Magistrate began again.

"The man with the rabbit is astonished. He believes himself now to be in possession of a magical rabbit. What should he do? He might think he has been especially favoured by Heaven to be in possession of such a magical rabbit. He might think he can obtain a far better price for this rabbit now he has found it to be magical. But is it right and fair that the noble family should be denied their

rabbit just because this rabbit now sits up and talks? Of course not. The contract has not been altered at all by the rabbit's new quality. This is because the contract was not specific as to the qualities of the rabbit that must be delivered up. Do you understand? It may be considered good fortune or bad fortune that this noble family is to be given a magical rabbit, but – and this must be emphasized – it is this noble family's choice whether they accept this magical rabbit into their household or not. And it is up to Heaven, in the fullness of years, as to whether this noble family will benefit or suffer through their choice.

"So the law is very clear, the contract for the rabbit must be performed."

"Similarly, whether Miss Tang has grown new qualities since the time of the signing of her mother's contract, and whether these qualities are supernatural or not, or granted by Heaven or not, is unimportant and legally irrelevant. It is wholly the choice of the family Zhou whether they still wish to accept Miss Tang as a concubine. They assure me that they still do.

"My decision is very simple and straight-forward then. Miss Tang is now to be delivered up forthwith to the family Zhou. She is to leave this court, go straight to the Zhou residence without further ado or complaint, and take up her concubinage as dictated in the contract."

There was an immediate buzz around the hall. Magistrate Zhu was forced to hold his hand up to silence the people. Trainee Legal Secretary Li made a note of this in the margin of his page, not knowing whether it should be recorded or not. He hoped further legal training would advise him in the future.

Magistrate Zhu continued.

"I also rule that Madame Tang should immediately pay the family Zhou compensation in the sum of twenty strings of cash for loss of two years of Miss Tang's concubinage."

Strangely, it was only then that Madame Tang cried out and fainted. She was quickly attended to by Madame Kong and several other women who were seated nearby.

Trainee Legal Secretary Li watched in awe as Jade Moon got up off the floor, standing tall, and stared at the Magistrate with incredible, fierce eyes, her face as hard as granite. She spoke then, her words sharp as a knife, edged with frustration and betrayal: "I am not a magical rabbit."

But the Magistrate looked only at his notes, making no motion or sign that he had heard anything at all.

Trainee Legal Secretary Li had no time to debate whether her words should be recorded also, for then a collective groan arose from the people in the Temple, horror and shock on the faces, as they belatedly realised the implication of the Magistrate's judgement. And Trainee Legal Secretary Li thought there was danger of a riot, when Patriarch Zhou and Second Son Zhou jumped up out of their seats clapping their great victory, paying little regard to how offensive their behaviour was or how they seemed to be the very opposite of what the noble born were supposed to be.

Only Sensible Zhou stayed in his seat, holding his head in his hands. The sooner he inherits the Zhou estate, the better for all, thought Trainee Legal Secretary Li.

Second Son Zhou took Jade Moon roughly by the arm. He dragged her unprotesting from the hall, seemingly oblivious to the jeers and the curses that were thrown his way. He was quickly followed by his father, Patriarch Zhou, holding his head high, and a most depressed-looking Sensible Zhou.

The Magistrate left the Temple quickly afterwards, accompanied by the grim-looking constables. Senior Scribe Xu also hurried after him, as if he had something important to discuss. Trainee Legal Secretary Li decided to do likewise, for the good of his own safety. The people were more than restless and unhappy, and Sergeant Kang had somehow contrived to disappear.

"Trainee Legal Secretary Li!"

He looked up from tidying his papers to see who had addressed him in such a forceful voice. It was Patriarch Yang, his old and wrinkled face very animated, eyes twinkling with excitement.

"Second Son Zhou will be dead before nightfall," said Patriarch Yang. "Write that in your stupid notes! Oh, and tell the Magistrate he can stay. Magistrate Qian was never as entertaining as this."

He then roared with laughter, and Patriarch Sun complimented him on his immaculate delivery and wit, before both left the Temple, apparently the best of friends.

"Oh, Huang Di, esteemed Yellow Emperor, creator of all that is civilised – you must preserve us all!" muttered Trainee Secretary Li, his paper and writing materials all gathered. He pushed his way through the mass of complaining people, out of the Temple, and out into the bright light of day.

CHAPTER 56

AFTERNOON, 27TH DAY OF THE 1ST MOON

"*H*orse, what are we going to do?" asked Fast Deng, anxiously glancing at the doorway, as if the barbarian horde itself was about to come pouring through.

His twin brother was just as worried. Only a short while before, a stone, thrown from the market-square, had bounced into the jail, and knocked his tea cup out of his hand. The cup had smashed into little pieces on the floor.

"Yeah, Horse, what are we going to do? We aren't going to survive the night at this rate. We'll all be thrown in the river and become fish-food. The Magistrate might have sent Jade Moon to the Zhou residence but he's as good as sent us all to hell."

Leaf was up for fighting – everybody and anybody. Little Ox had had to restrain him from racing out and chasing the stone-throwers down. Still, Horse mused, it would be something to do, and the people should not be allowed to throw stones at the jail or shout abuse. The people should be more respectful, regardless of their feelings; after all, to be a constable was to serve the people, and in a most honourable way. The people should recognise the difficult position in which they had been put.

Horse understood the people had good reason to be angry. They felt the Magistrate and the constables had let them down, and possibly consigned the whole of Tranquil Mountain to a terrible fate. Would not Heaven rain destruction down on them all for what had happened? Would the tea trees not all shrivel up and die, or White Dragon River run red with blood?

"Maybe we do deserve to go to the deepest of hells," said Horse, despairingly.

"Pig on a stick, Horse!" exclaimed Fast Deng. "That's helpful."

"Yeah, stop being so miserable," said Slow Deng. "Go and speak to the Magistrate again. Maybe now that he has seen the mood of the people he can find a different story in his law books – one that doesn't involve stupid speaking rabbits!"

Horse shook his head, realising that would be a waste of time. He was in fact barred from the Magistrate's office, for reasons he did not quite understand. When they had got back from the Temple, Horse had been surprised to see Tea Inspector Fang waiting for the Magistrate, his face still swollen and bruised from the beatings he had received from the bandits. The Magistrate had decided to speak in private with Tea Inspector Fang, ordering Horse to leave. Horse's despondency had deepened a short while later when Senior Scribe Xu went right into the Magistrate's office, followed then by Trainee Legal Secretary Li, as if they had been expected. None of them had been asked to leave.

"I thought the story about the rabbit was a good story," said Little Ox.

Fast Deng and Slow Deng looked askance at Little Ox, shaking their heads in disgust. They believed him to be quite altered, and not for the better, from what he had seen and done in Madame Wu's house. But Little Ox had been the only one of them to properly follow the Magistrate's reasoning, and had been forced to explain the meaning of the Magistrate's words to them all when they had first arrived back at the jail. In the Temple, Horse had hardly listened to the Magistrate at all. He had fixed his eyes on Second Son Zhou all through the reading of the judgement. And when Second Son Zhou had grabbed Jade Moon roughly by the arm and dragged her out of the Temple, it had taken all of his self-control not to run after them both and beat Second Son Zhou to the ground.

Leaf had listened eagerly to Little Ox's rendition of the Magistrate's judgement and explanation as to the meaning of the magical rabbit. Leaf had not been in the Temple – barred from attending by the Magistrate on account of his age – much to his fury and frustration. Instead, and to keep Leaf busy, the Magistrate had tasked him with delivering a series of letters: to the August Hall of Historical Records, to Tea Inspector Fang at the Inn of Perpetual Happiness, and to Patriarch Zhou, to be delivered to the Zhou residence itself. Even Horse thought this last especially pointless as the Magistrate could almost have leaned over from his seat on the dais in the Temple and passed the letter by hand to Patriarch Zhou.

Sergeant Kang was not even around to offer advice, helpful or otherwise. In fact none of the militia was anywhere to be seen. They had all either slunk back to their barracks to sleep through all the disturbances or were hiding out at the Inn of Harmonious Friendship, fortifying themselves for whatever was to come with wine. It was a most unsatisfactory situation.

There was a thud as yet another stone impacted against the wall of the jail. A voice in the market-square cried out, screaming: "The future of Tranquil Mountain has been stolen from the people!" Shouts of agreement could be heard springing up.

"We should have gone to Chengdu to seek our fortune," said Fast Deng.

"Without a doubt," agreed Slow Deng.

In the doorway leading to the Magistrate's office, Trainee Legal Secretary Li appeared, waving to Horse.

Horse got up from his chair, surprised to be summoned.

"What is it?" asked Fast Deng, of the clerk.

"Yeah, is the Magistrate now going to tell us a story about a weasel, a snake and a dancing pig to calm the people down and make us all feel safe?" asked Slow Deng.

Trainee Legal Secretary Li ignored this nonsense. "Have faith, constables," was all he said, with a slight smile on his face. He beckoned to Horse again, encouraging him to join the gathering in the Magistrate's office.

Horse hurried after him, trying to blank his mind to all that he felt, wanting the Magistrate to see that he was in control of himself and still available for duty.

In the Magistrate's office, Horse was astonished to see them all in good humour, even the Magistrate who sat at his desk. It seemed that the weight of the world had fallen from his shoulders. But that was not true for everybody. Senior Scribe Xu sat in his chair looking less than comfortable. Horse could not remember when he had ever seen the senior clerk so jittery and nervous.

"Senior Constable, it is good of you to join us," said Magistrate Zhu, forgetting the fact that he had barred Horse from the office in the first place.

"Ah yes, the young man with the most common sense in all of China," said Tea Inspector Fang, laughing.

Horse felt himself redden, not liking to be teased in this way, not at this time, not when his friend Jade Moon was probably being subject to Second Son Zhou's violence and unnatural desires. Horse took hold of himself. He ignored Tea Inspector Fang, and bowed to the Magistrate.

"Magistrate, do you have an order for me?"

"Yes, Senior Constable, I need you to come with me."

"Where to, Magistrate?"

"Ah, that shall become clear when we get there. But first you must promise me not to act in any way improperly, or open your mouth unless I bid it."

Horse nodded, uncertain, not sure if he had ever done anything improper in his life – unless the Magistrate was referring to how he broke in the storeroom to free Jade Moon's bow and arrow; an act he did not regret and would repeat in similar circumstances again and again, regardless of any order to the contrary.

"As you say, Magistrate," he said.

"Good, that is very good. First you must go back to the others and order them to be confined to the jail until I return. Passions in this district have become inflamed, unnecessarily so, and it is best that they stay indoors for now. And that applies doubly so to the boy, Leaf."

"Yes, Magistrate."

"Then you will accompany me and the others gathered here. Perhaps you can assist Senior Scribe Xu more so, as just now he has become quite suspicious of his balance. I suspect he needs a strong shoulder to lean upon."

Horse looked to the senior clerk, wondering why Physician Ji had not been summoned if he was in such distress. And if they were all going to walk some distance, and be about some important official business – just an impression he was receiving from all the faces upon him – then should Senior Scribe Xu be coming with them at all? His brain began to ache with the stress and mystery of it all.

CHAPTER 57

"*M*agistrate, this is quite unexpected," said Patriarch Zhou. "Welcome to my house. Your letter was waiting for me when I arrived home. The barbarian girl has been placed in isolation as you suggested and not spoken to. But you need not have worried. I have forbidden Second Son Zhou to be alone with her until Ritual Master Zhan returns from Chengdu. He is my son – one of only two – and such precautions are necessary, are they not? Who knows what kind of demon inhabits her body. I will have wine and tea brought presently, but what is so important you should arrive with Tea Inspector Fang, Senior Scribe Xu and this clerk? Is there some danger that I am not aware of? The people will grow less agitated by evening. They always do when it is time to cook and eat their dinners."

Patriarch Zhou had hardly finished reading the letter from the Magistrate when his guards announced the arrival of the Magistrate at the main gates. Patriarch Zhou had been quite flummoxed. He already had a splitting headache – a carry-over, he thought, from the tension of the Temple. And though his petition had been successful – his confidence in the law fully restored – he had already been forced to physically hold apart his two sons who wished at that moment to kill each other. Yes, he had wanted to give his sons everything in life, but even he was beginning to question Second Son Zhou's unwholesome desire for the barbarian girl. The moment she had been led into the Inner Quarters in the house, a great wailing had arisen there – whether from the she-wolf herself or from the other women he could not (and did not want to) know.

Embarrassed by the violence between his two sons, which the guards must have seen, he ordered the Magistrate's party be let in immediately and that his sons should sit at his side. It was possible, at least, he thought, that the presence of the Magistrate may return some modicum of harmony back into the Zhou household. Just in time he got his arguing sons seated in their chairs either side of him and facing the doors, as the guards showed the Magistrate into the room.

"We do not require tea or wine, Patriarch Zhou, but I thank you for the offer," replied Magistrate Zhu.

Patriarch Zhou frowned as he saw the grave expression on the Magistrate's face, the sickly sallow features of Senior Scribe Xu (who did not look at all well) and the junior clerk, excitable as always, carrying a bundle of papers. Then he began to scowl as he noticed Tea Inspector Fang's ugly and swollen face (why hadn't his guards mentioned his presence in the Magistrate's party?) and Horse too, who took up station with two of his own guards at the back of the room. He couldn't understand what was going on, what they could all want from him at this time. He chose to be polite, to cover his rising anxiety.

"You are recovered, Tea Inspector Fang – from your ordeal?"

"Oh yes, much recovered thank you, Patriarch Zhou."

"I did not see you at the Temple."

"Physician Ji advised against my attendance. I am to avoid all controversial and emotional scenes for some months to come. But I must congratulate you on your success. Your patience with the legal process has finally paid off."

"Ah yes, thank you."

"But Patriarch Zhou, you do not look overly satisfied," said Tea Inspector Fang, with a grin. "In fact this room seems to me rather chilly, and your sons do not look in the best of health."

Unhappy and confused by Tea Inspector Fang's presence, and the fact that the bandits – whoever they had been – had not killed the obnoxious official when they had had the chance, Patriarch Zhou decided to ignore him. He would not to be goaded into a show of temper and discourtesy. He fixed his attention on the Magistrate instead. After all, the Magistrate surely had the greater rank.

"Magistrate, what is it I can do for you?"

"Patriarch Zhou, I come on a matter of great urgency. I have been led to believe this town is in great peril."

"Again?"

"Yes, indeed."

Patriarch Zhou looked left and right, to each of his sons. "Have either of you heard of any peril? Have more bandits come to town? I know one or two escaped."

But before Sensible Zhou or Second Son Zhou could reply, Magistrate Zhu opened his mouth to speak again.

"Patriarch Zhou, I assume you are fully aware of what has gone on in this district in the last few days?"

"Yes, of course. A most regrettable business, Tea Inspector Fang's kidnap and the death of that old man…whose name escapes me at this moment, but—"

"Then I wish to explain what Senior Scribe Xu has explained to me…about sacrifice."

"Sacrifice? Is Senior Scribe Xu drunk, Magistrate? He doesn't look quite right to me."

Magistrate Zhu nodded in agreement. "The gravity of his concern has affected his health, Patriarch Zhou. But let me speak of what he explained to me just now, so you might understand why we have come here with such undue haste. He has told me that without doubt the bandits were defeated by the bravery of the constables and the soldiers and the people but that, as Magistrate, I had a responsibility to the future. You might look confused, Patriarch Zhou, for I was just as confused by his words. 'Whatever do you mean?' I asked Senior Scribe Xu. He replied: 'We must make an offering or a sacrifice to Heaven for our salvation. It is the least we can do.' Quite remarkable words, don't you think, Patriarch Zhou?"

"Yes, yes, of course, but what has this got to do with me?"

"Please be patient, Patriarch Zhou, I am coming to that. Senior Scribe Xu explained that only through the direct intervention of Heaven was my and Tea Inspector Fang's life preserved. The fact that we both stand in front of you today is surely testament to that intervention."

"Yes, yes, of course. Heaven was right to preserve your lives, but what has that got to do with me, Magistrate?"

"Senior Scribe Xu is adamant that a sacrifice has to be made to honour the intervention of Heaven."

"I don't understand, Magistrate. What sacrifice? Why come to me? I make offerings at the Temple, and send cash to the monks at the Serene Tiger Monastery. I even give cash to that madwoman, Miss Dai, who runs the Always Smiling Orphanage. What else can be done?"

"Patriarch Zhou, I have been told by Senior Scribe Xu that he is prepared to sacrifice his life-savings for the future of this district. But he says this is not quite enough. He has told me there must be a concomitant sacrifice from a man of rank in town – for surely Heaven would take more notice of an offering from a nobleman than from a common person."

"Man of rank? Sacrifice? Magistrate, you are talking in riddles. I am no scholar! Speak plainly to me. The day has been stressful enough, and we have yet to gather in the first tea harvest!"

"Very well, Patriarch Zhou. Senior Scribe Xu has offered up his life-savings in exchange for the future, as a measure of his compassion and concern for us all. But he wishes his cash to be well-spent. He also knows that a further sacrifice has to be made by a man of rank. And not wanting to see either you, Patriarch Yang or Patriarch Sun impoverished through this sacrifice – he believes the economy of this whole district is dependent on the wealth of your great families – he offers up his life-savings in exchange for your sacrifice. But he does understand that the cash will be little compensation for your loss."

"Loss? What loss?"

"Senior Scribe Xu believes it is imperative that you make this sacrifice, Patriarch Zhou – for the whole town. Neither Patriarch Yang nor Patriarch Sun has anything suitable to offer up. And he believes Heaven and the people will consider you a great man for making such a sacrifice, though in reality you will lose nothing."

"Magistrate, what is it you are saying? What have I to sacrifice?"

"Father, you should listen to the Magistrate," said Sensible Zhou, the shutters of his mind opening, his temper and his fight with Second Son Zhou now completely forgotten. He began to hope with all his heart.

"Patriarch Zhou," said Magistrate Zhu, raising his voice, filling the whole room, "Senior Scribe Xu offers to help you make your sacrifice to ensure the future harmony of the District by giving you his life-savings in exchange for the concubinage of Miss Tang. He then intends to give Miss Tang back to the people. The copies of the contract have already been drawn up by Trainee Legal Secretary Li. Tea Inspector Fang and I will act as witnesses...the very best kind of witnesses."

"Contracts?" Patriarch Zhou was confused, and began to feel angry because of this confusion. He looked from face to face for an explanation of what was happening to him under his own roof.

It was Second Son Zhou who next opened his mouth. "Father, do not let them—"

"Senior Scribe Xu will not take no for an answer, Patriarch Zhou," said Magistrate Zhu interrupting. "He is adamant that Heaven demands such a sacrifice. He will not leave until he has relinquished his life-savings in exchange for the young woman."

"Magistrate, what you say is impossible," said Patriarch Zhou, feeling a sharp pain in his chest. "We have only just received this girl after two years of waiting. I can understand the need for a sacrifice to preserve the future – who can't? – but I have some spare cash and Patriarch Yang doesn't need that old sword of his, and we could drag Patriarch Sun to the Temple more often. In fact we could cook up some of Patriarch Sun's precious fish from his pond. Surely Senior Scribe Xu could keep his cash."

"You have not quite understood Senior Scribe Xu's insightful thinking, Patriarch Zhou," said Magistrate Zhu. "He is adamant the people owe a great debt to Miss Tang for her courage and skill in defeating the bandits. He is in no doubt she is a heroine – an instrument of Heaven. Now, as magistrate I am concerned only with the law. I cannot comment on the will of Heaven. I also know next to nothing about heroes and heroines. Though I must say, and speaking as one man of senior rank to another, that Senior Scribe Xu has quite convinced me. Is forty strings of cash enough to release Miss Tang into the care of Senior Scribe Xu?"

"Forty strings of cash?"

"Father—"

"Shut up, Second Son, I am trying to think," barked Patriarch Zhou.

"It is a decent price for an honourable sacrifice, Father," said Sensible Zhou, now seeing the possibility of a bright future for the Family Zhou for the first time in years. If only Senior Scribe Xu would speak up, he thought, and help the Magistrate, and not look as if he was going to be sick....

"Patriarch Zhou, do you expect Senior Scribe Xu to sacrifice more of his life-savings to compensate you for letting go of Miss Tang's concubinage?" asked Magistrate Zhu.

"Magistrate, what are you talking about?" asked Patriarch Zhou, the tone of his words strained and anxious. "You said yourself the law is clear...in the Temple today. I heard you. Everyone heard you. My son has waited years for that girl. I will not—"

"Perhaps fifty strings of cash?"

"Fifty? Magistrate, I would not—"

"Sixty?"

"Magistrate, this is insane!"

"Seventy?"

"Magistrate, stop this nonsense…you are befuddling my mind. I would accept nothing less than a thousand strings of cash for that barbarian girl!"

Senior Scribe Xu fell right over to the ground in a deep faint. Horse rushed forward and knelt down to assist him. Trainee Legal Secretary Li did not move however, except to shuffle papers and to produce an ink-brush as if from thin air. He had his orders.

"Then the contract is agreed, Patriarch Zhou," said Magistrate Zhu firmly. "Senior Scribe Xu will sacrifice one thousand strings of cash from his life savings to compensate you for the sacrifice of Miss Tang's concubinage. I now believe… no, I am now quite certain…that the future of Tranquil Mountain and this district is preserved."

Patriarch Zhou looked to each of his sons, seeing relief on the face of eldest son but shock on the face of his second.

"Father, this is not right. You cannot sell her. She is mine. I have waited all these years," said Second Son Zhou. His skin was flushed, and he was having great difficult staying in his seat.

But Patriarch Zhou ignored him. He stared at the prone body of Senior Scribe Xu who was struggling to return to consciousness helped by the capable hands of Horse, and then at the Magistrate, whose confident and hawk-like eyes stared back at him, and finally at Tea Inspector Fang who continued to grin, but also to exude a quiet menace.

Why had Tea Inspector Fang come? He was not interested in sacrifices, or the people. He was only interested in the tea. Was he here to issue a subtle threat? That if he did not agree to this sale of Jade Moon the Agency would look at the Family Zhou as a problem to be dealt with, not necessarily now but some years hence….There was the future to contend with, and not just the fulfilling of Second Son Zhou's desires. And one thousand strings of cash was a phenomenal sum. The best concubines that Chengdu had to offer would only command four hundred strings or so. So much could be done with that cash. And wouldn't the people look at the family Zhou more sympathetically? After all, it was not as if he had lost out to Madame Tang. He was still to receive twenty strings of cash in compensation from her. He had still won in law.

"Magistrate, this new contract is…ah…acceptable to me," said Patriarch Zhou, softly, knowing he was beaten. "I am happy to make the sacrifice."

"Good," said Magistrate Zhu, satisfied. "The people will hold the family Zhou in the highest regard for what you have done this day. Surely Heaven cannot fail to notice such a sacrifice."

Trainee Legal Secretary Li stepped forward, offering up the contracts for signature, with the cost of one thousand strings of cash already inked in.

Not wanting to hesitate, not even for a moment, Sensible Zhou jumped out of his chair. He took the ink-brush from Trainee Legal Secretary Li, and said: "I am empowered to contract on behalf of my father," and made the signature on all copies of the contract without hesitation.

"Now we can all sleep easy tonight," said Magistrate Zhu. "Patriarch Zhou, I can say quite sincerely that I am proud to preside over a district that includes such a noble man as you in its number. I look forward in the near future to taking dinner with you one evening, perhaps at the Inn of Perpetual Happiness."

Patriarch Zhou was astonished. A private dinner with the Magistrate would certainly give Patriarch Yang and Patriarch Sun something to think about and could be enjoyable at the same time. "Magistrate, thank you, I would like that very much," he replied.

"Good, then we will leave you now. Senior Constable He will remain to escort Miss Tang immediately from your house. Trainee Legal Secretary Li will help Senior Scribe Xu home. I am sure his spirit will recover quickly after making this great sacrifice." Magistrate Zhu turned to Tea Inspector Fang. "Shall we go, and leave the Family Zhou in peace?"

Magistrate Zhu marched out of the room, and Tea Inspector Fang, with a laugh and a discourteous and inappropriate wave to Patriarch Zhou, followed him.

"Father, what have you done? What has just happened to us?" asked Second Son Zhou.

But Patriarch Zhou was not listening. Instead, he said out loud, so even his guards could hear: "I didn't think Senior Scribe Xu had so much cash."

❧

In the street, outside the gates of the Zhou residence, Magistrate Zhu steadied himself against a nearby wall, breathing deeply.

Worried, Tea Inspector Fang moved to support him. "Magistrate, are you ill? Shall I fetch Physician Ji?"

Magistrate Zhu shook his head. "Don't concern yourself, Tea Inspector Fang. It will pass. All things will pass."

"I think that if I'd just spent a thousand strings of cash on a girl I'd feel faint as well." Tea Inspector Fang was shaking his head, but smiling. "I hope she is worth it, Magistrate. For that amount of cash I could have bought twenty of the prettiest girls in all of China."

"Miss Tang saved both of our lives – it was a debt of blood, of honour."

"A debt of honour? One thousand strings of cash! Magistrate, you could have just bought her a pretty dress and a few gold bangles. I am more inclined to believe that you have just bought peace for this district. Though I don't agree with your methods, and certainly don't agree with you enriching one of the Patriarchs, I respect you for what you have done for Tranquil Mountain."

"I wanted to do at least one good thing in my life, to atone for mistakes made in the past. I have at least given this young woman her freedom. I thank you for extending me the credit at such short notice, so Senior Scribe Xu would not worry unduly about putting his name to a contract. And I thank you for your presence just now. Patriarch Zhou could hardly keep his eyes from you."

Tea Inspector Fang laughed again. "It's nothing, Magistrate. I know you are good for the cash and, after all, you were willing to exchange your life for mine, with the bandits. I also have a debt of honour to you – yet to be repaid."

"Just help me with the porterage list, and convince the Tea and Horse Agency to pay the best price it can for this district's tea."

"Now you are being quite ridiculous, Magistrate. I think you should get a tonic from Physician Ji, to wake you up. And in regard to Jade Moon, I fear you have been infected by some of Second Son Zhou's strange desires. Physician Ji may have something for that as well!"

It was many hours later before Magistrate Zhu understood fully what Tea Inspector Fang had meant by those final words. Fortunately, Tea Inspector Fang was then long gone from the jail, and only Little Ox, who had been serving him tea, noticed his embarrassment and discomfort.

"Magistrate?"

"It is nothing, Constable Wu. Now tell me, are my new orders ready to be put into action?"

Little Ox nodded. "He is to be followed and watched every moment, Magistrate."

"Covertly?"

"Yes, Magistrate."

"Very good – but remember, there can be no gaps in this surveillance, and no mistakes."

Little Ox nodded again, gravely, and then made the deepest of bows. All of the constables were well aware of the high stakes. To lose someone once was bad enough; to lose them twice was unforgivable.

CHAPTER 58

*H*orse hurried off, looking for where they had put Jade Moon. He had never seen such a large house, with so many rooms and corridors, and such luxury and finery. Not even in Senior Scribe Xu's wonderful home. However, he need not have been anxious about where to go, for the guards – all a superstitious lot, and wanting rid of *her* – happily pointed him in the right direction. And, when he found his way to the Inner Quarters, a door was readily opened and he was quickly pulled inside.

A lady, dressed in skirts of bright, green silk, held onto his wrist tightly. He did not recognize her, but she knew him. She spoke to him intensely, her fear palpable.

"I am Madame Zhou, wife to Patriarch Zhou. And I know you are Horse, a constable, reputed to be a good boy. Understand this, so you may tell all who ask: we are not a wholly stupid family."

"I have come to take Jade Moon away," Horse replied, with a shallow bow, thinking the woman deserved respect, and some explanation for his presence in this most private part of the house.

To his surprise, Madame Zhou smiled warmly. "Thank you, Senior Constable. I already know what has gone on, and that we have the Magistrate to thank for our futures. I do not know what to make of her, whether she is possessed by evil or a heroine reborn – but one thing is true, that Daughter of the Wolf does not belong here."

Madame Zhou led him down a dark corridor, and pointed though an open doorway. Horse looked in. Jade Moon was sitting on a small chair next to a narrow bed, her head bowed and her eyes closed. Whether she was praying or not,

260

he could not tell. But there was an atmosphere about the room he did not like. The room was filled with a dark foreboding, as if a thousand lightnings were about to strike. It was not a wholesome feeling. He believed then, if he had not already believed it before, that Jade Moon was far from ordinary. Whatever barbarian spirits or demons or gods whirled about her, they certainly did not want her in the Zhou residence.

"Take her away, constable," said Madame Zhou. "Before my family is destroyed and this house crumbles and the dust of it covers our rotting corpses."

Madame Zhou disappeared then into another room, leaving Horse to his duty.

"Jade Moon!" he hissed, not wanting to make a commotion. She did not open her eyes or look up or make any sign she had heard him at all. He wondered if the family Zhou, for their own safety, had fed her some narcotic. He stepped into the small room and shook her by the shoulder. "Jade Moon, you must wake up!"

Her eyes opened, jet black, in pain. He withdrew his hand swiftly.

"Jade Moon you must come with me. You don't belong here. You have been sold again."

She looked up at him, not understanding. And, feeling he was risking his own health, he leant over and took her by the hand, using all his strength to drag her to her feet as she resisted him, her face a mask of confusion.

"You don't belong here," he said again. "We must go. We must go before you cause Heaven to take vengeance upon this house and upon this family. They are not all bad, I think."

"I-I am no longer a concubine?" He words were faint, her mouth hardly opening.

Horse did not quite know how to explain what had happened, what he suspected. For surely Senior Scribe Xu did not have one thousand strings of cash to spend, and had never before shown a predilection for concubines. He was certain the Magistrate had pulled off a masterful trick – a trick that surely the Deng brothers, when they learned of it, would be proud of. Guilt gnawed at him though. He should have trusted the Magistrate more, should have known the Magistrate would not have abandoned her.

"Yes, you are still a concubine, Jade Moon. Senior Scribe Xu has bought you…but not really…well, I cannot explain now. We must go. We must leave this house immediately."

"Let go of my hand."

He did instantly, not wanting to fight her, or carry her out of the house bodily. "Please, Jade Moon, we must go."

"I don't want to be anybody's concubine," she said, meaning it.

"Good, good, but you can tell people later," replied Horse, anxious to be away. He glanced up to the rafters, thinking if they delayed any longer the roof would come down on him. "Please follow me, Jade Moon. Please trust me. I am aware I owe you a great debt for what you did for the Magistrate. I would not repay you by leading you into danger."

She saw his sincerity and finally acquiesced. With relief Horse led her from the room. He did not look behind to see that she followed him as he retraced his steps out of the Inner Quarters. Once again silent guards motioned him the route to take. After many tense moments, a hundred counted footsteps, he and Jade Moon were out of the house.

On the path through the courtyard, leading to the massive front gates, Horse heard a shout from behind. Thinking Second Son Zhou had completely lost his senses he turned, his fists bunched, ready to fight to defend Jade Moon. But it was Sensible Zhou who ran towards them, his hands out-stretched before him, signalling he meant no harm.

"Please excuse me, Senior Constable. I know what has happened here tonight," Sensible Zhou said. He was breathless, his eyes dancing with excitement and joy. "You must pass on my sincerest thanks to the Magistrate for what he has done for my family. It is as if a great shadow has been lifted from my life. Tell him not to begrudge us for our stupidity and intransigence. My father and brother will see the sense of all this in time. The Magistrate is welcome in this house at any time, day or night, and the thousand strings of cash...well, I will see the cash is used wisely, for the good of the town and the tea gardens. And you and the constables are welcome here too, for any reason...even the Deng brothers. Tell the Magistrate I will not forget. Oh, and I am sending each of you constables a present this very evening."

Sensible Zhou dipped his head slightly. Warmed by the nobleman's words, Horse bowed in return, but much more deeply. The people said the day could not come too soon when Sensible Zhou would inherit his father's mantle. Horse was forced to agree. Sensible Zhou turned back towards the house, not giving Jade Moon a single glance.

Horse looked at her, seeing even more confusion in her face as she tried to unpick the meaning of Sensible Zhou's words.

"Has the Magistrate bought me?" she asked.

"Of course not," replied Horse, sharply, proud he had learned at least something from the Magistrate. "It is forbidden by law for a magistrate to buy a concubine, or to take a wife, from the district over which he is presiding. But Jade Moon, this is no time for talking of the law. I must get you home safely."

"Home?"

"Yes, to your mother."

He strode off to the main gates, hoping she still followed, and nodded to the guards as they gladly opened the gates for him. Outside on the street, Trainee Legal Secretary Li was waiting for them, grinning, supporting Senior Scribe Xu whose long legs were still weak and wobbly.

"Horse, what kept you?" asked Trainee Legal Secretary Li. "I must get Senior Scribe Xu to his home."

The gates to the Zhou residence slammed shut, forcing Horse to glance back with a start, relieved to see Jade Moon still a few paces behind him, the right side of the gates.

"This has been a day to remember," said Trainee Legal Secretary Li, so excited still he did not want the day to end.

"Forgive me," replied Horse, "But the Magistrate would want me to deliver Jade Moon safely to her home and her mother."

"We all have to go the same way, Horse, down the Street of Heavenly Peace.

We may as well walk together," replied Senior Scribe Xu. Despite his continuing nausea, he was lucid enough to think that it would not hurt, for the sake of appearances (and for the lie that must be told) for the people to see him and Jade Moon together. He had bought her, after all. He should spend some little time with her, before giving her back to the people.

By the time they reached the door to Madame Tang's house, thankfully without incident, many people had come out of their houses, to stare silently at the short procession. Though it would be some hours before the details of Senior Scribe Xu's purchase of Jade Moon, and gift of her back to her mother and the people, would be fully understood, the people could all see that something wonderful had happened. Some even bowed quite solemnly as Jade Moon passed by, still dressed in her finery, still walking tall like a princess.

However, her mother's door was latched firmly shut, Madame Tang elsewhere, in mourning.

"I will leave you now, Jade Moon," said Horse, satisfied he had done what Magistrate Zhu had intended, and that with the people gathered around no harm would come to her. "Senior Scribe Xu will explain what will happen to you. I am glad you are free."

There was still incomprehension in her eyes, confusion as to her true situation. But Horse didn't want to delay further, thinking the Magistrate would chastise him for taking too much time. He smiled at Jade Moon, nodded to the clerks, and hurried on his way. When he reached the market-square, he began to laugh, a great tension leaving his body. He broke into a run, glad to be alive, wanting to join his fellow constables…his friends…as quickly as possible, and take tea, and enjoy the beginning of a wonderful future.

At Madame Tang's door, Trainee Legal Secretary Li released Senior Scribe Xu's arm, believing the senior clerk could now support his own weight – which thankfully proved to be true. Trainee Legal Secretary Li opened up the file he carried with him and extracted a few sheets of paper.

"Jade Moon, here is a copy of the contract of purchase for you from the family Zhou. This document makes you concubine to Senior Scribe Xu. I—"

"I do not wish to be concubine to anyone," said Jade Moon, looking at the clerks one by one, eyes cold, lips set thin and tight.

Trainee Legal Secretary Li swallowed, realising he had made the mistake of starting with the wrong piece of paper.

He tried again. "Jade Moon, I—"

"Trainee Legal Secretary Li, allow me," interrupted Senior Scribe Xu. Despite his physical weakness it was his responsibility to tell Jade Moon the truth of what had happened, but to insist she maintained the lie, for her own good and that of the Magistrate, and to abide by the confines of the law. For if surely proof was ever found that the Magistrate had supplied the cash for the purchase of a concubine, even if he had never used her as such, he would invite more than severe criticism, which would never do.

"Jade Moon, please listen to me carefully," continued Senior Scribe Xu. "You must accept these documents from Trainee Legal Secretary Li because they are proof for you of your new status. Tonight you were bought from Patriarch Zhou for the impossible sum of a thousand strings of cash, in my name, ostensibly for me. But I do not need a concubine. The ghost of my dead wife would not let any other such woman in my house. There is another document therefore in Trainee Legal Secretary Li's hands. This grants you release from my family, as concubine, and sets you free, so you can return to your mother without constraint or hindrance. You are free to live your life as you wish, and marry any you might choose, if that is your desire."

Senior Scribe Xu nodded to Trainee Legal Secretary Li, who happily passed the documents into Jade Moon's hands. She looked at the papers, still not understanding what had happened to her.

"You have bought me?" she asked softly.

"No, no," replied Senior Scribe Xu testily, irritated by Jade Moon's slowness on this matter. "Jade Moon, that is the lie that must be believed by the people. I don't have a thousand strings of cash. I have never had a thousand strings of cash. Even my wife never had a thousand strings of cash. I was only required to pretend."

Finally, realisation dawned on her. She looked straight into Senior Scribe Xu's eyes.

"Then the Magistrate has bought me and set me free?"

"Yes, but, Jade Moon, none are to know, and the documents do not support this contention. What has happened I think is not wholly lawful...or I should say that it is...but...forgive me, I cannot explain. I just ask you not to ever speak of this again. Begin your life anew. Now I must return to my house to recover, and Trainee Legal Secretary Li must return to his place of work."

"Senior Scribe Xu, how do I repay him?"

To his great surprise, Senior Scribe Xu thought she appeared more pained and upset than when the Magistrate had read out his judgement earlier that day in the Temple. Would he ever understand the workings of a woman's mind?

"You owe him nothing, Jade Moon. You should go into your home. I am sure your mother will soon learn of your new condition and return."

But Jade Moon was not thinking of her mother. She was calculating furiously, thinking of the hours she could work, and the cash she could earn. A thousand strings of cash! Such a sum was impossible. It almost hurt her mind.

"Senior Scribe Xu, it could take me fifty years to repay him," she said, eventually, stricken by the thought of the debt of freedom now hanging over her head.

"Jade Moon, there is nothing in those documents that states you owe cash to any. And if you offered cash to the Magistrate he would turn you out of the jail and deny any such debt was owed to him. You have been gifted your freedom because the Magistrate wanted it so. And I am certain Heaven wanted it so also. Now forget our words tonight. Keep this great secret close to your heart. And if any ask you why I supposedly did this thing for you, say that it is because I care for Tranquil Mountain, and I want to live the rest of my years here in peace and harmony – for surely such harmony would not come to pass if you had remained in the Zhou residence. At least that much is the perfect truth."

"But Senior Scribe Xu, my mother says it is a law of business that all debts have to be paid. I cannot live with the shame of—"

"Young woman, still your mind for once!" snapped Senior Scribe Xu.

Jade Moon shut her mouth quickly, more than surprised at the strength of Senior Scribe Xu's tone.

"Good," said Senior Scribe Xu. "Now learn to accept your new situation, for all our sakes. And please pass on my regards to your mother."

"Goodbye, Jade Moon," said Trainee Legal Secretary Li, grinning, showing every single tooth he had.

And with one last sickly smile from Senior Scribe Xu, who did not look well at all, Trainee Legal Secretary Li carried him off down the street towards the market-square and then on to his home.

Jade Moon looked down at the papers in her hand. The calligraphy was beautiful. She wished she had learned to write as well as that. Then she saw the reference to the one thousand strings of cash, and shook her head at the figure, not knowing how she could live with such a debt – which is what it was, despite the words of Senior Scribe Xu, who was a man and could not understand such things.

Why had the Magistrate done this for her?

She did not know.

She wanted to think kindly of him for it, but only frustration and anger welled up within her, and tears came to her eyes. One thousand strings of cash...fifty year's work, at least...to be repaid.

How could any woman be worth such a figure?

Why had he done this?

Why had he refused to look at her in the Temple?

Why had he insulted her by comparing her to a magical rabbit, and then paid over such an incredible sum?

It made no sense; he made no sense.

"I cannot live with such a debt," she said out loud. "It will have to be repaid."

She pushed on her mother's door, and walked inside.

CHAPTER 59

*H*ow the Magistrate knew, Horse could not say. But Tea Inspector Fang began to behave as the Magistrate said he would, by acting recklessly, by going out after dark to drink and gamble as before – as if nothing had happened. Only now, with his guards, the Bian brothers, dead, murdered, he had no protection at all.

It made no sense, not to Horse, not to Little Ox, not to the Deng brothers – and certainly not to Madame Kong or Chef Mo. There had been arguments within the Inn of Perpetual Happiness, furious arguments, but all to no avail. Tea Inspector Fang would not be denied his pleasures. Or so Horse thought.

"Magistrate, if gambling is against the law, then why do you not let us speak to Mister Long, the proprietor of the Inn of Harmonious Friendship? If he did not allow gambling then Tea Inspector Fang would have no place to go."

Trainee Legal Secretary Li, in the office at the time, had been very supportive of Horse speaking up in this way. Indeed, he had actively encouraged Horse to do so, being as perplexed as any.

The Magistrate was not angered by the question. He answered slowly, so Horse could consider carefully every word.

"Gambling is prohibited by the law, and quite rightly. By wasting their cash, gambling men bring ruin to their families. But, to take away all the pleasures of the people – evil or not – is to invite trouble; sometimes trouble of an unexpected kind. Also, if I chose to close down the inn even just for a few days, I am sure there are plenty of other dens of vice in town for Tea Inspector Fang to frequent. At least at the moment we will know where he will be. Be patient, Senior Constable – I am sure you will not have to observe him for long."

This was all very well for the Magistrate to say. Watching over someone without them knowing was not easy, especially when you were also looking out for someone else watching. Furthermore, as Tea Inspector Fang kept the hours of an owl, the constables had gone night after night with hardly any rest. This was not work that could be done in shifts. Two constables might not be enough.

Only the Deng brothers revelled in the task, seeing the observation of Tea Inspector Fang as more exciting than the usual plodding around town hoping to stumble across trouble.

"The Magistrate is dangling Tea Inspector Fang like a lure," said Fast Deng, early on.

At first, Horse could not believe this. Encouraged again by Trainee Legal Secretary Li, he had asked the Magistrate if this were true – and, moreover, if it was legal and right to do so.

This time the Magistrate paused before answering. He reflected for a long time on the large, patient and thoughtful constable who stood before.

"Your concern is noted, Senior Constable," the Magistrate finally said. "Just do not fail."

Which, Horse decided, was no answer at all.

On the third night of their observances, the Deng brothers sought to ease the difficulties of following Tea Inspector Fang covertly by dressing up in women's clothing. These clothes were borrowed from the maids, Peach and Pearl, both of whom were so excited to be part of the Deng brothers' secret and dangerous mission. Madame Kong offered no objections either, glad that the Magistrate was a man of such good sense that never would he let her special friend, Tea Inspector Fang, come to any harm. Unfortunately, this ingenious plan of the Dengs, in which even the usually cautious Little Ox saw some merit, was rendered useless before it had even properly begun. Walking out onto the street in their grand disguises, the Deng brothers were immediately accosted and propositioned by a drunken clerk. The Deng brothers shed the clothes promptly, shocked by what had occurred. And just as shocked was Trainee Legal Secretary Li, who, at dawn the next day, immediately wrote a letter of complaint to Senior Scribe Xu, naming the offending clerk and describing his dreadful behaviour.

Horse was less concerned about marauding clerks than he was about the weather. The last few days had turned nasty again – heavy rain and thick fog on most nights. A bandit could be hiding only a short distance away and would not be seen. And visibility wasn't the only issue. After Tea Inspector Fang had finished his long evening of gambling, he had developed the odd habit of not walking directly back to the Inn of Perpetual Happiness. Instead, he wandered the streets of Tranquil Mountain aimlessly for hours, seemingly unaware of both the poor weather and the danger. Horse had no choice but to enlist extra help.

Leaf had standing orders from the Magistrate that he must be safe in his bed at the Always Smiling Orphanage just after dusk. Horse, without seeking permission, temporarily suspended these orders. The boy had remarkable eyes. The fog and the rain appeared not to affect what he could see. Leaf also knew the streets of Tranquil Mountain as well as any of them – better, in fact – and had the uncanny knack of never getting lost, even in the narrow and confusing streets and alleyways of the poorer parts of town.

Leaf would have done anything Horse asked of him regardless, but he had the good sense to get Horse to promise, if they were successful, to provide him with a uniform and a sword. Each of the constables was now resplendent in a grand uniform, courtesy of Jade Moon and her mother, complete with good walking boots – as well as a sharp long sword each gifted to them by a very grateful Sensible Zhou. Though Leaf could not yet be a constable because of his age, or be allowed to carry a sword for the very same reason, Horse was still obliged to acquiesce to his demands. Leaf's eyes were just too valuable. And as Little Ox said, with some wisdom, about this: "Let Leaf's demands be next month's problem – we need him right now!"

On this night, the fifth following Tea Inspector Fang about town, Leaf demonstrated his worth. It was well after midnight. The fog was thicker than ever but thankfully the rain had slowed to just a persistent drizzle. Visibility was poor to almost non-existent. It was like they were walking through the clouds. Tea Inspector Fang had once more begun to wander around town after finishing an evening's gambling. They were following, maintaining their distance but still trying to keep him in sight.

"Horse! Look there!" whispered Leaf, tugging at Horse's sleeve.

Horse peered through the fog, trying to see what Leaf had seen. Leaf had pointed past the Tea Inspector, further along the Street of Quiet Reflection on which they now found themselves.

At first Horse saw nothing, except the back of Tea Inspector Fang and great billows of swirling fog. But then, further up along the street, he saw a solitary figure detach itself from a doorway. He knew this was it – this was the time – but he couldn't say why.

"Go get the Magistrate!" he ordered. Leaf, to his credit, did not argue. The boy took off at a run, disappearing in a blink of an eye.

Horse did not need to issue any other order. The plan had been agreed beforehand. The Deng brothers – the fleetest – raced forward, past Tea Inspector Fang, to intercept their prey. Little Ox – probably the strongest – ran to Tea Inspector Fang to restrain him from bringing danger to himself. And Horse followed on, hurrying forward as quickly as he could.

It worked perfectly. When Horse caught up with the Deng brothers, the twins had their swords at the throat of a heavily cloaked man, his face obscured by a cowl. A nasty, curved dagger could be seen in his hand.

"In the name of Magistrate Zhu, you are under arrest!" shouted Horse, loud enough to wake the dead, hoping the shock of his voice would provoke the bandit into dropping the weapon.

However, the bandit, who may as well have been deaf, paid no heed to him. Seeing Tea Inspector Fang so close, he pushed past the Deng brothers' swords, and lunged past Horse, trying to stab his intended quarry.

Horse had no instructions to kill anyone. So he did what he thought was best. He led with his fist, connecting instantly with the bandit's jaw. The effect was immediate. The dagger dropped and the bandit crumpled to the ground.

"Dancing Demon Kings!" exclaimed Fast Deng. "You've killed him!"

"Didn't the Magistrate want him alive, Horse?" asked Slow Deng, kicking at the inert body on the ground.

Frightened by what he may have done, Horse bent over the body and pulled the cowl away from the face. Thankfully he breathed still. The man's features were as deformed as the Magistrate said they would be – how had he known? – but what disturbed Horse most was that the bandit was young, a mere year or two older than him.

"Oh, tell me you have not killed him, Constables!" wailed Tea Inspector Fang. "Please let him go. He is a boy…just a boy!"

Horse glanced back at Tea Inspector Fang, still held securely by Little Ox. Horse could not be certain, but he thought that tears as well as raindrops coursed down the Tea Inspector's face.

The Magistrate was soon there, led by Leaf, holding a bright storm lantern before him. He ignored Tea Inspector Fang for the moment, wanting to peer down at the face of the unconscious bandit.

"Good – very good, Senior Constable. I am so pleased. You have apprehended the murderer of Mister Gong."

Mister Gong! Horse had completely forgotten. With his attention focused only on the protection of Tea Inspector Fang he had forgotten all about the terrible loss of the Gong family. A surge of guilt filled his body. But this was just as quickly replaced by a surge of joy as the Magistrate commended him again and the other constables. They had pleased him – they really had!

"Magistrate, you must be lenient with the boy," pleaded Tea Inspector Fang. "You must be a man of compassion – you must!"

Magistrate Zhu turned on him, furious. "Lenient? Do not presume to tell me how to proceed, Tea Inspector Fang! This bandit is responsible for the death of an innocent old man; and of your guards, the Bian brothers. And he was intending to kill again – you, in fact. I do not feelORSHorHor I have any leniency in me for him."

"But Magistrate – I am to blame! I alone am to blame."

"Take the Tea Inspector to the jail," Magistrate Zhu ordered Little Ox, who complied without hesitation, roughly hurrying the Tea Inspector along. The Deng brothers followed on, already having picked the fallen bandit up between them, intent on taking him to the cells.

"You must wake Trainee Legal Secretary Li," said Magistrate Zhu to Horse, a broad grin across his face.

How his temper had vanished so quickly, Horse could not guess. And neither could he guess whether the Magistrate was grinning because he was very happy with the turn of events, or was gaining some cruel pleasure from dragging Trainee Legal Secretary Li out of bed at this indecent hour.

"But first deposit this boy at the orphanage," added Magistrate Zhu, pressing a bright copper coin into Leaf's welcoming hands and patting him on the head.

Leaf did not mind being taken back to the orphanage. Though having boundless energy and enthusiasm, he was still just a boy. Working with the constables these last few nights had exhausted him. He went to sleep on the instant. As Horse explained to the fascinated Miss Dai all that had happened, Leaf dreamed of great and magnificent battles with bandits, pirates, goblins and vast barbarian hordes.

After, at his house on the Street of Glorious Destiny, Trainee Legal Secretary Li dressed quickly.

"Is it accomplished?"

"Yes," replied Horse.

"And no one is hurt?"

Horse shook his head, hoping that the bandit would recover consciousness from his blow. "It is odd though. I think Tea Inspector Fang would have been happy to be stabbed and killed. He is more concerned with the bandit's fate than his own."

"I dare say the Magistrate will soon reveal why this is so," replied Trainee Legal Secretary Li. "But for now, Horse, I am as confused as you."

Back at the jail, with Magistrate Zhu and Trainee Legal Secretary Li behind their desks and with the constables lined up against the back wall of the office so they could listen in, Tea Inspector Fang spoke again. This time only at the Magistrate's prompting. Tea Inspector Fang was slumped in the chair, tears still dripping from his face. Horse thought him a pale shadow of the man he once had been.

"This young bandit is the son, isn't he?" Magistrate Zhu's voice was sharp, condemning, though Tea Inspector Fang had committed no known crime. "He is the son of Tea Merchant Wen!"

Tea Inspector Fang raised sad eyes. "So you know."

"At first it was speculation only," said Magistrate Zhu. "On the trail, when I saw him try to murder you, I saw his rage to be personal. I guessed then that he was known to you...and you to him. And then I pondered Mister Gong's dying words, how he had named Scary Face Fu. I understood then that he had stumbled on an essential truth and seen the father in the son – the facial disfigurement somehow passed down from generation to generation."

Tea Inspector Fang nodded, wiping his eyes with his sleeve. "It is a great sadness. That poor boy has had to bear so much."

"Tell me his true name. I never again wish to refer to him as 'The Ghost of Scary Face Fu'."

"His name is Helpful Wen, Magistrate – born as gentle and kind a boy as there ever has been. He was once as dear to me as my own blood-kin. What he has become is my fault – my fault entirely."

"There is much that needs to be explained, Tea Inspector Fang. First let us start with Tea Merchant Wen and how he came by his alias."

"Scary Face Fu?"

"Yes."

"It started in a rough part of Chengdu, more years ago than I wish to recall. It was a cruel joke. Some of the people there started calling Tea Merchant Wen by the name Fu. You see he married a widow whose name was Fu. She was still young, and a good woman, I can tell you – so don't think badly of her for remarrying, Magistrate. I don't hold with what any scholar might say about this. The widow took his name, of course, but Tea Merchant Wen moved into her house, rather than she into his. It was the better house, you see. As a joke people began to call him Mister Fu, thinking him weak and in her spell. It was envy, nothing more. It was not the truth. She was a kind and respectful woman, and a good wife up until the day she died. But this is China, and some people here act little better than barbarians, beyond contempt. Then some began to call him Scary Face Fu and worse, Magistrate – I can tell you! And all because these fools envied his good fortune. You should know he was my friend and that I discouraged this behaviour and got into fights over this terrible name calling."

"And Mister Gong?"

"I cannot explain how he knew. The nickname did not spread to Tranquil Mountain, thank goodness. I would imagine, Magistrate, that he must have lived and worked in that part of Chengdu at that time."

Magistrate Zhu glanced across to Trainee Legal Secretary Li who nodded, making a note to consult the census records to confirm this. It seemed the only possible truth. Many from Tranquil Mountain went to the city to seek their fortune, only to come back in a year or so having discovered that home was a better place to be.

"Tea Inspector Fang, you get around town," said Magistrate Zhu. "You would have heard the gossip, that Mister Gong had named his killer as Scary Face Fu. Why did you not come to me and tell me the name was known to you?"

"Magistrate, my mind was on tea – always on tea. I also knew that my friend, Tea Merchant Wen, was dead. To my shame, not once did I remember the son. Scary Face Fu was a name from the past – best left there."

Magistrate Zhu nodded, accepting this. "I was mistaken too. At the time I didn't give Trainee Legal Secretary Li's researches as much credence as I should. I thought Tea Merchant Wen still alive. I thought him out for revenge, for you having taken away a tea contract from him back in 1072, the year you were both arrested for fighting in the street."

Tea Inspector Fang's mouth dropped open in astonishment.

Magistrate Zhu blinked. "Isn't this why the son has now come after you, to take revenge for what you did to the father?"

"Magistrate, no – that is not it at all! That fight…well, I hardly remember it. We had both been drinking, I expect. We were friends – the very best friends. You must believe this, Magistrate! We both loved tea. Yes, we competed for tea contracts – who didn't in those days? – but I loved him like a brother. Unfortunately, two years later, when the world changed for us in Sichuan, I forgot him as well as myself."

"You are speaking of the creation of the Tea and Horse Agency?"

"Yes, Magistrate. All the local tea merchants were put out of business. I was lucky to be recruited as an inspector by the Agency; Tea Merchant Wen, unlucky, was not."

"And he blamed you for this? And the son continued with this blame?"

Tea Inspector Fang shook his head. "No, Magistrate – there was no blame, not on his part, not then. It was just fortune – good and bad. He understood that, as did I. No, my crime came later. You see before all this, as his friend, I had pledged to care for his son, if he should fall on hard times or something should happen to him. You must understand that his wife had died only a few years after giving birth to his son. Apart from tea, his son was his whole world."

"Ah, then tell me about his death."

"Magistrate, to my shame I do not know. I was so taken up with my work as a tea inspector, and so full of my new importance, I did not seek out the truth." Tears once more began to roll down Tea Inspector Fang's face. "He fell down some stairs, or succumbed to the plague or some fever. It matters not now. With the end of his tea business, I think he became a broken man. I did not see this, or go to visit him, because I was so busy being an Agency man. He was proud. He would not have written to me or come calling to explain his distress. And, after his death, when the son – this good boy, Helpful Wen – came calling to my house in Chengdu looking for my help, he was turned away. To my shame I had forgotten all about my pledge. I was away on business. My servants would not have known him, for I was then so prosperous I had employed many new people who knew nothing of my old friendships. I only found out about this visit a few days ago. I never knew of it. Helpful Wen told me, as he raged at me after my kidnap and beat me for leaving him to suffer on the streets of Chengdu and survive in any way that he could. I do not know how Helpful Wen lived. I should have been a father to him. So he came here to Tranquil Mountain to take his revenge on me for failing in my duty to him, and to make cash as well, I think. That is what he had promised the youths he had brought with him. What he has become is my fault alone. You should have let him kill me, Magistrate. It is what I deserve."

"And did Mister Gong deserve to be killed as well? And what about your guards, the Bian brothers? Let me decide, Tea Inspector, what is deserved and what is not."

"Magistrate, you must let him go! I will pay any fine. I will take him away from here, and into my house. I will—"

"No!" interrupted Magistrate Zhu, firmly. "You will return to the Inn of Perpetual Happiness where you will make your peace with Madame Kong. And then you will return to your work. What you do to make peace with the spirit of Tea Merchant Wen is up to you. But, when my report is completed, Helpful Wen will be sent with the militia to Chengdu. He will stand trial before Prefect Kang for murder. I am but a rural magistrate – a capital crime is far beyond my purview."

"Then I will make my applications for leniency to Prefect Kang."

"That is your prerogative, Tea Inspector Fang – if he will hear you."

"Are you going to question Helpful Wen further, Magistrate?"

"Yes."

"Please do not beat him to extract a confession, Magistrate. He has suffered enough."

"I have suspicions that he had help from within Tranquil Mountain."

"Magistrate, you could beat him the requisite twenty strokes of the rod but he will not confess to that. And even if he did, it would be his word – a youth and a bandit – against Patriarch Sun. Forget this supposed connection, Magistrate. I know this is not Kaifeng, but even here the great and the noble have powerful protectors. I abuse the Patriarchs, I know, but I am careful not to go too far. Please, Magistrate, for your own—"

Magistrate Zhu raised a hand, having heard more than enough. "Return to your lodgings, Tea Inspector Fang. Senior Constable He will escort you. And think on this: if I had allowed you to be murdered this night because of your guilt over Helpful Wen's sad fate, then all sorts of repercussions would have been brought down on the people of this town by the authorities in Chengdu. The loss of an important official is never something that can be ignored. Years ago, you thought only of yourself when you ignored the plight of Tea Merchant Wen and his son. Tonight, you were still only thinking of yourself when you thought to assuage your guilt by allowing him to murder you. Both times, you ignored the needs of the people. Both times you were mistaken."

Shaken by the admonishment, and the truth that Magistrate Zhu had somehow plucked out of the air, Tea Inspector Fang rose weakly from his seat. He bowed towards the Magistrate and began to shuffle out of the office. But, before he was out of the door, he turned one last time.

"Magistrate, in spite of all that has happened, I still remember that you came for me even though now I expect it was for the good of the people. I would wish us to be friends. I do not make friends easily as you know, and I have lost the friends I once had. But I would like to try again."

Magistrate Zhu nodded, his face still severe. "I would like that also, Tea Inspector – when my temper is somewhat diminished. I, too, am not without fault. I have committed grievous errors in my life – errors that I will take to my grave and that continue to colour all my expectations of life. It is only the unshakable moral correctness of Miss Tang, and the consistent attention of my constables to their duties, that leads me to believe that – in spite of flawed men such as us – there is indeed still hope for China. Tomorrow, after I have examined Helpful Wen, I am going to visit the sons of Mister Gong, to pay my respects and explain to them – as much as is possible – how their father came to be murdered. I would appreciate it if you would accompany me to pay your respects, and to speak of what you know as well. I am sure the Gong family deserve nothing less."

Tea Inspector Fang nodded, sadly. "Magistrate, I will be there. I give you my word." Then he disappeared out of the doorway, quickly followed by four tired but contented constables, much lifted in their spirits by the Magistrate's unexpected praise.

Trainee Legal Secretary Li quickly finished the notes he had been making, feeling emotional, overcome by the sadness of life.

"Your conduct has been exemplary too," said Magistrate Zhu, shuffling his papers for his immediate review in the morning.

"Thank you, Magistrate," replied Trainee Legal Secretary Li, brightening.

"For a clerk, that is," added Magistrate Zhu – who then began to laugh, continuing to laugh as he left his desk and then took himself off to bed.

Trainee Legal Secretary Li grimaced. There were many things to admire about Magistrate Zhu, but his unnatural, unpredictable and cruel sense of humour was certainly not one of them.

CHAPTER 60

"*M*agistrate, may I speak to you in confidence?"

Magistrate Zhu had been expecting a question. Trainee Legal Secretary Li had been restless at his desk all morning, and the dark shadows under his eyes spoke of a sleepless night.

"Ask any question you wish. I could do with the distraction. I have just been reading the latest memorials from Chengdu. It appears that Prefect Kang is in the process of drafting new city ordinances in regard to street traders. I find myself quite anxious to read them."

Trainee Legal Secretary Li wasn't sure whether the Magistrate was joking or not. A simple smile from him could hide a multitude of sins. He decided to press on with his question. "It concerns Scary Face Fu, Mister Gong and Patriarch Sun."

"Go on."

"Magistrate, I do not know what to think."

"About?"

"Well, the Ghost of Scary Face Fu – who is really Helpful Wen – is caught and will be tried before Prefect Kang for the murder of Mister Gong. He has confessed to this."

This was true. When Helpful Wen had woken from being punched to the ground by Horse, he had confessed immediately to the murder of Mister Gong. Not even the threat of a beating had been necessary. Helpful Wen had said: "Magistrate, it is my only regret. He bumped into me and startled me and I struck out without thinking." He had then tightened his mouth like a clam, rolled his eyes like a mad person and refused to answer any more questions. It was enough to prove guilt before Prefect Kang, but Magistrate Zhu was intending to add in his full report that this confession was still only half the truth – that the beating of Mister Gong had been savage and merciless, surely not just the innocent and startled flailing of fists.

"And Magistrate," continued Trainee Legal Secretary Li, "now that his murderer is caught, Mister Gong will be able to continue his travels in the afterlife, confident he has found justice."

"Yes – naturally."

"But, Magistrate, I understand that there is no evidence of any wrong-doing… that we have only suspicions…but what am I to think of Patriarch Sun? What if he or his men did assist Helpful Wen in the kidnap of Tea Inspector Fang? How am I supposed to greet him in the street?"

"With politeness, Trainee Legal Secretary Li! This is China. We are not barbarians. Under the law no one is innocent or guilty unless proven otherwise. There is really no need to think any other way."

Trainee Legal Secretary Li thought on these words for many hours but finally concluded he could see no wisdom in them. He was a clerk, used to mountains of paperwork and the holding of petty – sometimes major – grudges. He decided that if he met Patriarch Sun in the street he would certainly look the other way.

EPILOGUE

EARLY MORNING, 10TH DAY OF THE SECOND MOON

*I*t was dawn. The constables were in their cots after a long night of patrolling. She came as she had the previous two mornings, holding a small purse in her hands. She hurried, not wanting to be seen by too many people – her own troubles a private affair. She left the purse on the doorstep of the jail, and then turned her back, wanting to get away, back to her home and her work.

"What is it that you think you owe me?"

The question was spoken, not shouted. But his voice was one she could not ignore. She stopped before the gate leading out of the jail forecourt onto the market-square. Some of the traders were already setting up their stalls. She turned, conscious she did not look her best, but confident also that she did not look the mess she might have done. Her hair was combed but still loose about her back and shoulders, and though the grey work-clothes she wore were made of rough cloth, there was not a rip or stain upon them.

He was standing in the doorway of the jail, alone, dressed in his plain black robes, ready for his day of work at his desk. She was glad to see his eyes and skin spoke more of vitality than of overwork. She had heard he kept very long hours at his desk, reading, thinking, writing, and thinking some more. It would not do that he ruined his health before time.

"A debt must be repaid, Magistrate," she said, the words having been rehearsed in her mind over and over again.

"You were not supposed to discover where the cash had come from," he replied.

He considered her, her long hair moving gently in the breeze, the subtle cosmetics that had been applied to her face. Exotic, yes; unusual, yes; barbarian,

276

unmistakeably; but an exquisite and expressive face just the same. Her eyes were deeper still than he remembered, and her lips thinner, more sensitive. Seamstress of unrivalled talent; descendent of a long line of warrior queens – both could be true. He forced himself to remember that this young woman had dealt out death from more than a hundred paces.

"Magistrate, did you think that I or the people could be deceived by you for long? This is a small town."

She did not choose to add that it was Senior Scribe Xu who had told her directly what had happened, where the thousands strings of cash had truly come from to purchase her from a life of concubinage.

Magistrate Zhu bent down to the doorstep and picked up the purse she had left there. And out of his sleeve he retrieved the purses she had left the day before and the day before that. He moved towards her, holding the purses out to her.

"Please, Miss Tang – there is no debt. I know that life is hard enough for a seamstress."

"I am a good worker – I will never starve."

"Miss Tang, there is no debt."

Seeing his resolve, she accepted the purses from him. They contained very little, barely twenty coins between them – all she had earned up to now – hardly enough to make even a little dent in the mountain of cash that was owed. He had negotiated a price of a thousand strings for her freedom; but to her, freedom was priceless, if freedom it truly was. She was no longer bound in contract to the Family Zhou. She was now bound in a different way – a very different way! – to this young and handsome official, who had been sent to them…to her…by Heaven, all the way from Kaifeng.

"I will never forget," she said, dipping her head in a simple bow.

Then she turned away and walked quickly through the gate, trying to keep her nerve and her poise, trying to walk tall. Before she left the market-square to enter the Street of Heavenly Peace, she glanced back towards the jail, and saw him still standing there, his eyes still upon her.

"And Magistrate, you will never forget me too," she spoke to herself. "Not if I can help it."

Then she began to smile, for perhaps the first time in many years, and felt the colour come into her cheeks. She put her hands over her face so that the neighbours would not see.

Inside her house, her mother was busying herself with breakfast, in the foulest of moods, still begrudging the twenty strings of cash she had had to pay as compensation to Patriarch Zhou. "Daughter, where have you been? Do you not know we have a mound of work to do today?"

Jade Moon did not reply. She merely sat in her chair, took up her needle and thread and began to hum an ancient melody. Madame Tang began to scratch her head, thinking she should seek out Physician Ji. A happy spirit had somehow invaded the body of her daughter.

The End

~

Lightning Source UK Ltd.
Milton Keynes UK
UKHW022245110219
337131UK00005B/181/P